COBRA
KILLER

COBRA KILLER

GAY PORN, MURDER, AND THE MANHUNT TO BRING THE KILLERS TO JUSTICE

Andrew E. Stoner and Peter A. Conway

MAGNUS BOOKS

Magnus Books
Cathedral Station
PO Box 1849
New York, NY 10025

Library of Congress Cataloging-In-Publication Data available.
Printed in the United States of America on acid-free paper.

First Magnus Edition 2012

Edited by: Don Weise
Cover by: Linda Kosarin

ISBN-13: 978-1-936833-01-6

www.magnusbooks.com

CHAPTER 1
A Murder on Midland Drive

"At first glance, this may look like just a lurid saga on the margins of a far-flung subculture. But the tabloid headline of the tale may conceal a larger truth...a reality where the participants hoped to realize their most outrageous sexual fantasies, where screen names and avatars enable endless reconstruction of selves: a fluid, identity-less existence that many millions of people have chosen as their primary model for seeking sex and love."
—Michael Joseph Gross, *Out* magazine, October 2007

During the third week of January 2007, Bryan Kocis boarded an airplane in San Diego for a long flight back home to Pennsylvania. He was filled with excitement and hope. It was a trip he had taken many times before over the last several years as his home-based gay pornography business began to grow. He'd found financial success in producing gay porn in the most unlikely of all places—tiny Dallas Township, Pennsylvania—and his company soon rivaled anything being produced in the porn capital of the world: the San Fernando Valley of California.

He carried with him on this return flight to Pennsylvania a signed copy of a legal settlement that he thought ended an issue that had nagged him for more than a year. He thought he was nearing the end of a protracted and bitter fight that had brought him scorn and to the brink of arrest on federal child endangerment laws.

The settlement settled a lot. But it ended nothing.

Five days later, Kocis, forty-four, was dead, his head nearly severed from his body, his body curled into a fetal position and pierced with twenty-eight separate knife wounds to the abdomen and chest. His body was charred with second and third degree burns that would render him unrecognizable. Police retrieved dental records to identify him. His life had ended on the leather sofa in his living room as his home was reduced to a smoking hull of burned up dreams.

Bryan Kocis was dead and the hunt for what had brought such unparalleled violence to Dallas Township, Pennsylvania was just beginning. The violence that took Kocis' life would send shockwaves across the community and across the country. His murder would reveal more about Kocis than most people ever knew and even more about an unexpected enterprise operating from a base in placid, conservative northeast Pennsylvania.

As details emerged, first neighbors, then the community and everyone would know that Bryan Kocis had built a successful gay pornography business from his modest home—an undertaking that may have contributed to his death. His secrets would unfurl for all to see, revealing the sometimes complicated life Kocis had led, and the hastily planned and executed conspiracy that cost him his life.

The long road to justice begins
There was never any question the investigation into

the murder of Bryan Kocis would be a joint effort. Dozens of officers from local, state, and federal agencies would be involved, led by the Pennsylvania State Police Major Case Investigations.

"Right from the outset we worked with the police and this investigation rested with the state police, as it should have," assistant district attorney Michael Melnick said. [1]

Pennsylvania State Trooper Michael Boone, a fifteen-year veteran, was one of the first to arrive at the murder scene, a simple one-and-a-half story home at 60 Midland Drive at about 9:45 P.M. on Wednesday, January 24, 2007. Snow flurries had begun to fall. His job: process any evidence that could be collected from the scene.

Boone, a member of the state police's Forensic Services Unit, took measurements, made diagrams, and captured the scene in photographs and on videotape. His first photographs included exterior views that showed intense burning to the front porch and entry to the home, burning so intense the ceiling and roof of the small porch began to collapse before firefighters could extinguish the flames. Outside, two small snow shovels were leaned against Kocis' BMW parked next to the house. The intense fire had damaged the car, even melting headlamp casings. On the porch itself, a charred wooden bench and the remnants of what appeared to be a melted plastic one-gallon gas tank.[2] The front door was burned and charred; the exterior "storm door" melted in place. Neither of the doors showed signs of forced entry. Inside the blackened living room, a portion of the ceiling had collapsed and heavy melting damage had occurred to a giant big-screen TV and entertainment center Kocis had just purchased a few weeks prior as a Christmas present to himself. The room's picture window was blown out, the metal bar separating the panes dumped onto the sofa below. It was just part of the fire debris that fell upon the sofa, and Kocis' lifeless body, as the fire raged.

"(Kocis is) still lying on the couch," Boone said in describing the scene. "He's found lying on his back. This debris would have come down on top of him."[3] Boone's photographs showed that most of the sofa's cushion and stuffing had burned away, the frame being all that remained of the couch. "Mr. Kocis' body (was) lying here," he reported.[4]

Close-up photos of Kocis' body showed his severely slashed throat, his skull almost severed from his body, as well as knife wounds to his left chest and abdomen. After Deputy Luzerne County Coroner William Lisman removed the body, a large pool of blood and other biological fluids remained.[5]

As snow showers continued until after 1 A.M. and a slight accumulation began to show, investigators decided to place plastic tarps over exposed areas of the house to preserve all the evidence they could. One long, cold night of investigating was coming to a close, but days of hard work in the Pennsylvania winter lie ahead.

Assistant DA Michael Melnick got his first look at the scene in the morning light of Thursday, January 25. "It was bitterly cold that day," Melnick said, recalling that as he stepped under a yellow police line tape surrounding the Kocis home, he was greeted with a stern "welcome" from State Police Detective Steve Polishan, who didn't know Melnick from Adam.

Melnick recalled Polishan telling him, "Very nice to meet you. We'll meet you back at the Dallas Township Police Department." Melnick took the hint to back off and waited to meet the detectives later in the tiny squad room of the Dallas Township Police Department, just a mile east of the murder scene.[6]

It would be two more days before investigators from the District Attorney's office were allowed in the scene. State fire marshal and homicide investigators spent those two days painstakingly combing the burned rubble of the Kocis home, some detectives down on their hands and knees sifting for clues.

Among the pieces of evidence collected by Trooper Boone

was "a small little razor blade knife" found underneath the burned love seat. Behind the front door, on a small half-circle table, police recovered Kocis' untouched wallet, a money clip with $60 cash in it, sunglasses, a pocket knife, and keys to his prized BMW. Police also found loaded handguns stashed throughout drawers in cabinets and end tables in the home. Kocis' family members would later recover $1,800 in cash left in a kitchen drawer. In the kitchen sink, two long-stem wine glasses and a broken wine bottle (damaged in the fire) and cocktail shaker were found.

Investigators did not find any fingerprints on any of the items collected. It was no surprise. "Heat is very bad for a latent print," Boone said. "The latent print is going to be as a result of secretions from the body and the pores of the fingertips." Boone said the heat destroyed any remaining sweat or oil needed to leave a print from anyone who was in the room before the fire was set. "Especially excessive heat is going to dissipate that away to the point where it's either going to be obliterated or just destroyed totally."[7]

Further, collection of trace DNA evidence from any body fluids was impossible. As Melnick said, "The place was just incinerated where the victim was."[8]

The state fire marshal for this portion of Pennsylvania, State Police Trooper Ronald Jarocha, offered the official ruling: the cause of the fire was arson. Jarocha determined that the front door of the home had been left open, providing oxygen to a small fire started behind a love seat adjacent to the sofa on which the victim was found deceased.[9]

Jarocha said in all likelihood an open flame was used to ignite combustible materials stuffed behind the love seat and that a burn pattern on the floor was created, along with heavy charring on the back of the love seat. Jarocha concluded that if the fire started elsewhere in the room, the area behind the love seat normally would have been a protected area from flames.[10]

Among the combustibles found piled and burned in

the room were a small throw pillow with tassels, paper and cardboard products. "There was nothing there to accidentally cause this fire," Jarocha said.[11]

Trooper Jarocha noted one other odd finding: smoke detectors had been removed from their mountings throughout the house and placed on the dining room table. The batteries, however, had not been removed, so they sounded as normal when smoke and fire began filling the home.

Jarocha and Boone supervised the painstaking effort to comb the house for evidence. Burned debris and ashes were carefully shoveled away from the living room and searched for any possible clues.

Kocis' friend Robert Wagner came back to Dallas Township from New York City at the request of investigators, and Polishan led him in a walk-through of what was left of Kocis' home. Wagner's purpose was to help investigators locate and verify what items were normally present in the home and were now missing, Polishan said. Wagner, as it turned out, was the last known person to go inside Kocis' home, having spent the weekend before as Kocis' house guest.

Polishan said Wagner verified that Kocis used his dining room table as a desk. The dining room, adjacent to the living room, was less damaged by the fire, allowing some computer screens, a scanner, and a keyboard to remain intact. The hard-drive towers were missing, pulled violently from the connecting wires left behind.[12]

Valuable paper records that told the story of Kocis' business and his key contacts, although stacked on his dining room table, were badly burned or charred, but some remained readable. Wagner helped investigators make sense of what remained.

Wagner also pointed out an empty Rolex watch box—evidence that an expensive Rolex watch was missing. The watch, which Kocis rarely removed from its box when he wasn't wearing it, was also missing from his body.

Polishan said investigators scooped up multiple documents

from the living room and dining room area, along with three tapes stowed inside a fireproof Sentry safe.[13] The three "mini DV tapes" seized from the small safe contained master tape images of a porno Kocis was producing. Eventually, detectives would recover a matching fourth "mini DV tape," identical to the three in Kocis' safe far from Midland Drive. The fourth matching tape was contained inside a Sony camera seized weeks later during a search warrant served on a Virginia Beach, Virginia home.

The brutal manner of death: Homicide

While detectives took their initial steps into determining what had happened at Bryan Kocis' home and why, pathologists were determining how he died. Dr. Mary Pascucci, a clinical pathologist, conducted an autopsy on Kocis' body on the morning of January 25, 2007 in the morgue of the Wilkes-Barre General Hospital. Luzerne County Coroner Dr. Jack Consalvo observed, as is standard practice.

As Kocis' remains were removed from the body bag, investigators continued to photograph the body. One picture showed Kocis badly charred body lying lifeless on the morgue's examination table with fabric from his clothing and the sofa still clinging to his corpse. Dr. Consalvo determined the cause of death was a near decapitating wound to the neck, and ruled the manner of death was homicide.[14]

The autopsy revealed Kocis also suffered second degree burns on his back, and third degree burns on his legs, hands and arms. His fingertips were completely burned away. Fragments of his clothing were burned into his skin. Kocis' genitals were also heavily charred and there was a stab wound to the left side of his groin area.[15] The gruesome neck wound "completely severed" Kocis' windpipe, his esophagus and the carotid artery serving his brain and heart. He had been stabbed twenty-eight times, mostly in the area of his sternum and abdomen. Dr. Consalvo said the autopsy showed Kocis was dead prior to being set on fire. The autopsy was complicated, however, by the post-mortem burns over eighty percent of the victim's body.

Consalvo also ruled Kocis was dead from his neck wound before he was stabbed repeatedly elsewhere on his body. This matched observations by Deputy Coroner Lisman at the scene of "frothing, bubbling" body fluids around the neck wound, consistent to what he has witnessed with other fire victims as a veteran of the county coroner's office. Lisman said the "frothing"(normally seen from the mouth of fire victims) came from the gaping wound to Kocis' throat, indicating where his boiled body fluids erupted amidst the fire.

Toxicology results showed Kocis' blood alcohol level was .035, the equivalent of having consumed two one-ounce drinks, Dr. Consalvo said. No illicit drugs were found in Kocis' system.

Melnick said the manner of death was one of the few known answers early on. "The only thing we could say with certainty (at the start) was that it was one fell swoop, as Shakespeare would say. One fell swoop. It was a terrific blow."[16]

A motive was not clear, but it was clear that this was not a simple robbery gone bad. It looked and felt more like a "planned hit," investigators believed. "Whoever did this we knew was interested in destroying Kocis," Melnick said.[17]

High tech chatter, high tech investigation

As the days between Bryan Kocis' death and any news or public update stretched on, the Internet buzzed with speculation and "reporting" on the case. The murder was being discussed nationwide on gay blogs and news sites of all types, making the investigation more complicated, said Capt. Fred Hacken of the Pennsylvania State Police. "Technology has changed the process of policing to a certain degree, that's something that makes the case more complex...and you're dealing with people associated all over the country."[18][19]

But technology would prove to be helpful too. E-mail traffic, Melnick said, led investigators almost immediately to their prime suspects.

Pennsylvania State Police Corporal Leo D. Hannon, Jr., who eventually was named the chief criminal investigator of the case, credited the department's computer crimes analysts with producing many of the important first e-mail and computer leads needed in the case. Hannon said the computer analysts generated a lot of key leads that "were invaluable to building the case."[20]

State Trooper Bryan Murphy and Assistant DA Shannon Crake worked long hours sifting through the "cyber" elements of the case. As Melnick put it, "This was the most complex case ever for me both legally and factually. Legally because we had some very tough issues with the criminal conspiracy, and there was a lot of computer evidence that had to be sifted through."[21]

As the investigation shifted away from the house on Midland Drive, authorities turned the property over to the victim's father, Michael J. Kocis, Jr. as the daylight gave way to night on January 26. The police also returned the five loaded handguns found inside the home.

To secure the site, Michael Kocis hired a contractor to nail plywood boards up against the burned out doors and windows of the home. He went home to share his grief with his wife, Joyce, and his daughter Melody. All three returned the next morning, to walk through what remained of Bryan's physical possessions.

During their visit to the burned out house, Melody (who knew more about her brother's gay pornography business and personal life than his parents did) immediately noticed the missing computer towers. She also noticed that the key documents proving the age of Kocis' porn actors were also missing.

The documents, commonly referred to as "2257 forms,"

are a result of strict federal law covering the production, distribution, and possession of adult content under the Child Protection and Obscenity Enforcement Act of 1988. The 2257 law requires producers of adult content, such as Kocis, to obtain proof of each performer's true age, to certify that the person is above the age of eighteen, and to maintain the records permanently. The only exception is adult material produced before July 3, 1995.

Melody's information, along with that provided by Wagner, proved very helpful to investigators. Their knowledge of what was missing from the house told a story about what may have been behind this horrible act.

Kocis' cell phone records would also provide good leads for investigators. Cell phone calls to and from the victim—just before, after, and possibly even during the murder—provided a specific roadmap to possible suspects' activities and movements.

Combined, computer and cell phone evidence would lead directly to two suspects—and in the words of Assistant DA Crake, "all of a sudden, things started to fall into place."[22]

Investigators tapped the Federal Bureau of Investigation—high-level help arranged by Luzerne County District Attorney David Lupas—to obtain needed search warrants. (Lupas later resigned as district attorney before the case was closed to accept appointment as a judge.)

Early on, with no clear suspect identified, the ability of the Pennsylvania investigators to enlist the help of the FBI was particularly helpful, Melnick said, because they had already impaneled a grand jury that could possibly review evidence and even order subpoenas if the case went federal.[23]

As other detectives canvassed neighbors and talked to Kocis' known associates, police learned that Kocis was last seen outside of his home at 2:05 P.M. on January 24 when he picked up a "to go" order at the Really Cooking Café in Dallas, an establishment he visited often.

As investigators dug deeper into the records and materials

salvaged from Kocis' home, Trooper Murphy obtained information about the victim Kocis from his regular e-mails and web traffic. Just seventy-two hours after the murder, detectives had already interviewed Kocis' Florida-based webmaster who reported that Kocis almost always used an e-mail address known as kingcobra@cobravideo.com or kingcobra@aol.com for all company-related business. E-mail messages from that mailbox were captured, as well as model applicant information sent to Kocis' Cobra Video operation via its website.

The investigation quickly showed the very last contact Kocis had with anyone online was with a model named "Danny Moilin," who allegedly lived in the Philadelphia suburb of King of Prussia, Pennsylvania and wanted to work for Kocis' company. "Danny's" application came in at 10:18 A.M. on January 22, 2007. The application came from a free Yahoo e-mail account under the address of dmbottompa@yahoo.com and included photographs of "Danny" submitted for Kocis' consideration.

Tracking down "IP addresses," or an Internet Protocol address for everyone associated with Kocis' e-mail and website was key. "(The IP addresses) gave us a specific internet connection location," Murphy would later testify. "There's over four billion possible IP addresses (in the world), and no two IP addresses can be connected to the Internet at the same time."[25]

In simplest terms, IP addresses led to the front door of the key suspects.

The investigation goes public

Progress on the case, it would seem, first came fast and then slowed to a crawl. How would detectives learn who this "Danny Moilin" was, and what was his connection to the case? Stymied by a lack of information about the would-be model beyond what the e-mail records revealed, police used a tried and true method: they asked the public for help.

On February 2, now more than a week after Kocis was slain, they released one of the photographs "Danny" had submitted as part of his model application. Not only did media throughout northeast Pennsylvania pick up the story and run it, but gay media across the U.S. broadcast the image as well.

It didn't take long for more information to surface.

The next day, a Norfolk resident called police and said he knew who "Danny" was—Harlow Raymond Cuadra. The informant said he knew Cuadra well, and even helped authorities track down Cuadra's MySpace profile page and the separate escort and gay porn sites he owned: www.boisrus.com, www.norfolkmaleescorts.com, and www.boybatter.com. Together, the information provided by the Norfolk source was a jackpot—the pictures matched: "Danny" was Harlow Cuadra.

Detectives also surfaced, for the first time, the name of Cuadra's lover and business partner, Joseph Manuel Kerekes, also an escort and actor for their burgeoning home-based gay porn and male escort enterprise.

Ironically, the website postings by Cuadra also revealed a photo taken after a Las Vegas dinner meeting just days before showing Cuadra embracing former Cobra Video star Sean Lockhart—a well known gay porn star first "discovered" by victim Bryan Kocis. Lines were beginning to be connected.

Another Virginia man notified authorities after reading about the Kocis murder online and recognizing Cuadra's picture, saying Cuadra lived in nearby Virginia Beach and often operated under the alias "Drake."

"Drake" himself popped up in a telephone interview with Sarah Buynovsky, a reporter with the local ABC affiliate television station in nearby Scranton, WNEP. Buynovsky reported that Harlow Cuadra confirmed that he was the person in the picture of the so-called "Drake."

Buynovsky reported that Cuadra said he never knew Bryan Kocis personally and that he had never used the name "Drake" and was in Virginia the night Kocis died. Cuadra told WNEP that his image online is often stolen and used by other people. [26] Buynovsky reported what detectives were just learning: Cuadra was a male escort and went by various aliases.

"My clients are always calling saying, 'You're in Atlanta, you're here, you're there,'" Cuadra told Buynovsky. "I have to say, 'No, that's not me.'" [27]

The *Citizen's Voice* of Wilkes-Barre tracked down Cuadra *and* Kerekes. Reporters Wade Malcolm and Robert Kalinowski spoke first by phone to "Mark" (later identified by the reporters as actually Kerekes), who answered the phone at Norfolk Male Companions. He confirmed the "Drake" picture was actually Cuadra and that Cuadra worked for the escort service. [28]

Malcolm and Kalinowski then had luck getting Cuadra on the phone. He promptly denied ever knowing Kocis and that he was "freaked out" that his image was being linked to a murder investigation. "That picture (the police) are using, I've used everywhere. It's my cover picture," Cuadra said. Repeating that he did not know Kocis, he did acknowledge meeting with Lockhart, one of Kocis' former actors, just a few weeks prior in Las Vegas. [29] "We talked about working together, but nothing really came of it," Cuadra said to the reporters. [30]

Cuadra told them he had no plans to contact the police investigating Kocis' murder, and although he was talking freely with television and newspaper reporters, he said he planned to follow his lawyer's advice and not talk to the police. [31]

At the time, police investigators would say only that they were still checking to determine who "Drake" was, and that Cuadra's conversations with the media did not represent the kind of "coming forward" they were expecting from a "person of interest" such as "Drake".

More computer work—more leads

Just as helpful tips from the public were coming in, Detective Murphy's computer work and the federal subpoena power in hand were about to yield more clues. A search warrant served on Cox Communications linked the dmbottompa@yahoo.com e-mails to Kocis in the hours before his death from an IP address linked to Cuadra's home address in Virginia Beach.

A separate search warrant served on America Online revealed that Kocis, through his kingcobra@aol.com account, had contact with dmbottompa@yahoo.com several times between January 22 and 24. As one more measure of proof, Murphy confirmed through a subpoena with Yahoo.com that the e-mail address of dmbottompa@yahoo.com was only ever used for contact with Kocis—strongly suggesting that the e-mail address was created solely for the purpose of contacting Kocis leading up to his murder, investigators would later allege.[32]

IP logs for the dmbottompa@yahoo.com e-mail address showed the e-mail address was first created at 4:00 P.M. on January 22 through a free account set up on Yahoo.com by "Danny Moilin." Twenty-one minutes later, at 4:21 P.M., an e-mail was sent to the dmbottompa@yahoo.com account from webmaster@boybatter.com. The subject line of the e-mail was listed as "yoyo" and the body text of the message read, "jjjjjjjjjjj."

Ten minutes later, dmbottompa@yahoo.com sent an e-mail to cobra@cobravideo.com, another e-mail address used by Kocis. The subject line was sure to catch Kocis' eye: "would like to model :)" and the text, complete with punctuation, grammar and usage errors, perhaps meant to further the lie that it was from a teenager, read:

> hi my name is danny vissiting family for the next week in the king of Prussia area. a friend of mine told me that you guys are close to there. would like to meet you and talk about filming and stuff. don't have much experience with this at all. may need to be taught first.

Use of the word "taught" likely burned brightly in Kocis' mind. Kocis liked younger guys, and he had also demonstrated a willingness to help young guys explore their sexuality on camera through his Cobra Video productions. Police uncovered another e-mail from dmbottompa@ yahoo.com to Kocis, sent on the day of the murder:

> good morning, I have to take my dad a few things to center city (Philadelphia) then I will be free...so if you want to meet up earlier, that would be great! I am real excited about meeting and hangin with you. Danny.

Kocis answered this e-mail, writing:

> Hi Danny. I have a few meetings later this afternoon so I was thinking about 7-8 PM to have you here. I guess you'll bring an overnight bag and don't forget those two Ids. My address is 60 Midland Drive Dallas PA 18612.

"Danny" answered quickly, complete with a smiley face, saying, "see you around 7:15 depending on traffic."[33]

Other potential suspects

While circumstantial evidence seemed to pave a wide path to Cuadra and Kerekes, investigators did not rule out other suspects, at least not initially.

Early on in the investigation, State Trooper Hannon and Dallas Township Detective Douglas Higgins flew to Palmdale, California, a tony community in the Antelope Valley, separated from Los Angeles by the San Gabriel Mountains. There they met a young man who detailed for them a troubling conversation he had once engaged with one of Kocis' top discoveries: porn actor Sean Lockhart.

This new source told investigators that in October 2006, Lockhart, who performed in Cobra videos under what would become a famous name—Brent Corrigan—had talked about getting rid of Kocis. Police were learning that Lockhart may have felt Kocis had ruined his life.[34]

Informants also told police that Lockhart said his friend and one-time lover, Grant Roy, could find a "cleaner" to take care of Kocis, something the informant said Roy strongly chastised Lockhart against saying in front of other people.

While the emerging story of Lockhart's animosity toward Kocis matched what Kocis' Los Angeles-based attorney, Sean Macias, would also tell authorities in subsequent interviews, it lacked knowledge or awareness of how Lockhart and Kocis had begun to reach a settlement in the days just before the murder. The alleged conversation with Lockhart, after all, had occurred months earlier in October 2006, when emotions between Lockhart and Kocis were extremely hostile. Detective Higgins confirmed through Bryan Kocis' father that he was involved in a tumultuous lawsuit with Sean Lockhart, Grant Roy, and their business partner in California, but Kocis' kin never implicated any of the men as possible suspects.[35] Kocis' father also revealed that the lawsuit had been settled just days before and that "Bryan seemed happy and upbeat," Detective Higgins said.[36]

Soon, Grant Roy would meet face-to-face with Corporals Mark Filarsky and Gerald Williams of the Pennsylvania State Police in the San Diego office of his lawyer Ezekiel Cortez. Roy confirmed he had been surfing the web looking for potential partners to work with Lockhart in a new porn production once the Cobra Video suit was settled. He came upon Cuadra's image and website and encouraged Lockhart to invite him to meet with them during the Adult Video News confab in Las Vegas in early January 2007.

After meeting with police, Higgins eliminated Roy and Lockhart as potential suspects. "They were one-hundred percent truthful with us and they told us everything they knew."[37]

Roy proceeded to tell detectives that he and Lockhart had

met with Cuadra and Kerekes just a few weeks before. He detailed a dinner meeting in Las Vegas in which the idea of filming porno scenes together was discussed, "but I informed them that we could not do anything at this point because of pending litigation with Bryan Kocis," Roy said.[38]

Roy went on to tell a story he would repeat verbatim many times over; it was Cuadra and Kerekes who suggested getting Kocis "out of the country," not Roy and Lockhart. "Sean had a few drinks in him and I don't think he understood what Harlow was saying," Roy said. "I looked at Harlow and knew that he was talking about getting rid of (Bryan Kocis), killing him. I grabbed Harlow by the knee and told him, 'No, we don't need Bryan to leave the country.'"[39]

Roy said that after the Las Vegas dinner meeting, they next heard from Cuadra on the day after Kocis' murder. He said Cuadra called Lockhart on his cell phone while Lockhart worked a temporary job as an office assistant. "Harlow told him to go to the WNEP-TV website," Roy said. "Sean went to the website while he was still on the phone with Harlow. Sean saw the information about the death of Bryan (Kocis) and became upset. Harlow told Sean, 'I guess my guy went overboard.'"[40] Roy said the disclosure from Cuadra upset Lockhart so much he had to leave work immediately.

The investigation would continue to clear Lockhart and Roy from any part in the despicable acts that took Kocis' life, but it would not relieve them of participation in the complicated journey toward justice.

CHAPTER 2
The Kocis Secrets Revealed

"Bryan was a good, honest person in a bad, dishonest business."
—Melody Bartusek, Kocis' sister

When a person dies as a result of a homicide, it is likely his secrets, if any, will soon be revealed. That certainly was the case as investigators probed deeper into the life of Bryan Kocis and the events leading up to his grisly murder.

Summarily dismissed as a "pedophile" by some of his neighbors and even some competitors in the gay porn industry, Kocis was a great deal more complicated than such a pejorative description of him. Nineteenth century physician and sex researcher Magnus Hirschfeld (1868-1935) is credited as one of the first to advance a more precise understanding and knowledge of people with sexual tastes such as those Kocis demonstrated. Scholars credit Hirschfeld as among those who coined the more specific term "ephebophilia," defined as sexual attraction to post-pubescent adolescents. Hirschfeld distinguished the commonly abused term from "pedophilia" that is broadly used today to describe any sexual contact between an adult and a child or adolescent.

Hirschfeld's definition of "ephebophilia" is helpful to understanding Kocis' sexual identity. Kocis was not, in the truest definition of the word, a pedophile as described by some. But his sexual and romantic interest in post-pubescent boys and young men left him vulnerable to personal complications and even criminal charges. Age-of-consent laws exist but vary from one U.S. state to the next. In the Commonwealth of Pennsylvania where Kocis lived, age-of-consent laws are less clearly defined than other states. For example, Pennsylvania's criminal code defines the age of sexual consent as sixteen years of age. But it offers an exception, allowing thirteen-fourteen-and fifteen-year-olds to engage in consensual sexual contact with others who are no more than four years older. That exception did not help Kocis, who as a man in his thirties and forties had acted on his sexual interest in post-pubescent teens—actions that had led him into legal trouble.

Police alleged that during the months of May and June 2001, Kocis met a fifteen-year-old boy from South Whitehall Township, a western suburb of Allentown, Pennsylvania, about sixty-five miles south of Kocis' home in Dallas Township. Police said Kocis and the boy met online in the "Male to Male" chat room on America Online. It would be those chat room exchanges that would reveal the details of their interactions and bring Kocis in contact with the police.

The *Allentown Morning Call* reported at the time that Kocis had promised to give the boy a modeling job when he turned eighteen and that he had encouraged the boy to send "dirty pictures of himself and others" via e-mail. The boy allegedly complied, sending several pictures, including one displaying his nude buttocks.

Later, police said, the boy and Kocis agreed to meet and police learned Kocis drove to South Whitehall Township to pick up the boy and take him back to Dallas Township. Initially, investigators believed Kocis "groomed" the boy by offering him work preparing mail orders for gay porn videos that Kocis produced and distributed from his home under the name Cobra Video.

During one encounter in May 2001, however, the boy reported that Kocis invited him to watch some of the videos and they engaged in sexual contact. The boy alleged Kocis videotaped the exchange. A second encounter a few weeks later may have been less consensual, investigators believed. On their second encounter, Kocis showed the boy a porno video, a probable cause affidavit filed by police alleged. In addition, the affidavit claimed that Kocis brought the boy an open can of soda and that after he drank it, he felt very tired and his body became partially paralyzed. It was then, investigators alleged, that Kocis took the boy to the bedroom where they engaged in sex.[1]

At a later hearing in Luzerne County on the matter, the boy, by then sixteen, told the court the sexual encounters with Kocis had occurred in the upstairs bedroom of Kocis' home. During the hearing, Kocis' attorney Al Flora, Jr. asked the boy, "Did you engage in sexual activity? Did you do it freely?" and the boy replied, "It was freely done, but it wasn't anything I wanted to do."[2] As a result of Flora's questioning, a charge of child rape against Kocis was dropped.

As part of their investigation, Luzerne County investigators served a search warrant on Kocis' Midland Drive home on July 12, 2001, the same day they arrested him on a variety of charges, including statutory sexual assault, aggravated indecent assault, involuntary deviate sexual intercourse, sexual abuse of children, and unlawful contact or communication with a minor.

Former Dallas Township Police investigator Fred Rosencrans, who led the probe into the allegations against Kocis, said Kocis and the boy had chatted frequently via the online chat room and that he believed the chats and contact with the boy indicated Kocis viewed him as a possible sexual mate, although it was not clear if Kocis ever intended to recruit the youth to perform in any of Cobra's videos.[3]

Bryan Kocis' 2001 arrest

Finding video evidence of the alleged assault would later prove to be a critical piece of Rosencrans' investigation. At the time of his arrest, Kocis was not completely unknown to local authorities. Beyond a previous property line dispute with a neighbor, Rosencrans said one neighbor told him that there seemed to be a lot of men and boys going in and out Kocis' home.[4] Rosencrans said Dallas Township Police "kept an eye" on Kocis, "but without anything solid to go on, we didn't just barge in. Once we had the break with the victim, we could serve the search warrant and go forward with a case." [5]

The break came when the young man's parents called police in Allentown. Rosencrans met Kocis for the first time when serving the search warrant, and Kocis acted surprised that the police were at his door, but also seemed to Rosencrans to be "cocky" and "standoffish." Rosencrans said Kocis seemed annoyed by the number of people in his home, which included investigators from the Luzerne County District Attorney's office.

Police read Kocis what the specific charges against him were as well as his rights, but Kocis was not talking to police. "He just seemed very arrogant to me," Rosencrans said.[6] Kocis was lodged in the Luzerne County Correctional Facility in Wilkes-Barre until his father posted his $75,000 bail.

Rosencrans, meanwhile, pored over seized records, computers, DVDs, and video tapes taken from Kocis' home. Rosencrans shared Kocis' records with federal authorities hoping to find something that would link him to federal charges, ranging from child pornography to possible tax evasion. No federal charges were ever leveled. The local investigation stalled, and the case quickly fell into a "he said-he said" argument with Kocis through his attorney, flatly denying the boy's allegations.

The key clue would come in a tiny micro-DVD cartridge, stuffed in a box away from the presumably legal videos being produced and distributed for the Cobra Video enterprise. "That was a huge break that broke our case," Rosencrans said. On the microcassette was a sexual encounter between Kocis and the boy that matched the encounter described earlier by the accusing boy.[7]

"We were just going on the victim's statement, but that (videotape) solidified this for us," Rosencrans said. "I looked through thousands of tapes and scenes and finally I found this tape and showed it to (Kocis' attorney Flora) and they couldn't deny it; it was on the microcassette."[8]

On April 4, 2002, Kocis pleaded guilty to a single count of corruption of a minor for producing and possessing the sex video of himself and the fifteen-year-old boy.[9] Luzerne County prosecutors dropped the other charges against Kocis. Assistant District Attorney Jeff Tokach conceded that there was a valid "mistake of age" defense to almost every charge. Flora told the court the boy had repeatedly lied to Kocis about his age and that Kocis was unaware he was only fifteen.[10]

The boy's reluctance to participate in the prosecution of Kocis was a key stumbling block as well, as Tokach learned his family didn't want to be involved in any more than they had to. "The reason why he pled to the sexual abuse of children charge is because the victim, at the last minute, before the trial, did not want to testify," Rosencrans recalls. "He didn't want the embarrassment. It would have been public in an open court. (So) the only thing we could have (Kocis) plead to and would stick was the sexual abuse of children and that was only because we had it on video."[11]

On May 15, 2002, Luzerne County Judge Michael Conahan approved Kocis' plea agreement and sentenced him to a year of probation. Conahan did not require Kocis to register as a sexual offender under Pennsylvania's sex offender registry law. That failure to require Kocis to register as a sexual offender with state and local authorities would later prove controversial as questions were raised about whether the law was followed regarding a Pennsylvania mandate that he register as a sex offender.

Attorney Al Flora told reporters in 2007 (as the investigation into Kocis' murder went forward) that the DA's office "never intended Kocis to plead guilty to a charge that would have made him register as a sex offender."[12] Flora and Tokach agreed that a "clerical error" led to Kocis pleading guilty to the wrong charge (sexual abuse of a child) and that a change was made to the sentencing order in 2006. At that time, Kocis' guilty plea was downgraded to a single count of "corruption of a minor" and included an unusual written note on Kocis' court record from Judge Conahan that Kocis was "not subject to any Megan's Law provisions."[13]

Kocis seeks to move on

With the legal struggles behind him, Kocis moved on to rebuild his life. His parents, Michael and Joyce Kocis, and his sister Melody Bartusek remained loyal by all accounts. They may not have fully understood the nature of Bryan's new business, but the Kocis family stayed in close contact with one another.

Bryan Charles Kocis was born May 28, 1962 in Fairbanks, Alaska, before the family settled in Larksville, Pennsylvania. He was raised in a simple home on East Main Street in the northeast Pennsylvania town of Larksville, a community about ten miles southeast of where he eventually settled as an adult in Dallas Township. Situated on the Susquehanna River, Larksville is a typical Pennsylvania town with a mostly white, aging, and stagnant population just two miles west of the regional centers of this part of the state, Scranton and Wilkes-Barre, Pennsylvania.

The son of a typical post-war American family, Kocis' father served eight years in the U.S. Air Force before settling into a comfortable middle-class family life, paid for with his salary as a food inspector for the U.S. Department of Agriculture. As a youth, Bryan Kocis was active in church, serving as a youth Deacon, and in the Boy Scouts of America, rising by age seventeen to the rank of Eagle Scout (the highest Boy Scouts rank) from Pennsylvania Troop 247. He graduated in 1980 from Wyoming Valley West High School in nearby Plymouth, Pennsylvania, where he was reported to be a good student.

An avid photographer as a young man, Kocis won a nationwide photography contest and later attended the Rochester Institute of Technology, a private institution of about 8,000 students founded in 1829 at Rochester, New York, focusing on academic majors in the fields of art and design, computer science, medical sciences, and engineering. RIT was then and now ranked among U.S. colleges and universities as "very competitive" in terms of admissions.[14]

Upon graduation from RIT in 1984 and until the mid-1990s, Kocis worked as a biomedical photographer for Pugliese Eye Care in Kingston, Pennsylvania. Company mergers and management changes at work caused Kocis to pursue other interests, including a failed effort at selling cell phones. Still, at age twenty-four, he was able to purchase his own home at 60 Midland Drive for about $56,000. Attempts to start his own businesses were not successful, however, fueling his 2001 Chapter 7 bankruptcy filing that sought relief from $200,000 in debts from credit cards and a $20,000 loan from his father. In his bankruptcy filing, he listed limited personal assets, outside of the value of his mortgaged home, at about $6,000 and monthly income of only $1,800 from online video sales. The filing revealed that in the midst of this personal and professional reorganization, Kocis was launching Cobra Video—his new vocation and avocation.[15]

Beyond his financial struggles, his 2001 arrest had likely

confirmed for his loving family what they had suspected in the past: Bryan was gay. But like a lot of gay men of his generation, he kept his life compartmentalized. He interacted with his family much as he always had, but when away from them, he moved toward a more openly gay life. His embrace of his sexuality seemed to coincide with the development of his interest in gay pornography as a business enterprise, something his family was initially unaware of. Bryan's family eventually learned of his business interests, but as his father said, "I had very little knowledge of what he did in his business. I know now, but then, I didn't have a clue."[16]

The base for his business was his Midland Drive home, a locale no one entered unless invited. Kocis' neighbor and friend Nancy Parsons was aware of his meticulous efforts to remodel his home by himself, but said his arrest and subsequent bankruptcy had altered his outlook. "He changed a lot," she said.[17]

Kocis eventually created and registered the Business Entity Name "Cobra Video LLC" with the State of Pennsylvania on September 20, 2002, listing himself as president and his home address as the business location. In 2005, he also registered Cobra with the Corporations' Division of the State of Delaware, a state known for its business-friendly laws.[18]

Kocis focused his efforts with Cobra Video on the type of guys he liked: young, white, thin, clean-cut guys under the age of twenty-one. He easily found an audience for his videos. As Cobra grew, his financial stability did as well. He bought a Rice Township parcel in 2004 for $159,900 and another one in 2006 for $225,000. No mortgages were ever listed for the purchases, supporting neighbors' statements that Kocis claimed he paid cash for them.[19]

Kocis demonstrated other signs of his growing wealth. His family recalled a once-in-a-lifetime trip Kocis organized for his parents and sister via limousine to New York City for Independence Day 2004.

Several expensive and showy cars were spotted at various times at Kocis' home, including a Maserati convertible, a BMW SUV, and a V8 Aston Martin. Always well coiffed, Kocis dressed himself in expensive, semi-casual clothing and often sported a Rolex watch emblazoned on the back with his initials "BCK."

Prior to his 2001 arrest, Kocis was well-known to many neighbors, sometimes attending block parties where he was described as intelligent but overly confident, maybe even a little too arrogant or slick for his small community.[20]

Michael and Nancy Parsons recalled he attended neighborhood cook-outs in their backyard on several occasions. "He used to walk in the neighborhood," Nancy Parsons said. "He was nice to everybody."[21]

His arrest changed all of that.

Nancy Parsons remembered that day well. "My husband came up and he woke me up from bed and he said, 'There's cops all over!' We looked outside our kitchen door and this policeman said, 'Wait until you find out what's living next door to you.' So then (the police) start telling us, because this kid, well, you know, had accused Bryan of molesting him or whatever, and I thought, oh Bryan is so proud and everything, I never thought he'd come out (of his house), I thought he'd shoot himself. But then he came out and he was arrested, his mug shot was on TV and he never was, like, apologetic or embarrassed. He just acted the same, like it never happened."[22]

One neighbor, Jeanette Niebauer, told the *Citizens' Voice* that when she and her husband moved to Midland Drive in 2003, other residents pointed to Kocis' house and warned her that a "pedophile" lives on this block.[23] "Of all the people on this block, we were probably the only ones he stayed friendly with," Nancy Parsons said. Her husband did yard work for the increasingly reclusive Kocis in return for money, holiday gifts, or an occasional case of beer exchanged on a hot summer day.[24]

As the *Citizens' Voice* reported, "Most others in the

neighborhood came to regard (Kocis) as a strange outsider, a square peg among these well-groomed homes with roundly trimmed shrubs."[25]

A secluded life

The sexual abuse charges had served to make Kocis more guarded and secretive than before, but did not stop his quest for new models above the age of eighteen in online AOL and other online chat rooms. An online exchange from two young gay guys in San Diego, California would, in fact, prove too tempting for him to resist and would serve as the introduction of Sean Lockhart to Bryan Kocis.

By all indications, Kocis' personal life also grew as guarded as his professional conduct in the years following his arrest and guilty plea. Kocis accepted no unexpected visitors to his home. "We just couldn't drop in on him," Kocis' father Michael said. "We had to notify him beforehand. If it was out of the ordinary, say we were passing by, we would call him from the down the road."[26]

His friend Deborah Roccograndi confirmed the same. She had only twice been inside Kocis' home in the twenty-five years she knew him—normally meeting him at a restaurant or outside his home.

Kocis refused to answer the door for FedEx and UPS deliveries and pick-ups that were part of his business. Packages were picked up and left on the front porch. On at least one occasion, Kocis enlisted the help of neighbor Michael Parsons in delivering prepared packages containing videos and DVDs to the Dallas post office.

As comfortable as Kocis may have been with the Parsons, Michael reported that the friendship had strict, unspoken rules. "If I went over and knocked on his door, he wouldn't answer the door. I'd come back and I'd call him on the phone, and most of the time he wouldn't even answer the phone, he'd just let it go to the answering machine, and I'd just leave a message and then a couple of minutes later he'd call back or he'd be knocking on my door."[27]

After his murder, investigators reported that Kocis concealed numerous loaded firearms throughout his residence, which they said further illustrated his concern with his personal security, and the unlikely idea that he would allow unknown visitors to enter his home.[28]

One of Kocis' former actors told *Out* magazine that Kocis was "just a smart, nice guy. Not the sleazy, overbearing producer. There was nothing stereotypical about him."[29]

Some of Kocis' other neighbors, however, painted a significantly more negative view of him as a secretive man. They told detectives that the curtains and blinds in Kocis' home were almost always drawn, regardless of the weather or time of day.[30]

Amy Withers, one of Kocis' neighbors, told the writer from *Out* magazine that "he slept during the day and worked at night. I would hear car doors at three in the morning. I would hear him having sex in the Jacuzzi on his deck, right below my bedroom window. He always scared the hell out of me: always wore aviator sunglasses and a baseball hat. Everything that you would ever think of a creepy porn guy? That would be him."[31]

It was Withers who confronted Cobra Video star Sean Lockhart outside Kocis' home while he stayed there during the summer of 2004. Lockhart quoted her as questioning him about his age and warning him, "Are you aware you're living with a pedophile? He's not supposed to have any contact with any child under the age of eighteen."[32]

Lockhart recalled that Kocis seemed to have few friends.

"It got to a point where all we were doing was sitting in his dark house, barricaded away from the public," Lockhart said. "We hardly ever left the house."[33]

Those who did gain entry to Kocis' home described it as a typical 2,000 square-foot home of a marginally fastidious bachelor. The "hominess" of the place, however, was at times overrun by growing stacks of paperwork, DVDs and videos related to his business.

Detective Rosencrans, who arrested Kocis in the home in 2001, said the first floor living area of the home was set up as a regular home, but the basement contained several studio "vignettes" or scenes for Cobra Video productions. By the time he was murdered six years later, the basement was little in use, detectives believed, and the burgeoning cottage industry of Cobra Video operated out of the dining room.

As time went on and Kocis began seeking out locations beyond his own home for making videos, his home's basement became overrun with "storage of everything imaginable, tons of porn," Kocis' friend Wagner said. "He would be getting porn from all sorts of studios that would ask him to review it. He would look at it (and then) throw it down there. Everything, he was continually buying stuff, so it would all get chucked in the basement.[34]

A successful yet controversial cottage industry

Cobra Video was growing, but not necessarily distinguishing itself. Kocis lived and worked far from the center of the adult entertainment industry in California observed J.C. Adams, a Los Angeles-based journalist and blogger on the gay porn industry and a former editor of *Unzipped* and *Inside Porn* magazine. Adams' online site, www.gayporntimes.com, closely followed the Kocis case and is considered one of the definitive news and information sites on the gay porn empire. "He wasn't well known at all. There are so many small, little companies like his that they tend to blend together," Adams said.[35]

Veteran gay porn producer Kevin Clarke was no fan of Bryan Kocis, calling him "a pariah in the porn business." Clarke said "there are two types of people who make porn, those that are in it for the work and those that are in it for the boys. It is obvious which one of those Bryan Kocis was," he wrote in an open letter posted on March 25, 2009 on the DeWayne in San

Diego blog.[36]

Clarke contends Kocis only goal was "getting into (the) pants (of young men) as much as it was shooting them in porn. He was a predator and an abuser."[37]

Clarke, the director of several eighteen to twenty-three year old twink videos such as *The American Way, A Young Man's World, Ashton Ryan's B-Boys,* and *The Seduction of a Surfer,* said "More often than not I would talk a young man out of doing porn if I thought it was not something they should do." He adds, "If your goal is to bed them, you come from a different place.(Kocis) was not concerned with their welfare, he was concerned with their ass." Clarke said, "His legacy of barebacking twinks stands as a homage to the debased mind of a predator," referring to Kocis' practice of filming gay sex scenes without condoms. "We as an industry should protect the youngest in it; we should have stopped Bryan by speaking out."[38]

The argument over using condoms in gay porn films has been brewing for a long time. Since HIV infection and AIDS swept the gay community in the 1980s, activists have continually called on porn companies to require condoms in all filmed scenes. Health officials have told the *Los Angeles Times* as recently as 2009 that they believe as many as half of the performers in gay porn movies are HIV-positive. As early as 2004, the *Times* reported that "A small number of producers, catering to customers who eroticize risk, have begun to produce so-called 'bareback' videos that featured actors without condoms. Industry insiders say this market—though still a niche—is growing in popularity."[39]

Titan Media, one of the largest producers of gay porn, say they require condoms and believe it is a good policy. More and more younger models are applying to work for Titan with the interview process revealing they have done bareback videos in the past, reported Keith Webb, a Titan vice president. Webb noted "an upsurge of eighteen-, nineteen-, twenty- and twenty-one-year-olds making unprotected-sex movies, which to me is horrifying, absolutely horrifying."[40]

Adams believes that despite Kocis' place as an early producer of "bareback porn," he likely leaves no lasting legacy on the industry. He cuts through the bareback versus condom use argument in the industry. "People who hate barebacking and think it is unsafe hated Bryan," he said. "It depends on who you talk to and their feelings on the issue."[41]

The same holds true for the typical age of Kocis' performers. Use of barely-legal performers is a time-honored sub-genre of adult content, whether it's gay or heterosexual content, Adams said. Reactions from porn customers varies. "It's about the same as the way people who feel about bareback react—if they don't care for younger guys, or twinks, then they don't care for Bryan's videos," Adams said.[42] Kocis' productions "were popular in that genre, that sort of twink sub-genre that he specialized in, but in the broader sense of the industry, he was not well known and was not a 'player.' I would say he was virtually unknown in the industry."[43]

Adams believes the porn industry is open to "cottage" entrepreneurs such as Kocis because of the ready availability of advanced home-computers, affordable video cameras, desktop video editing systems, and the Internet as a natural distribution network. "This is a dramatic change from the past," Adams said. "Anyone can set up a company anywhere and be successful and mine their own small sphere of influence. They just want to do their own thing, hire boys they think are attractive, and make the films they want to make. They are not necessarily interested in being part of the porn industry at large, or moving to California or to the San Fernando Valley, which is ground zero for the industry."[44]

Revenue streams for Kocis' operation were varied, Adams stated. Beyond traditional distribution deals such as the one Cobra had in place with Pacific Sun Entertainment, direct distribution to members or visitors to the Cobra website meant more money directly into Kocis pocket. "He likely had very little overhead," Adams said.[45]

Remembering Bryan

In the end, those who had loved and knew Bryan Kocis best of all were heartbroken and dumbfounded by the fate that had become his life. They never knew him as the "pariah" or "predator" described by others, and they never could have imagined the terror that took his life.

In the days immediately following his death, the Kocis family grew frustrated with increasingly sensational coverage of the case. "I think it tears them apart when they perceive public attention may be focused on things other than bringing the perpetrator to justice," said Bryan's former attorney, Al Flora, Jr.[46] Flora issued a statement on behalf of Kocis' family that said, "Now is not the time for insinuating that his life is worth something less because of his involvement in a lawful adult entertainment business or his lifestyle. Our society demands that justice be achieved. Public attention and media concern should focus on the murder of this young man and the devastating impact that this crime has had on his family. No court has ever determined that Bryan Kocis was a pedophile or sexual predator subject to Megan's Law restrictions or that he was operating an illegal Internet porn business."[47]

In later interviews, Bryan's parents and sister attempted to paint a more complete picture of the man known to most only as a gay porn producer with an appetite for younger guys killed in a murder.

"He was the type of person that did things for people," his mother Joyce Kocis tearfully testified at a sentencing hearing for his convicted killer. "We heard stories after (he was killed) about the generosity he would do."[48]

His father Michael, sputtering his words between deep sobs of grief at the same hearing said, "I broke down and cried" when learning of his son's death. "He was basically burned beyond recognition...(and) I couldn't do a damn thing about it."(49)

Michael Kocis described his son as a companion on hunting trips and someone who had saved his life during an earlier heart attack. "He would drop everything to help me out."(50)

His mother reminded those following the case, "He was a very loving and giving person. He wasn't like the media portrayed him, as a gay pornography producer. That was not Bryan."(51)

One of his two sisters, Melody Bartusek, said, "It never mattered to us if Bryan was gay or not because that was his own personal life and not ours. He never flaunted (being gay), and what he did in private was up to him. All that mattered was how well he treated us (his family), and he was an amazing son, brother and uncle. He always put us before himself, and he would do anything for us." (52)

Bartusek said her brother was "a good, honest person in a bad, dishonest business."(53) She added, "He was the most thoughtful person I ever met."(54)

Kocis' parents said their son had promised he would end his adult porn business in 2008 and focus instead on his dream of a restaurant. "When he made a promise to his mother, he always kept it," Michael Kocis said.(55)

Unfortunately, it as a promise he would not live to fulfill.

CHAPTER 3
The Rise and Fall of the Cobra Empire

"Although Cobra Videos are categorized as amateur, you're not gonna find anything amateurish about these hot young guys auditioning for a talented, up and coming production company."
—Radvideo.com review of Cobra Video

During the years 2001 and 2002, major events were happening in the life of Bryan Kocis that would foretell how he would live the rest of his life. Amidst a bankruptcy filing and the humiliation of his arrest on child sexual abuse allegations, Kocis had pressed "play" on his dreams of creating a gay porn company specializing in twink videos.

For those unfamiliar with the vernacular of the gay porn world, "twink" describes clean-cut, thin, smooth young men, usually between eighteen and twenty-four years old. In earlier gay decades, they would have been described as "chicken." Whatever you call them, "twinks" are popular content for gay porn in the youth-obsessed American culture. Bryan Kocis was fond of twinks too, and he intended to use that interest in launching porn venture, Cobra Video.

The company got underway in earnest in 2001, with the video release of *Casting Couch I, Austin's Beach Buddies, Outdoor Boyz, Ethan's College Buddies,* and *Campus Boyz I and II.*[1]

In his earliest releases, producer/director Kocis is credited as "Bryan Phillips," a nom de plume he later dropped for his real name.

The scenario for *Casting Couch I* runs eerily familiar to the earlier allegations brought by a fifteen-year-old boy in a criminal investigation of Kocis and showcased the gay porn genre he was perfecting. *Casting Couch I* consists of nine scenes, seven of which feature young men seated on a futon sofa in Kocis' home, answering introductory questions about themselves, their sexuality and their sexual interests. As Kocis himself described it on the Cobra video website and in other promotional materials, "We do some close shots and, of course, the 'Mystery Hand' has to give him a lil (sic.) grope." Kocis himself never appears on camera, though his voice is heard asking questions off-camera and his hand sometimes intercedes on camera to touch the men.[2]

Kocis discloses in his description of *Casting Couch I* on Pornteam.com that "I had to get three forms of ID on little Jonathan as this nineteen-year-old guy looks much younger than his years." He adds that in one of two duo scenes in the video, the pairing of an actor named Tim with Austin required "an early session we had done for practice" when Tim "had just turned eighteen."[3]

Kocis' commitment to casting young guys in his videos found a welcome audience among gay porn buyers. An online review posted of one of Kocis' early efforts noted that "although Cobra Video videos are categorized as amateur, you're not gonna find anything amateurish about these hot young guys auditioning for a very talented, up and coming production company."[4]

A description of *Casting Couch III* contains a troubling reference from Kocis. Whether true or just suggested to help sell the video, he notes that one of the actors will "tantalize you when you hear him talk about his first experience at eight years old and then how he purposely was bad at school so he would get sent to detention with a very special teacher." *Casting Couch III* shows scenes filmed around various parts of Kocis' home, including his upstairs bedroom and the living room (where he would later be murdered).[5]

Campus Boyz I was reviewed at Radvideo.com as "the video that started the ball rolling from this great studio (Cobra)" and dubbed it "a true classic for its time, and a real trailblazer when the amateur bareback niche first made a comeback."[6]

Austin's Beach Buddies, starring one of Kocis' most popular discoveries, "original Cobraboy" Austin Sterling, broke the mold of earlier Cobra productions and was filmed away from Kocis' Midland Drive home, partially on the Delaware shore, presumably during the summer of 2000 or 2001. The video features single-named "Cobraboyz" Justin and Kaipo who appeared in several other Cobra productions and again featured bareback, or condomless, anal sex that would become a trademark of Cobra videos. The Radvideo.com reviewer of *Austin's Beach Buddies* gushed when he dubbed it "without a doubt one of the best twink videos you will ever purchase."[7]

In 2002, the year Kocis served his criminal probation for his earlier arrest, it appears video production at Cobra continued, but at a slower pace. That year Kocis released just two titles, including one that summed up his ever-growing controversial place in the gay porn world, *Bareback Twink Orgy.*

By this time Kocis had also found a new filming location, a local beauty salon loaned to him by the owner that he used after the salon closed for the day.

Bareback Twink Orgy was originally released as *Bareback Beach Boyz* and appears to also have been taped at a shoreline cottage or resort, and includes external beach shots with the actors enjoying the sun and surf. It was edited at a later time to remove one scene that included a light, sadomasochistic bondage three-way scene featuring actor "Aaron Phelps" ball-gagged and chained to two posts on a patio. The bondage scene was inexplicably pulled from a new version of the tape renamed *Bareback Twink Orgy*.

In his video notes Kocis posted online at Pornteam.com about *Bareback Twink Orgy*, he reported that one of the actors, credited as Armon, "just turned eighteen the week before this trip and we promised to throw a birthday party for him, though he didn't quite realize the type of party it would turn into." Kocis notes the orgy scene that follows took more than two hours to film and features two camera angles (though it is unclear if Kocis ever employed anyone other than Robert Wagner to assist in taping scenes).[8]

Kocis' disclosure that Armon had just turned eighteen, if accurate, indicates he would have recruited the teen to participate in the video prior to the teen becoming legal. However, given the genre Kocis had tapped into, the dangerously-close-to-illegal-age references in some of the video descriptions could have been just salesmanship or marketing to attract a devoted audience of gay porn video buyers.

In similar fashion, an online posting boasted that actor Ethan Armstrong was "a newly-turned-eighteen guy" and was "the first real poster boy for Cobra Video" starring in *Ethan's College Buddies*.[9]

Another early film, *Outdoor Boyz* released in 2001, wandered briefly into kink by featuring one actor using a corn husk as a dildo (a variation not repeated in later Cobra releases).[10]

In his notes on the production of *Outdoor Boyz*, Kocis revealed some of the control he would later be accused of exercising over his actors with a heavy hand. He noted that "I will admit I was a bit ticked off about (actor) Ashton getting his skinhead haircut right before this scene." Contracts signed later between Kocis and Sean Lockhart would reveal Cobra requirements that the actors not dramatically alter their appearance before or during taping.[11]

Bryan's friend Robert Wagner

Robert Wagner met Bryan Kocis in the fall of 2000 when he was still a computer science major studying at prestigious Cornell University in Ithaca, New York, although Wagner is originally from northeastern Pennsylvania, not far from Kocis' home.

Wagner said he first met Kocis at the Steamtown Mall in Scranton, Pennsylvania, a location Kocis preferred and continued to use because "it was a nice, neutral location where he would determine if (young men) were cut out" for making porno videos, Wagner said.[12]

"Initially it started out that I was a model and then it grew into a friendship," Wagner said. "I made a few videos early in college, then we just became friends."[13]

Even after moving to New York City after 2004, Wagner remained in close, daily contact with Kocis via e-mail, phone, texting, and frequent visits to his Midland Drive home. For Cobra Video, Wagner said he did a lot of "second camera work" and helped Kocis in organizing model applications and reviewing applicants for the porn videos.

Wagner said he managed and organized the 2257 forms for Cobra Video, assisted in checking IDs at model shoots, and picking up actors from the airport and delivering them to video shoots.[14]

Wagner, in fact, spent the last weekend of Kocis' life at the Midland Drive home visiting his friend and helping organize IDs and 2257 forms for several hours. Wagner said he was scanning hard copies of the 2257 forms into a back-up computer and making sure all records were in order.

Kocis wanted to digitize and backup the records, Wagner said, because he had heard a rumor that federal authorities were opening new investigations into porn companies. "Investigators were coming, making sure all the reports were in order, so I wanted to make sure that everything was in perfect shape," Wagner said.[15]

Enter Sean Lockhart as "Brent Corrigan"

Bryan Kocis' ambitious efforts to build Cobra Video continued and a string of new videos followed, with the 2002 release *Charmed* nominated for "Best Specialty Video" at the Gay Adult Video News Awards. The 2003 release *A Boy's Raw Urges* stripped away all pretense about whether safe sex practices were in use—the video ventured freely into raw porn territory with bareback sex, including the highly risky practice of reinserting a penis into the anus with ejaculate still present.[16]

Cobra's most popular titles were still to come, however, and coincided with the arrival of Sean Lockhart in 2004, always cast as "Brent Corrigan" in Cobra productions. Lockhart wrote about his earliest days working for Cobra Video in a four-part "guest column" titled "A Siren's Tale" posted after Kocis' death on the popular gay blog, www.jasoncurious.com. In it, a poetic Lockhart declared that "at the heart of every shipwreck is a siren."[17] Describing himself as "young, supremely naïve and misguided by those who were once close to me," he says that at age sixteen during the summer of 2003 he began an Internet chat with Bryan Kocis with the "help" of his then-twenty-one-year-old boyfriend.[18]

Lockhart said the summer before the start of his junior year in high school was one of newfound freedom. His boyfriend represented "the first relationship ever in which a person outside my family held precedent in my life."[19] Lockhart said a live webcam was used to send pictures of Lockhart in the nude to Kocis, which served to entice him to approach Lockhart for a video shoot. Kocis was instantly interested, Lockhart said, and began an extended online chat and other contact with the then-sixteen-year-old boy. "Bryan's pursuit was on as he began to recruit me with subtlety," Lockhart said. "He gained my trust and sparked my curiosity by showering me with compliments, giving me the kind of undivided attention of which the likes I had never seen before."[20]

Kocis learned Lockhart's "hopes and dreams" and "presented the ways in which I could achieve these things by joining him at Cobra Video," Lockhart said.[21] Lockhart admitted he participated in an initial effort to mislead Kocis about his real age, allowing Kocis to believe that he would turn eighteen in October 2003 (rather than his actual seventeenth birthday). Lockhart attributes pressure from both his boyfriend and Kocis for deciding to go ahead with the deception.

Believing a lie about his actual age was "no big deal" and that "nobody would get in trouble and that it was common that boys worked underage in the industry," Lockhart went forward with sending tapes and participating in private webcam shows in order for Kocis to "audition him" via the Internet.[22] "Bryan was intent on remaining in contact with me," Lockhart said. "This became an almost daily event from the first time we were introduced, until the day I gave him official notification of my true age (in the autumn of 2005)."[23]

The underage issue surfaces

At the same time Lockhart was creating a new cross-country connection with Kocis, forty-year-old Grant Roy had begun plans for how Lockhart could cash in on his good looks and strong sex appeal to gay men. Roy's plan was for Lockhart to not only star in gay adult videos but to produce and own them. "That way, when you're old and gray, if we do it right, this thing's still gonna be paying,'" Roy recalls telling Lockhart.[24]

While Roy's plans for Lockhart's career were in their infancy, Bryan Kocis was moving full steam ahead. In February 2004, Lockhart says Kocis paid to fly him to Fort Lauderdale, Florida to tape scenes for a new video, *Every Poolboy's Dream.*

Lockhart describes the weekend as a flurry of activity with sex scenes filmed at a local gay resort, followed by external still photo shoots on the beach with the cast of the video for the DVD box covers.

"At the end of the weekend and upon completion of all

production, Bryan gathered up all the models to present their IDs and have everyone sign contracts and model releases," Lockhart said, noting this reflected Kocis' standard practice of "shoot now, ask questions later."[25]

Lockhart said while Kocis personally inspected the IDs of each of the other actors used in the films, he assured Lockhart to "not worry about it" and that he had already reviewed his documents via an e-mail attachment. That e-mail attachment, a PDF, contained false information added to a Washington state driver's license and an altered Idaho birth certificate using Adobe Photoshop.[26]

Veteran gay porn director Kevin Clarke notes, "No reputable person would ever shoot anyone on the basis of an e-mailed picture of an ID. Ever. Those of us that shot in the eighteen to twenty-three year old age group were especially careful. We always went the extra mile."[27]

Lockhart said, "After the shoot, all I really wanted to do was to quietly fade away; something Bryan did not necessarily agree with."[28]

The artist known as "Brent Corrigan"

Disagreement still exists over how Lockhart's stage name "Brent Corrigan" was created. It would be a disagreement that would grow to epic proportions. Lockhart claimed in interviews and in court documents that he selected the name "Corrigan" from a phone book because of it sounded Irish.[29] Kocis claimed the "Brent Corrigan" name was created by him early in 2004 "to be used in the creation of a series of premier adult content DVDs/videos for Cobra" and that he "is the owner of this trade name, has invested time and money in the promotion and creation of this trade name for a character to be premiered in its adult gay films and serials."[30]

The fight over the name "Brent Corrigan" would come later, but for now, *Every Poolboy's Dream* was an instant hit for Cobra. For Lockhart, he said "it only complicated matters.

Bryan's promise of anonymity from the industry started to crumble as person after person in the gay community began recognizing me from my debut film."[31]

Lockhart claims it was at this point when Kocis first began to learn of his underage status at the time of the Fort Lauderdale shoot for *Every Poolboy's Dream*, a major and potentially criminal violation of federal law. Lockhart believes, however, that Kocis was intent on scaring him into compliance and silence with the risk of a federal charge hanging over his head and by exposing his involvement in gay porn to Lockhart's mother and family. Amidst his ever growing behind-the-scenes pressure on Lockhart *and* growing DVD sales, Kocis kept *Every Poolboy's Dream* on store shelves and for sale online.

"Though I was worried, confused, and felt utterly alone and conflicted, Bryan remained a constant entity in my life," Lockhart said. "With all the questions and uncertainty surrounding my age, he made it a priority to maintain tabs on me."[32]

Kocis also acted quickly to get Lockhart back in front of the camera based on the sales success of his debut video for Cobra. Another video was proposed, *Schoolboy Crush*. This video, shot in April and May 2004 in La Jolla, California, would cast Lockhart's "Brent Corrigan" character opposite another rising gay porn star, Brent Everett. In fact, the Corrigan character's fascination with Everett would form the basis of the "plot" of the film.

The highlight of *Schoolboy Crush* would be a rare double-penetration scene with Corrigan bottoming without condoms for two men at the same time. Just like *Poolboy*, the *Schoolboy* video was an instant hit and won a 2005 nomination for "Best Overall Gay Video" via Adult Entertainment Broadcast Network's first-annual "Video on Demand Awards." At the time of the awards and brisk sales of the video, no one knew one of the stars of the film had appeared in it while underage and still completing high school.

Signs of strain surface

During the weekend of the shoot for *Schoolboy*, Lockhart said Kocis introduced him to alcohol and "made a move on me"—a sexual encounter Lockhart would later claim embarrassed him and one that he did not disclose to anyone.[(33)]

At the conclusion of taping for *Schoolboy*, Lockhart described a new ritual Kocis employed, asking each performer to hold up, on video, a copy of his driver's license or other legal ID and to say, "I am at least eighteen years of age" and then state his date of birth. "This was not something (Bryan) had asked me to do on the first shoot," Lockhart said. "I was caught completely off guard, and I panicked when Bryan finally requested to see my driver's license. I tried my best to pretend I was looking for it in my baggage and could not find it."[(34)]

Kocis grew impatient with Lockhart's inability to produce an ID upon demand and so settled for a called up image of Lockhart's ID on his laptop computer and taped Lockhart making his "I am at least eighteen years of age" declaration next to the laptop. But that didn't satisfy Kocis. As Kocis drove him home that day, Lockhart said he ordered him to obtain a California driver's license that showed he was eighteen years old, and to send it to him in Pennsylvania immediately.

Lockhart said he remained in constant worry that the truth about his age would become known, "but it was still only an abstract possibility," noting that the real worry was his family would learn of his porn activities. "That was there and then, in my face, I was living it every day," Lockhart said.[(35)] Still, Kocis pushed forward with production.

"(Bryan) just wanted to make more movies," Lockhart said. "He didn't want me to tell anyone the truth. He had too much to lose if I did. I trusted him about a lot of things, including when he told me that I was the one who was going to go to jail over all the lies, not him."[(36)]

Lockhart moved to keep things from "unraveling any

further" and set out to obtain exactly what Bryan Kocis wanted: An ID that indicated he was eighteen years old.

Making a promise many a regretful porno performer has undoubtedly made *after* the filming stops, Lockhart said "I promised myself I would do the work to get where I needed and then turn my back on the industry until I felt my bad decisions could no longer haunt me."[37]

For $200, Lockhart said he bought himself an ID from a man in a Los Angeles park that showed him to be eighteen a year *before* he actually turned eighteen in October 2004, and sent it to Kocis. Forging ahead to "do the work to get where I needed," Lockhart had signed a rudimentary one-year modeling contract with Kocis in July 2004 that promised to pay him:

- Monthly Sprint cell phone payments of $75 per month (with any charges over $75 each month deducted from a monthly "monetary payment" promised);
- A monthly "monetary payment" of $150 per month;
- An undisclosed "signing bonus"; and
- The "usual fee for all modeling engagements for Cobra Video LLC."[38]

Lockhart said, at least initially, his relationship with Kocis was based in trust. The 2004 contract reflects that: Nowhere does it specifically state what Lockhart must do in order to receive the reimbursement promised in the document. It was later reported that Lockhart claimed he was paid $3,500 for his first scenes for Cobra in *Every Poolboy's Dream* and *Casting Couch IV*.[39] "I did not have a strong father figure in my life," Lockhart said. "My stepdad was no longer there. Bryan knew that I was in a very vulnerable, exposed state and that it was very easy for him to slide in there and assume the position.

It started as something of a mentorship but all it takes is to get someone's trust before you can hook them and get exactly what you want out of them."[40] Lockhart would go on to star in other Cobra videos, including several titles legally filmed after he turned eighteen, such as *Creamy B'Boys* and *Naughty Boy's Toys*, both released in 2005.

In July 2005, Lockhart signed another one-year exclusive modeling contract with Kocis and Cobra Video, one he later described as "shoddy." Although the second contract between the two men was somewhat more "lucrative" for Lockhart than the 2004 version, it still reflected the personally complicated relationship between the two men. In the new version, Kocis and Lockhart agreed to list Lockhart as "an independent contractor" and specified terms the latter had to meet in order to get paid $20,000, almost all of the money tied to the transfer of title for a 2002 Volkswagen Jetta from Kocis to Lockhart. In exchange, Lockhart agreed to six individual action scenes, one non-action scene (presumably a masturbation scene) and still photography to promote the video. The work was to be "completed to the satisfaction of the company" and "the type and amount of still photographs" to be determined by the photographer.[41] The terms further called for Lockhart not to radically change his hair style or color or place any tattoos or piercing on his body without Kocis' prior approval until the contract was completed. It also specified that Lockhart would be "required to be STD and HIV-negative to complete work" and would submit to "regular testing" at "regular intervals." Kocis added a line that Lockhart's compensation would be reduced if he contracted an STD that rendered him unable to complete the terms of the contract.[42]

The contract included terms that would later prove critical in the fight that was about to erupt between Kocis and Lockhart: "The Model will be exclusive to Cobra Video... (and) the Model will not perform in any adult work (nude) with any other Adult company and will not pose for any nude photographs for any other person or company."[43]

A contract amendment entered at the same time as the second deal in July 2005 indicated Kocis immediately transferred the Volkswagen Jetta to Lockhart and paid an insurance premium immediately, acknowledging work completed to date.[44]

The same month Kocis signed his new deal with Lockhart, Kocis registered the website domain, www.brentcorriganxxx.com to combat use of the "Brent Corrigan" character on other websites, and to maximize his profits from the growing popularity of "Brent Corrigan" among gay porn customers.

Only a month later, however, unknown to Kocis, Lockhart was back in San Diego with his now-lover Grant Roy and began in earnest to try and make a break from Kocis, or at least to recast their relationship as strictly one of business, with no expectations of personal intimacy, which Lockhart alleged Kocis often pushed. After several angry phone calls, e-mails, and texts between the two, Lockhart said he told Kocis of his plans to go public with the news that he had performed in adult videos for Cobra while he was only seventeen years old. Kocis surely knew Lockhart was slipping from his control and intended to go out on his own as "Brent Corrigan." In addition, friends and family reported Kocis finally had to face the reality that Sean Lockhart was planning to betray him.

The battle reveals "the" secret

Once back in California, Lockhart enlisted Roy to participate with him in an online chat on a porn fan site known as www.juicygoo.com. In that chat, Lockhart confirmed he planned to produce and release his own content under his now growing stage name, "Brent Corrigan."[45]

The Internet would become "ground zero" for the Kocis-Lockhart battle, with Kocis posting scathing online statements about Lockhart under the screen name "King Cobra," and Lockhart's version being represented in posts created by Roy under the handle "Cobra Killer."

In response, Kocis got serious and filed a U.S. Trademark and Patent application for the name "Brent Corrigan"(a trademark that was never granted). He intended to stop Lockhart and Roy from profiting from the identity of "Brent Corrigan," an identity he believed he created and owned.

By September 2005, the Lockhart-Kocis fracture *really* went public, and Cobra's run of luck in producing extremely popular gay videos was about to hit a landmine. Lockhart broke open the Cobra Video empire with his voluntary public disclosure that he had performed in adult videos for Cobra and Kocis when he was only seventeen years old and a junior in high school.

News of Lockhart's possible illegal performances first broke in the *Adult Video News* publication, *GayVN*, when Chad Beville, a Tempe, Arizona-based attorney, told a reporter he was in possession of Lockhart's legal birth certificate listing his date of birth as October 31, 1986. This meant any videos produced before October 31, 2004 would be illegal under unforgiving federal law that not only held producers and distributors liable, but also customers.[46] Beville told *GayVN* in an e-mail that "four titles...appear to have been produced before (Lockhart) turned eighteen. There may be other titles he appeared in after he turned eighteen...Anything made before (October 31, 2004) would be, by definition, child pornography."[47] Lockhart's goal, Beville said, was to get the illegal videos off the market. The four videos in question were listed as *Bareboned Twinks*, *Casting Couch IV*, *Every Poolboy's Dream*, and *Schoolboy Crush*.

If Kocis was prepared for the allegation, it didn't appear so in his response. He told *GayVN* that "these are just allegations" and referred any further questions to the Pennsylvania attorney who had defended him in his earlier criminal trial, Al Flora, Jr.[48]

The scandal-sensitive porn industry wasn't waiting to see if Lockhart's claim held any validity. The Free Speech Coalition (a trade association for the adult entertainment industry) issued its own statement saying that it recommended "until the facts in this case are clarified, all (affected titles) and promotional materials should be immediately removed from circulation and distribution, and all content, online and offline, that contains the performer named Brent Corrigan should be removed and sealed for attorney review and consultation."[49]

Kocis needed to act quickly to control the damage, including potential damage to a valuable distribution arrangement he had in place with Pacific Sun Entertainment, a giant, industry-leading wholesale adult video distributor based in North Hills, California. Kocis assured everyone that Cobra Video has "color copies of the three state-issued forms of identification that Mr. Lockhart presented, including a birth certificate, all indicating a birth year of 1985." Cobra also apologized to all retailers and customers "for the inexcusable hardship and disruption in business that (Lockhart) has caused." Kocis singled out his undoubtedly nervous distributor, Pacific Sun Entertainment, noting they had handled "a difficult situation in a very prompt and effective manner."[50]

Cobra Video's news release said that all of its requests for an original copy of Lockhart's birth certificate had been rejected. Cobra's statement said the issue was further complicated by the fact that the state Lockhart was born in Idaho, a state that did not make birth certificates available under public records law, and could only be requested by the individual or an immediate family member.[51]

At the same time, Lockhart's attorney complained that Kocis continued to "harass Sean with e-mails and phone calls" and that Lockhart would not cooperate with producing an original copy of his birth certificate until Kocis ceased his contact.[52] Beville would later confirm to a reporter that Lockhart had presented Kocis a forged ID before performing in the adult videos produced for Cobra. If Lockhart's claims and statements to the FBI about his underage status were having an effect, Kocis wasn't letting on. He claimed that he had not been contacted by federal authorities about any alleged violations of the 2257 codes and said that he planned to release additional scenes Lockhart filmed for Cobra after December 2004 and that those would be distributed in later videos (later pasted into the *Brent Corrigan's Fuck Me Raw* and *Take It Like A Bad Boy* DVDs).[53]

The strict federal law known as the Child Protection and Obscenity Enforcement Act of 1988, most normally referred to as the "2257 law," typically resulted in a disclaimer posted on all adult content by producers that:

> This video contains explicit sexual material which may be offensive to some viewers. You must be eighteen years or older to enter this content. All models, actors, actresses and other persons that appear in any visual depiction of actual sexual conduct appearing or otherwise contained in this adult content were at least eighteen years of age at the time of the creation of such depictions. With regard to the remaining depictions of actual sexual conduct appearing or otherwise contained in this video, the records required pursuant to 18 U.S.C. 2257 and C.F.R. 75 are kept by the custodian of records of (company name) at (company address).

Lockhart and Roy hit a roadblock

By October 2005, Lockhart's new partnership with Grant Roy, a former Texan transplanted to sunny San Diego, California, resulted in the formation of LSG Media, LLC, and a registered domain name, www.brentcorriganonline.com.

Kocis reacted strongly to the bold move by LSG Media, launching a federal trademark lawsuit in the U.S. District Court of Southern California against Lockhart and his partners.

The suit sought damages and injunctive relief to stop Lockhart, Roy and LSG Media, LLC from releasing new titles

using the name Brent Corrigan. The latter issue addressed a
long-simmering argument over the Corrigan stage name.
Lockhart claimed in interviews and court documents that he
selected the name Corrigan from a phone book because it
sounded Irish. Kocis claimed that he chose the name in early
2004 "to be used in the creation of a series of premier adult
content DVDs/videos for Cobra" and that he was the owner of
the trade name, and had invested time and money in the promotion and creation of the character name Brent Corrigan.[54]
The suit repeated Kocis' claims that Lockhart had used forged
documents in order to work for Cobra Video in four productions and had "misappropriated (the Brent Corrigan) name to
compete in bad faith against Cobra Video."[55]

Kocis went forward in 2006 with the release of two films
Lockhart had filmed prior to their split, each of which bore
titles that reflected the contempt that had grown between the
two. *Brent Corrigan's Fuck Me Raw* featured a crude cover photo
of Lockhart exposing his anus with sperm running from his
sphincter (a Photoshop alteration to the photo allegedly added
in later) and *Take It Like A Bad Boy* (alternately named *Take It
Like A Bitch Boy*). *Take It* would be Kocis' final production for
his Cobra enterprise, covering an extraordinarily lengthy 140
minutes.

Lockhart took exceptional insult from the degrading video
titles and cover images. It was an annoyance he would have
to live with. "It bothered me…(but) I knew what (Kocis) was
trying to do, and it didn't get to me," Lockhart said.[56]

Lockhart's counsel Beville was unimpressed, noting that
the biggest problem facing Kocis and Cobra was the fact that
they had allegedly never inspected the actual ID, in violation
of federal law. "In order to prove their civil case they have to
give factual evidence of a felony committed by themselves,"
Beville claimed.[57] "I believe Bryan Kocis is doing this to keep
the other models that he may have photographed underage
from coming forward," he added. Kocis called that claim "a

baseless allegation" and urged Beville to produce any proof of any other underage performers having worked at Cobra.[58]

Kocis, through his new California counsel, Jeffrey Douglas, made it clear who he felt was at fault in the underage performance saga: Lockhart. He accused Lockhart of having committed fraud and possibly serious crimes by knowingly appearing under the age of eighteen in the videos, and "feloniously" obtaining a fake driver's license, Douglas said.[59]

In April 2006, Pacific Sun Entertainment withdrew two more Cobra Video releases, *Campus Boyz I* and *Campus Boyz II*, from distribution, offering no explanation as to why. The move did nothing to quell swirling rumors that Kocis had engaged other performers besides Lockhart under the age of eighteen. No other confirmed allegations about any other Cobra performers being underage were ever raised publicly, however.

A very personal, ugly fight

Months of nasty e-mail and blog postings followed on both sides of the Kocis-Lockhart fight, with wild allegations and personal assaults raised on each side. Supporters of Lockhart even started a blog devoted to his side, www. friendsofbrentcorrigan.com.

Roy went a step further: in the early months of 2006 he launched a blog under the unfortunate name, www. cobrakillerblog.com. Roy said he created the site because the fight with Kocis had gone public, and he was bitter. His postings to the site, he said, were "to shed light on the difficulties we were having in the lawsuit…just to shed a little light on what was going on."[60]

Jason Sechrest, who owns and operates the "Jason Curious" blog and a casting agency for gay porn actors in Southern California, wrote about the public fracture that erupted between Kocis and Lockhart. In initial postings, he seemed to take Kocis' position, but incidents to follow seemed to push Sechrest and others in the "gay porn establishment" toward Lockhart's position. A July 2006 incident at Sechrest's "Cocktails with the Stars" event at Micky's Bar in West Hollywood seemed to turn several against the reclusive Kocis. Sechrest said "Cobra continues the lies" and clarified that Cobra Video did not hold an event with Brent Corrigan at Micky's, but instead attempted to crash the weekly "Cocktails with the Stars" event.[61] Sechrest described a "pathetic cry for attention" by Cobra when one of the two men passed out free copies of a bareback video featuring Lockhart, while another posed as a fan asking for a photo to be taken with Lockhart. "Just before the flash went off, (they) threw up a copy of a Cobra video to make it look like Brent was promoting it. They ran out quickly…as Cobra continues its fork-tongued lies."[62]

Lockhart would later accuse Kocis of stealing passwords for his MySpace account and engaging in instant messaging chats with fans and others, posing as Lockhart, and sullying his reputation. "He would, like, IM all my friends. My brother IM'd him and that's how my brother found out about my adult work, he sent him a (picture), and he started soliciting sex with my brother. He didn't know it was my brother. So, after that happened, I just stopped using instant messaging," Lockhart said.[63]

Roy also was playing rough—he reportedly approached the FBI Field Office in San Diego, California on two separate occasions, filing complaints against Kocis and his Cobra Video company, alleging they were employing underage performers. No public disclosure of any FBI action was ever revealed, and no charges were ever brought.[64]

By August of 2006, gay porn giant Falcon Studios began promoting one of its major releases of the year, *The Velvet Mafia*. The film featured the name of an actor new to the industry, Fox Ryder, but his face was very familiar. Fox Ryder was Sean Lockhart. The battle for the name Brent Corrigan still in full swing, and Lockhart not backing away from the gay porn industry, a savvy Falcon Studios found a way to move Lockhart's image (under the new Fox Ryder name) onto the DVD box cover. Gay porn industry insider Sechrest said he believed the "scare tactics" of Cobra Video forced Falcon to abandon any ideas of using the Brent Corrigan name. "(But), I think the drama and mystery will only help to sell the movie more. Brent's fans know what the hell he looks like and he's on the box cover for God's sake. And if this isn't life imitating art, I don't know what is: in *The Velvet Mafia*, two porn companies are violently vying for the exclusivity of (Lockhart's) character, Fox Ryder."[65]

More troubles for Lockhart

In October 2006, abandoning the new stage name of Fox Ryder given to him by Falcon producers, Lockhart finally launched www.brentcorriganonline.com, described as a members-only site that would allow Lockhart to produce and distribute new adult material. Just a short time later, however, the site went dark when its online payment coordinator, CC Bill, allegedly canceled his billing contract reportedly under pressure from Kocis, and his attorneys determined to maintain control of the Brent Corrigan name.

The billing contract stalled and with no way to create a members-only site, Kocis had successfully stymied LSG Media with their newest venture. Further complicating matters would be internal struggles within LSG Media. The fight centered on who made the decisions about the site and how each of the partners was being paid.

In a March 2007 interview with www.Gaywired.com, Lockhart claimed he had filmed more than twenty scenes for the new website, but was only a thirty percent owner of the overall project. Lockhart explained that he started the company in which he was a part owner in order to have "something to show for continued adult work in the industry." Lockhart told Gaywired.com that "Grant (Roy) and I want to take pride in producing wholesome adult work where no one is degraded, embarrassed or exploited," he said. "We pay attention to good pairing and we only produce condom work."[66]

Does Cobra Video live on?

In June 2007, less than six months after Kocis' murder, "Jeffrey" at Cobra Video sent an e-mail blast to Cobra's fans from the King Cobra e-mail account addressing the murder of Bryan Kocis and a new "transitional period" for the company:

> This year we lost Bryan to a senseless crime. Bryan devoted the last six years to developing Cobra Video into what you know it to be today. Bryan kept working and making movies as that is what he loved to do. He had a vision and as devoted Cobra fans, you were loyal to his product.[67]

With that, the beat seemingly went on uninterrupted at Cobra with fan e-mail noting that "the company and the website will live on" with re-releases of *Take It Like A Bad Boy* and a slightly reworked later version, *Take It Like A Bitch Boy* becoming available within days. "We welcome you back to the website and we invite you to visit us often for news, upcoming sales, and new titles from Cobra Video" the e-mail added. "And don't forget about our Cobra Models! Fresh new faces are on the horizon!"[68]

No new Cobra Video titles were created or released after 2007, however, with the company's websites still listing previously released titles and about a dozen photo shoots of Lockhart (many shot during a trip to Hawaii by Lockhart and Kocis) advertised on the site.[69]

The publicity surrounding Kocis' murder apparently did serve to drive some further interest in Cobra Video. Eurocreme USA, a New York City-based retail and wholesale distributor of adult content, announced in June 2007 that it would distribute the "last Cobra Video production by director Brian (sic.) Kocis before his death," *Take It Like A Bad Boy*.[70] "We're happy to put this movie out because we've always been fans of Brian's (sic.) work," Eurocreme's sales manager Hugo Harley said. "His movies have always been best-sellers."[71]

In July 2007, the Adult Entertainment Broadcast Network (or AEBN) announced it was becoming the exclusive "video on demand" home for the Cobra vehicle, *Take It Like A Bad Boy*, reported to be Kocis' twenty-second video overall.[72] AEBN offered the video through its PornTube.com website and noted it had enjoyed "a longtime relationship with Cobra Video" and that the murder of Bryan Kocis "has affected me deeply," said Chris Baker of AEBN. "I feel honored to have a chance to showcase his last work this way."[73]

Kocis' murder doesn't end the controversy

Although the "collaboration" of Lockhart and Kocis had produced some of the best-selling gay videos of their time, it also produced a vicious and very personal fight between them that would prove difficult to reconcile. Despite that reality, Lockhart took the high road upon news of Kocis' unexpected death in January 2007. In a February 2, 2007 posting on his site, www.brentcorrigan.com, he wrote a brief statement under the heading "Pay your respects to Bryan Kocis." In it, he reported he had been advised by attorneys not to comment on the matter, but noted, "The settlement documents were signed and all parties were looking forward to moving on to a mutually beneficial arrangement. Please pay your respects to Bryan Kocis, his family and friends. It is time to show them all the love and support you have shown me."[74]

Kocis' death did nothing to quell controversy surrounding the videos he left behind. A fervent Lockhart supporter and blogger operating under the online name DeWayne in San Diego was not letting matters go. In September 2007 (a full nine months after Kocis' death), DeWayne in San Diego reported on his blog that he had sent a new letter to the Child Exploitation and Obscenity Section of the U.S. Department of Justice. In the letter, DeWayne raised issue with whether proper 2257 records were even available for the Cobra videos still in distribution and produced between 2001 and 2007.[75]

Cobra's online records' statement indicated the 2257 documents were held by the Pennsylvania State Police, although Pennsylvania authorities repeatedly denied they held the 2257 records at the State Police Barrack at Wyoming, Pennsylvania. For his part, DeWayne believed the records were either destroyed in the blaze at Kocis' home or they were seized by police.

Wherever the records were, DeWayne clearly wanted authorities to swoop in and stop Cobra from continuing to sell videos, particularly ones featuring Lockhart (even though they were presumably legal, if produced beyond the date Lockhart turned eighteen and was still in the Kocis stable).

As of 2012, the 2257 Compliance Statements still posted online for Cobra Video and its companion site, www.brentcorriganxxx.com, listed 62 Dallas, Suite 238 in Dallas, Pennsylvania as the site where records were held. That address cannot be found on web-based or state-issued paper maps, and no such site exists in Dallas, Pennsylvania. The sites still list "B. Kocis" as the "custodian of records" at his former Midland Drive home (now gone) in Dallas.[76]

Beyond restating the copyrights Cobra claimed on the videos, the Cobra website noted that "All models appearing on this website, and in our videos, were at least eighteen years of age at the time of production. Proof on file as required by law. Cobra Video LLC complies with Federal Law 18USC2257 and Federal Regulations 28CFR75."[77]

The site also noted, "Use of the words 'boy, boi, boyz, twink' etc. are popular gay terms and do not in any way, shape or form indicate that the model is under the age of eighteen. This website uses adult(s) models and warrants the use of these materials for adults as a visual fantasy or education in the Privacy (sic.) of their homes."[78]

A toll-free number listed on the site is now "out of service."

The last of the Cobra empire

On January 8, 2008, almost one year after Bryan's death, his father Michael Kocis, Sr. (as the executor of his estate) filed a wrongful death lawsuit against two men, Harlow Cuadra and Joseph Kerekes, for the murder of his son and the burning of his home. The suit sought unspecified monetary damages for funeral, burial, estate, and property damage costs from Cuadra and Kerekes. Whether the Kocis family actually ever expected to receive any compensation was unclear, but the action did represent that the Kocis family was not willing to give up on pursuing civil remedies against the men they believe murdered Bryan, family attorney Conrad Falvello said.[79]

In April 2008, the Kocis family and estate won a default judgment of "undetermined damages" against Cuadra and Kerekes after no one representing either defendant responded to the civil filing in the Luzerne County Court of Common Pleas.[80]

The last remnants of Bryan Kocis and the Cobra Video empire he built came tumbling down as a bulldozer and front-end loader reduced his fire-ravaged home at 60 Midland Drive in Dallas Township to rubble on August 17, 2007. As the *Citizens' Voice* reported, "The half-charred home, guarded by no trespassing signs and crime scene tape had been a haunting sight for residents of Midland Drive, a constant reminder of the night seven months ago when police found (Kocis) slashed and stabbed to death inside his burning home."[81]

Neighbor Nancy Parsons, told a reporter that she felt sorry for Bryan and that "once the ground is smoothed over, it's like you're erasing him."[82] The lot containing Kocis' former home was eventually purchased by Parsons and a grassy lot is all that remains of the site today.

CHAPTER 4

Virginia is for Lovers

"Harlow said something to me once...he said, 'Bo-bo, sometimes I forget what Harlow I am.' I didn't think that much about it at the time, but I think there was so much pressure on Harlow, even pressure I put on him, to be so many things. I think he may have just went off a little."

—Joe Kerekes

Since 1969, tourism officials in Virginia have attempted to lure visitors to the state by reminding them that "Virginia is for lovers." The phrase has helped boost tourism to the state *and* it accurately describes the relationship between Harlow Cuadra and Joseph Kerekes. Although Cuadra and Kerekes have said they still love each other, they will spend the rest of their lives apart from one another.

Outside of their personal lives, the two men attempted their own form of luring visitors or "tourism" dollars to their own Virginia enterprise. They were so successful, in fact, that at one point local officials in Norfolk became concerned when a Google search of the city's name would most often pop up with Norfolk Male Companions at or near the top of the search list. It reflected the huge investment the couple put into marketing their escort business not only in Virginia but all across the Atlantic seaboard—fueled by online links and more than $120,000 annually in advertisements placed in gay publications in Baltimore, Richmond, and Washington, D.C.[1]

They also invested in themselves—spending most mornings at Big House Gym in Virginia Beach. They chose that gym because it lacked all the clients and "fans" of Cuadra found at Gold's Gym. Kerekes called their new gym "this little shitty thing (where) you slide your card, and no one is ever there, and if they are it's just great guys, like bartenders and bouncers."[2] Cuadra said he liked the gym because "you can do whatever you want in there."[3] Doing whatever they wanted is just what they did—including filming Cuadra's first solo gay porn video on the site. It was the start of more to come.

Cuadra was the star on the Norfolk Male Companions and the www.boisrus.com website touted him as "Virginia's Hottest Gay Male Escort." On a profile next to photos of Cuadra clad only in revealing underwear, he falsely listed his age as nineteen (he was well into his twenties), his height and weight, the size of his penis, and that he was a "skater" and "surfer," basically "an All-American next door bad boy" of Cuban-German descent.[4]

Another posting on the site listed Cuadra as "Stud Wonder Harlow" and declared him as "the hottest 'top' in teen porn and escort world as voted by user review sites."[5]

A boy named Harlow

Harlow Raymond Cuadra was born August 5, 1981 in Miami, Florida to a fragile and struggling family, ultimately led by his mother, Gladis Zaldivar. With Harlow's birth father out of the picture and never a presence, Mrs. Zaldivar attempted to build a normal family for her growing brood of four children. But poverty, a divorce and a struggle to learn English and assimilate contributed to continued challenges. The family eventually settled in nearby Homestead, Florida—a town perhaps best known for having been leveled by the devastating Category 5 Hurricane Andrew in 1992.

During his trial for the murder of Bryan Kocis, a psychologist who examined Cuadra described his childhood as a nightmare, a description confirmed by Cuadra's older brother, José.[6] "We were living on welfare, living on food stamps, it was bad," José Cuadra said.[7]

An April 1985 marriage for Cuadra's mother provided financial support but created new tensions that remained a secret for years to come.

"(Our stepfather) had a fixation with Harlow," José Cuadra said.[8]

José said his stepfather, would use the ruse of sending him to the store so that he could have time alone with the younger Harlow. Despite these and other allegations, Cuadra's stepfather was never charged or convicted of child molestation or any related offense.

Gladis Zaldivar said she did not know about the alleged problem for years until she one day decided to open a letter her husband had written to her son, now away at boot camp for the U.S. Navy. Cuadra said when he was in the Navy, his stepfather wrote him many letters—in Spanish—"love letters…like a man would write to a woman. One day, he gives the letter to my mother and tells her to mail this for him," Cuadra explained. "Well, my mom opens the letter because she wants to add her letter (in) and…she opened the letter so she can add her own and reseal it and she read it and she was—it knocked her out. That terminated their relationship."[9][10]

Though the repeated years of alleged childhood molestation had been difficult, Cuadra said, "I just grinned and bared (the molesting) because it was better me than my little brother and sister."[11]

Cuadra said he went to visit his stepfather in 2001 and came out to him as a gay man. His stepfather reacted poorly,

Cuadra said, calling him a "faggot." Cuadra added, "I didn't understand (his reaction). He threw me out of the house and I had to walk to get a cab."(12)

It was shortly after this Cuadra dropped out of all contact with his family. A phone call from his mother, who Cuadra said repeatedly stated her unconditional love for her son, was no help. "I couldn't accept it, so I got off the phone with her and I threw the phone into a river…I canceled my phone account and I went with another service, and that was the last time I spoke to my parents, in 2001, and my entire side of the family."(13)

In the interim, Cuadra and Kerekes gravitated toward Kerekes' parents who lived nearby in Virginia Beach, whom they called Momma K and Pappa K. "They were my parents and they loved me," Cuadra said. "They would bring it up, 'Harlow, you have to meet your mom. You know, we want to meet your mom. You have to find her, Harlow. You have to get to her.'"(14) Despite such encouragement, Cuadra said he still resisted. "I couldn't deal with it," he said.(15)

That separation would last until 2007 when Cuadra's younger brother ran across his name on the Internet as a possible suspect in the murder of Bryan Kocis. His mother and family reached out to him again, reconnecting via MySpace. Cuadra's youngest brother, David, said he and his sister ran across Cuadra's name on MySpace and sent Cuadra an e-mail, but reports he received an odd reply: "Sorry, I don't know any fourteen-year-olds." David didn't give up, instead asking his older brother José, now in his late twenties, to send another e-mail, prompting a reunion.

Discovery of Cuadra on MySpace also meant his family discovered his career in gay porn and escorting. "It was weird at first, but he's my brother," José testified at Harlow's trial. "He was scared that we would reject him because he's gay. He's my brother."(16)

Cuadra cut off family contact after he got out of the Navy, concerned that his sexual orientation on top of his work as a male escort would be too much for them to handle.[17]

Shortly after the e-mail exchanges with his siblings, however, the five years of silence were ended as Cuadra visited his mother's home in Greenville, South Carolina, with his partner and lover, Joe Kerekes, along. The visits would continue even as authorities began to close in on Cuadra and Kerekes on a charge of murder. For Cuadra's youngest sibling, David, "I didn't care about that, him being gay. I was happy to get my brother back."[18] His sister Melissa felt likewise: "Harlow told us he was afraid we would reject him because he was in the pornography business and he was gay."[19]

In and out of the Navy

Cuadra reported for duty in the U.S. Navy in January 2000, and served two years, eleven months and eight days, including receiving training as a hospital corpsman. His last assignment was at the Oceana Naval Air Station at Virginia Beach, Virginia. It was during this time that Cuadra met Joe Kerekes.[20]

A civilian spokesman for the U.S. Navy confirmed at Cuadra's trial that he sought separation from the Navy in 2006 on the basis of his admitted homosexuality—a violation of the military's controversial "Don't Ask, Don't Tell" policy that outlawed service in the military by openly gay individuals. After a short legal struggle, he received an honorary discharge.[21]

Cuadra described being in the Navy like being "watched over by a loving yet strict parent who kept me fed, clothed and cared for."[22]

Shortly after leaving the Navy, Cuadra moved in with Kerekes.

It was a quick romance. "(Joe) was my first and only, definitely my first and only," Cuadra told film producer John Roecker in his documentary film *Everything You Ever Wanted to Know About Gay Porn Stars*.[23] Cuadra talked about his first date with Kerekes, which consisted of a public meeting at a Virginia

Beach shopping mall. "(Joe) thought I wasn't interested (in him)," Cuadra said. "Like I met him in the mall just to walk around and entertain him and all and not to let him down? But, no, I was really interested, I liked him. It was kind of like my first date. I didn't know how to act."[24]

It would be Kerekes who would draw the still closeted Cuadra out of the closet. "(Joe) sat me down on my bed and he grabbed my fingers and just interlocked them (with his) and all of a sudden everything was, like, muted and I couldn't hear anything," Cuadra said. "(Joe's) eyes were all teary, his searching brown eyes. Then he goes, 'Harlow, Harlow, I want to be jealous over you.'"[25]

The "I want to be jealous over you" line was one Kerekes made up, and one that would closely match how he would deal with Cuadra for the forthcoming years.

Cuadra's post-Navy years, however, were not ones he completely enjoyed, life becoming difficult with the $10-an-hour jobs he was able to get.[26]

Attempting to go to school to train as a hospital medical technician, along with a high cost of living in the beach community of Virginia Beach, made making ends meet a challenge. "It was out of free will that I escorted, entirely subject to the law of necessity. I needed a job."[27]

Looking back, not only does Cuadra point to Kerekes' influence over him in coming out, he also credits Kerekes with leading him into escorting—a career that Kerekes had already undertaken. "Well, I wish(ed) I could go to school, but...I met Joe and he got me involved in male escorting, which is like being a call-boy, literally," Cuadra said. "They called me and I went to their homes. It was the first time I had ever done anything like that. I didn't know that anything like that even existed, at least not something that organized."[28]

Early on, Harlow and Joe used "stage" or "performer" names to meet with their clients. "(When) I started working for Joe way back in the day, it was, like, alright 'Call me Chris,'"

Cuadra said, but clients would be confused. "I would have to sit there and convince them that I'm Harlow, and so I said after a while, I was, like, screw it, just use my name 'cause it's easier for you."[29]

Cuadra says his very first client was a man claiming to be a former professional football player with an intense foot fetish. "He wanted me to just lay back and play with my feet. He even forbid me from clipping my own toenails."[30]

Before long, Cuadra reports he ceded much of the control of his life to the slightly older Kerekes, his lover but also perhaps a father figure he had never known. Kerekes took care of "booking" Cuadra, all the while keeping Cuadra's image front and center on the web. "Running the escort service, we were making a lot of money on a daily basis," Cuadra said. "We thought that as long as the escort business was on the up-and-up, we do not need to send (porn) content out to be printed on DVDs by factories. We didn't need anybody's help; we could do it all in house. That was how the whole thing took off."[31]

In Roecker's documentary, Cuadra's voice, recorded over a phone from inside a correctional facility, rises with excitement as he describes how he would e-mail webmasters at gay porn sites and ask them to attach links from their site to Cuadra and Kerekes' new enterprise.

There were problems, however.

Criminal records in Virginia indicate that Cuadra's escort career led to at least two criminal citations during a September 28, 2004 arrest. At that time, police in Norfolk, Virginia charged him with violations of state law covering body massage enterprises and for operating without a city license (two typical citations used by local authorities to crack down on prostitution). A small mountain of civil complaints against both men—primarily tracing back to their difficulty in paying their bills on time—continued to grow through the years as well. Joseph Kerekes had previously filed a Chapter 7 bankruptcy in 1998 that discharged an undisclosed amount of personal debts in April 1999.[32]

Cuadra said he and Kerekes also did not worry about the widespread problem plaguing most adult sites: piracy of content by users. Cuadra said his philosophy was "basically if you are going to steal it and share it, at least leave my logo on there and everyone will know where you got it. I wasn't going to be greedy about it. I got my money, my share, and it became kind of fun."[33]

Cuadra also knew how to enjoy the fruits of his labor. An avid car collector and self-professed "motor head," he posted messages and photos frequently on Dodge Viper Club forums, gloating about his vehicles. In July 2004, he joined the Viper Club forums online, announcing his purchase of a 2004 red Dodge Viper. He gloated that "over at Tysinger (Dodge in Hampton, Va.), I only pay the sticker price. They don't add anything in. I could get a better deal off of E-bay, butt (sic.) I cannot wait."[34] In a February 15, 2006 posting under the screen name of "Quickysrt," Cuadra gloated that "(I) got the new Vette…but kept the Viper. Picked it up yesterday at Colonial Chevy."[35]

Another forum member asked Cuadra to compare the Corvette to his Viper. "It is very comfy…I bought it as the daily driver in mind with some track use in the future. The ride is very soft (like a caddy) yet it has no body roll and feels great above 2500 rpm. It does not scare the shyt (sic.) out of me like the Viper.(I) have the navi system which is pimp but I'll never use. Great insulation (quiet ride), lots of power, I recommend it."[36] Ever mindful of the attention he could gather, he posted that "nobody looks at me in the Vette. The Viper is the attention whore."[37]

He closed out his postings in the Viper forum on December 6, 2006 responding to a club members' prompt that asked members "What have you done this past year that's worth mentioning?" Cuadra posted (complete with smiley faces) that he "got off drugs and (was) living life better. 2007 is going to be a real money maker."[38] Despite the online posting, it was never clear whether Cuadra or Kerekes used any drugs, although both enjoyed drinking alcohol.

Lights, camera, action at BoyBatter

Cuadra claims the original idea for doing gay porn was for him and Kerekes to videotape, produce, and distribute it under the "BoyBatter" name. The name, Cuadra said, was a "tongue-in-cheek (reference) for young men's semen."[39] "BoyBatter started as a hobby, I was bored," Cuadra said. But over time, BoyBatter became "Joseph's prized cash cow," he said.[40]

Kerekes convinced Cuadra that he should not only be producing gay porn videos but that appearing in the videos himself would help sales. Cuadra started with a solo masturbation scene Kerekes filmed of him. "We were just having a good time," Cuadra said. "It did not sink in until we started receiving the orders for the movies and I recognized a couple of the names on the those order forms and I was, like, 'Oh, alright, this is different. Here it goes.' I remember as (the video) was uploading to the website my palms were sweaty. I said, 'Oh boy, this is it!'"[41]

Cuadra said shortly after launching the BoyBatter site, it made money and quickly became the daily focus of Kerekes, who took over the site's business operations. "That was it," Cuadra said. "(Joe) took possession over it and that was the last time I saw it the way it was."[42]

Gay porn journalist J.C. Adams of the online *Gay Porn Times* believes despite the amateur nature of the site, Cuadra had some porn star potential. "In gay porn it's said you have to have a great face, great body, or a great dick. You have to have one of at least those three things to work. If you have two of those things you can become famous. If you have all three, you can become a star. I think in the case of Harlow Cuadra, he had at least two of those qualities."[43]

It wasn't all fun, Cuadra confessed. "A big part of me was sad.

It was like, this is the mark that I'm leaving."[44] He expressed similar sadness surrounding some of his escort assignments that took him to the homes of married men where he sometimes saw family pictures displayed around the house. "It made me feel like a home-wrecker, like I was sort of facilitating that family's downfall."[45] He adds that a "melancholy moment would place its cold hand" on his shoulder from time to time, but that he overcame his occasional guilt and shame to continue all the while "condemning my desires even as I acted them out."[46]

In its heyday, BoyBatter.com purported to provide access to "the hottest college and military studs on the planet." Under a section called "Boy Batter Boys," the website announced "this section is our claim to fame. The Boy Batter Boys section is updated weekly featuring only hot military and college stud boys in Norfolk, Virginia. These amateur young bucks are filmed using the very best in professional lighting and camera equipment."[47]

Its first actor, gay-for-pay Army veteran Justin Hensley, was paid only $50 for his first appearance on the site, Cuadra said. Eventually, more content was added—all of it of the amateur variety—"but the sex scenes were good" even if the story lines, such as using the tried and true "seduce the pizza delivery boy" scheme, were corny. But that was all part of the plan. "We tried to be as corny as possible mocking the bigger video houses," Cuadra said. "I paid the guys very little money. They wanted to do this."[48]

At its peak, the BoyBatter site offered its approximately 7,500 members fifty-one originally-produced videos (with scenes culled from about fifteen separate video shoots) and forty-four photo galleries that included solo, couple, and group action (including many scenes shot with Cuadra or Kerekes). Kerekes gloated that the BoyBatter site eventually pulled in between $9,000 and $10,000 a month on DVD sales. Three DVDs were marketed from the site (and eventually elsewhere through other porn distributors), including *Major Hardon, Boy*

Splatter, and *Young Bucks in Heat.*

Young Bucks in Heat earned a controversial nomination by DVD distributor Pornteam.com as one of the Best Films of 2008, even while its producers and stars, Cuadra and Kerekes, remained jailed on murder charges.[49]

Kerekes said his job was to keep the BoyBatter site going on a daily basis, and he employed an unusual (and possibly illegal) tactic to keep the site's name in front of potential clients on a daily basis. Kerekes said he would use the credit card numbers of former clients of their escort businesses, www.boisrus.com and Norfolk Male Companions, to buy refundable, one- or three-day passes to various gay porn sites where he could drop in ads and "reviews" of BoisRU and its services. He would quickly cancel the orders before the "introductory period" ended, keeping the customer's credit cards from being charged.

In addition, up to forty PCs and laptops were fired up each day from inside their home, he said, with "spam" ads running in chat rooms all over the Internet. America Online, MSNBC, Yahoo, and MSN chat rooms were especially targeted but had to be "rebooted" each day because of aggressive efforts to kick commercial "chatters" out of the various chat rooms.

Kerekes said keeping the website and related enterprises going each day was hard, demanding work. "Whenever I would complain to Harlow about how the escorting was going, he'd tell me to go back and take care of the computers."[50] Later in prison, a jailhouse informant would report that Kerekes said Cuadra had to do most of "the mule work" of the escorting business, while he ran the business side of things.

Cuadra's good looks and large endowment won notice from others as well. Jason Sechrest reported that Falcon Studios, the "big daddy" of the gay porn world, approached Cuadra when it was casting two of its 2006 productions, *Riding Hard* and *Dripping Wet.* Cuadra was never cast, however, in any Falcon productions.[51] Sechrest quoted a Falcon casting agent as saying when they approached Cuadra about "becoming a porn star," he replied by e-mail that he "already was a porn star" because of his work on Boybatter.com.[52]

Joseph Manual Kerekes

While Cuadra was the up-and-coming "twink" star in the BoyBatter stable, it was Kerekes who was the star of *Major Hardon*. Cashing in on his brief, one-month military career that ended when Kerekes was kicked out of boot camp, Kerekes sported a traditional high and tight Marine haircut for his role as the slightly older and bossy Trent in the movie. As the DVD's cover describes it, *Major Hardon* tells the story of "three young marines (sic.) determined to find a way to release their tensions and end up helping each other achieve their mission!"[51] Kerekes appears in all three of the movie's scenes featuring three other more "twinkish" actors credited as Jason, Justin, and Seth. Kerekes in the role of Trent leads the climatic three-way orgy to end the epic.[53]

The BoisRUs escort website listed Kerekes as "Stud Marine Trent" and twenty-four years old (about ten years younger than his actual age). His description noted (falsely) that he was a Marine and emphasized other characteristics such as his muscle tone, hairiness, his tan, and the fact that he was a "dominant" lover.[54]

Another listing for "Chris" on "All American Escorts" showed Kerekes' picture and described him as a twenty-one-year-old college student who was sexually versatile and promised: "Currently a college student. Please call me for after school fun. You will not be disappointed."[55]

It was a long way from Kerekes' initial career path as a youth pastor that he said put him in the pulpit of the Hampton, Virginia mega-church, Bethel Temple Assembly of God. The Bethel Temple congregation, which describes itself as "a multi-cultural, interdenominational church that exists to bring people into dynamic relationship with Jesus Christ," apparently saw potential in a young Kerekes.[56]

The Kerekes family landed at Bethel Temple at the end of a trail of various other churches his mother Rosalie took him and his two younger siblings to as a "Navy widow." Her husband often away on long deployments, Mrs. Kerekes raised her children in a "strict and Godly manner"[57] and "We went from church to church (during) most of my childhood," Joseph said. "At seventeen, I started faithfully attending Bethel Temple and soon thereafter began an intense discipleship under Pastor Ron Johnston."[58]

Joseph Manual Kerekes was born December 30, 1973 in Butte, Montana while his father was on Navy assignment in the northwest. In 1982, the family settled in Virginia Beach, Virginia where Kerekes' father Fred was assigned by the Navy.

Kerekes describes his childhood as "wonderful" because he believed he had the best mother and father in the world. "Dad was gone a lot, he served twenty-four years in the Navy with long deployments, but mom stayed home with us."[59] He would tell others that the family didn't have a lot of extra money, even rationing use of their air conditioner to save money.[60]

In school, Kerekes was outgoing and popular and scored good grades into high school. Upon high school graduation, he won financial support from Bethel Temple to attend Valley Forge Christian College in Phoenixville, Pennsylvania (ironically, just over 100 miles southeast of the site where Bryan Kocis would one day be murdered). The school traces its start to revival meetings started in a Pennsylvania campground in 1931. It claims as its mission "To prepare individuals for a life of service and leadership in the church and the world" and tells prospective students, "If you hear God calling you to full-time, vocational ministry, or if you sense him leading you to serve him in the marketplace," then VFCC is for them.[61]

Kerekes says he earned Dean's List citations for each of the three and a half years he attended the school. He never graduated, however, after angry outbursts and struggles with his impulsive behaviors caused him friction among the evangelical and fundamentalist students and faculty. He left the seminary and eventually the church amidst his struggles.[62]

Kerekes "falling out" with the church occurred when he was just twenty-three. It would not be the last time his temper and behavior would do him in. Kerekes takes the blame on himself, saying many people in the church and his family were supportive and encouraging of him despite his anger problems. "I received unspeakable favor from the senior pastor, Ron Johnston," Kerekes said. "I was the youngest person ever to stand and preach in Bethel's pulpit (in a) 6,000 seat sanctuary."

Kerekes recalls his preaching as a "magnificent" experience where the characteristically charismatic Pentecostal worshipers "rose to their feet in tremendous applause."[63] He added via a 2007 blog posting while awaiting trial that "I rose quickly in the church and was ministering on a weekly basis and there were some who did not like this, so there was controversy over it, but when I left the ministry, my love for people remained the same, thus energizing my escort career."[64]

His church mentor, Bethel Temple's former senior pastor Johnston, told *Out* magazine that he sensed Kerekes was in a struggle between good and evil in his life. "There's a dichotomy in Joseph," Johnston said. "There are two Josephs. I would see a Joseph that on one side was extremely kind and good, and on the other side he would lose it. I've seen this before with people that were demon-possessed."[65]

Johnston's stark description of Kerekes is one that Kerekes agrees with himself. "I've done some really bad things in my life," he said. "I have not lived a life that has pleased or served God."[66]

The dichotomy of Joe Kerekes goes all the way to his sexual identity as well. Although he spent most of his adult years in a sexually intimate relationship with another man, performed in gay porn videos, and worked as a prostitute for male clients for many years, he does not consider himself gay. The most he will say about his sexual identity is: "I still struggle with some issues of lust, but the only man I have ever loved was Harlow."[67]

Does this mean he was just "gay for pay" as some performers and escorts say? Kerekes says no. "I still do not call myself gay. I just love Harlow. I have never loved another—man or woman. Through high school, ministry years—I never even thought of myself as anything but straight."[68] Kerekes said his feelings for Cuadra remain strong, though there were noticeable tensions between the two men under the strain of their criminal cases. "We are still hot and heavy. I have hundreds of letters (that) I have received since our arrest (from Harlow).… We 'made love' together and simply 'had sex' as male escorts or in porn. (Harlow) was/is my lover, my mate, my better half."[69]

Pastor Johnston recalls a day when Kerekes came to him a few years after leaving the church and after washing out of the U.S. Marines being declared "unfit for duty." He said Kerekes confessed he had started a male escort service and was in a sexual relationship with Cuadra. It was a stark contrast from the young man he once thought could be a successful, and charismatic, pastor for an Assembly of God parish. Johnston said he told Kerekes "You have the call of God on your life. It doesn't matter how far you've gone or what you've done, God never takes back what he gives you. God is always there, no matter what happens or what happened, to forgive and help you."[70]

The pastor would not hear of Kerekes again until the spring of 2007 when news broke of his and Cuadra's arrest for the murder of Bryan Kocis.

Joe Kerekes' ambition

Kerekes' journey to that low point had taken him from Bible college, studying to become a personal trainer and nutrition specialist, one month in the Marines, to a lucrative career in male escorting. "I was feeling like a failure; ministry, Marines, many good vocations, all failed," he said.[71]

Escorting then, he said, filled the desperate need for money and he declared matter-of-factly, "I knew I had the gift of 'people skills,' so I escorted."[72] Kerekes' ambition to succeed served him well in escorting, as he worked with as many as ten different escort services advertising him under various names and various sexual identities: straight, bisexual and gay. Most of the time, however, he operated under the names Mark or Trent. "I was pretty much the all-around gay, bi, straight male escort for all of Norfolk and Virginia Beach, because I was available 24/7," he said.[73]

It wasn't all easy. Kerekes started out living in "transitional" neighborhoods of Norfolk, including a $300-a-month apartment at 3125 Jersey Ave. and spent his nights without escort calls working the gay clubs and bars of the Hampton Road areas of Virginia.

Cuadra, who was living in Virginia Beach at the time, later joined Kerekes in an apartment at Hague Towers in nearby Norfolk. Referred to by them as a "penthouse apartment"(they actually lived on the twentieth floor, not the top floor), they later moved to a custom-built home on Stratem Court in Virginia Beach. "We started raunchy, but ended up being high-class," Kerekes said.[74]

Kerekes today makes strong claims that he and Cuadra pulled in more than $1 million in 2005 and 2006 from their growing escort and amateur porn empire. Investigators would later confirm that the escort service was bringing in money in at least the six figure range, if not a lot less than the $1 million Kerekes claimed. Kerekes and Cuadra capped their investment efforts in the escort business in 2005 by buying the house at 1028 Stratem Court meant to be the base for their growing enterprise.[75] "What Harlow and I built and earned (was) with only the skin of our asses, escorting," Kerekes said.[76]

Kerekes continues to deny he and Cuadra faced any financial difficulties as 2007 dawned, but he told a different story on a secretly taped intercept of him and Cuadra explaining their financial woes to Grant Roy and Sean Lockhart.[77]

"We almost lost our house," Cuadra said.

"Yeah, we were behind, we were behind two or three moths, they were about to take it," Kerekes added.

"The Viper, everything was back in payments," Cuadra said, noting they caught up on payments just enough to keep it from being repossessed.[78]

Despite all the financial challenges, Cuadra said "any chance (Joe) can take to act like a big shot, he'll do it. That is (why) Vegas is the only town that makes him feel comfortable in his skin. It's over the top. That's Joseph Kerekes."[79]

The employees of BoisRUs

A list of eighteen to twenty-two year old "boys" was employed occasionally by Kerekes and Cuadra, but it is unclear how many "employees" were ever a part of the escort service beyond Cuadra and Kerekes themselves.

Three of those men were called as witnesses in the 2009 murder trial of Harlow Cuadra. Justin Hensley said he was out of work in April 2005 when he answered an ad for male dancers placed in the classified section of the *Virginian-Pilot* newspaper, and Kerekes offered him work.

As he started working with Cuadra and Kerekes, "it was (just) an escort business, and then it picked up into the gay pornographic production, gay porn videos to be specific," Hensley said, by July 2005.[80]

Hensley, a soldier in the U.S. Army, would later be deployed on two tours of duty to U.S. military operations in Iraq. But before leaving to serve his country, he spent time serving male clients procured for him by Cuadra and Kerekes— escort work that brought him a maximum of $250 an hour. Hensley described clients of the escort business as high-level executives, military officials, and political figures. His claim that a U.S. Senator was among the clients for BoisRUs was never confirmed.

"Mr. Kerekes pretty much was the boss of (BoisRUs), he

mostly answered the phone and set up everything, but he occasionally went on calls with myself. Mr. Cuadra pretty much did the escorting full-time," Hensley said.[81]

His escort work eventually led to at least one on-camera performance with Cuadra in the very first BoyBatter gay porn production. Despite his growing involvement with the gay business enterprises of Cuadra and Kerekes, Hensley said he was engaged to be married to a young woman and was only "gay for pay." "I grew to be a friend of Cuadra because he took care of me," Hensley said.[82]

Another young man affiliated with Cuadra and Kerekes' enterprises said he earned up to $250 for an hour spent with clients and that he witnessed a well-oiled operation where Kerekes ran the booking for the escorts under the BoisRUs company, and Cuadra ran the pornography company.[83]

Andrew Shunk, who regularly worked out with Cuadra and Kerekes at the Big House Gym in Virginia Beach, said the couple "usually worked out once a day, usually in the morning for at least an hour, and it was mainly muscle building," he said.[84]

Shunk and Hensley described a tight relationship between the men, with Kerekes acting as the muscles and Cuadra as the brain.[85] They said Kerekes worked to keep Cuadra happy and pleased, an assessment confirmed by Kerekes mother. "Joe went out of his way to make Harlow happy," Rosalie Kerekes said.[86] His efforts to keep Cuadra happy, however, did not prevent Kerekes from continued angry outbursts in their home and elsewhere. Joe's temper remained legendary.

The nature of Harlow and Joe

Needing a place to stay, Hensley said he began living with Cuadra and Kerekes in September 2005, first at their townhome on Link Court in Virginia Beach and the later at their Stratem Court home. He would describe, however, a less-than-ideal living condition. "They both pretty much wanted me to stay there and work all the time and not have a social life," Hensley said. "I couldn't go out. I (could) go down the street to get lunch, but I had to come back. I could only leave on the weekends."[87]

Hensley rejects suggestions that Kerekes was domineering over Cuadra. Kerekes could be "a loud mouth," Hensley said, and Cuadra "just kind of put up with it."[88] "I grew to be, you know, a friend of (Harlow), because he took care of me and (Cuadra and Kerekes) had their disagreements about things, but I don't think Harlow would do *anything* for Joe," Hensley said.[89]

Hensley said he finally decided to leave in March 2006 when a fight between Cuadra and Kerekes went too far, with Kerekes firing off a Glock 9mm handgun inside the house during a fit of rage. Kerekes himself admits to throwing table lamps, computers, and other items at Cuadra during other arguments.[90]

Hensley left, he said, because "I was worried about my well-being."[91]

He said he did not witness the gun being discharged, but heard it from an adjacent room as Kerekes and Cuadra engaged in a disagreement that quickly grew to yelling and screaming.[92] Hensley said he could be certain that it was Kerekes who fired the gun "because I walked in there afterwards. He was the one with the handgun in his hand. I'm pretty sure if he wanted to shoot Harlow in close proximity, especially with a handgun, he would have hit him."[93]

Shunk would also later confirm he saw bullet holes in the walls of the Stratem Court house and "from what I was told, Joe discharged the weapon in the house."[94]

Whether Kerekes had the will to kill Cuadra or just scare him, no one will ever know. The relationship between Harlow and Joe could be complicated. The partnership of Cuadra and Kerekes was punctuated by their declarations of intense love for one another. Joe had Harlow's last name "Cuadra" tattooed on his buttock. But they also were haunted by periods of growing jealousy as outside sexual partners were constantly being introduced because of the demands of their escorting and porn enterprises.

Hensley recalled another frightening experience when Kerekes' temper exploded. He described a scene where he and Cuadra were riding in a car driven erratically by Kerekes. "When they picked me up (that day), I don't know what (Kerekes') attitude problem was...but when they picked me up, we jumped on the Interstate ...and (Kerekes) was flying through lanes, swerving through traffic and then got over to the HOV (high occupancy vehicle) lane and punched it; and he was going well over 140 miles-per-hour," Hensley said. [95]

Hensley also recalled a day when Kerekes was drinking heavily and grabbed him by the throat and pinned him, briefly, against a wall inside the Stratem Court home. Earlier in the same day Kerekes had kicked in the door to Cuadra's bedroom and punched a hole in the wall. "(Kerekes) snatched me up and said, 'If I ever needed you to do anything for me, would you do it?' And I just kind of stopped and stared at him," Hensley said. "I was worried about my physical well-being pretty much. I mean, I wasn't going to let the man sit there and try and manhandle me, because I can defend myself." [96]

Hensley said he overcame his initial intimidation and fear of Kerekes. "He looks like he's on steroids and, honestly, I saw the kind of weight he was lifting, and, you know, his anger and attitude problem," he said. "But when I got to know him, no, I wasn't intimidated by him. It was all size and mouth and that was it." [97]

He said he also witnessed instances where Cuadra stood up to Kerekes' verbal harangues and told Kerekes to "shut up."

Cuadra, while on trial for the murder of Bryan Kocis, described Kerekes as "a sociopath" and said as a result, "We don't have any friends." Sociopath or not, Cuadra never left Kerekes and stayed by his side until the moment of their joint arrest on murder charges. [98]

Harlow and Joe's business model

Kerekes described Norfolk Male Companions as "a large, impressive and proficiently working machine" that had the potential to make millions. By all indications, the escort business desperately needed to be successful. Between the two men, Kerekes and Cuadra had racked up a mountain of $988,695 in debt by the time it all came tumbling down in 2007. "Yes, our bills were massive, but only because we wanted them to be," Kerekes tried to explain. He claimed the couple needed daily income approaching $3,900 to meet their personal and business expenses.[99]

The "earn it—burn it" style in which they lived was noticed by others. Kerekes father, Fred, told a magazine writer that the couple ate out at most every meal, often favoring Boston Market for a quick dinner. But other times they went all out, dropping thousands of dollars on meals. "Joe had a $6,000 chinchilla coat he bought in Vegas," Fred Kerekes said. "It was leather inside—reversible. He had a 3.5 carat diamond stud in his ear. Harlow's was 2.5 karats. They always wore Rolexes."[100]

Kerekes' father also knew where much of the money came from—credit card cash advances or purchases and a second mortgage on their home. "I knew they were out of control," he said.[101]

Pennsylvania State Police Corporal Hannon, who led the Kocis homicide investigation, said of the two men, "It was obvious these were two individuals who led an extravagant lifestyle and followed through with it in all facets of their life."[102]

Their "success" was reflected in the four vehicles they leased or were purchasing: a BMW M-5, a Corvette Z06, a Dodge Viper, and a Honda S-2000.

The "work" of the escort agency, though, continued to cause strife between the two men. "I hated it when he was with a client," Kerekes admitted. "I was jealous a lot. Even though we were in the escorting business, it seemed like he was cheating on me in a way."[103] Kerekes said he particularly became angry when he thought Cuadra would spend too much time with any one client. "Harlow and I would disagree about how to do escorting. I was very committed to doing it one way, and he was often doing it another way."[104] When Cuadra had stayed too long with a client, Kerekes would begin paging him with messages that said, "The hour is up, time to leave."

Kerekes admits that Cuadra's approach with their loyal client, Captain Joseph Ryan, who he first met in the summer of 2003, turned out to be correct. Cuadra thought Captain Ryan, a retired Naval shipmaster and maritime consultant, had the potential to be generous, regular customer of the escort service. He was. Right up until the end, Captain Ryan was in there trying to help Cuadra—eventually donating $7,500 to his defense fund.[105]

"Harlow said to me, 'Joe, we have to give people their money's worth, we have to make them feel that we really want to be there and that we really like them,'" Kerekes said.[106]

The jealousies grew greater when Cuadra, on his own, decided to move away from their previous "company policy" of faking ejaculations and prohibitions against participating in anal sex or performing oral sex without a condom. (Cuadra would later testify at his trial that he did not prefer using a condom when performing oral sex on another man because the spermicidal lotion on latex condoms would irritate the inside of his mouth.)

Kerekes said the "company policies" were in place during their first years in business, but Cuadra was pressuring him to take the escorting in new directions—under the motto of "giving people their money's worth."[107]

During one fight over what limits were appropriate with clients, Kerekes said he "blew up" and threw more than $2,000 in cash off the balcony of their Hague Tower apartment. "I did that to show him that the money didn't mean anything, that the clients don't mean anything," Kerekes said. "The only thing that mattered to me was him, and if he was going to escort, we needed to do things a certain way."[108]

Kerekes, who acted as the pimp for Cuadra and for his own alter-ego escort, Mark or Trent, found himself doing fewer and fewer calls over time as most of the clients wanted to book Cuadra. This seemingly only added to Kerekes' jealousy, as on one occasion he followed Cuadra to a client's home and peered into a bedroom window to see what was happening. Kerekes said he burst into the client's home unannounced, demanded that Cuadra leave, and frightened the elderly male client considerably. Kerekes grew angry, he said, because he witnessed Cuadra engaging in oral and anal sex against the "company policies."

Kerekes "burst in" another time Cuadra was with a client, this time in their Stratem Court home. He worried that not only was Cuadra going too far with the client, but that he may have been developing feelings for the client. As a result, Kerekes said he hid inside large cherry wood cabinets in their client rooms and burst in on the two. "What the fuck are you doing?!" Kerekes recalls shouting. "The client was obviously scared to death, he was jumping into his clothes and trying to get out of there as quickly as possible."[109]

Kerekes eventually "gave in" to Cuadra's ideas about how to run the business, although the new rules included a hidden camera in the bedroom used for sexual encounters with clients. The camera was not for security. "I just wanted to make sure I knew what Harlow was doing," Kerekes said.[110]

Eventually the cameras allegedly served a new purpose. Clients who wanted could purchase a DVD of themselves having sex with Cuadra for an additional fee. While the potential existed for Cuadra and Kerekes to use the tapes to extort money from closeted clients, no indication has ever surfaced that they took their escort business in that direction.

Near the end, as many as 150 regular clients kept the

company going, making their requests via e-mail off the website or by phone.

When a client called, they almost always dealt directly with Kerekes. "Harlow didn't talk to people on the phone," he said.[111] "When they would call, I would ask them where they lived or where they were staying," Kerekes said. "I know the Virginia Beach and Norfolk areas very well, so if they were calling from some area where the houses aren't even worth $100,000, I knew we weren't even going to bother with that person. That person probably wasn't going to able to afford us."[112]

Keeping the clients happy

Client reviews, if what is posted online can be trusted, were favorable. Between 2005 and 2007, postings on websites such as www.daddysreviews.com and www.whoboy.com sung the praises of Cuadra and Kerekes. In one, a client claiming to be a thirty-six-year-old male said he liked the added touch of being picked up at his hotel in a nice car for his "date" with Cuadra. "Harlow's pictures don't do him justice, he has a nice tight body, broad smooth chest, defined stomach, and of course a very nice butt," the client review read. "We talked and got to know each other. We then spent some quality time in the Jacuzzi. After he got me all hot and bothered we decided to hit the bed and I had one of best times I have ever had. After several hours of fun we had a nice shower and went out to dinner. Harlow is a nice young man with a great personality. I would recommend (sic.) any one wanting a great expericence (sic.) to try him out."[113]

Another review purporting to be from a sixty-year-old man said, "I have been wanting to have an experience with a man, Harlow was my first. I was very nervous, and he put me at ease with a massage to start. His body is unbelievable, and his cock is the greatest. He came three times, and I think he could have gone on. He made me feel like a stud that I am not. I have returned for more since, and will return again."[114]

A forty-three-year-old businessman was also apparently satisfied. He wrote online that "I preset my appointment with Harlow for two hrs. in-call two weeks in advance before my conference in Virginia Beach. The arrangement was made through Mark, the agent who did a very good job in arranging the time and presence of the models requested. The in-call place is located in a very private, first class neighborhood. The indoor facility is above par with all the amenities available and nice furnishing. The place also has it's (sic.) own video equipment on hand for photography and movie production. The service provided by Harlow was superb and excellent. He was very versatile and came thrice during the session. He looks much younger than his age and has the most perfect body."[115]

Almost every client review seemed to make mention of Cuadra's triple-ejaculations during each session. Whether those were actual ejaculations or the "faked kind" that Kerekes said the couple had perfected is unclear.

Kerekes himself received a couple of favorable online reviews as well. Called Mark or Trent by his customers, one who described himself as "fat, almost fifty" wrote, "Trent was even more perfect than his pics. He was wearing a white muscle shirt and black shorts. His muscles were bulging. And on top of being a major hunk, he was so amazingly nice to me! He showed me into his place and we just hugged and then we kissed and then we stripped and then we climbed into the big bed and then we hugged some more and kissed some more. I was really happy and excited to be with this total stud. Tent (sic.) has a wonderfully muscled chest with just the right amount of hair on it and a beautiful hairy ass." Describing a "flip" sexual scene where both men bottomed for each other, the customer concluded, "After we cleaned up and dressed, he walked me back out to my car. What a gentleman! This was such a wonderful experience that I was eager to see Trent again as soon as possible. I will have to find another time to get away to the Virginia shore to see Trent again. I loved my time with Trent! Hot, muscled, hard, fun, kind, considerate, the perfect escort gave me the perfect session!"[116]

Another customer was pleased to have hired both Cuadra and Kerekes for a three-way scene at his hotel room. "The guys even stuck around afterward to chat," he wrote.[117]

Ironically, the Daddy's Review website featured not one, but two separate reviews of Cuadra posted on January 29, 2007, just five days after the Kocis murder. Both of them sounded dramatically similar in their descriptions of the claimed sexual encounters with Cuadra, prompting the question: were the reviews posted by Cuadra and/or Kerekes themselves? Insiders say that it is not uncommon for escorts to go online and post favorable reviews of themselves as a means of drumming up business.

If any of Cuadra and Kerekes' clients worried their covers would be blown by the growing seriousness of the charges against the two men, Cuadra tried to put that doubt to rest while still jailed in Luzerne County awaiting trial. "I just wanted for everyone to know that there are no black books with client lists, there are no senator, congressman or others that will be named here... Joe and I never kept a book with client names in it," Cuadra posted online.[118]

One of Cuadra's regular monthly customers, Captain Ryan, said he greatly enjoyed his personal time with his escort, but did not appreciate Kerekes. Ryan said Kerekes "was the controlling part of the business...he did have, I'll say, a domineering tone even in terms of setting arrangements in that he was denying certain calls in his manner or very forceful, not very good customer service, if you will."[119]

In fact, Kerekes "fired" Ryan as a client on at least three occasions for attempting to get too close to Cuadra, he said, only to relent and agree to let him see Cuadra for additional meetings. Kerekes would not allow, however, the weekend or out-of-state trips Ryan occasionally suggested for himself and Cuadra.

Part of Cuadra and Kerekes' rules for their escort business was for their "boys" to avoid local gay bars. "It's bad to be seen (at gay clubs), you lose business. I tell all my guys, like the open ones, I'm, like, 'Ya know, don't frequent gay clubs, and if you do, then you want to stop,'" Kerekes said. Staying away from clubs helped clients keep their secrets, even secrets kept by gay men from their lovers. "I hate seeing those kind of clients, the ones you know they're cheating on somebody else, I hate that," Kerekes said.[120]

Eliminating competitors was also nothing new for Cuadra and Kerekes. When they started their escort adventures, as early as February 2002 when the www.boisrus.com domain was registered, they partnered with Jon Ross of Norfolk. Ross had made a name for himself as the owner of Elite Escorts, a company specializing in introducing women to men in the Navy-dominated beach communities around Norfolk. Today it still operates under various names such as Penthouse VIP Escorts and 24-Hour Escorts.

At one time, early in his escorting career, Kerekes worked for Ross as one of his few male escorts—available for female or male clients. He parted ways with Ross, he said, after feeling Ross did not appreciate his time or talent. "One night he called me and wanted me to go to Richmond, Virginia on a call," Kerekes recalled. "I said, 'John, I know I can make that kind of money right here in town tonight without having to drive all that way.'"[121] An argument ensued and Ross, Kerekes says, fired him on the spot. Ross would later suffer an eerily similar knife attack to the one that killed Kocis—but Ross survived. According to Matthew Childress, a former investigator with the Virginia Beach Police Department, "assailants attempted to kill (Ross) by slitting his throat. Our informants stated that Kerekes boasted about forcing Ross to sell BoisRUs.com to him."[122] Childress said Norfolk Police investigated the attack on Ross because it happened in their jurisdiction, but they weren't able to make any connections between the incident and Kerekes-Cuadra. This may be due to the fact that Ross was unable to provide a detailed description of the assailant at the time of the attack, Childress said.[123]

Regardless, Ross relented on the BoisRUs domain name, and Kerekes was off and running with his own escort enterprise.

The world starts to close in on Harlow and Joe

Unknown to them, at the same time Pennsylvania authorities were looking closely at Cuadra and Kerekes for any possible involvement in the Kocis murder, Virginia detectives were moving forward on their review of their escorting activities.

In January 2006, the Special Investigations Unit of the Virginia Beach Police Department began its own probe of a "citizen's complaint" concerning Norfolk Male Escorts and Norfolk Male Companions (the enterprise sometimes operating under either name). The complaint alleged that the operators, Cuadra and Kerekes, were running a prostitution ring disguised as a legitimate escort service, Childress said. He said the complaint originated from an unhappy former employee of Cuadra and Kerekes.[124]

Virginia Beach detectives took an unusual approach in their investigation. "We decided not to investigate this complaint like a traditional prostitution sting," Childress said. "We decided to treat this as a money laundering investigation. The informant was very close to Cuadra and Kerekes, and we were able to generate several sworn affidavits for subpoenas (to allow us) to initiate our financial investigation."[125]

Review of financial records for Cuadra and Kerekes quickly helped investigators make an inter-state link to activities of possible illegal money laundering, and the Internal Revenue Service was contacted as the investigation began to mirror a federal RICO probe. A RICO probe, named for federal and state Racketeer Influenced and Corrupt Organizations Act, allows federal and state prosecutors wide latitude in reviewing conspiracy and other activities involving several criminal statutes, including money laundering.

As 2007 unfolded and the investigation into the Kocis murder began, open suggestions that Cuadra and Kerekes had something to do with the case, according to Cuadra, had a *positive* effect on their escort business. "It's been busy, it's been crazy, it's been crazy and ya know people are booking like extended time, 'cause they all wanna talk about (the murder case)," Cuadra said. "So I have like this BS version of it, like a Cliff Notes."(126)

Claiming he was tired from his escorting work and the pressure of being under suspicion for murder, Cuadra believed as late as April 2007 (one month before he was arrested) that "We've survived the worst of it" and that things "can't get any worse."(127)

Kerekes said he and Cuadra were initially quite frightened of being arrested, especially after they drove by their home during the execution of the February 2007 search warrant. "Fifteen or sixteen police cars, the big black tanker truck with the gyro cam on top and a big white truck were all sitting in front of our house. We said, 'Oh my God, how many people get to ride by their own house and see the SWAT team in there?'"(128)

Former detective Childress said he was present for both the February and May 2007 searches at Cuadra and Kerekes' residence. "Their home was large and was set up like a business," Childress said. "They had camera equipment both up and downstairs, they had a production room with a lot of computers, and they were mass producing their DVDs in their home."(129)

Childress also recalls that a private room was clearly set up for in-call escort services. "It was elaborate," he said. "They had a king-sized bed, massage table, spa and a huge shower. They had the finest alcohol and expensive cigars available for their clients. They also recorded their in-call sessions (on DVD), something I don't know whether their clients knew or not."[130]

Following the February raid, Cuadra and Kerekes were spooked and fled Virginia Beach for three months. "We got out of town, we were scared," Kerekes said.[131]

The couple sold diamond rings and watches to raise cash. "We sold everything that was valuable to us, gone," Kerekes said.[132]

Cuadra's assessment that "the worst of it" was over would prove to be very wrong.

On May 15, 2007, he and Kerekes were locked in handcuffs and shackles and charged with the murder of Bryan Kocis. After his arrest, those who knew Cuadra well, including his personal attorney Barry R. Taylor, remained unconvinced that he could be a killer. "Harlow does not seem to have the character to commit a crime like this," Taylor said.[133]

Once extradited to the Luzerne County Jail, Cuadra's family and a few remaining friends kicked into gear the idea of an auction to help raise funds for his defense. Cuadra said, "For the supporters that I have, thank you for standing by me in my time of need. As for all the others, I still wish you the best in life, there are no hard feelings."[134]

Cuadra took issue with online speculation going on outside the jail that he and Kerekes were open to any sort of plea agreement for the charges they faced. "There are no deals for Harlow and Joe, there haven't been any deals for Harlow or Joe, and Harlow nor Joe will be taking any deals," he said, noting the prosecution's case included "to (sic.) many loopholes."[135]

Cuadra's confidence about no deals would eventually be shattered. That would come later. As the summer gave way to fall in Luzerne County and he sat out his time in an isolated jail cell, he had no reason to believe otherwise.

During his time in jail, Kerekes joined Cuadra in posting missives to a web blog via emissaries outside the jail. In a November 20, 2007 posting, Kerekes said, "I want everyone to know that I am innocent of the charges against me" and that

"I was arrested for heinous crimes that I am innocent of."[136]

Cuadra said his imprisonment convinced him of the need to begin to take "prayer a little more seriously," acknowledging that letters received from his lover Kerekes indicated a growing fear that they would both spend the rest of their lives apart from one another.[137]

CHAPTER 5
Harlow and Joe Seek a Solution

"What if Bryan left the country? What if he went to Canada?"

—Harlow Cuadra

"Harlow knows someone who would do anything for him."

—Joseph Kerekes

Dallas Township Fire Chief Harry Vivian was still at the fire station at 8:35 P.M. on Wednesday evening, January 24, 2007, when the 911 dispatch center reported a fire very near the station on Midland Drive. It took firefighters only moments to arrive and they found flames shooting from the porch and front window of the structure.

By 9:45 P.M. as firefighters knocked down the last of the hot spots still burning, snow began to fall as Dallas Township Police officers strung a police line tape across the frontyard and street in front of the house at 60 Midland Drive. The fire ravaged the small Cape Cod style house, stretching up to the second floor and the roof of the home. As the quiet snow fell, the only noise heard over the idling fire trucks was the sound of an electrical truck setting floodlights in place on the scene so that investigators could work into the night.

On a night like this, particularly a weeknight, people in the north can normally be found inside their homes. But on Midland Drive, a handful of neighbors bundled up against the winter wind and snow, looking on as firefighters rolled up fire hoses and police and coroner investigators began the grim task of figuring out what happened.

This kind of noise and disruption was unusual for Midland Drive—a narrow paved street that climbs a small incline as it moves northwest from East Center Hill Road and ends at Fern Knoll Cemetery at the bottom of a slight incline, adjacent to the campus of Misericordia University. This kind of activity was unusual, really, for all of Dallas Township and the town of Dallas—a twenty-two square mile area of Luzerne County in the Pennsylvania foothill mountains that is home to some 15,000 residents.

The house at 60 Midland Drive was as typical as they come in Dallas. "It was quiet, nobody knew what was going on," said neighbor Donna Yachim.[1]

That certainly was true on that snowy January night. Just beneath the smoldering hole that used to hold a picture window at the front of Bryan Kocis' well-kept home was his body, slashed and burned lying curled up on a leather sofa. It was a grisly scene worse than any horror film producer could ever conjure.

The pathologist would later say that Kocis was dead before the fire was set, but none of that removed the feeling of disrespect reflected in stabbing and setting a dead man's body on fire. By morning, detectives would have dental records from Dr. John Evans, Kocis' dentist, who along with forensic dentist Dr. John Hosage would confirm the dead man's identity.

Early on it was clear to investigators that Bryan Kocis' past and his porn business were key to determining who had killed him, and why.

A challenging investigation from the start

Dallas Township Police Detective Sergeant Doug Higgins, the first detective on the scene, quickly called on the Pennsylvania State Police to come in and assist. Lieutenant Frank Hacken of the Wyoming post (later promoted to captain) responded and said the early focus of the probe was to learn as much as possible about the victim and his associates. "The victim's past is going to lead us to solve this crime," Hacken said. "We are definitely interested in his pornography business. We're not stating pornography is the reason for this, but it does make it more complex."[2]

State Police Corporal Leo Hannon, a veteran of more than a decade of state police investigations (who is also cross designated as a Federal Agent with the U.S. Department of Homeland Security) summed up the challenge this way: "It was a very difficult and complex investigation for a number of reasons. Not specifically to the line of business Mr. Kocis was involved in but mainly (because) his associates were spread out over a vast geographical area. It made interviews difficult."[3]

Despite growing information about their victim, police were not limiting the scope of their probe to the adult film world. A roadblock was put in place along East Center Hill Road one night after the murder, just a block away from Kocis' home. East Center Hill Road is a major east-west thoroughfare. Police asked passers-by if they had been in the area the night before and whether they had seen anything unusual. Pennsylvania Crime Stoppers also stepped in and offered a reward of up to $2,000 for anyone providing information leading to the arrest of the person or persons responsible for the murder.[4] "We're just asking that anybody who has any kind of information... whoever they may be, they may be a potential witness," said

State Police Trooper Martin Connors. "They may not even realize they've seen something. We need that information. No matter how insignificant something might seem, when put together with our information, it might be a case-breaker."[5]

There would be few calls to police, however.

As it turned out, police were getting plenty of information on their own. "My feeling is that there wasn't a lot of time for people to call in and say, 'Hey, I saw this or that,'" Detective Higgins said. "By hitting the streets really hard the next morning, interviewing the family, the friends, the neighbors, we learned where Bryan would eat, where he went here, where he went there. Everyone you talked to took you someplace else. And hitting it so hard with so many investigators…meant we gathered information quickly."[6]

The aggressive investigation was in place from Day One. The tiny Dallas Township Police Department, less than a mile from the crime scene and tucked into the back half of the township's town hall, served as the central command post for investigators. The squad room would fill to capacity during investigators' daily briefing meetings.

It was at the bustling police department where Bryan Kocis' parents and his sister Melody went early on the morning of January 25, 2007. After watching the morning news on TV they realized the news of a house fire they were seeing reported was at the home of their loved one. They had been unable to get Bryan on the phone (unaware that he was already dead) and went to the police department looking for answers.

"They actually just showed up before we could confirm who our victim was," Detective Higgins said. "In reality we knew who's house it was, but we didn't know for sure who was on the couch because nothing was confirmed yet."[7]

The family was distraught, but cooperative, and eager to help investigators. They quickly helped in locating dental records for a positive identification of Bryan's body, for example, since burn injuries to his body were so severe to his fingers and hands, fingerprint identification was impossible.[8]

The two Midland Drive neighbors who knew Bryan best, Michael and Nancy Parsons, did not arrive home from a trip to Florida until several hours after the fire was put out. As they drove up their normally quiet street after a long drive home, the crime scene unfolding at Kocis' house next door shocked them.

Other neighbors on Midland Drive provided key bits of information. At least two neighbors reported that minutes before they saw the fire bursting through the front of Kocis' home, they saw a "light colored" SUV back out of the driveway and drive away.

Los Angeles-based attorney John R. Yates, Jr. was also talking to police and reporters. Investigators had already uncovered Yates' name and the names of his clients, including Sean Lockhart and Grant Roy, and were beginning to untangle the lengthy legal dispute the men had fought with Kocis. Yates described his clients as "shocked" to learn of Kocis' death and told the *Citizens Voice* that "Various law enforcement officers have been in touch with me. My clients are fully cooperating with police."[9]

Luzerne County Judge Peter Paul Olszewski, Jr. had already granted a police request to seize all cell phone, home phone, voice mails, text messages and e-mail records attached to Kocis. The police request was specifically focused on Kocis' communications during the week of January 18-25, 2007.

Did desperate people seek desperate solutions?

It's said desperate people and desperate acts are not often far apart. That is one explanation for the "solution" investigators believe Harlow Cuadra and Joe Kerekes hatched for their problems at the end of 2006 and the beginning of 2007. But such a simplistic take leaves out a great deal of what has been revealed about the pairing of Harlow and Joe.

There is no question life had become increasingly difficult

for the couple as 2006 drew to an end. In Kerekes' own words, the couple had a spending habit that required them to bring in as much as $3,900 a day in income.[10]

Despite acknowledging the need for a substantial daily and weekly income just to keep their heads above water, Kerekes insists that as things stood in January 2007, "We needed no partnership (with Sean Lockhart), no single actor, no outside help whatsoever" to meet their financial obligations. Going further, he said, "We did not need to murder Kocis at all. Neither did we need (Sean) Lockhart at all. We simply saw something we wanted, as pointless as (the) $30,000 Daytona gold Rolex I wear, so we took it. Oversimplifying? Maybe. True? Yes."[11]

Cuadra, seemingly conflicted about his life and its twists and turns, had pushed forward in escorting and porn. He had also set out to find solutions to help salve the financial hemorrhage he and Kerekes faced. Andrew Shunk said he met Cuadra and Kerekes for coffee in early January 2007, and the two began talking about a "new deal" they were crafting for their company. The "new deal" meant bringing the Brent Corrigan name (aka Sean Lockhart) to their fledgling porn operation—contradicting Kerekes' later claims they were not interested in Lockhart. "They thought that by bringing in Sean Lockhart or Brent Corrigan, that it would bring a six-figure profit within the company," Shunk said. "(They thought) that combining Brent Corrigan's experience in the pornography industry as well as Harlow's, that it would be (a) phenomenon."[12]

Shunk said Cuadra told him about the Las Vegas meeting he and Kerekes had with Lockhart and shared their plan to try to lure Lockhart to them with a per-scene payment—as much as $50,000 each—for porn videos made with their company. Shunk said they also planned to cut out Bryan Kocis and Cobra Video.

Shunk next heard from Cuadra, he said, via a text message indicating he and Kerekes were headed up to Pennsylvania. "I assumed it was to see a client," Shunk said.[13]

Kerekes said it was Cuadra who "discovered" Sean Lockhart, alias Brent Corrigan online and came up with the idea that Lockhart had superstar potential in the world of gay porn. "To tell you the truth, I never knew who (Lockhart) was until Harlow told me who he was and told me they were (instant messaging) and texting each other," Kerekes said. "Harlow was very excited about him. I was unimpressed with Sean. He's very short, and I didn't see him as anything very special."[14]

Cuadra would offer a conflicting version of his actual interest in Lockhart. Cuadra said it was Lockhart who pursued matters online, by phone, via text messages and agreed to a meeting for all the interested parties—Cuadra, Kerekes, Lockhart, and Grant Roy—as part of a trip to the Adult Video News Expo in early January 2007 in Las Vegas. Cuadra said it was Lockhart who wanted the meeting to occur, and not him. Cuadra and Kerekes said they had no plans to attend the AVN event until Lockhart enticed them to do so. "The Vegas meeting was something that came up completely out of the blue," Cuadra posted on his post-arrest blog. "The night before AVN, (Lockhart) came online stoked about his trip to Vegas. 'I am surprised you're not going Harlow,' (Lockhart) said and how it was all a big industry party or something like that."[15]

Cuadra claims Lockhart continued to entice him to Vegas, including an offer to show him the town. If Lockhart would agree to dinner, Cuadra told Lockhart he and Kerekes would make the trip. "(I) figured that if I could include some type of business matter into it, (Kerekes) would be a willing sponsor of the trip," Cuadra said. He figured correctly, he said, reporting that Kerekes immediately ordered two tickets on Southwest Airlines for them to fly almost immediately from Virginia to Las Vegas.[16]

Cuadra describes a rather raucous "business dinner meeting" at Le Cirque Restaurant inside the massive Bellagio Casino and Hotel in Las Vegas on January 11, 2007—including two crystal champagne glasses broken during overly enthusiastic toasts. He originally suggested on his blog the glasses were broken in a drunken moment of frivolity. He later claimed, however, the glass breaking was his signal to Kerekes that he wanted to leave the dinner meeting because he claimed Lockhart and Roy were suggesting that Kocis should be killed.[17]

Oddly, if Cuadra was anxious to get out of the company of Lockhart and Roy, as he would later claim, it didn't stop him from having Kerekes "take some pics of us mostly for use on MySpace"—ones that were quickly posted online showing a seemingly inebriated Cuadra with his arm lazily wrapped around Lockhart's shoulder. The same picture was also sent later on by Cuadra to a newspaper reporter at the *Times Leader* in Wilkes-Barre who was covering the murder of Bryan Kocis.

Putting a plan into motion

Once back in Virginia from their quick Vegas confab, investigators believe Cuadra and Kerekes wasted little time setting in motion an elaborate plan to move "the artist known as Brent Corrigan" away from Kocis and Cobra Video and to their struggling enterprise. On January 14, just three days after their Las Vegas meeting, Kerekes, writing under his oft-used fake name Mark, reported "a huge update" for subscribers to BoyBatter site:

> Harlow and Mark just returned from the AVN Awards in Las Vegas where we sat down with Porn Twink mega star "Brent Corrigan" and discussed a partnership in filming and collaboration in porn site efforts and DVD distribution. WOW! So look forward to exciting announcements as we follow down this unknown path with some of the biggest names in our industry. :)

Kerekes ended the post with a big lie—noting that "sensation Harlow is currently on duty in the field with the marine corps (sic.) but was able to take leave for this important meeting and will return to escorting soon."[18] This would be the first of at least two announcements about Harlow's availability for escorting as the days clicked down to when they hoped to be in Pennsylvania to make the Bryan Kocis roadblock go away.

Kerekes outlined the start of that effort openly in his jailhouse interview with the *Times Leader*. "We got back from the AVN and we were in our office," Kerekes said. "I was updating our advertising for our (website) and Harlow was on the other side and did his thing. He set up an account using the name 'Danny Moilin' and e-mailed Bryan with a picture." Kerekes said Kocis was immediately interested. "Bryan instantly e-mailed back asking (Harlow) to send more pictures and pictures in different sexual positions, so Harlow did all that," he said.[19] On January 20, Cuadra placed an online order using his Discover Card, an order that would be impossible to explain away later. Cuadra purchased background information on Kocis, including his home address, phone number, financial information, and criminal history. Two days later, an e-mail account was created on Yahoo.com from the PCs inside Cuadra and Kerekes' home with the screen name dmbottompa@yahoo.com. Records would later reveal the account was used only to communicate with two recipients: one a test message sent from Cuadra's e-mail account, and a series of e-mails sent by "Danny Moilin" to victim Kocis.

That same day, at 11:18 A.M., "Danny Moilin" filled out and sent in an online application via Kocis' Cobra Video website seeking a modeling opportunity. At 1:23 P.M., a second application was sent via the Cobra site, including revealing, nude images of "Danny Moilin," later determined to be Cuadra.

Kocis must have been pleased about the new arrival. He immediately forwarded to his friend Robert Wagner a copy of the "Danny Moilin" e-mails and photos and told him they were scheduled to meet at his home two days later.

Joe and Harlow go to Pennsylvania

In reality, the timeline between Cuadra's initial contact with Bryan Kocis and Kocis' death is amazingly short. Confirmed by January 22, 2007 e-mails sent between Kocis and who he thought was a young man named Danny Moilin, Cuadra and Kerekes were in Pennsylvania within forty-eight hours of having made their initial contact.

Prior to leaving for Pennsylvania, Cuadra and Kerekes appeared to be men carrying out a plan, however poorly crafted.

At 9:40 A.M. on January 23, the couple rented and picked up a Nissan Xterra SUV from the Enterprise Leasing Company in Virginia Beach, using the driver's license and Discover credit card of Harlow Cuadra.

A short time later, videotape shows Cuadra and Kerekes entering the Superior Pawn and Gun Shop, just 1.2 miles east of the Enterprise office, where they are video recorded purchasing a Sigarms model FX1SG lock-blade folding knife and a Smith and Wesson .38 caliber revolver and ammunition. The purchases were paid for with a Visa card carrying the name of Harlow Cuadra.

Hours later, at 7:26 P.M. a pre-paid Verizon wireless cell phone is activated and used for the first time, relaying its call off a cell tower on Bells Road in Virginia Beach, just 200 yards from Cuadra and Kerekes' Stratem Court home.

Kerekes said in a newspaper interview that he and Cuadra left town almost immediately after those purchases, en route to their destination in the Wilkes-Barre area (about 377 miles from their home in Virginia Beach). They checked into the past-its-prime Fox Ridge Inn (one of the only motels in the area accepting cash as payment) in Plains Township, Pennsylvania and waited.

Pennsylvania detectives recovered a receipt from the Fox Ridge Inn carrying the name and driver's license number of Joseph Kerekes. The address listed started with "1028 Stra…"

but was scratched out, replaced by a fictitious address and zip code.

Kerekes said the couple ate dinner at Kentucky Fried Chicken on their first night in Pennsylvania. But they had more on their agenda. Police would later allege the couple ran reconnaissance on Kocis' home by driving by his Midland Drive home on January 23, 2007, but did not proceed with approaching him at that point.

The next day, Kerekes said the two ate lunch at a Friendly's Restaurant, visited a gym, and went to a nearby Wal-Mart store.

On the day he would die, Kocis sent another e-mail at 2:23 P.M., this time informing his one-time nemesis Sean Lockhart that a new male model was due at his home later that day for an "interview."

As the day wore on, Kocis' cell phone rang frequently. At 5:51 P.M. Kocis took a phone call, ironically, from the estranged business partner of Lockhart and Roy. Just eight minutes later Kocis took a call from the pre-paid Verizon cell phone Cuadra had purchased. Kocis thought he was talking to his expected guest, Danny Moilin.

Moments later, at 6:01 P.M., Kocis spoke again by phone with Lockhart and Roy's business partner. The content of those conversations was never revealed but may have related to the settlement just reached between all of the involved parties.

At 6:26 P.M., Kocis' friend Robert Wagner placed his last call to his friend.

At 6:35 P.M., another call from the pre-paid Verizon wireless cell phone is recorded making its last phone call, this one bouncing off a cell tower on Country Club Road in Dallas, Pennsylvania—just 500 yards and within view of Kocis' home. Cuadra was apparently near Kocis' home but was too early for his appointment.

Kocis took another call at 6:49 P.M. from a car dealership that was repairing his Aston Martin.

Kocis answered even more calls from Lockhart and Roy's former business partner at both 7:23 and 7:34 P.M.

His final call, at 7:50 P.M., came from attorney Sean Macias and lasted only a few minutes, as Cuadra had arrived for his appointment.

The 8:12 P.M. call to Kocis from his friend Deborah Roccograndi went unanswered. It likely was coming in as Kocis was in the last moments of his life or was already dead.

At 8:34 P.M., one of Kocis' neighbors dialed 911 to report flames and smoke pouring from the front of his home. At that same moment, a cell phone registered to Kerekes recorded a call going to the cell phone held by Cuadra. Investigators never determined the meaning of this particular call placed between the two phones held by their top suspects.

"Harlow had a job to do"

"In all honesty, when Harlow left me there at the hotel in Wilkes-Barre that night of January 24, 2007, I was relaxed and lackadaisical and considered Harlow's 'outing' as any normal escort call, an hour with a gentleman for sex for a profit," Kerekes said. "The only difference was that in this instance, packed with lubricant and condoms was a 30% serrated $300 Sig Sauer knife and a revolver. As Harlow walked out of the room, I waved goodbye. He did not make eye contact, he had a 'call' to do. I turned back to my computer and conducted, as normal, business, sending e-mails, canvassing chat rooms and fielding calls to potential escorts."[20][21]

In as straight-forward a manner as can be, Kerekes said, "Basically, as real and true of a picture that night that I could portray to you is (this): I had work to do, and so did Harlow, to kill Bryan Kocis, a task we had prepared two weeks to perform since the idea's inception between Sean Lockhart and Harlow at that business meal at Le Cirque in Vegas at the Bellagio." Kerekes insists that Cuadra and Lockhart "forged a bond, a cohesiveness and understanding, both fully aware of the job, its details and its aftermath."[22]

He further attempted to demonstrate that Lockhart and Grant Roy were "in" on the planning by saying, "We thought our agreement and desire, conceived in Vegas, was formidable enough to bear the weight of the forthcoming investigative onslaught. Neither the promises from our West coast friends (Lockhart and Roy) or the figurative iron in their backs was strong enough to honor loyalties that were clearly established that night in Vegas."[23]

Kerekes lamented that missing from the documents used to charge him and Cuadra was any mention of a conversation he alleged occurred between Cuadra and Lockhart that night in Vegas. He claimed Lockhart said, "I'll believe it when I see it," about the ability of anyone to bring down Bryan Kocis. "It wasn't said in a frivolous undertone, but was a crystal clear challenge to Harlow to proceed," Kerekes said. "We did."[24]

After the murder, new developments surface

On Thursday morning, January 25, Virginia Beach detectives were still conducting their own separate investigation of Cuadra and Kerekes related to their home-based escort business. They likely had no knowledge that a vicious murder had occurred less than twelve hours earlier in Dallas Township, Pennsylvania. In fact, Virginia Beach Police Department patrol officer Brent Riddick was just doing his normal follow-up when he ran a license plate that morning. He ran the plate on a silver/grey Nissan Xterra SUV with dark trim that was parked in the driveway of 1028 Stratem Court in Virginia Beach, the home of Cuadra and Kerekes. The plate on the SUV came back to Enterprise Leasing Company of Virginia Beach. For Virginia authorities, although it was just a routine check as part of their pending RICO investigation into the activities of Cuadra and Kerekes, it would ultimately provide a direct link between the men and the violence perpetrated at Kocis' home some 377 miles north.

Just over a week later, on February 2, police investigators told eager reporters covering the case that there were "new developments" to report. That same day they released a photo of a man they knew as "Drake," who they believed was from either Philadelphia or Allentown, Pennsylvania. Investigators believed "Drake" was the young man who had an appointment with Kocis on the night he was killed. Bryan Kocis' former attorney Al Flora, Jr. speculated to reporters that the man known as "Drake" "could hold some answers to a complex and puzzling investigation."[25] Detectives would soon learn that "Drake" and "Danny Moilin" were the same person: Harlow Cuadra.

The long hours of hard work was beginning to pay off for detectives. Along with the information gathered from Kocis' family and friends and his phone and computer records, tips poured in from the gay community once the Danny Moilin picture was made public. Several calls came into the Pennsylvania State Police identifying the young man in the photo as Harlow Cuadra.[26]

Pennsylvania authorities wasted little time in contacting their Virginia counterparts, and on February 9, just sixteen days after the Kocis murder, detectives from both states began preparing a search warrant for the Virginia Beach home of Cuadra and Kerekes.

Just after 5:30 A.M. the following day, the Virginia Beach SWAT Patrol led a raid on the Cuadra-Kerekes home at 1028 Stratem Court. The SWAT team was used to gain entry but wasn't needed to secure the site. Cuadra and Kerekes weren't home. Lead investigator Leo Hannon said ninety-one separate items were seized from the home, including clothing, duffel bags, and a variety of video equipment. "Specifically what was brought to my attention were two video cameras, which had serial number plates forcibly obliterated," Hannon said. "I observed no other items from the residence had serial numbers removed."[27]

The cameras were returned to Pennsylvania, cameras detectives were convinced were the ones missing from Kocis' home. A concerted effort was made to try and identify the original serial numbers. Hannon first sent the cameras to the FBI Academy-based laboratories in Quantico, Virginia. At the same time, he made contact with Sony Products in Japan. Hannon wanted to know if there was any type of hidden serial number found within the seized electronics equipment. No hidden serial numbers were found by the FBI—and for a good reason—Sony officials later verified that no additional serial numbers were placed inside the cameras beyond the one that police found obliterated.[28]

Prelude to a trap

In the weeks following the February 10 search warrant on their home, Harlow Cuadra and Joseph Kerekes were rarely, if ever, seen at home. The search warrant had not only served to chase them into a hiding of their own choice, it also crippled their escort and porn operations.

Associates of the couple would later report that Harlow changed his cell phone number and made his MySpace profile private, two moves that made it almost impossible for his loyal clientele of escort customers to reach him. Both men were convinced by their lawyer and their own fear that they needed to steer clear of the tightening noose that was emerging in Pennsylvania and Virginia.

During this period, Kerekes' parents were observed by police going into and out of the Stratem Court house, gathering up what valuables remained after the police search. Were they collecting items to pawn and sell in order to raise money for the couple? Perhaps. Cuadra and Kerekes were verging on a level of broke they had not known for awhile. Although they had always had a mountain a bills, now they had little or no means to raise money.

In early April 2007, Cuadra's attorney Barry Taylor sent

a letter to Michael Melnick, assistant district attorney. In it, Taylor demanded Pennsylvania authorities release the 2257 forms that were seized from the Stratem Court house. It's not stated in the letter, but it's clear without the 2257 forms, Cuadra and Kerekes were unable to legally operate their BoyBatter website, a last refuge for some possible income.

Melnick said he told Taylor that the 2257 forms were no longer in his possession and were being reviewed by the FBI, and "it would take a long time for us to get those forms."[29] Taylor, no doubt, was irritated and dissatisfied with the reply, but didn't have any choice but to accept it.

It was the second part of Melnick's answer, however, that may have caught most of Taylor's attention. "I made the comment that 'We kind of put the investigation on the back burner' and that 'We're working with a skeleton crew on this case,'" Melnick said. "I was perfectly honest with him."[30]

The statement was true, if not leading.

The Kocis murder investigation *had* started with as many as twenty-five to thirty investigators when it first was opened. More than three months removed, however, the group of investigators looking into the matter had settled down to about six. Some observers may have assumed that meant no one was spending much time on the Kocis probe. Nothing could be further from the truth.

One factor that may have fueled the "backburner" idea rested on the fact that one of Luzerne County's other most historic criminal cases was making its way back into the headlines and dominating the work of law enforcement officials. Investigators faced the possible restart of the ongoing saga of Hugo Selenski, a convicted bank robber implicated in the deaths of at least five people whose bodies were found buried on his Kingston Township property in June 2003. Years of legal wrangling and appeals combined with the federal indictment and resignation of two Luzerne County judges on unrelated theft and corruption charges, helped to stall the Selenski case for years. A long-awaited appeal hearing regarding evidence in the Selenski case appeared at hand in the spring of 2007, fueling speculation that the Kocis murder investigation was fading as a top priority for police and the district attorney.

With all eyes focused on Selenski saga, Melnick said "What I learned later is that Taylor, after my phone call with him, called his clients (Cuadra and Kerekes) and stated basically what I had told him about the back burner." Whether the comment was intended to root Cuadra and Kerekes from their hiding place or not, it served that purpose. "The next thing I learn, Corporal Hannon and Sergeant Higgins and the boys were on an airplane flying to California. I was shocked, but they said our suspects were on the move and going to California."[31]

State police computer forensics experts would later uncover e-mails between Kerekes and Roy that proved the two prime suspects were emerging from hiding and were headed to California. Unknown to Cuadra and Kerekes, Roy was in a mood to help police, if only to get speculation moved off him and Lockhart, once and for all.

"I had the impression that (Cuadra and Kerekes) were down in Florida, but then they thought the coast was clear and it was time to forge ahead with their ambitious plan to film with Brent Corrigan," Melnick said.[32]

Cuadra and Kerekes confirmed that growing confidence when they re-emerged for their late April meetings with Roy and Lockhart.

CHAPTER 6
Shock and Awe in San Diego

"It was culture shock. Not even in the Navy had I ever been in front of so many people naked…Lots of laughs were had tossing the ole (sic.) football around and frolicking around in the nude. My favorite part was how Brent melted in my arms, cuddling on a beach blanket."
—Harlow Cuadra, blog entry about his day at Black's Beach

To be clear, suspicion about who killed Bryan Kocis did not immediately settle on Harlow Cuadra and Joseph Kerekes. Speculation online and among porn insiders almost immediately centered instead on Sean Lockhart and Grant Roy because of their well-known and public feud with Kocis.

Blogger Jason Sechrest posted on his blog that many people reported having heard Roy talk out loud about wanting to "get rid" of Kocis. Sechrest, who then as now claims to be a friend and supporter of Lockhart, compared the young actor in one blog posting to Sharon Stone's evil character in the psychotic thriller *Basic Instinct.* "(Sean) has every quality that made (Stone) one of the more lovable villains in cinematic history," Sechrest wrote. "He's overtly sexual, frighteningly intelligent, highly manipulative, and he has an addiction to risk in seeing how much he can get away with…and yet we root for him every time."[1] Sechrest said he was concerned that "it doesn't look good at all" for Lockhart and Roy, writing, "I wouldn't like to think that either of them would ever be capable of involvement in such a crime. But I also know that when I take my personal feelings for the two of them out of the equation and look at this on paper, it doesn't look good for them, and that worries me."[2]

Sechrest also raised a frequent theory about who killed Kocis: "It could have been any number of those boys who came back seeking revenge upon him. Or even perhaps one of their fathers."[3]

How it may have looked didn't matter except for the fact it helped prompt Lockhart and Roy to actively participate in helping police trap the real killers: Cuadra and Kerekes. Blogosphere speculation aside, police had long ago satisfied themselves that Lockhart and Roy had nothing to do with Kocis' murder and instead focused their entire attention on the men from Virginia Beach. Among other factors weighing heavily in favor of their innocence, Lockhart and Roy were confirmed by police to have been in California at the time of the murder in Pennsylvania.

Harlow and Joe ensnared—on tape

Grant Roy and Sean Lockhart had previously agreed to notify Luzerne County detectives if they had any contact from Cuadra and Kerekes. As early as March 2007, the contacts were coming fast and furious by phone and e-mail. "Harlow and Joe were itching, itching to get work done with us," Lockhart said. "And we took the opportunity to have them come out to San Diego to open up a dialogue with them in a wiretap setting."[4] Lockhart said his attorney advised against getting involved in the wiretap. "I chose to take part because I knew that this was the only act, this was the first thing and the biggest thing I could do despite the risks to my safety or anything else," Lockhart said.[5]

The time had come for authorities to take Roy up on his offer to wear a wire and help gather specific evidence against Cuadra and Kerekes that implicated them in the death of Bryan Kocis. San Diego Police Department authorities planned, supervised, and executed the wiretap since it was to occur in California, and Roy was a resident of that state. "Roy consented to wearing a body wire, he never withdrew his support," the state would later argue in its in-court motions to keep the recorded tapes in evidence against Cuadra and Kerekes. "He was under no pressure from any law enforcement agency regarding consent. Law enforcement officials made no promises or threats. Roy received no compensation for acting as an informant and had no charges pending against him at the time."[6]

Investigators met as a group at 8 A.M. on Friday, April 27, inside the San Diego City Police Department to make hasty but needed final plans to get key evidence on Cuadra and Kerekes. Pennsylvania state detectives Hannon and Yursha, along with Dallas Township Police detective Higgins, led a briefing for representatives of San Diego city and county authorities, as well as representatives of the FBI, the Drug Enforcement Administration (DEA), and the Naval Criminal Investigative Service (NCIS).

At 12:30 P.M. that day, Grant Roy reported to the gleaming glass and steel office building in downtown San Diego that houses the city's police force. There he met with investigators discussing a wire that he would wear during planning meetings with Cuadra and Kerekes.

Planning for the San Diego wiretaps, at both the Crab Catcher Restaurant and Black's Beach, would require quick work on the part of investigators who brought in help from the San Diego City Police department, the San Diego County

District Attorney's Office, and investigators from the DEA and NCIS. The meeting locations were both calculated by authorities to try to put Cuadra and Kerekes at ease, perhaps prompting them to talk more openly about the Kocis murder.

San Diego detective Robert Donaldson, investigator Ronald Thill, and NCIS Special Agent Kim Kelly would finalize Roy's instructions, including the execution, security, and safety measures they would employ should any problems arise. Following that, detectives told Roy to meet them at 2:15 P.M. at the Marian Bear Memorial Park, a 467-acre natural parkland in the San Clemente Canyon of San Diego County. As Roy's black 2003 Ford Expedition entered the park, Sean Lockhart was with him. DEA Special Agent Andrew Pappas installed the wire for Roy and gave final instructions. Pennsylvania state trooper Yursha assured him he would be followed by police at all times. From there, Roy and Lockhart set off north on the seven mile drive from the park to the San Diego-La Jolla Marriott Hotel near the Regents Marketplace in La Jolla.

During the drive, a nervous Lockhart is recorded asking Roy to stop chewing his gum in a certain way and remarking, "I don't feel well." It would be the first of several indications that Lockhart was noticeably uncomfortable in his role as an "undercover agent" for the police.[7] For his part, Roy remained cool, if not determined, and instructed Lockhart to explain his nervousness or apparent ill-at-ease appearance by saying he had just visited with his parents and an uncle and that "you're not in the best of spirits."[8] Roy also cautioned Lockhart, "There's probably gonna be lots of things brought up that you're not gonna understand, you just need to go, go with it as far as what we've been talking about for the past couple of weeks, what for shooting and stuff...just let it go."[9]

Just before the couple reached their destination, Lockhart offered a soft "I love you" to Roy, who replied, "I love you too. Just be strong, be strong, be yourself, don't let (Cuadra and Kerekes) get under your skin..." He further advised that if Cuadra's "buttercup shit" continued (an apparent code word for open sexual flirting Cuadra had initiated with Lockhart during their first visit and subsequent contacts), he should "let him do it a little bit…(and do) whatever you would normally do."[10]

Four for lunch

At 2:45 P.M., fifteen minutes late for their luncheon appointment, Roy and Lockhart picked up their passengers, Harlow Cuadra and Joe Kerekes, from the front drive of the Marriott. From there the foursome battled San Diego traffic down Torey Pines Road to the tony Crab Catcher Restaurant perched on a cliff overlooking the ocean in La Jolla.[11]

The car ride consisted of casual conversation about the accommodations Cuadra and Kerekes had engaged at the Marriott Hotel, local gyms, background information about La Jolla and San Diego, and the weather. Cuadra and Kerekes would hardly have known the friendly conversation had a much wider audience. Also unknown to them, undercover officers were not only following the vehicle, they were strategically located both inside the restaurant and at all of its exits.

The luncheon group would end up being seated near a window in the Crab Catcher Café rather than the main dining room because they didn't arrive until after 3:00 P.M., more than a half hour late for their original reservation. Outside, investigators used telescopic lenses to photograph the entire meeting, further evidence to go with the concealed wire audio recordings.

As they discussed what to have for lunch, Lockhart volunteered during a discussion of planned photography and taping at San Diego's infamous Black's Beach that the entire Kocis murder had caused him "to lose a lot of friends." Without prompting, Cuadra said, "Same here" followed by an apology from Kerekes: "Sorry man, sorry 'bout that."[12]

It was Grant Roy, though, who brought the conversation

over lunch into focus on areas that interested police listening and recording nearby. Roy brought up his and Lockhart's struggles with their new venture LSG Media.

Cuadra was right on cue referring to Lockhart and Roy's business partner, he asked: "What's this guy's problem? Why doesn't he want to make money and get on the bandwagon?"[13]

The answer to that would be the troubles surrounding the Kocis murder, Roy suggested, and beliefs by some that Roy and Lockhart had somehow played a role in the murder. "When *this* happened, right around the first ten or thirteen days (after the murder), (our business partner) avoided us, and then when I finally forced a meeting with him, he said he was going a day or two later...to meet with (Kocis' attorney Sean) Macias," Roy replied. "*This*," according to Roy, was the murder of Bryan Kocis.[14] Roy also indicated an earlier business investor interested in helping Roy and Lockhart "buy out" shares of LSG Media held by their partner, had "become scarce" since "*this*" happened.[15]

The conversation would not linger on the murder long, as Cuadra and Kerekes pumped Roy for details about the settlement Lockhart had reached with Kocis and how it might impact future projects using the name Brent Corrigan.

Roy discussed his concerns that the settlement was still in effect because Kocis' estate now held the rights to Cobra Video's interests, and they might challenge or sue any new Brent Corrigan ventures.

Cuadra was unimpressed: "Fuck it, I say bring it."[16]

Kerekes felt similarly: "You guys should just break away, man, just do it, break away."[17]

The conversation captured on tape revealed an odd reality; Roy, Kerekes, and Cuadra talked openly and freely about what Lockhart could or would do in porn. Lockhart, of all four men, had the least to say on the subject. Whether that reflected his nervousness about the undercover operation or just how things always operated is unclear, but Roy would even sometimes paternally answer questions put directly to the younger Lockhart.

Given the Cobra settlement challenges that remained, Cuadra and Kerekes quickly turned the conversation into schemes that would allow them to work with Lockhart for their BoyBatter company and avoid having to pay anything to Cobra or the Kocis estate. At least for the purposes of this conversation, the schemes were ones Roy seemed to entertain, including one that would show Lockhart as being paid only $10 for a porno scene, meaning Cobra would only receive $2, the actual full payment would be paid under the table directly to Lockhart, cutting Cobra out.

Kerekes sought to reassure his potential new business partners: "One thing, Grant, we don't, we're not in this to hurt you guys or to screw Brent (Lockhart) at all, and the way I see this, if we film and we put it on our site, you guys are getting any money from CC Bill (one of the nation's largest Internet credit card and check payment processing systems)."[18] Kerekes offered to give Roy and Lockhart the pass codes to the existing CC Bill accounts supporting the BoyBatter and BoisRUs "so you can see what…we've made over the past two years, and you could see instantly how much it goes up because Brent's on the site."[19]

Despite his later claims of being lackluster in his interest in having Brent Corrigan appear with Cuadra, Kerekes continually pushed the idea of linking up with Lockhart, trying hard to lock down a price for at least three porno scenes between the two performers. Kerekes started the bidding at $2,000 per scene but could not get a firm commitment from Roy. The price quickly rose from $5,000 per scene to $6,000, all for a performer Kerekes claimed wasn't important to him. Still, with no firm commitment in hand, Kerekes tried to sweeten the pot: "If you guys can give us, like, a word right now, and a time right tomorrow, I'll give you an extra grand, seven grand cash, if you could gives us a time."[20] His desperation showing,

Kerekes said, "I just wanna keep you guys happy and I wanna maybe secure some more stuff down the road, too."[21]

Kerekes wasn't done trying to secure a deal, as the group walked toward the restaurant exit, he posited a new idea: "Keep in mind the option too, of, like, we could do a two-year thing, like, where I pay you a grand a month, that, that turns out to be twenty-four thousand or as long as you want. I mean, that's also an option."[22]

To show their readiness to begin working with Lockhart, Cuadra revealed he had even thought up a story line and plot for their planned epic. Based on the 2001 film *The Fast and the Furious* starring Vin Diesel, Cuadra said he had lined up members of his classic car club to provide automobiles for the needed non-sexual "action" scenes.

As the group prepared to part, Roy excused himself to the men's room and made a quick call to the detectives listening in. He was concerned about the quality of the audio via the intercept because a news helicopter was circling nearby as fire rescue crews worked to pluck a wayward surfer out of the La Jolla Cove as the tide continued to rise.

Lockhart remained tense. "I couldn't mask my fear and nervousness, and I kept my mouth shut for the duration of (the luncheon), and I was visibly upset."[23]

When he returned, Roy showed no signs of nervousness, and in fact returned with a new aggressiveness, challenging Cuadra and Kerekes directly about online references to Brent Corrigan as "Super Twink of the Millennium" and the male escort components of their website.

"What's the deal there? I mean, I asked ya not to do it," Roy said confrontationally. "That's part of my reluctance in this whole thing, and ah, ya know the hell, the pure fuckin' hell that we've been through the past three months, y'all don't even know."[24] Roy went directly to the point of the Kocis murder and how it had directly impacted both him and Lockhart. "Ya know, when I told you in Vegas, when we were sitting there, and I said, '*That* doesn't need to happen because they're gonna come to me first,' and that's exactly what the fuck has been happening," Roy said. He lamented what he and Lockhart had had to deal with regarding the police and that Lockhart "doesn't deserve it, 'cause he had to fight this Cobra shit for the past two years and now this (murder) shit."[25]

For once, Lockhart jumped in and added a dramatic flare: "My career is ruined…once everyone wanted to work with me, and everyone wanted to be involved with me, and now no one wants to touch me."[26]

The tactic seemed to be working, at least to elicit sympathy from Kerekes and Cuadra, if not a confession. "I understand if you guys want to leave us alone," Kerekes said. "Do you want us to go home?"[27]

Roy also took the occasion to confront the "threats" he said Kerekes had made against them following the Kocis murder, and the long period of silence that resulted between the two sides. Roy's actions continued to put Kerekes and Cuadra back on their heels.

"I didn't mean to threaten," Kerekes said.[28]

Kerekes' impulses seemed to fail him at this point. Instead of continuing down the line to reassure Roy that he and Cuadra could pay the funds needed to secure Lockhart for the joint venture, he began detailing the financial struggle he and Cuadra were facing, including another possible bankruptcy, because of the scrutiny they faced following the murder.

Roy seemed unmoved. He said, "I can't understand, ya know why? I was in Vegas (with you) and we got everything, everything I wanted out of that meeting, and we got it and the following week when you're putting the pressure on (Lockhart)…*all this shit happens.*"[29]

Later, Roy would direct the issue again to Cuadra and Kerekes: "When we had dinner and you brought *that* up, I said, 'No, *that* doesn't need to happen.'" He added, "If anything happens to fuckin' Bryan (Kocis), they're coming after me and

(Lockhart), and me most likely because I was the one that's been most fuckin' vocal about this since day one, screaming for everybody to do their fuckin' jobs."[30]

There it was. Roy laid it out openly and succinctly. He laid the responsibility for the murder of Bryan Kocis at the feet of Kerekes and Cuadra.

Kerekes managed a weak reply, "I wish I could change a few things with the situation, I can't," he said.[31]

Perhaps to lighten the mood, or to offer some hope amidst the now tense discussion, Cuadra and Kerekes began gloating that their attorney Barry Taylor had told them Luzerne County officials had failed in their effort to gain more federal search warrants.

"Yeah, the judge wouldn't issue (one)," Cuadra said. "They wanted to take it federal so they could come and get another warrant to search our place again."[32]

It is here again where Taylor's relaying of information from Luzerne County authorities didn't well serve Cuadra and Kerekes. In addition to the erroneous idea that Luzerne County authorities lacked the ability to get more search warrants, the "back burner" idea surfaced as well. "Barry said the Lieutenant (likely Leo Hannon) called him and (the police) put it on the back burner, and they said there's other pressing things like a mass grave they just found up there," Kerekes relayed. He expressed confidence that Pennsylvania authorities would soon be returning their prized 2257 age of consent forms, and computers taken during the February raid on their home.

"I jumped for joy when the federal judge said 'not good enough,'" Cuadra said.

In fact, Cuadra and Kerekes had regained the guns taken from their home during the search, but their other property would never be returned.

Their falsely claimed optimism bubbling over, Kerekes said, "Our lawyer's actually very happy right now, the way things are going...that's why we came (to California), we're not looking over our shoulder right now."[33]

At 4:42 P.M., the group finished their lunch and walked the half mile down Prospect Street to a small shopping district located there, near popular La Jolla Cove Park. Roy seemed intent on driving home his point, noting that he and Lockhart woke up from the "bad dream" of dealing with the legal struggle with Kocis to a "fuckin' nightmare" regarding his murder.

Kerekes asked sheepishly, "Want to throw me (off) the cliff?"

Cuadra jumped in and answered for Roy: "Yes, he does. It's getting better though, especially with the news that we got the other day. Everything's getting better."[34]

As the group ended its after-lunch walk, Kerekes seemed to regain his confidence. Kerekes said he understood Roy "need(ed) to vent" his frustrations, but said, "You understand why I'm not talking more about *anything*, right? I don't know if there's a wire on you."[35]

Roy laughed nervously and said "No," and Cuadra seemed intent on removing the tension again. "Well, anyways, anyways, the news is good now," he said.

It seemed to work. Kerekes never returned to his "joke" about Roy wearing a wire and said, "Yeah, it's all good, it's all good now. We're home...and we told ourselves that, when we go home from this, we're gonna start sleeping there."[36]

Before the group parted, Kerekes was again swinging back into an apologetic mode, offering: "I apologize, Grant, for hurting you guys and messing things up, I really do. I messed up our lives, too."[37]

As the day wound down, Lockhart's uneasiness seemed to reach a pinnacle. "I'm gonna go home and I'm gonna throw up," Lockhart declared to no one in particular. He would blame it on drinking coffee, eating lobster bisque for lunch and worries about his family. It was more likely the culmination of the pressure he felt carrying on a conversation intended to get Cuadra and Kerekes to implicate themselves.

There would be no direct admissions of guilt this day, Kerekes noted that "We have some information that…we'll tell you the whole beans once we're naked on the (beach) and filming, but ah, let's just say after we have a sure word, there's some things that you really need to hear …."[38] Kerekes was alluding, in a rather clumsy manner, to a claim Cuadra had made that Kocis was working on a separate deal behind Roy and Lockhart's back, even while settlement negotiations were continuing.

As one might expect after an afternoon of negotiations over producing a gay porn video, the conversation ended with Lockhart discussing anal douches and baby hair trimmers that Cuadra could use in order to prepare for the next day's potential sex scenes.

Once Cuadra and Kerekes were dropped off back at the Marriott just after 6:00 P.M., Roy and Lockhart began debriefing between themselves as they drove to the park to have the wire removed. Lockhart was still in agony. "I'm scared of them," he said. "I have never felt like this before. This is probably one of the hardest things in the world."[39]

At 6:15 P.M., detectives removed the wire from Roy's body and began planning their next move.

A day at the beach

Roy and Lockhart weren't done with their clandestine role in the investigation. Both agreed to participate a second time, on Saturday, April 28, at a scheduled meeting and "photo shoot" at Black's Beach in San Diego County.

Roy and Lockhart met up with investigators again at 1:26 P.M. behind a Von's Supermarket in La Jolla. There Roy was provided "a tape recording key fob" or a key remote for a vehicle holding a recording device. "The key fob was being used because Roy would be executing the wiretap at a nude beach and therefore couldn't be body wired," State Trooper Hannon wrote in his report. The key fob activated, Roy and

Lockhart set off for a second day in a row to the Marriott Hotel to pick up their guests, Cuadra and Kerekes.

The group traveled to the Torrey Pines State Nature Reserve, noted for its "outstanding natural scenic views and as the home of the rarest pine tree, *Pinus torreyana*," a tree that reportedly only grows at Torrey Pines and on Santa Rosa Island off the coast near Santa Barbara. The park also boasts that it preserves the last salt marshes and waterfowl refuges in Southern California.[40]

For tourists of all kinds, including gay men, the park is known for its nude and semi-nude beaches. The high broken cliffs and deep ravines on headlands overlooking the ocean provide a true challenge for hikers to reach Black's Beach, and did for the monitored party as well, taking them about fifteen minutes to climb down to the water's edge.

Again unknown to Cuadra and Kerekes, police were listening and watching their every move at the beach from boats far off the coast, and from officers strategically located in the cliffs surrounding the beach.

The group would spend only about two and a half hours at the beach under mostly cloudy skies overhead, but what they discussed, and what Cuadra and Kerekes ultimately disclosed, would prove pivotal.

Getting Cuadra and Kerekes to the beach was a task; both were immediately impressed and somewhat intimidated with the height of cliffs overlooking the ocean beach. "God, I'm actually scared, I've never seen anything like this," Kerekes exclaimed. "Oh yeah, this must about twenty stories in the air if you were in a building," Cuadra added. "I will never forget this."[41]

As the group climbed down the rocks to get to the beach, Kerekes cautioned Cuadra to slow down; "You don't wanna get dirty or scratched, alright?"[42]

Cuadra successfully climbed the rocks wearing sandals, not shoes, and caused more concern when he had to slip away once on the beach to find somewhere to urinate.

It didn't take long, though, for "the shoot" to start, with Roy and Kerekes in the role of co-directors, both giving their partners frequent instructions on what to do, how to stand, or how to act.

Cuadra and Lockhart wasted little time in getting to know one another, although initially everyone remained clothed. Eventually, Lockhart, Cuadra, and Kerekes would strip. Roy would only remove his shirt, according to the tape. "Let them get to know each other a little bit," Kerekes suggested as Cuadra and Lockhart walked ahead on the beach.

Starting off with still photos, Roy and Kerekes can be heard giving the duo directions on how to pose. "Let me see one with a pout, relax boys," Roy said. "It's the beach, take your shoes off, relax, they're gonna get nasty."[43]

The still photos completed, videotaping began with both Roy and Kerekes operating the camera, capturing about seven minutes of "set up shots."

As time wore on, the conversation drifted repeatedly into "business talk" as the men discussed troubles with keeping their porno websites up and running. Unknown to Cuadra and Kerekes, a key fob in Roy's waistband and later on a beach blanket where Cuadra and Lockhart sat, captured every word spoken.

The tape soon captured Cuadra volunteering information he said he had heard from Kocis discussing by phone an idea of how to get Roy away from Lockhart and how to get Lockhart back in alignment with Cobra Video. Cuadra also claimed Kocis referred to Lockhart behind his back as "a little bitch." Whether real or made up, the effort was in earnest: Cuadra and Kerekes wanted to drive a wide wedge between them and anyone else wanting Lockhart's talent and time.

As the conversation moved on, Roy mentioned as an aside that he gave his business partner copies of all of the necessary 2257 release forms for various shoots that had already occurred.

Roy's casual remark inadvertently succeeded in opening the floodgates of incriminating information. Cuadra, apparently misunderstanding, assumed Roy was referring to Bryan Kocis and the 2257 forms belonging to Cobra Video, and started to volunteer that any such documents at Kocis' house and were now gone.

Cuadra still didn't get it and talked on, "Well, if you guys wanna take care of Cobra once and for all, I mean, I don't think there's a real hurry on it, unless (Kocis) had a copy of all that paperwork at his lawyer's office, it's all gone."[44]

How would an innocent man with no involvement in Kocis' murder and the blaze at his home know that? This was just the *first* incriminating statement Cuadra would volunteer that day.

Roy seemed surprised that the information was coming out so easily.

"Really? All his records?" Roy asked.

"It's all gone," Cuadra declared. "He had, umm, a big box of master tapes, DVD tapes. That's all gone. Yeah, so, unless he had a copy of it somewhere, it's all gone."

Cuadra went on to suggest that since he knew Cobra's consent forms were now gone, "you guys could contact the FBI somehow, discreetly, and go, 'Hey, I think someone else is underage,' (and the FBI) is gonna go up to them (and say), 'We wanna see model releases.'"

Cuadra at that point turned to Lockhart and said that he had watched the master tape from Kocis' collection that included the scene with Lockhart and Cobra's other major "star," Brent Everett.

"We watched them all at our house," Kerekes chimed in.

"Yeah, yeah, and they're gone now…they're disintegrated," Cuadra added, being unspecific about how he had destroyed Kocis' master tapes and DVDs.[45]

In all, Cuadra and Kerekes admitted on the Black's Beach tapes to having seized as many as fifty-five of Kocis' tapes (presumably taken during the murder, burglary and fire at

Kocis' home), and watched them over a period of two days at their Virginia Beach home and then destroying them. "I saw all I needed to see," Cuadra said. "I was gonna keep one of them and give it to you (Lockhart and Roy) as a gift…but it's too hot right now, let me just get rid of it."[46]

He added that he had been "given" from Kocis "a couple of (other) items that are disintegrated now, also…(Kocis) had a Rolex, ah, 'BCK' (engraved on the back), and, and well it's gone."[47]

Cuadra had spilled the beans on a key piece of evidence unknown to anyone who hadn't held Kocis' Rolex watch in their hands. The initials "BCK" were carved into the clasp of the watch—something only those closest to Kocis knew.

Kerekes urged Cuadra to continue gloating, and he did, mentioning that all of Kocis' editing software and three computer towers and two laptops were also taken and later destroyed. Cuadra, apparently comfortable that he wasn't being taped because of his nudity and that of Lockhart, was on a roll and really opening up. He openly criticized statements by police investigators that they had seized Kocis' computers that provided solid leads and that whomever was admitted to Kocis' home the night of the murder had to have known him.

"That's bullshit," Cuadra said. "Because we did some recon work, and the door doesn't have a peephole in it…it has two square blocks of, ah, windows, way up on the top, and Bryan's not tall enough to see through that."

As if it were an afterthought, Cuadra leaned into Lockhart and added: "It was quick. He never, he never saw it coming."[48]

Roy saw the opening that Cuadra had created, openly implicating himself in Kocis' murder.

"You were in there with him for a little while?" Roy asked.

"Yeah," Cuadra confirmed.[49]

Repeating his claim that Kocis referred to Lockhart behind his back as "my little bitch" and "the product," Cuadra again turned to Lockhart and said, "So don't feel too bad, man."[50]

Cuadra said he had thought about not telling Lockhart what he alleges Kocis was saying: "(You) might as well have a decent memory of the guy, but fuck it, two drops in a bucket, fuck it now, ya now. That, that dude was all about making a buck, that's it."[51]

Kerekes added his opinion that there's nothing wrong with wanting to make a buck, "but ya don't hurt kids along the way. I don't screw kids over, that's one thing they could come back to me, we don't have any bad blood between us and the kids. It's, like, 'I got your two grand in my pocket for today's scene and a little bonus,' and you know 'I'm gonna do you guys right' and I'm gonna do every kid that ever works for us, right?"[52]

Business talk aside, Cuadra and Kerekes again drifted into dangerous territory, providing investigators listening on the key fob wire (and for jurors later) a rather detailed account of Cuadra's one-night stand that ended in Kocis' murder.

Kerekes noted that Kocis had prepared a contract for Cuadra prior to his arrival and was ready to pair him with other actors he had in his Cobra line-up. "And (Kocis) acted like he didn't know him, of course, but he had planned on instantly writing Harlow a contract," Kerekes reported.

Investigators later came to the conclusion (or at least agreed with it by accepting a guilty plea from Kerekes) that Kerekes' knowledge on what transpired inside Kocis' home must have been based on details told to him by Cuadra. Not everyone would agree—the argument about whether Kerekes had actually been inside Kocis' house the night of the murder would go on and was never decided, in no small part due to the evolving story offered by Kerekes.

There was never any argument, though, that Cuadra had been inside the home. "I'm used to drinking with my clients, I only have a sip or two," Cuadra said, setting up the scene between himself and Kocis.[53] "I only have like a sip or two while I keep pouring it and pouring it for them, so by the time the doorbell rang, and (Kocis) got up, he was kind of stumbling, and ah, that was it."(54)

His version would be the one repeated later at trial—that "someone" burst into Kocis' home that night and committed the murder in Cuadra's presence. Kerekes never seemed fully on board with that version, later trying to make it seem Cuadra "happened upon" the murder, and always insisting he was never present.

Cuadra had more details to offer, though.

He reported Kocis had just purchased a 65" Sony plasma TV for his living room—a new item delivered just days before. He also said the room was equipped with a $20,000 sound system. Other details he reported were Kocis' upcoming plan to go to California for business and details about the upstairs bedroom and the steep roof-ceiling line in the Cape Cod-style house. "It was all there," Cuadra said. "It must look like shit by the time what's his name was done, but yeah, he was trying to figure out how to operate it while I was there."(55)

At times, the photo and video shoot would intercede back into the conversation. Kerekes thought Lockhart and Cuadra should kiss, but "you're not allowed to fuck (on the beach)," Lockhart said.

A further few drifts of the conversation, and Cuadra disclosed he had been molested as a child, "and it's what kind of made the whole decision kind of easy, almost a little too easy."(56)

Unknowingly, he may have just disclosed a key factor in the Kocis murder, the amount of "over-kill" present with the victim suffering twenty-eight stab wounds after his head was nearly decapitated from his body. Forensic profilers have learned over time that when victims are found with such intense mutilation, suspects are likely to be found unsurprisingly among those harboring enormous amounts of rage.

Did Cuadra substitute Kocis for the man who had allegedly molested him as a boy? Only Cuadra knows that for certain, but his remarks that kept coming reveal that "the whole decision" to kill Kocis was apparently made easier by either perceived mistreatment by Kocis of Lockhart and other young men or by Cuadra's projection of an image of his own childhood molester upon Bryan Kocis.

"Being molested…is, like, a very controlling type of thing, where you couldn't really talk to anybody about it, ya know, just live with it, ya know?" Cuadra offered to Lockhart.[57]

Cuadra did have moments of doubt, openly expressed, but they seemed more intended to apologize to Roy and Lockhart for implicating them in the crime. "I should have thought a little bit more of where all those fingers would have pointed," he said. "I remember looking at all the press…I'm just glad that shit's over with."[58]

Cuadra's disclosure about his alleged childhood molestation prompted an impromptu discussion among the men about growing up and figuring out that they were gay. Cuadra doesn't blame the molestation for that. He confessed he had feelings for other boys prior to that. But he would synthesize that statement with one that would convince most anyone who heard it that Harlow Cuadra was the killer: "I think (the molesting) is why it took me a while for me to accept my sexuality because of all of that," Cuadra said. "Ummm, actually, seeing that fucker (Kocis) going down, actually it's sick, but it made me feel better inside. It almost felt like I got revenge and I know that sounds really fucked up, really fucked up, but I still couldn't sleep for a week."[59]

Insomnia or not, Cuadra was convinced getting Kocis and Cobra Video out of the way not only solved Roy and Lockhart's problems with him, but possibly also the emerging problems with LSG Media. "I don't think that if we all would have just sat back and you would have done it the legal way, I don't think it would have turned out the way you wanted, honestly," Cuadra said.[60]

At one point, Kerekes even appears to threaten others who had struggled with Roy and Lockhart on financial matters.

Kerekes offers that challengers should "bring it, I'll dance with that all day long."[61]

Cuadra also boasted that Kocis was in a hurry to meet his new potential model "Danny Moilin." Cuadra reported, "He was in a hurry, he had to go to California. That's why it was all done so quick."

Modeling would interject itself in the conversation again, with Roy giving instructions on how Lockhart and Cuadra should toss a football between the two men (a talent that Cuadra apparently did not possess). Roy described it as "if that wasn't a couple of fairies playing catch, I don't know what was."[62]

Kerekes encouraged the two to kiss on the lips, to which Cuadra replied, "Don't worry, we'll get all warmed up in a second."[63]

Cuadra wanted to know if he could "suck dick" on the beach, only to be reminded again by Roy that no sex acts were tolerated, even though it was a nude beach.

At one point, Cuadra also picked up Lockhart and carried him on his shoulder.

"It seemed effortless," Lockhart said, commenting on Cuadra's strength in picking him up.[64]

It may have seemed physically effortless for Cuadra, but Lockhart said it was anything but effortless for him regarding his own demeanor toward the more aggressive Cuadra. "I was very guarded, very cold with the exception of when I had to play it up to make them comfortable so they (could) speak," Lockhart said.[65]

Cuadra was "doing everything and saying everything that he could to warm me up and make me feel better about what had happened to Bryan," Lockhart would later say.[66]

The preliminaries over and the cloudy skies hanging on, the four men made their way back up the rocky cliffs over Black's Beach and Cuadra and Kerekes were returned to the Marriott. There were discussions about the subsequent sex scenes that needed to be filmed between Lockhart and Cuadra. Giving excuses of needing to clean their house and go get the proper lights for the shoot, Roy and Lockhart extracted themselves from the other two and returned to be debriefed by police investigators.

No "million dollar sex scene" would ever be filmed between Cuadra and Lockhart. Within a month of their walk on the beach, Cuadra and Kerekes would be in handcuffs and shackles and facing multiple charges stemming from the murder of Bryan Kocis.

Cuadra-Kerekes react

Harlow Cuadra may have inadvertently picked up on Lockhart's trepidation during their April meeting in California. He had posted on his blog while he was awaiting trial: "That last time Brent and I played footsies...our elders (Kerekes and Roy) discussed the boring paper work and financial deals. All the 'boy wonder and stud wonder' wanted was to fuck and make some memorable movies while we (were) at it...This time it was even difficult to look at each other's eyes."[67]

For his part, Kerekes was convinced that the microphone used to record both the Black's Beach and Crab Catcher Restaurant conversations in Southern California was planted in Lockhart's sunglasses. "The speaker was in sunglasses Brent wore at the beach. It was cloudy out and he never took those glasses off," Kerekes told the *Times Leader*.[68]

Kerekes was wrong.

Cuadra offered perhaps the most ironic take on all of the events, but did so before he would soon be arrested and later would be sentenced to life in prison.

"I'm a person that believes that scars are signs of living... and that everything tells a story," Cuadra said to no one in particular during his day at Black's Beach, long ago.[69]

CHAPTER 7
Sean Lockhart in the Role of Brent Corrigan

"I think one of the biggest lessons I've learned through all of this is simply that often times in order to fix your mistakes and learn from them, you must wear them, and in a sense, embrace them."

—Sean Lockhart

Sean Paul William Lockhart was born on October 31, 1986. If that fact had always been reported and known by anyone who met Sean, a world of controversy that has surrounded his gay porn career would not have existed. But when it counted, Lockhart admits he lied about his birthday and said he was born in 1985 and that one year of difference made all the difference. He almost, singlehandedly, set the gay porn world on its head.

Lockhart's personal bio on his website, www.brentcorriganinc.com, notes that he has driver's licenses from two states, a passport, Social Security card, and a citation for underage drinking on his twentieth birthday to, once and for all, prove his age. The true birth year is no longer a secret and

Sean has moved beyond that.[1]

Lockhart was born the second of four children in Lewiston, Idaho, a tiny southeastern Idaho hamlet located about 280 miles south of Spokane, Washington. "I grew up in the suburbs... under an older brother who drove me up the wall...I have a younger brother and sister (and) I drive them up the wall (but) I know they love me."

Lockhart describes his as a loving family, if not a close one. Now though, "We don't talk often and scarcely see each other even on a yearly basis," he reports.[2]

Lockhart said he has never met his biological father, and his mother and stepfather divorced when he was in third grade. "After that, my mother really wasn't there very much. My stepfather raised me."[3]

Seeing his mother on "holidays and every once in a while," he believes his mother was "over" with being a parent and moved to San Diego, California, hundreds of miles away from her children.[4]

In school, Lockhart said he was a good student with a 3.2 GPA and was active in the drama society, student government, and some school athletics, although "I got sidetracked a bit and didn't keep up with the sports as I'd have liked." He credits his stepfather with doing a good job of raising him and his siblings, even without their mother present.[5]

Sean starts a new life in California and meets Bryan Kocis

At the age of sixteen, Lockhart himself moved to San Diego to be closer to his mother. By now, Lockhart was self-identifying as gay but was still closeted to his family. His dashing looks, however, had begun to get him noticed, and a common comparison was born: Lockhart indeed looks a lot like teen heart-throb Zac Efron (just one year older than Lockhart). "I told myself that since I wanted to direct (films), I needed to be in Southern California," Lockhart reported. "I'd come here, do my two years in high school, get residency established and then go to UCLA or someplace similar. Between me and my dream lay a few major obstacles."[6]

Once in California, life was a struggle. Lockhart said "my mother failed to provide me with the stable home environment every growing, young adult sorely needs" which forced him to take numerous part-time jobs in retail to make enough money for food and everyday essentials.[7]

During this time, Lockhart says an older boyfriend "introduced me to a lifestyle that wasn't very fitting of a sixteen-year-old. He was nothing but the worst influence on me. But I thought this was what gay people did."[8] Exposed to drinking binges, illicit drugs and as much ready-anonymous sex as he'd like, "I didn't know that most of the gay community isn't into drugs and being evil to each other, that there is a side of the gay community that actually takes care of each other."[9]

His exposure to the grown up world of gay men included nude webcam videos of Lockhart sent to Bryan Kocis whom he had never met before. "(My boyfriend) was online with (Kocis)," Lockhart explained. "He whips around the webcam, points it at the bed, and rips my clothes off. I'm instantly hard because I'm a sixteen-year-old and this means sex. I'm pointing at the ceiling and he's, like, 'You're on webcam.'"[10]

The images of Lockhart were ones that caught Kocis' intense interest.

Lockhart and Kocis started up an almost immediate friendship, propped up by texting, e-mails, and phone calls. Lockhart's boyfriend, however, quickly grew unhappy with Kocis' intense interest in Lockhart. The answer? Lockhart says his cell phone was cut off by the jealous boyfriend. Enter Kocis. "Bryan understood (that he) would nearly lose all communication with me," Lockhart said. "To avoid that from happening, (Kocis) sent me a Sprint cellular phone, validating it by offering me a job. By sending me the phone, Bryan knew it would be easier for me to get independence..."[11]

By January 2004, Lockhart said Kocis requested and

received two personal casting tapes from him in addition to a private webcam show. "He told me he wanted to see how I would look on camera and spent a great deal of effort shipping his personal camera to me from across the country. He did not, however, spend any effort obtaining my identification."[12]

By February, Lockhart was flying to Fort Lauderdale, Florida to shoot scenes for the infamous *Every Poolboy's Dream* and *Casting Couch IV.* Lockhart was only seventeen and a junior in high school at the time.

After *Every Poolboy's Dream* hit the shelves and was made available online via Kocis' video site, things got "complicated," Lockhart said.

Kocis eventually began asking him about his actual age, Lockhart said, but "Bryan's concern appeared to be centered more on what would and could happen to me if it was verified I was seventeen. He spoke of fraud; that it was a federal crime. He told me that if the FBI were to get involved that I would be held solely responsible for the crime because he had done everything in compliance with the law."[13]

Lockhart says Kocis' entreaties to him also included threats to "out" him to his family, and advice that no other video company would employ him for porn productions because he had done "bareback scenes" for Cobra (just as Kocis wanted it). "The things Bryan told me made me feel like Cobra was the end all, be all for me in the adult industry," Lockhart said.[14]

The success of *Every Poolboy's Dream* quickly prompted Kocis to propose another film, this one titled *Schoolboy Crush.* Lockhart said filming of *Schoolboy Crush* left him with a feeling of doom.

"At the time, I was not out and I was still somewhat ashamed of my homosexuality, let alone having participated in gay porn," Lockhart said. "Bryan knew this and was aware that if my family were to learn of my adult work, I would be shamed and embarrassed. At age seventeen, these types of feelings rule your world!"[15]

Despite the feelings of worry, doom, and shame, Lockhart was determined to get rid of the secret problem of his underage status. He obtained a fake California ID showing him to be eighteen years old and promptly showed it to Kocis. It was a move Lockhart says he regrets, he was now part and parcel to the lie. "I believed my only option was to provide him with an ID that read I was eighteen. Looking back now, armed with the truth, I understand it was yet another wrong decision on my part," he said.[16]

Lockhart stays with Cobra Video

Kocis tapped into Lockhart's stated interest in film school to entice him to come back east to work for Cobra Video so that he would gain "real-world" experience. With a forged "work study" letter in hand (one that purported to be from a university art school), Lockhart fooled his mother and set off for a whirlwind weekend in New York City at Kocis' expense. "I arrived in New York to find a lavish setting," Lockhart said at the Hudson Hotel in mid-town Manhattan. "Bryan had gifts of clothing to wear…at all the swank little gourmet dining places he brought me to. That weekend Bryan showed a world to me I had only seen portrayed on TV and in movies."[17]

Lockhart said his introduction and connection to Kocis grew quickly because Bryan focused on every detail of his life and that "the absence of a strong, positive male figure (or any parental figure for that matter) in my life left me wide open to anyone's advances; advances of any kind."[18]

After the fact, Lockhart has been upfront about his entrance into gay porn at age seventeen, becoming the "Traci Lords," as it were, of gay porn. But perspective is needed, Lockhart believes. "When I did the work underage, it was two shoots within one month of each other, for one studio," he said. It was also for a porn producer, Kocis, who was far from the center of the gay porn empire of Southern California.[19]

His foray into gay porn was very much a part of the

relationship with his boyfriend at the time, the first of what would be several relationships he would form with older gay men. Getting free from his boyfriend in California meant landing in another immediate relationship with Bryan Kocis, one that would hang over his young life for years long after the two summers he spent at Kocis' home in Dallas Township, Pennsylvania. The summer trip to Pennsylvania was again perpetuated with a fake "art school" letter shown to Lockhart's mom who asked no questions.

"I spent the summer in a small town tucked away in the middle of nowhere," Lockhart said. "The first three weeks went smoothly." But things changed quickly.

Kocis' plans went beyond teaching Lockhart the business. They included a romantic partnership where Lockhart would permanently relocate to Pennsylvania, go to college there, and maybe even help run Cobra Video.

An emotional and sexual relationship developed with Kocis, Lockhart acknowledges, but today says the sexual interaction was "expected" and that he believed Kocis' "help and support would end if I didn't do it."[20] He also admits Kocis showed him a lifestyle he had never known when I was growing up, including fine dining and elaborate vacations. "I went to places I never had been (before)."[21]

Kocis' "detailed plans" scared him, Lockhart said. "I did not like the idea, and I told him it would deter me from my focus on mainstream film. As soon as Bryan began understanding I was not going to relocate for him and his business, our arrangement there in Bum Fuck, Pennsylvania changed."[22]

By the end of the summer of 2004, Lockhart says things had truly soured between him and Kocis. He accused Kocis of holding hostage his return airplane ticket to California after Lockhart fled Kocis' home to go stay with another Pennsylvania man he met online.

His resentment of Kocis ran deep. In "A Siren's Tale" published online by blogger Jason Sechrest, Lockhart refers to Kocis as a "forty-three-year-old, flat-faced, pig-nosed producer."[23]

Venturing out on his own after leaving Kocis, Lockhart returned to San Diego and found home life with his mother none the better. While he was away, his mother had relocated to a new apartment, one that did not include a bedroom for Lockhart. Forced into working part-time to rent his own apartment, Lockhart struggled to complete his senior year of high school.

By December 2004, Kocis would be back in his life. Desperate for cash, "I agreed to film a scene for Bryan in La Jolla, California."[24]

The offer of employment and cash also came with an offer for a Christmas get-away to Hawaii for Lockhart and Kocis. Lockhart took the offer, all the while trying to "make it plain and clear to Bryan, we were traveling as friends and that I was merely giving him the opportunity to fix things between us."[25]

Kocis had other plans—booking a room for the two with just one bed. A confrontation ensued and Kocis backed off, avoiding the sexual advances Lockhart said he made on him previously.

While in Maui, Hawaii, Kocis rented a Ford Shelby Cobra for photo shoots featuring the sparkling Pacific Ocean in the background. The photo shoot was successful, but included a car ride in which Lockhart claims Kocis threatened his life.

Approaching the subject by telling a hypothetical story that matched their own struggles, Lockhart said Kocis' story included references to a "producer hiring 'waste management' to go after the boy. Bryan was planting in my head that I could never allow the truth to come out," Lockhart said. "If I did, my life would be in danger."[26]

Kocis' death, however, makes it impossible to verify the interaction Lockhart described on a high cliff overlooking the ocean on Maui. Kocis' family members denied that he was ever violent with anyone or that he would ever threaten anyone.

Again, despite his fears and concerns and now of legal age, Lockhart continued to do various scenes for Cobra Video to get by as the months passed, believing Kocis' claims that Cobra Video was his only option.[27]

Finishing his senior year in high school with perhaps the most unusual part time job ever, Lockhart said he grew more frustrated with having "nothing to show" for his work with Cobra. All the money he made went to pay daily expenses such as rent, gasoline and food, all necessities Lockhart said his mother had long ago stopped providing with any regularity.

Lockhart's new partner: Grant Roy

Lockhart's return to California coincided with his meeting a new lover and partner, Grant Roy, a Texas native twenty years Lockhart's senior. Roy is credited by Lockhart into "making me into a man."[28]

Roy said when the couple started dating, he told Lockhart, "First of all, I'm not gonna be your San Diego Bryan (Kocis)."[29] What emerged was a variation on an open relationship— although that is not a term the couple embraced. They came to an agreement that if outside sexual contact happened, they would talk about it with each other afterward. "It doesn't make any sense to throw away a perfectly good relationship, just because you enjoy someone else's company," Lockhart said. "Grant knows that I'm twenty (years old) and I have needs."[30]

Roy said he knew Lockhart was performing in gay pornos and "I can't expect (him) not to act on urges that happen sometimes, cause ya know, I told him, I end up in some of those situations sometimes, too, and it's not fair and I wouldn't want somebody taking that away from me when I was younger."[31]

Lockhart said he believed that "part of our problem in the gay community is that we're constantly trying to adhere ourselves to straight principles or relationships, monogamy for instance, and we're men and we're built differently and our brains are different, and we have different urges."[32]

Eventually Lockhart and Roy, they said, transitioned from lovers into just friends and business partners and all sexual contact between the two men ended—though they continued to live together.

Lockhart's plan to leave Kocis and Cobra Video behind, however, was not only a product of personal necessity, but also because he began noticing for himself his potential and popularity. It would take that sort of personal belief to help Lockhart overcome a withering assault from Kocis and others who saw him as a danger to all of gay porn because of his history in bareback porn.[33]

For Lockhart, the venture did not come without cost. Sued in federal court and recruited to be a key undercover witness in a cross-country murder investigation, Lockhart experienced a lifetime of living before he turned twenty. "Being nineteen and twenty and having to experience these things, it was as if the weight of the whole, raw and real world was compressed and grinding down upon my shoulders," Lockhart said in a May 2008 interview.[34] Lockhart credits his partner Grant Roy, not his family, for helping him get through. "Grant is the one who has liberated me and he's been here ever since," he said. "In some ways, these trying times have humbled me and taught me how to better regard the world and all it has to offer, good or bad."[35]

Lockhart as a producer

Lockhart proclaims he's "the youngest, most eager, most determined and creative young porn producer" in the history of gay porn. "Porn can be a bad business, but not my company," he said. "Since I know what it's like, I treat models right. I treat my models with the utmost respect from the beginning to end."[36] His video shoots have covered as long as two weeks where he played host to guys in multiples of twos and fours. "On those shoots, it's all about the boys," Lockhart boasted. "I do everything from feeding them, keeping them entertained, housing them, and filming the intended work."[37]

Part of the respect he is insistent on offering his models, he says, is making videos that feature no bareback scenes. "I consented to doing bareback (with Cobra)…because I was falsely led to believe I was being 'protected' by the producer and the boys he was pairing me with. Fortunately, I got out of that alive and HIV-negative." He added, "I chose against doing bareback and chose to save myself from a fate so many young people are falling victim to even today."[38]

But gaining respect has been difficult, and comes and goes it seems. Criticism of his stint as an underage gay performer still popped up during the 2009 Gay Video News Awards.[39] Despite the struggle, Lockhart says finding work and being taken seriously as an actor in or out of the porn industry is not a major concern. He declared, "I'm a porn star, and my life is deeply rooted in that."[40]

Proof of that was his cover-image emblazoned on the 2006 Falcon Video release, *The Velvet Mafia*, with Lockhart appearing as "Fox Ryder"(rather than Brent Corrigan), described as "a striking youth from a broken home who was raised on an Iowa milk farm" who gets discovered by a gay porn producers.[41]

Not to be outdone, at the same time Kocis' Cobra Video relaunched *Take It Like a Bitch Boy*, a video he had released previously under a less vulgar title, apparently as a reminder to the industry that Lockhart and his alter ego, Brent Corrigan, were still officially a part of the Cobra Video stable.

This was followed a series of other Lockhart films Kocis rushed to market earlier in 2006. Kocis' titles included *Cream B-Boys*, *Naughty Boy's Toys*, and the troubling *Brent Corrigan: Fuck Me Raw*, a video by its very title meant to demean Lockhart.

New struggles emerge with LSG Media

Lockhart acknowledged the setbacks created by the Cobra suit and the struggle for control of his new effort under LSG Media, a limited liability corporation formed by Lockhart,

Roy, and a third partner who held a fifty-one percent interest.

In June 2007, Lockhart wrote on his blog that he had been prevented from releasing DVDs featuring his image while the Cobra legal fight went forward. "One of the elements to the settlement was that we were not permitted to release DVDs during settlement mode or until the settlement agreement was completed," Lockhart explained. But Lockhart assured fans "I'm around, I'm kicking (hard) and I still have not given up. When I called myself determined, I meant it. I'm built for hard work and I intend to use that to my advantage."[42]

His determination to move on away from Kocis and Cobra Video, a move he thought he was negotiating with the settlement talks with Kocis in the weeks before Kocis' murder, did not mean an end to struggles.

Originally set up to support Real Boys Online, Lockhart said LSG Media had planned to specialize in amateur scenes available only online. "I think the priority (was) to get to the meat of what you're doing, good adult scenes, before you get artistic. When it's all said and done, it's all porn and that's what you're watching...there will be a good mix of twinks and young muscle jocks, anything attractive under the age of twenty-five."[43]

What was envisioned and what came to be soon were separate ideas. The newly formed LSG Media became a new source of stress and irritation to Lockhart. "Just to keep the record straight, I have not yet been paid one cent for my work here on the blog, the scenes I have filmed that you enjoy in the Member's Site, or any of the promo work I have done for this website and this company," he wrote on the new www.brentcorriganonline.com blog on June 22, 2007. He acknowledged his only payment so far were sporadic donations given to him by fans.

It seemed history was repeating itself. Lockhart's struggle to be paid and have control of his work was back again, in his view, this time in the form of LSG Media. "After a year and a half…this is how the star of the site is repaid for all his hard work! Paid nada, nothing, zilch, zippo!" Lockhart said.[44]

Lockhart took the dramatic step of recommending that his fans not purchase memberships on the site and promised that BrentCorriganOnline and related blogs and member sites would go dark soon as memberships and traffic began to evaporate. "After all, what use is Brent Corrigan Online when Brent Corrigan has left the building?" Lockhart asked.[45]

In the months that followed, the site did in fact dwindle and Lockhart's absence was noted by at least one blogger, industry journalist J.C. Adams. He referred to Lockhart as "laying low" since the murder of Kocis, a description Lockhart took exception to. "I'd just love to see how effective and productive (Adams) would be while weathering a storm like the one I've experienced in the last year," Lockhart wrote on his blog at the end of November 2007, taking umbrage at Adams' assessment of the situation.[46]

Earlier in July 2007, however, he had launched a new website and blog known as www.brentcorriganinc.com, a slight variation on the name of the one launched earlier by LSG Media. "Here, you'll get it all. Just be advised, from here on out, you have absolutely no reason to continue your regular visits (to the old site)," he told his fans. "I wash my hands of that filthy failure, and I beg the same of you."[47]

The slow months of 2007 did provide Lockhart with two non-porn acting opportunities, including a small part in the independent film *Tell Me* and a part in an unaired TV pilot *Didn't This Used To Be Fun?* [48]

As 2007 came to an end, Lockhart used his blog to take issue with large stories published first by *Rolling Stone* writer Peter Wilkinson in September 2007, followed the next month by another take in *Out* magazine by writer Michael Joseph Gross.

Lockhart noted alleged errors or omissions in both articles, and accused particularly Wilkinson of having "an individual

THE CRIME SCENE – The burned out remains of Bryan Kocis' home, 60 Midland Drive, Dallas, PA. *(Citizens' Voice photo, used with permission)*

FRONT PAGE NEWS – The murder of Bryan Kocis was big news in Northeast Pennsylvania. *(Citizens' Voice front page images used with permission)*

THE VICTIM – Murder victim Bryan Kocis, circa 2001, following a court appearance on child endangerment charges brought in Luzerne County, PA. *(Citizens' Voice photo, used with permission)*

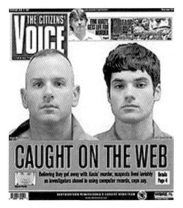 

FRONT PAGE NEWS – The arrests and convictions of Harlow Cuadra and Joseph Kerkes made front page news. *(Citizens' Voice front page images used with permission)*

AT ARREST – Harlow Cuadra (at left) and Joseph Kerekes were both arrested in Virginia Beach, VA and fought efforts to be extradited to Pennsylvania to face murder charges. *(Times-Leader photos used with permission)*

FACING FACTS – Harlow Cuadra (front, right) and Joseph Kerekes are led to an initial hearing in Luzerne County, PA for the murder of Bryan Kocis. *(Times-Leader photo used with permission)*

CENTER OF THE PROBE – The squad room of the tiny Dallas Township Police Department served as the central point for investigators probing the murder of Bryan Kocis. *(Photos by Andrew E. Stoner)*

THE COURTHOUSE – The historic Luzerne County Courthouse, site of the Cuadra trial, dominates the skyline of Wilkes-Barre, PA. *(Photo by Andrew E. Stoner)*

GUILTY – Jail guards lead an unemotional Harlow Cuadra from the Luzerne County Courthouse after jurors found him guilty of murder. *(Times-Leader photo used with permission)*

WAITING – Prosecutors proved Cuadra and Kerekes paid cash for a room at this motel, the Fox Ridge Inn in Wilkes-Barre, PA, the night before the murder of Bryan Kocis, just 11 miles away. *(Photo by Andrew E. Stoner)*

CUADRA-KEREKES HOME – The once active home of Cuadra and Kerekes, 1028 Stratem Court, Virginia Beach, VA. *(Photo by Peter A. Conway)*

WITNESS FOR THE STATE– Gay porn actor "Brent Corrigan," whose real name is Sean Lockhart, walks to a courtroom inside the Luzerne County Courthouse as a prosecution witness against Harlow Cuadra. *(Times-Leader photo used with permission)*

OTHER KEY WITNESSES – Prosecutors also called (from left) Grant Roy, Mitch Halford, and Robert Wagner as key witnesses in the Harlow Cuadra murder trial to buttress their case. *(Times-Leader photos used with permission)*

CUADRA DEFENSE TEAM – Public defenders enlisted to lead Harlow Cuadra's defense against murder charges, from left, Paul Walker and Joseph D'Andrea. *(Times-Leader photo used with permission)*

A GUILTY PLEA – Joseph Kerekes is led from the murder trial of Harlow Cuadra after refusing to testify in the case, despite having earlier pled guilty to murder. *(Times-Leader photo used with permission)*

THE DA – Michael Melnick, a deputy district attorney for Luzerne County, accepts congratulations for the conviction of Harlow Cuadra from the victim's father, Michael Kocis (at left). *(Times-Leader photo used with permission)*

HEARTSICK – José Cuadra (right, back to camera) attempts to shield his mother Gladis Zaldivar from reporters and photographers as they exit the courtroom shortly after the jury announced its guilty verdict against Harlow Cuadra. *(Times-Leader photo used with permission)*

THE JUDGE – Former Luzerne County Judge Peter Paul Olszewski, Jr. who presided over the Cuadra murder trial, and sentenced both Cuadra and Kerekes to prison. *(Times-Leader photo used with permission)*

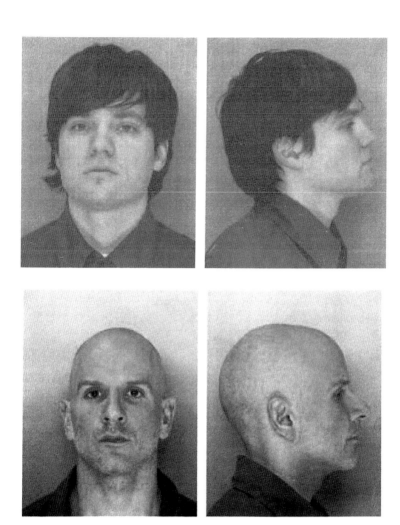

Pennsylvania Department of Corrections inmate photos of Harlow Cuadra and Joseph Kerekes. (Photos by Pennsylvania Department of Corrections, Coal Township Correctional Institution and Huntingdon State Correctional Institution)

DEMOLISHING THE PAST – Wrecking crews removed what remained of Bryan Kocis' home months after his murder. *(Times-Leader photo used with permission)*

ALL THAT REMAINS – All that remains of Bryan Kocis' home is this landscaped lot along a quiet neighborhood street in Dallas, Pennsylvania. *(Photo by Peter A. Conway)*

SCATTERED REMAINS – Bryan Kocis was cremated and his ashes were later scattered over this lake known as the Ice Ponds in rural Luzerne County, PA. *(Photo by Peter A. Conway)*

agenda" in his story, noting that "I should not have ignored Wilkinson's tinge of disdain that lightly emanated from him upon our first meeting. I really got a clear dose of journalism and what it really means when *Rolling Stone* and *Out* took their chance to tell their idea of what has ensued in (and around) my life," Lockhart said. "There is no justice in journalism."[49]

Approaching a settlement

Months of fighting were coming to an end late in 2006 as Lockhart and Kocis began seriously considering a settlement. For Kocis, his patience and his wallet were growing weary of expensive legal bills from California lawyers, all with no known resolution in sight. Depositions from both sides were taken in the contentious lawsuit in September 2006, giving everyone a chance to have his say.

A month later, after reading the transcripts of depositions given by Lockhart and Roy, Kocis approached his friend Samuel Hall, a Milwaukee-based entertainment lawyer who had befriended Kocis earlier in 2005. Apparently Kocis appreciated the demeanor of the depositions from Roy. "They expected (Roy's deposition) to be very hostile," Lockhart said. "He wasn't. So that really paved the way. Bryan took the first step and Grant returned the call (and)...the proceedings started happening."[50]

Hall was never officially an "attorney of record" for Kocis, the two had enjoyed a platonic friendship that included trips to Florida, Costa Rica, and Las Vegas.

"He had contacted me for advice and to bounce things off of," Hall said. "I was never formally retained as his lawyer, more so (I) became friends with him, (I) was somebody he could bounce questions with (about) the legal system."[51]

Hall said Kocis eventually was calling him by phone almost daily in 2005 and 2006 as the legal battle with Lockhart and Roy grew uglier.

But time has a way of changing things.

"It became clear that Bryan really wanted to settle the case by around November of 2006," Hall said, and that he had begun to focus on other things. "You know, up until that time, probably consistent with other lawsuits, it just consumed his life," Hall said. "It was something that he talked about, was concerned about every single day. By the time November of 2006 came, he became more interested in moving on with his life."(52)

Getting on with his life, though, meant Kocis would have to go face-to-face with Lockhart and Roy after a lot of angry, hurtful words and accusations had been exchanged between the trio. Regardless, Kocis green lighted the idea of having Hall approach Roy to have an open conversation about what could be done to resolve the case that would make both sides happy, Hall said.(53)

Hall described his role as trying to help all sides identify "how you can make money going into the future."(54)

Hall's efforts resulted in a draft Memorandum of Understanding written in the waning days of 2006 and the first few days of 2007. It was the MOU that served as the summons for all parties to meet at Hall's Las Vegas Boulevard condominium to start more detailed negotiations.(55)

Kocis showed up at Hall's Las Vegas home with an expensive gift for his friend, a Rolex watch. He remained nervous, though, that Lockhart and Roy may decide to back out of talking about a settlement.

On January 11, 2007, Kocis and Hall had a long dinner meeting, one in which Hall could see Bryan was ready to move on. "Bryan would talk about this lawsuit every day, and I said, 'You know, I can't talk about this every day. I need to talk about other things.'"(56)

The next day, Hall accompanied his friend/client to the Bellagio Hotel. There they met only with Roy. Lockhart did not show with Roy explaining that Lockhart's "personal feelings with respect to Bryan" made him reluctant to show.

A settlement this close in hand, Hall again stepped up and suggested Kocis return to the condo, while Hall talked to Roy alone. "We all came to the conclusion that if the case was going to be resolved, Sean (Lockhart) was an integral part of it and he needed to be there and he needed to take part in this meeting," Hall said.[57]

Soon Roy was convinced of Hall's good intentions and talked Lockhart into joining him at the condo for a long-dreaded but absolutely necessary face-to-face meeting with Kocis.

Around Hall's kitchen table that Friday afternoon, the group reviewed the proposed settlement. "Initially, everybody was a little tense," Hall understated. "There was a lot of distrust between these guys." The desire for a settlement, however, seemed to override that distrust. It also drove the meeting along into a four hour affair, ending around 8:00 P.M.[58]

Lockhart agreed to participate because he had become convinced that Kocis "had no intentions of preventing me from moving forward outside of what he wanted to do together. We agreed that he had a certain amount of fair stake in what I was doing because of my popular start at Cobra Video."[59]

Progress had been made, Hall said, "but we realized we weren't at a meeting of the minds and frankly, you know, we weren't close but we were making good progress. So we decided to go to dinner."[60]

The group went first to the Wynn Casino for dinner, a trendy Las Vegas nightclub in what now is the location of the Planet Hollywood Casino for drinks.

Seated in a "VIP booth" at the club, Hall described the meeting as friendly and optimistic. While no agreement was yet reached, Kocis and Roy had already started talking about possible projects they could do together, "and how their businesses could co-exist, work together (and) possibly even collaborate in the future," Hall said.[61]

The following day, the group met again at Hall's condo

starting at noon. "It was a long day, it took seven or eight hours," Hall said. "Most of the concessions were made by Bryan during that meeting."[62] Hall said Kocis wanted distribution rights to any videos LSG would make for market—a concession Lockhart and Roy were unwilling to make. Kocis eventually relented on that request after several hours of talking, "and everything (else) fell into place," Hall said.[63]

By Saturday evening, a final agreement was in place, another Kocis concession paving the way. Kocis had earlier insisted on creation of a new LLC to handle distribution of not only Cobra Video products featuring Lockhart, but also LSG videos with Lockhart. Hall said Kocis eventually relented by receiving other considerations, such as payment for the licensing fee for the trademark of the Brent Corrigan name.

The only remaining item was a planned visit by Kocis to LSG in San Diego to view what videos Lockhart and Roy had produced themselves and to determine how those could be distributed going forward.

The agreement finally in place, Hall reported all parties were ecstatic. "Sean gave Bryan a hug, which, you know, shocked me because I saw it the day before," Hall said. "There was so much distrust, and I think everybody was just really happy that the thing was done and (were) optimistic."[64]

The optimism even spread to Lockhart and Roy suggesting good places to have lunch when Kocis came to their hometown of San Diego to see the videos. As Hall said, "It was neat to see, because Grant was, you know, talking to Bryan, things within the industry, not necessarily looking for advice, but bouncing ideas off. Bryan was doing the same thing."[65]

Kocis' excitement was palatable. After discussions ended and the group broke up, Kocis coveted a large and expensive $25,000 Rolex watch at a shop inside the Bellagio Casino and Hotel. Kocis was in a mood to buy it as a gift to himself. Hall and Kocis' friend Robert Wagner, who had flown out from New York, prevailed on him to wait and not buy the watch on an impulse. Wagner described the aftermath of the settlement discussions this way: "It was very amicable...The weight of the world had just been lifted from Sean, Grant and Bryan's shoulders."[66]

The goodwill lasted, Hall said, through Kocis' subsequent visit to San Diego to see the Lockhart videos and up until when the final documents were signed on January 18, in Kocis' suite inside the W Hotel in downtown San Diego. "I mean, these guys weren't going to barbeque every weekend, but they had an ongoing professional relationship, like I said, (that) relied on each other in order to make money going into the future," Hall said. "They all understood that, and they all knew that, and they looked forward to working together."[67]

Agreement or not, "Sadly, there were forces unseen to all of us at work that converged and someone lost their life," Lockhart said. As he and Roy ended their battle with Kocis, they had already begun looking for new models to work on future projects. Part of that search, included the elaborate dinner meeting with Harlow Cuadra and Joe Kerekes at the same time the Kocis battle was concluding. The fury that meeting would release—resulting in Kocis' murder—would be realized later. For now, the settlement between Lockhart and Cobra was real.[68]

The end to the struggle with Kocis did not come without a final flair, however. A bottle of Kocis' favorite champagne, Veuve Clicquot, was opened and before the documents were signed between all parties on January 19, Kocis asked for a moment alone with his former friend and protégé, Lockhart. The two talked alone, outside the company of Roy and their lawyers, for about two minutes. "He took me aside," Lockhart said. "He hugged me and I hugged him back."[69]

"He said 'I'm truly sorry for all of this. I should have handled it differently; and if I had, then none of this would have happened,'" Lockhart said. Kocis' words to him were "hard to hear," Lockhart said, because of the friction that had existed for so long between the two. "It doesn't just go away," he said, "but at that moment, it was pretty clear that this man was, had no intention of carrying on the kind of hurt and pain he had caused me."[70]

Roy was also convinced it was time to rethink his previously unflattering views of Kocis. "I'm thinking, ya know, maybe (Kocis) was a demon or a pervent or whatever...maybe we turned the tide for him," Roy said.[71]

It wouldn't matter for long what anyone thought of Bryan Kocis.

With all of the documents finalized and signed by all parties, the unthinkable happened. Bryan Kocis was murdered.

Even though everyone was now playing nice, some tension remained. "You can't dial down that immediately," Kocis' friend Robert Wagner said. "It had become a business relationship where they needed to learn to work together. They all had to share a sand box."[72]

Lockhart said his "strong feelings of hate and hurt that coursed from both sides had begun to dull and lose their fervor" and that the agreement included a component where Lockhart would have allowed him to "boost my production into overdrive" and to gain valuable producer and director credits.[73]

An added bonus for Lockhart included his provision that any new productions with Cobra would be shot using condoms. "I was going to be able to continue to go on shooting my work using condoms, the safe way," he said.[74]

Lockhart said the deal would free him from Kocis' control, and would be a relationship governed by a legal settlement. He said he regretted, "there was never a time before Bryan's death that we were able to change the public tide about each other," Lockhart said.[75]

Specific details of the settlement were private and financial penalties were built in for both sides to keep the agreement private. It would have stayed that way except for startling events about to occur.

After the fact, Lockhart and Roy were required to disclose many of the aspects of the agreement they had reached with Kocis to police and later to a jury, including a plan to produce three DVD projects together with Cobra Video, paid for by Kocis (per film costs as much as $60,000 per project). In return, Kocis would take a twenty percent interest in all earnings Lockhart made appearing in gay porn as Brent Corrigan for a four year period. Lockhart would also gain a directing and producing credit for one of the projects—something he had prized since he first met Kocis, who had also agreed to promote any projects completed by LSG that he thought were suitable for his company. Lockhart's continued HIV-negative status would also have to be confirmed prior to shooting new scenes.[76]

Little personal contact would have been required with Kocis, Lockhart believes. "Nothing could have happened that would have put Bryan back in my life the way he once was," he said. "But there was no reason to feel that we could never develop a new, more professional relationship governed by legal laws and clear-cut boundaries."[77]

Dinner with Harlow and Joe

Lockhart and Roy's trip to Las Vegas was jam-packed full of important events. Beyond touring the Sands Expo Convention Center displays by adult entertainment and technology companies of all types and the marathon meetings with Bryan Kocis, Lockhart and Roy had planned to meet with Harlow Cuadra and Joseph Kerekes on Thursday evening, January 11, 2007, just prior to the start of formal settlement discussions with Kocis. It was all a part of moving onward and upward with LSG Media. It's a meeting that may not have happened at all, except for the persistence of Cuadra and the growing panic he and Kerekes faced against a mountain of unforgiving debt.

Roy had previously tried to reach out to Cuadra, in 2006,

via a male escort site, www.men4rent.com, but had been rebuffed. At that time Cuadra considered himself his own gay porn producer and didn't entertain entreaties from other producers, such as Roy.

Something changed, though, and by November 2006, MySpace and AIM instant messages were coming in from Cuadra, not to Roy, but to Lockhart. And it was Cuadra who was trying to take the lead—trying to recruit Lockhart to come over to his emerging BoisRUs and BoyBatter sites to film with them.

Cuadra's efforts to interest Lockhart included promises to house him in what he claimed was their $2 million "beach" home in Virginia Beach during the shoot, "pay you very well," up to $10,000 cash for two scenes, and promised spins in his new Viper or M5. "No joke, we have some cool toys to play with, cars, boats, etc., I'd love to host you," Cuadra boasted in one e-mail.[78]

Lockhart said his brief "online" friendship with Cuadra started via MySpace and continued with a few follow-up phone calls. Lockhart said the phone conversations with Cuadra remained friendly in November and December 2006 and included discussion of both men's experiences in the gay porn industry, and even mention by Cuadra of Lockhart's past work with Cobra Video. "This is all about work," Lockhart said Cuadra insisted. "It's about how ready he was. He was ready right then. There was no delay to do some shooting. They wanted to hire me to shoot for them."[79]

Discussions moved along quickly, including Cuadra and Kerekes figuring how they could meet Lockhart's interest in tapping into residual earnings from DVD sales, rather than just one lump, upfront payment for appearing in scenes.

Cuadra and Kerekes would later indicate that they viewed Lockhart's residual payment request as obnoxious, but their interest in the emerging porn star remained high. Evidence of that: Cuadra and Kerekes became quite agitated when Cuadra mistakenly was dropped from Lockhart's online front page "friends" listing on MySpace, a prominent spot on the better-known Lockhart's page coveted by Cuadra-Kerekes.

Perhaps sensing or fearing waning interest in working with BoyBatter, Cuadra rushed copies of his latest production, *Young Bucks in Heat*, via overnight delivery to Lockhart and Roy. Lockhart and Roy watched the tape, rating its production quality "poor" but admitting "Harlow was a good performer."[80]

Lockhart said he was upfront, however with Cuadra about the need to tone his look. "There was a lot of conversation surrounding my objectives in the industry and the models I was looking for," Lockhart said. "There was a lot of discussion about both of us (Cuadra and Lockhart) being in the best shape possible if a collaboration were to ever come about." As part of that, Lockhart was direct with Cuadra: he was dissatisfied with his look. He told Cuadra, "Tone up a little bit more. A little bit more muscle (was needed), but definitely more defined abs."[81]

The settlement nears closure

As plans were finalized for a joint dinner for the four men, Lockhart-Roy and Cuadra-Kerekes, Lockhart and Roy continued their nearly simultaneous discussions toward resolution with Kocis and Cobra Video.

The four met at the Le Cirque Restaurant inside Vegas' Bellagio Hotel on January 11, 2007. Lockhart and Roy said they viewed the dinner meeting as mostly social, a chance to meet in person and learn more about one another. Cuadra and Kerekes, from their actions before, during, and after the dinner, obviously viewed the meeting as a key "make or break" meeting for their financial and business future.

Cuadra's enthusiasm, it seems, bubbled over at times with him embracing Lockhart upon meeting, calling him "buttercup" and openly flirting. Lockhart said he tolerated the behavior, but didn't enjoy it.[82]

The three-hour dinner conversation quickly centered on

the gay porn business, with Roy and Kerekes driving most of the discussion. Lockhart and Roy both said they made a concerted effort to avoid discussing their near-settlement discussions upcoming with Kocis. "It was a very sensitive time in the mediation and the settlement mode," Lockhart said. "We couldn't afford (revealing details,) but what we could tell (Cuadra-Kerekes) was that it was going well, and we were heading in a very successful direction. That was all they needed to know."[83]

Their best efforts didn't seem to satisfy the increasingly aggressive Cuadra and Kerekes. Lockhart said, "It was pretty clear that (Cuadra) was frustrated, that it wasn't as simple as just shooting, just going in and doing whatever he wanted. He failed to recognize the time constraints that we had."[84]

Roy also noticed the aggressive push from Cuadra and Kerekes. "Harlow and Joe both seemed a little eager to get this production underway," Roy said. "I really wasn't sure (of the) necessity of the rush, and at various times, I tried to explain to them that I didn't think it was going to be a problem (to go forward) as long as we were able to get out of this mediation." Despite this assurance, Roy said, Cuadra and Kerekes remained "eager, excited" and "a little pushy at times."[85]

It was at this point, Lockhart and Roy both would confirm later, that Kerekes suggested that settlement talks with Kocis could be sped up if "he went to Europe." Cuadra changed that up a bit, Lockhart said, suggesting Kocis could "go to Canada" and "never come back" with Kerekes adding, "Harlow has this guy who will do anything for him."[86]

Roy immediately understood what the "Europe" and "Canada" suggestions meant. "I just said, 'Look, guys, this has been an ugly, bitter dispute. It's been highly publicized online'…I said I felt this (battle with Kocis) had gone far enough, it got ugly enough, and if we continue down that road, somebody is going to get hurt."[87]

Roy insists he told Cuadra and Kerekes that "nothing

needed to happen" and that he remained confident they would reach a settlement with Kocis and Cobra Video. Roy nervously laughed off the suggestion he fully understood—one that included causing physical harm to Kocis. "I said, 'No, it's been ugly, it's been nasty, it's behind us, nobody needs to go anywhere in this thing,'" Roy said he told Cuadra and Kerekes.[88]

Lockhart admits his intoxication prevented him from fully understanding what Cuadra and Kerekes were suggesting. Lockhart said he had downed three vodka cocktails at his hotel room before leaving for dinner because he was only twenty years old and feared getting carded, and denied, a dinner drink. He wasn't carded, as it turned out, and he drank a glass of wine with every course of the elaborate dinner. At the end of the meal, Lockhart claims his intoxication rendered him "pretty much inoperable. I had a difficult time walking, seeing."[89]

Regardless, Cuadra wanted photos taken of him with Lockhart, one of them with Cuadra's armed slung over the shoulder of his new "buttercup" and another one showing him flipping the finger to the camera. Within hours the photos showed up on the BoyBatter website.

CHAPTER 8
Two Stand Accused

"One of our citizens was murdered. It was a business hit, period. That's the long and short of it. They had a plan to commit the murder, a plan to carry out the robbery, a plan to destroy evidence, and a plan to profit from the murder. They had a plan for everything."
—Assistant DA Michael Melnick

As Harlow Cuadra recalls it, Joseph Kerekes was hungry on the morning of May 15, 2007, so they did what they usually did: jumped in the car and headed for one of their favorite spots, Boston Market on Virginia Beach Boulevard. At least that is where they said they were going.

Police investigators in Virginia Beach who had been trailing the couple for weeks thought otherwise. Boston Market was not open at that hour of the morning, causing them to notify Pennsylvania authorities that the couple was "on the move."

Coincidentally, authorities back in Luzerne County were just wrapping up the final pieces of felony arrest warrants for

Cuadra and Kerekes. By 9:30 A.M., they had filed their charges and were underway. "We were going to go down to Virginia Beach anyway," Dallas Township Police Detective Doug Higgins said. "We had our bags packed and in the car when the Virginia Beach guys called and said, 'Hey, these guys are on the move, in the car, they look like they have some luggage with them, what do you want us to do?'"[1]

Fearing Cuadra and Kerekes would possibly fall out of sight again, one of the police investigators in Virginia made the decision to stop them. Pennsylvania authorities moved immediately to get to Virginia, driving straight through.[2]

As Virginia Beach Police surrounded their car with lights and sirens and weapons drawn, Cuadra and Kerekes apparently paused for a moment, trying to decide whether to stop for the police cars that now surrounded them. It was a brief delay, and the two were arrested without incident.[3]

Now officially charged with criminal homicide, conspiracy to commit criminal homicide, abuse of a corpse, robbery, burglary, theft, and two counts of arson, Cuadra and Kerekes were separated at the Virginia Beach Police Department and waited alone in interview rooms for detectives from Pennsylvania to arrive for questioning.

Attempting to "interview" Harlow and Joe

Detectives Higgins and state police detective Daniel Yursha were sent in to attempt to question Cuadra, while state investigator Leo Hannon and FBI Special Agent James Glenn met with Kerekes.

Cuadra was in no mood to talk. "He said, 'I have an attorney, I want an attorney, I have Barry Taylor,'" Higgins recalled. "We said, 'OK, but we're going to read, if you want, we're going to read these charges to you.'"[4]

That done, questioning of Cuadra stopped and Higgins and Yursha left the room to prepare to book Cuadra at the Virginia Beach lockup to await extradition to Pennsylvania.

"What I remember the most is that we left the room and when we were going back in, (Cuadra) says to us, he looks up at us and says, 'Joe didn't do this.' He just volunteers this as we walk in the door to tell him he is going to go to the lockup and that he would be hearing from us again," Higgins said.[5]

Prevented from questioning him further because of his request for an attorney, Higgins told Cuadra that if he and his attorney decided they wanted to make a statement, Pennsylvania detectives would return immediately to Virginia. "I told him, 'We would love to sit down with you and hear your side of the story,'" Higgins said. That never happened.[6]

In the short time they did spend together, Higgins came away unimpressed with Cuadra. "He is a male prostitute, and he comes across as soft, by the way he speaks and his mannerisms, but I can see right through that," Higgins said. "I can see him for what he is, he is a prostitute. He acts like that to get people to do what he wants, to manipulate people."[7]

Hannon and Glenn would fare no better with Kerekes, though there were more fireworks. Kerekes would later describe the exchange as a "soap opera" as he and his lawyers successfully sought to suppress statements the always talkative Kerekes made to the officers. He said his first and only words to investigators were, "I want a lawyer."[8]

Hannon and Glenn filed a report reflecting a very different type of meeting. Their report shows they first approached Kerekes in an interview room at the Virginia Beach Police Department at 8:20 P.M. and continued talking to him, on and off, until at least 10:04 P.M. that spring evening.

Hannon said he followed his normal procedure, informing Kerekes that he was under arrest, read him his Miranda rights, and informed him that he intended to read him the actual charge from the court. "I told him I didn't want to hear it," Kerekes would later say. "I just put my head down and he went on (reading)." Kerekes insists no one read him his rights, and they ignored his twice repeated requests for an attorney. "I asked twice for a lawyer, I never once interrupted…my head was down, I was just listening," Kerekes said.[9]

During a July 2008 suppression hearing on the matter, Hannon testified about his version of the interaction with Kerekes, and outlined his normal procedure in such instances, including reading the Miranda rights statement to an arrested person, and reading the full criminal complaint against them. He said he also confirmed Kerekes date of birth and Social Security number.

Hannon said Kerekes repeatedly said he understood that he was under arrest and that he understood his rights. In a synopsis report he wrote about the interview later, Hannon stated that Kerekes said, "I understand the words, but I don't understand why I've been charged with this. This is sad, but I never knew Bryan Kocis. All I've ever known of him is what I've read in the newspapers." Kerekes posture during his denials was "upright. His expressions were direct, and his speech was lucid and confident," Hannon said.[10]

When Hannon attempted to read the full criminal complaint and probable cause affidavit to Kerekes, he was repeatedly interrupted. When Hannon read from the report that computers seized from Kerekes' home "proved to contain valuable investigative information," Kerekes said that would be "impossible" because the computers formerly within his home were "dummies" and "didn't contain anything."[11]

Kerekes interrupted again later, saying the Las Vegas meeting between him, Cuadra, Roy, and Lockhart was "a harmless meeting" and challenged assertions in the complaint based on information obtained from Lockhart. "Are you gonna believe the words from the lips of that boy?" Kerekes reportedly said. "It wasn't about money. We have money."[12]

Kerekes would again challenge information in the complaint about the Nissan Xterra rented by Cuadra in the hours before Kocis' murder, saying, "We rented that for the weather. We had some bookings to get to."[13]

When the detective reached the point in the probable cause affidavit outlining Kerekes' e-mails to Roy that investigators uncovered—e-mails where Kerekes said "we'll tell them (the police) that you hired us"—Kerekes blurted out that he sent the e-mail in "a drunken rage" resulting from his anger on how Roy and Lockhart had stopped talking to them after Kocis was found dead.[14]

As he continued to read the criminal complaint and reached the part detailing the actual murder of Kocis, Hannon said Kerekes began to weep, swearing on his mother's name that he had not killed Kocis. He reportedly said to Hannon, "What are you looking for?" Hannon replied, "I want the truth.(Kerekes) started talking but I cut him off and advised him to speak with a lawyer if he wanted to make a statement (because of Kerekes' earlier assertions that he wanted counsel present)."[15]

Hannon said he also explained the extradition process Kerekes would face in being removed from Virginia and returned to Luzerne County, Pennsylvania. Asked if he had any questions, Hannon said Kerekes only inquiry was: "Are (Sean) Lockhart and (Grant) Roy in custody?" which was answered in the negative.[16]

Trashing the evidence

Kerekes and his attorneys at the time, Shelley Centini and John Pike, argued that reading the formal criminal complaint to Kerekes constituted "the functional equivalent of interrogation" and that the detectives were attempting to set up "a situation they should have known would likely elicit a response." Kerekes opinion was that "(Reading the complaint to me) was inflammatory. They highlighted these parts. They wanted me to say something."[17]

Centini and Pike were also seeking to block admittance of any evidence taken from Cuadra and Kerekes' home during the February 2007 search, and sought to suppress recordings of their conversations with Grant Roy and Sean Lockhart in

California in April 2007. They attempted to argue that all of this evidence was not collected consistent with Pennsylvania law, and therefore should be thrown out.

Taylor frequently raised similar concerns during the time he represented Cuadra and Kerekes. At the time of their initial arrest, Taylor said there were serious questions "about how strong the evidence really is."[18]

Taylor also raised allegations that the Virginia RICO investigation was used mostly to advance the Pennsylvania murder case. Graydon Brewer, an attorney briefly engaged by Kerekes, agreed, saying, "I believe it was a coordinated effort between Virginia authorities and Pennsylvania authorities that the search warrant and seizures were intentionally timed with the arrest, so that they would not have any assets to retain the counsel of their choice."[19]

Former Luzerne County District Attorney David Lupas commented on the unique nature of the Kocis murder investigation. "(This was) not your run of the mill, but again the investigators followed the leads and follow the evidence wherever it takes them," Lupas said. "This investigation basically, literally, went from coast to coast from Virginia to California."[20]

Assistant DA Michael Melnick insists that the search warrant of the Virginia Beach home was carried out consistent with Virginia law because he said that is where the home is located. The tape recordings were done consistent with California and federal law because that is where they were conducted.

One more call to Sean Lockhart

Before Cuadra and Kerekes even knew they should be on the run, and less than twenty-four-hours after Bryan Kocis' throat had been slit from end-to-end, they couldn't resist notifying Lockhart how they believed his "Kocis problem" had been resolved.

Lockhart said he reported to his temporary job as a clerical production assistant at a construction company on January 25, 2007 as normal. The day was about to fall apart.

Around 9:00 A.M., Lockhart's cell phone rang. The number popping up on the screen was Harlow Cuadra's. "I hadn't heard from Cuadra in a couple of days, in a week maybe," Lockhart said, indicating he was irritated to be hearing from them again.

When Lockhart answered, it was Kerekes on the phone. "Joe says, 'Hold on, Harlow wants to talk to you,' and Harlow comes to the phone and I guess he was in the shower or something and he says, 'Go to WNEP.com.'"[21]

Lockhart did as Cuadra suggested and called up the TV station's news site. "The center article, the main article, right there was (this) major fire at 60 Midland Drive and I clicked on it and read the first few lines," Lockhart said. "I just got the feeling in my stomach where something terrible, out of your control had happened. I shut (the laptop)."[22]

Lockhart said Cuadra blurted out, "I guess my guy went a little overboard." Shocked by what he was hearing, Lockhart said he had to go, and quickly hung up the phone.[23]

Frozen in fear by what he had read and what he now knew Cuadra was suggesting had been done to Kocis (a man he had talked to less than twelve hours earlier), "I left work immediately and I went home to Grant," Lockhart said.[24]

Lockhart and Roy had a tense conversation, with Roy also calling up the WNEP website to see what was being reported. "We had no clue, but I just remembered our feelings of fear and confusion," Lockhart said. "We didn't know what was going on."[25]

Roy said he was "scared to death" by the unbelievable news they were reading online about Kocis' death and "concerned that we might be next."[26]

Lockhart and Roy decided it was best to "go along" in order to avoid any danger for themselves, but Roy put into motion immediately a plan to contact attorneys Ezekiel Cortez and

Bernard Scoble of San Diego, but eventually also the police in Pennsylvania.

The lawyers offered good advice: keep away from Cuadra and Kerekes and don't talk to anyone alone. Roy also told Cuadra and Kerekes directly, by phone, to leave him and Lockhart alone. For once, the Virginia Beach couple complied, at least temporarily.

Meanwhile, lawyers for Lockhart and Roy approached local and federal police authorities indicating their clients had information relevant to a pending homicide investigation back in Pennsylvania. Roy would eventually make six separate trips to Pennsylvania, and Lockhart three of his own to assist authorities.

Harlow and Joe on the run

During the weeks between the February 10, 2007 search warrant on their home and their arrest on May 15, 2007, Cuadra and Kerekes worked to keep a low profile. "We ran for our lives," Kerekes would tell Roy and Lockhart during a luncheon meeting taped by authorities. "We were living in the ghetto in South Beach, okay, and ah, it's been horrible, we act like we have all this (money), we don't…we cash advanced everything. We're in so much debt, we're probably going to have to do another bankruptcy, it's just horrible…it's been hell. We haven't slept at home in three months, we're at hotels every night," Kerekes said.[27]

Cuadra admitted he couldn't sleep at home for fear the police would burst in at any moment. "We don't sleep there, we're back home during the day, but can you imagine sleeping there? No, we started sleeping in hotels," Kerekes said.[28]

Both men said their reportedly $500-an-hour attorney, Barry Taylor, told them to stay out of sight in Miami. "He was telling us to stay in South Beach, to stay there, it's not safe," Kerekes said on the Black's Beach police tapes. "I said, 'Barry, everything looks good for us here, I wanna go home, I don't wanna lose our house.'"

Kerekes admitted on the same tape that he had lied to Taylor about having at least $100,000 to pay his legal fees. The couple even authorized Taylor to conduct a never-conducted auction of their personal possessions, but called it off after an argument ensued over how the proceeds would be used. They also conducted an on-camera interview with TV producers from MTV's *Real Life* program to tell their side of the story, but the segment was never aired.[29]

Police had their last contact with the duo over the phone on February 12, as they visited with Kerekes' parents at their Virginia Beach home. During that visit, Joe Kerekes called his parents' house at least three times, detectives reported, but refused to come there to answer their questions in person, instead asking his parents not to talk to the detectives (a request they complied with, the elderly couple asking the detectives to leave their home).

About a month later on March 9, with funds running very low, a new video was posted on the BoyBatter.com website titled *Drake & Harlow: Beach Bubbles Bird*. Review of the video indicates it was shot at the Clinton Hotel in South Beach Miami, Florida and even shows a Miami Beach police car in the background while the two actors are on the beach. On March 16, another video was posted to BoyBatter.com, this one titled *Drake & Harlow Jack Off, Part I*, clearly shot inside a room at the Clinton Hotel.

Kerekes later provided more detail about their flight to a reporter from the *Times Leader*, saying how the couple stayed for a time in a condo rented with cash for a year in a friend's name to try and throw off authorities.

It was during this period, however, that Kerekes kept up regular e-mail contact with both Grant Roy and eventually Sean Lockhart, his messages getting more and more aggressive and threatening. On March 3, at 10:14 A.M., a strange message purporting to be from both Kerekes and Cuadra arrived in

Grant Roy's mailbox from Harlow Cuadra's MySpace e-mail address: "Hey grant, its harlow so when we gonna start filming? I know we had an agreement. Joe."

A minute later at 10:15 A.M. another e-mail came in to Roy saying, "you need to make some king (sic.) of contract with us before I tell them you hired us joe."

Apparently convinced threatening was the way to go, another e-mail at 10:17 A.M. was sent to Roy saying, "and we all know what u said to us at the avn in vegas and we have it on tape recorder and out (sic.) conversation at le cirque is recorded as well dont fuck with us."

Given time to cool off, at 10:43 A.M. another e-mail arrived announcing: "we are going to visit san diego this week or next and we need to meet we hope to see u soon."[30]

By early April, Kerekes was playing nice. In a very businesslike April 3, e-mail from Kerekes to Roy, he further approached the idea of a collaboration on a porn project involving Lockhart and Cuadra. Kerekes even queried Roy about whether his settlement with Kocis (prior to Kocis' death) would prevent a collaboration.

Roy responded by reminding Kerekes that the settlement with Kocis was strictly confidential. He sought to reassure Kerekes—whether in truth or as part of an effort to keep him on a string—that "any proposal that is presented will be in full compliance with the settlement and trademark license issues as they pertain to Brent Corrigan and Cobra Video."

Roy must have known the desperation Kerekes and Cuadra were under, but still offered, "If this does not provide you with enough reassurance to move forward with the shoot, then we will have no other choice but to cancel or postpone current plans indefinitely."

Roy promised a forthcoming "proposal" but admonished Kerekes not to "make any announcements, or insinuations on any of your websites or other websites or public forums as already seems to be the case."[31]

At the same time, Roy continued his discussions with law enforcement. "They were interested in getting us, having us get together (with Cuadra-Kerekes) for a meeting so they (could) possibly intercept the conversation and see if they would indicate what happened during the crime," Roy said.[32]

Kerekes described his months in hiding as just hanging out in "the gay ghetto in South Beach" Miami, where they saw some openly gay churches. Although still claiming not to be gay, Kerekes said, "Harlow said to me that I should have focused on being a pastor in a church like that."[33]

Cuadra said Kerekes would walk daily across the street from their rented South Beach condo to a Haitian restaurant called Tap Tap, just five blocks west of the beach. Barry Taylor, like clockwork, called every day around the same time, general checkup, Cuadra said, providing updates on what was happening back in Pennsylvania and Virginia. It was through Taylor, Cuadra said, that the couple learned that no warrants had been issued for their arrest, and that police investigators appeared to be scaling back their investigation of the Kocis murder.

It was just the start of the emergence from hiding Cuadra and Kerekes would enact. The couple went back to their Virginia Beach home, finally, where they found the remnants of the SWAT team entry into their home, including a small hole in the wall and burned carpeting, Cuadra said. Before returning home, however, Cuadra constructed a reunion with his mother and siblings by stopping off at her home in South Carolina en route back from Florida.

At the end of April, just one day after the infamous Black's Beach meeting and before he was arrested, Cuadra amazingly answered an e-mail from a reporter from the *Times Leader* in Wilkes-Barre. He gloated that all of the publicity surrounding the case and allegations linking him to the crime had helped him make more money (a similar claim he made to Lockhart and Roy on tape). He told reporter Ed Lewis, via e-mail, that the "world was ready for Brent Corrigan and me to film, so here is a preview pic taken yesterday of Brent and I on a nude beach in San Diego before our first shoot."[34]

Meanwhile, back at Stratem Court

Simultaneous to their arrests in May 2007, Virginia authorities executed a second search warrant on their Stratem Court home. This second search was a result of an ongoing Virginia RICO investigation launched in January 2006 after police received a complaint that Cuadra and Kerekes were running a prostitution service from their home. Items seized during the second search included a knife, laptop computers, a camcorder, tapes, and a Sprint mobile air card (all later turned over to Pennsylvania authorities).

Virginia investigators said their search was intended to uncover evidence related to booking escort clients, including ledgers or appointment books, lists of client names and phone numbers, and financial records related to Norfolk Male Companion, Inc., Norfolk Gay Escorts, and personal financial records of Cuadra and Kerekes.

After Virginia authorities completed their search of the home, Pennsylvania detectives also took a look around, including Sergeant Doug Higgins from Dallas Township. He described the home as "unimpressive" and noted that "There was a first floor weight room (where a living room normally would be) with a bunch of weights in it" and upstairs bedrooms contained an unusual amount of shoes and boots. "There were a whole bunch of shoes, I mean just a ton of shoes, sneakers," he said. "Another downstairs room was used to store car parts, and upstairs on the balcony is where all the computers were, about forty of them." Higgins said one of the bedrooms was set up as a "shoot room" with a bed, lights, cameras, and a surround-sound system all in place. Cuadra and Kerekes' personal bedrooms "were a mess," he said.

The Cuadra-Kerekes home was short on the normal

furnishings, in the living room, no couches, chairs, or tables. "It was a nice house, but in my opinion it was nothing fancy," Higgins said.

Earlier in the day, Higgins said he questioned some of the neighbors on Stratem Court. Few, if any, knew Cuadra and Kerekes at all. "They all said they noticed them washing their cars a lot. They said they noticed people coming and going sometimes and that sometimes they would wave," Higgins reported.[35]

Pennsylvania detectives who remained in Virginia Beach for a few days after the search warrant assisted in processing materials seized from Cuadra and Kerekes' home and their car. In their car, a knife identical to the one the pair were videotaped purchasing at the Superior Pawn Shop was found. "The knife found in their car was a staged knife," assistant DA Melnick said. "After they murdered Mr. Kocis, Joe Kerekes returned to the pawn shop and the thinking was that he needed to buy a replacement knife in case the police captured them. The Sig Sauer knife in the car was completely clean and (Kerekes) freely admitted that was a fake out. No one believed that they would be carrying around the murder weapon some five months after the crime."[36]

Cuadra apparently was convinced that the knife recovered actually helped exonerate the couple. He didn't count, apparently, on anyone knowing Kerekes returned to the Superior Pawn Shop for a second time and to buy a second knife. Cuadra wrote on his blog while jailed that "the knife that (Kerekes) bought at the pawn shop that day was in the glove box of the BMW, still in the paper and box it was sold to him in, never used, kind of amazing that he could buy the knife, use it to commit a very heinous crime and then restore the knife back to original condition and put it back in the box without a trace of DNA on it…the reason there is no DNA on the knife was 'cause the knife was never used and was in the glove box of the BMW since the day it was purchased."[37] The actual knife used to slay Kocis would never be found, although detectives tried hard to locate it. The cops also tried to find Kocis' Rolex watch, taken from his body the night he was killed, but never succeeded. "One of the statements from Kerekes said the watch was thrown off a culvert somewhere on a Virginia Beach highway, in a swamp-like area," Melnick said. "Low and behold, while we're interviewing witnesses, Leo Hannon is marching through the swamp months after the crime looking for that doggone watch (or knife)."[38]

Cuadra and Kerekes prepare to defend themselves

Cuadra's attorney Barry Taylor openly predicted that both Cuadra and Kerekes would eventually require the services of public defenders because their assets were seized. Taylor said he believed investigators did so to deprive the couple of the ability to hire a private attorney on their own.

Taylor vigorously defended the duo, at least initially, but eventually fell back into the background as the criminal case against the men moved away from Virginia to Pennsylvania (and their ability to pay a lawyer continued to dwindle). Cuadra and Kerekes would eventually work their way through many attorneys, paying for them with what resources family and friends could provide, and eventually relied upon public defenders. "Captain Jack"(whose real name is Joseph Ryan), acknowledged he was an active client of Harlow Cuadra's escort services, and reportedly also provided initial financial help for the defense.

An initial hearing was conducted for Cuadra and Kerekes in Virginia Beach on May 17, in which both men indicated they would fight extradition to Pennsylvania. During a subsequent hearing on June 7, bond was denied for both Cuadra and Kerekes. Kerekes said he could stay with his parents while he awaited trial, but bond was not possible, as Virginia Governor Tim Kaine had already signed an extradition warrant request from Pennsylvania Governor Ed Rendel. Joe and Harlow were going back to Pennsylvania.

The duo was not done fighting. Kerekes' new counsel, James P. Brice, Jr. of Virginia Beach, told reporters that his client had "certain rights under the constitution. If these rights are violated, the state must release them."[39]

Brice and Taylor succeeded in earning yet another hearing on the matter to determine whether Cuadra and Kerekes were the correct individuals sought by Pennsylvania authorities, whether they were fugitives, and whether the charges were valid and correct. The lawyers were also fighting to keep authorities in either Virginia or Pennsylvania from seizing their home, bank accounts, and other assets.

During the hearing, Kerekes' parents attended and as he left the courtroom, Kerekes turned, winked, and smiled at his mother. "She sat crying in the front row," according to a report aired by WTKR-TV in Norfolk, Virginia. Their attempts to line-up a bail bondsman for their son were unnecessary. No bond would ever be set.

On July 17, Cuadra and Kerekes were finally returned to Luzerne County, Pennsylvania to answer to the string of charges. Both men would soon employ the first of a series of various Pennsylvania attorneys.

As he strode into court ready to start his case against the men, assistant DA Melnick put it simply: "One of our citizens was murdered. It was a business hit, period. That's the long and short of it." Melnick and fellow assistant district attorney Tim Doherty noted that the plan they believed Cuadra and Kerekes had hatched and carried out against Bryan Kocis had succeeded on almost every mark. Except one: firefighters responded quickly and put out the fire meant to hide evidence in the case and preserved the grisly crime scene for investigators, most particularly Kocis' business records.[40]

Kerekes had something to say as well, yelling out to reporters as he was led from a police car in handcuffs and hand-restraint mittens to a state police post at Wyoming, Pennsylvania. "To answer your questions," Kerekes told reporters, "No, I didn't do it."[41]

Cuadra kept it simple as well: "Not guilty" is all he would say as he was led to court.[42]

Cuadra and Kerekes were arraigned before Magisterial District Judge James E. Tupper shortly after arriving back in Luzerne County, but it would be the last time the two men would see one another in a long time. Cuadra was ordered held without bond at the Lackawanna County Prison in nearby Scranton, while Kerekes was jailed at the Luzerne County Correctional Facility in Wilkes-Barre.

Cuadra, while mostly silent when reporters peppered him with questions outside court hearings, was prolific in his views on his short-lived web blog, www.harlowcuadraonline.com. Presumably dictating the entries to supporters on the outside who posted them, he often went beyond the frequent requests for money to fund his defense to address other issues.

Cuadra used the blog to openly suggest that it was Sean Lockhart and Grant Roy who were responsible for the death of Bryan Kocis. "You shouldn't always believe what you read 'cause a lot of things in our business are made up," Cuadra cautioned. "(D)on't believe the story Brent Corrigan tells the police for his limited immunity he received in reference to the statement he gave. Brent did what he did to cover his ass, he had a motive, everyone knew this and he needed to get the heat off himself, so he did, he diverted them to me, and made his self (sic.) look innocent."[43]

Cuadra also referred to what he believed were discrepancies in Lockhart and Roy's version of the infamous January 2007 Las Vegas discussion about making Kocis "go away." Unfortunately for Cuadra, however, the only conversations on tape were the April 2007 ones in which he and Kerekes openly implicated themselves. (E-mail claims uncovered later where Kerekes attempted to make Roy believe the Las Vegas and San Diego conversations were taped were never produced in Kerekes or Cuadra's defense.)

Cuadra incorrectly predicted that Lockhart would someday "be sitting right next to me in Luzerne County here" and that "he can't keep weaseling his way out of this, there is to (sic.) much stuff linking him."[44]

Later, Cuadra would again surface, this time in the November 2007 "Letters to the Editor" of *Out* magazine in a surreal letter "thanking *Out* for publishing the article on the death of Bryan C. Kocis" and doing so in "an unbiased form." He told the editor, "Joseph M. Kerekes and I were at our most vulnerable when the interviews for that article took place. Your writer could easily have exploited us for information or cast a darker cloud over us in order to make the story entertaining. He did neither." Cuadra signed his letter eerily, "Your new *Out* reader 4 life."[45]

Paying for a defense

Attempts to raise the funds needed to enact a Cuadra plan for acquittal included auctions operated by Cuadra's family and friends via the "Free Harlow Cuadra Blog." Items listed for the October 2007 auction was a chinchilla fur jacket, other pieces of clothing, paintings and model cars, and "to the highest bidder," two forty-five-minute exclusive interviews with Harlow and Joe for the news media or general public. The interview exclusive had a starting bid of $500 but no one ever purchased it. "The dollar amount to defend a capital case is over $250,000 combined," Cuadra wrote to supporters on his blog. "We have tried requesting donations and putting up our many personal items for auction to raise these funds. We have not been successful in meeting this demand (as) the donations and items that were purchased have not covered any where close to the funds required."[46]

A family auction site also went up online, headed by Cuadra's mother Gladis Zaldivar. She begged of readers to "please help free my son, he been (sic.) accused of murder and I don't have the money for the attorney fees." She added, "We all know the profession my son is in regardless of my son's sexual orientation that is not what is at hand today. Gay or not I will always love my son Harlow. I except (sic.) the fact that my son is gay, I will not except (sic.) the fact that he is being wrongfully accused of murder."[47]

Kerekes' parents, Fred and Rosalie, were also active in trying to raise funds. They posted checking account routing numbers online, along with MySpace and PayPal accounts to make it easier for donations to come in to benefit their son's defense. "They seized all their property and assets," Joe's father Fred Kerekes told the *Times Leader*. "Right now, they don't have any money for lawyers. I'm hoping to raise $150,000 for my son and Harlow (Cuadra)."[48]

Fred Kerekes said his son called him just before they were arrested. "He said, 'There are twenty officers out there, they are arresting me.' I talked to him in jail and he said they never read him his rights or told him why he was arrested."

Fred Kerekes also aired a similar complaint to Cuadra and Kerekes' attorneys regarding the freeze Virginia investigators placed on bank accounts and other assets held by the couple as part of their ongoing RICO investigation. "I believe the police trumped up these charges to seize everything they own," Fred Kerekes said. He said he did not believe his son was involved in the murder, and spoke up as well for his son's partner, Harlow Cuadra. "Harlow is a very nice young man. Both he and my son come to my house occasionally. We had them there on Thanksgiving, Christmas and they were here on Mother's Day."[49]

Other help was on the way. Former gay porn actor turned producer, Jason Ridge, and his fellow performer Danny Vox also attempted to help pay for the defense. Ridge said, "I am on a campaign along with a few other people to help the accused Harlow Cuadra fight this unjust accusation toward him."(No mention of Kerekes' situation was made.)[50] Ridge, who starred in at least six gay adult films between 2003 and

2007 (including *Nasty, Nasty* and *Gunnery Sgt. McCool*), started Ridgeline Productions in 2007. "We are making a defense fund to help (Harlow) get an attorney to fight this all the way through. I felt compelled to do this because as a fellow performer in the business, we have to look out for one another," Ridge said. "Harlow deserves a fair trial and he is desperately in need of money. As an American, everyone deserves a fair trial, unfortunately that means you need a lot of money. This is just my way of trying to help and once again, innocent until proven guilty."[51]

If others in the gay porn world were concerned about the fate of Cuadra and Kerekes, they never made that concern known as the porn industry continued operating while barely missing a beat.

While Cuadra and Kerekes sat in jail, their Norfolk Male Companions business crumbled. The *Virginian-Pilot* reported that there was no doubt the company was a front for illegal prostitution. A confidential informant told police that he worked as a prostitute for the business and performed sexual acts with clients while Cuadra was present, and confirmed that Cuadra and Kerekes were the primary escorts working from the home.[52]

The informant allegedly told police that the escort service charged $200 per hour for escort services performed at the home, or "in calls," and $250 an hour for services elsewhere (such as at a client's home or hotel), considered an "out call."[53]

Virginia authorities eventually dropped their probe into whether Cuadra and Kerekes had conspired to violate the state's RICO act, and related money laundering charges, but not before a second RICO-related search warrant was served on the home four days after the arrest of Cuadra and Kerekes. Reports from the May 18 raid noted that the escort service operating there provided "a massage table, multiple head shower, king-sized bed, leather couch, and hot tub."[54]

During the raid, investigators collected desktop and laptop

computers and monitors; a variety of digital still and video cameras; a printer; a Bose media center and stereo system, including CD changers and surround sound speakers; an iPod; numerous pieces of jewelry, including watches, gold necklaces, cufflinks, and bracelets; a Louis Vuitton bag; racing tire rims and various accessories for a Honda S2000; four vehicles: Honda Civic S2000, Dodge Viper, Chevrolet Corvette and a BMW; and $26,585.25 in cash.[55]

All of the vehicles in Cuadra and Kerekes' possession were sent back to the lenders who still held leases or loans on them, according to Virginia Beach Senior Commonwealth Attorney Scott Alleman.[56]

Cuadra and Kerekes would later complain loudly that the cash and other assets were not available to them to hire defense counsel as they prepared for trial. State and federal investigators believed the items seized from their home and bank accounts were the result of criminal activity and therefore not available to the defendants. "No one will ever talk about what happened to all that stuff," Kerekes complained from inside a Pennsylvania prison. "They just took it and it's gone and we never could get it so we could hire proper attorneys."[57]

State and federal authorities insist all assets seized from the couple's home were forfeited because they were gained as part of an illegal operation. The base for the Cuadra and Kerekes enterprise would also soon be gone. Public property records in Virginia showed Cuadra and Kerekes' home at 1028 Stratem Court was held on two mortgages totaling $533,400.

In August 2007, the house was listed for sale because prosecutors determined Cuadra and Kerekes owed almost as much as the assessed value of the home: $542,683. The original listing price for the home was set at $679,000 by Virginia Beach real estate agent Kelley Bass, noting that "this home is priced to sell! Motivated seller!" Unfortunately, there were no motivated buyers at that price, especially in a U.S. real estate market hemorrhaging from the sub-prime lending crisis that swept the industry.[58]

After about two years of struggling on the market, in July 2009, the house sold at a Sheriff's auction sale to a mortgage lender specializing in repossessed property at a listed price of $573,434. The buyers, apparently hoping to flip the house for profit, promptly put the house back on the market at a highly reduced price that continued to fall as the months drifted by.[59]

The house was not seized by Virginia investigators, Alleman said, because "the house would have been more costly to pursue than it would have to just give it back to (Cuadra and Kerekes)."[60]

The police raids on their home seem to particularly anger Kerekes. "They took everything, they took a four-hundred pound safe. They pried it open…with the jaws of life.(The police) called the fire department over, our neighbor was there and you know, they were giving us a play-by-play (of the search)," he said.

Kerekes said that during the search, his mother Rosalie confronted investigators as they hauled away computers and other valuables from the home. Among the seized items was a "state-of-the-art" Sony video camera, one Cuadra called his "baby." Before police took it, however, its contents were backed up online. "The only reason BoyBatter survived," Kerekes said, "is because we took the two computers that had all the movies on them over (to) my mom's house."[61]

In October 2007, under a heading "We are Innocent!" Cuadra and Kerekes announced they were selling Norfolk Male Companions and its related websites. It was unclear how much those "assets" would even be worth with Cuadra and Kerekes behind bars facing murder charges, but the website sale plowed forward. "The sale of Norfolk Male Escorts is intended to be sold to someone that would like to run an escort service, a legitimate escort service," Cuadra posted to his web blog. He claimed he and Kerekes "made a lucrative living off" the escort service and "the traffic the site brings on the Internet alone would keep someone busy for a long time."[62]

Both Kerekes and Cuadra attempted to reassure their families, friends, and supporters of their innocence. "I do not want people to judge Joe or I before all the evidence has come to light," Cuadra wrote. "I do understand that some things that are out there do not look good, but there are always two sides to every story and people should stop and think before judging anyone else."[63]

CHAPTER 9

Building the Case against
Cuadra and Kerekes

"This letter is for your eyes only. Thank you so much for your help…like I said over the phone, if my lawyer needs you to testify for me in court, your transportation and salary will be covered."

—Harlow Cuadra letter to potential alibi
witness Nep Maliki

Lawyer roulette

Cuadra and Kerekes worked their way through a dizzying array of defense attorneys engaged from just before their arrest until their convictions almost two years later. The "lawyer roulette" that took place was a direct result of financial resources the couple either never had or resources that would soon be out of their reach. Complicating matters, public defenders identified and appointed for Cuadra and Kerekes in small-town Pennsylvania had prior connections to the victim,

Bryan Kocis.

Prosecutors continued to raise conflict of interest concerns in the closing months of 2007 as both men moved closer to an ever-changing trial date. One obvious conflict was presented immediately with the appointment and then withdrawal of Al Flora, Jr. to represent Kerekes. Flora had represented the victim, Bryan Kocis during his 2001 arrest on previous criminal charges. Another potential public defender, Jonathan Blum, also had prior contact with Kocis.

The troubles would continue when defense attorney Demetrius Fannick sought to be installed as Cuadra's chief counsel, filing with the court on January 29, 2008 to replace his existing court-appointed defenders, Stephen Menn and Michael Senape.

Luzerne County prosecutors complained loudly, asking that Fannick be disqualified to serve Cuadra since he had met privately with Kerekes on at least eight previous occasions between October 26, 2007 and January 11, 2008. Fannick denied any "details about the offenses or possible defenses were discussed in the meetings," and that the two limited their eight discussions to how to pay Fannick for defending Kerekes.[1]

Fannick insisted there would be no conflict and questioned the prosecutor's motives for raising the issue. "I simply think they're raising it because I kicked their ass in the last homicide case I did. I think the DA is just doing it out of spite," Fannick told the *Times Leader*.[2]

Fannick *had* been a bit of a thorn in the side of the state, after having successfully defended notorious accused Luzerne County serial killer Hugo Selenski in 2006. The DA was adamant that Fannick should not represent Cuadra because of a potential conflict from his meetings with Kerekes, insisted Luzerne County's newly elected District Attorney, Jackie Musto Carroll. Fannick was not backing down, noting that in his view the DA had no standing to raise this issue. "I don't think the DA should be arresting people, and then decide who their lawyer is going to be," he said.[3]

On February 21, 2008, during a hearing to consider eventually unsuccessful motions filed by Kerekes to dismiss the charges against him for a lack of evidence and to require the state to reveal whether they viewed him as the principal killer, the issue of Fannick's participation blew up. All of the lawyers and both defendants summoned to Luzerne County Court of Common Pleas before Judge Peter Paul Olszewski, Jr. sought to resolve the issue of Fannick's participation. During the hearing, whatever agreement Fannick had with Kerekes, his plans now included defending Cuadra and revealed a new problem, a possible split in the united front Cuadra and Kerekes had heretofore proffered.

Kerekes had an outburst in court as the matter was discussed, requiring jail guards and his attorney, John Pike, to calm him. Kerekes yelled near the start of the hearing that he didn't want Fannick to have anything to do with the case if he planned to use anything the two had discussed during their meetings. The *Times Leader* quoted Kerekes as shouting out, "Harlow won't roll on me."[4]

Even assistant DA Melnick was in an uncooperative mood. He told Judge Olszewski that he was hesitant to proceed with calling witnesses to rebut Kerekes' dismissal motions because the issue of Fannick's participation remained unresolved. Olszewski agreed, and delayed hearing evidence on either side of Kerekes' motions until he had ruled on the other state motions about whether Fannick could remain as Cuadra's counsel.

To buttress its claims to get Fannick thrown off the case, the DA offered a series of conflicts they said were raised by his participation, notably:

- Fannick had issued a news release on November 28, 2007 stating that he planned to represent Kerekes in the Kocis murder trial. In the statement to the media, he said, "I would certainly like to get involved in Mr. Kerekes' case. I believe it is very defendable. But I can't do anything until I am retained. There are certain limitations on my conversations with him. I do not want to overstep my bounds. I don't want to in any way interfere with Mr. Kerekes' representation unless I am retained."

- Fannick met with Kerekes eight times for a total of five hours at the Luzerne County Correctional Facility, including October 26 and 30, 2007; November 7, 2007; December 6, 7 and 14, 2007; and finally on January 11, 2008.

- Kerekes' state-appointed attorneys at the time, Shelley Centini and John Pike, had reservations about anyone meeting with their client prior to trial, but they acquiesced because they believed Fannick was about to enter himself as Kerekes' chief defense counsel.

- After filing an appearance on behalf of Cuadra in January 2008, just eighteen days after he last met with Kerekes, Fannick told reporters, "I'm on board and it is my understanding (there) will be a trial. I don't see any other way it is going to be resolved unless the DA's office drops the charges. My client (Cuadra) maintains his innocence."

For his part, Fannick continued to insist he never officially represented Kerekes in the matter, and only met with him for the purposes of deciding whether he should or could be retained (according to Kerekes, for fees in excess of $100,000 that he was unable to raise).

In a March 2008 hearing before Olszewski to resolve the Fannick issue, Kerekes would back that claim saying the two "absolutely" never discussed a defense strategy, never discussed his whereabouts on the day Kocis was killed, never discussed the merits of the commonwealth's case, never discussed any possible cooperation with the state, and never accepted any legal advice or opinions from Fannick.[5]

Melnick apparently had doubts and peppered Kerekes with reminders that he had blurted out previously in court he didn't want Fannick using anything they discussed in defense of Cuadra. Kerekes explained away his outburst as saying he was "emotional" on the day of the original hearing.

Kerekes was the only witness called in the hearing to resolve Fannick's participation, and so Olszewski would have to base his decision solely on that testimony. Fannick did not testify under oath as to his discussions with Kerekes. Kerekes would later contradict himself again, admitting in a state prison interview that he lied in court, and that his discussions with Fannick went far beyond the fee structure.[6]

Melnick implored Judge Olszewski to rule a conflict existed. "The appearance of fairness…is paramount. To condone this conflict of interest is just wrong."[7]

Olszewski issued his order on March 19, 2008, disqualifying Fannick as Cuadra's counsel. He said his decision reflected his commitment to "promote and protect the truth seeking function of the judicial system." Olszewski's order said that Kerekes' in-court outburst when he saw Fannick, "If you try to use anything we spoke about, I'll have you removed," convinced the court that "a lawyer-client relationship exists between Fannick and Kerekes."[8]

Describing Kerekes' testimony as "unpersuasive" and "unconvincing," Olszewski dumped Fannick from any possible participation in Cuadra's defense. In a statement accompanying his order, the judge said "had attorney Fannick testified under oath that no substantive discussions occurred, today's ruling may well be different. That attorney Fannick elected not to do so made this court's decision clear."[9]

Fannick told reporters that he had underestimated the value of his own testimony to buttress Kerekes' claim that no conflict had been created.

A week later, supporters of Cuadra posted a notice on his blog that an appeal was planned and that Fannick would be representing him in his upcoming trial.[10]

Apparently irritated by the role Kerekes' "unpersuasive" testimony had played in the matter, Cuadra was quoted by his supporters as saying that "As for Joe's outbursts in court, well, as we all know that is Joe, and no one can stop him from running his mouth, whether it be truth or fiction."[11]

Later, during pre-trial proceedings, one attorney for both Cuadra *and* Kerekes were removed when it was "discovered" that the two were now employed by the same law firm. Attorney Mark Bufalino, one of three lawyers working for Kerekes, and attorney Paul Galante, working for Cuadra, were removed from the case, causing further delays.

The episode did reveal publicly for the first time the growing schism between Cuadra and Kerekes. Galante told Judge Olszewski that Cuadra was holding some hostility toward Kerekes, and Kerekes' attorneys alleged the same hostility existed on the part of their client as well.

It was clear, the one-time lovers might eventually have to turn and implicate the other in the Kocis murder. The pre-trial exchange confirmed what observers could already see in court during the pre-trial phase, that although seated near one another, Cuadra avoided direct eye contact with the more animated Kerekes. The two men looked only briefly at one another, and they never spoke directly to each other (even during break periods when the judge was outside of the courtroom).[12]

The families of Bryan Kocis and Joe Kerekes were the most visible in the court throughout most of the proceedings, including the pre-trial hearing. Joe's father donned a baseball cap emblazoned with the word "JESUS" on the front with Joe and Harlow's names on the back.

As expected, the parade of attorneys on and off the case created a blizzard of motions on behalf of both defendants, all but one unsuccessful. Attorneys for Kerekes and Cuadra lost on efforts to have separate trials, to have the trial moved out of Luzerne County, to keep victim autopsy and crime scene photos sealed, to suppress any statements either man made to police during their arrests, to exclude evidence seized from their Virginia home, and the lynchpin to the prosecution's case, to exclude tape recordings of conversations the defendants conducted over two days in San Diego in April 2007. The only effort that did succeed was to keep a portion of Kerekes' remarks to state police detectives while under arrest in Virginia Beach away from a jury. In the end, it mattered not: no jury was ever called in Kerekes' case after he accepted the state's plea agreement.

Harlow goes in search of an alibi

One of Cuadra's best clients, certainly his most generous, businessman Howard Mitchell Halford of Atlanta, Georgia, said Harlow told him that "a bad alibi is better than no alibi."[13] Cuadra, who initially attempted to deny he was ever in Pennsylvania and then shifted it to say he was there for a camping trip and/or modeling appointment with the victim, needed someone to back up his story.

One of his proposed alibis was to come from Halford, a man who said he loved Cuadra. Halford later told detectives that Cuadra approached him at the end of January or early in February 2007, saying he was upset about his picture being circulated on the Internet as a "person of interest" in the Kocis investigation.

Halford said Cuadra was concerned because Cuadra claimed he was at home the night of the murder and therefore had no alibi. A week later, Cuadra contacted Halford again and said he needed someone to act as an alibi witness for him, and Halford said he agreed to help, knowing that, in Cuadra's words, his original statement to police "had not gone well."

Cuadra asked Halford to call his attorney, Barry Taylor, and let him know that he would be an alibi witnesses, and Halford even met with Taylor about the alleged alibi. "Halford stated that he went to Barry Taylor for Harlow because they are very close companions, have an intimate relationship, and he was concerned about Harlow's well-being," detectives would later write in a report. "Halford (said he) felt underlying pressures that if he didn't cooperate there may be a problem with Joe Kerekes. Halford stated that Kerekes was very aggressive and a controlling individual toward Harlow. Halford was concerned about his and Harlow's welfare in this regard."[14]

Halford would later drop any pretense of an alibi, and backed out of providing any information that would be useful to Cuadra placing himself away from Pennsylvania on the night Kocis was killed. He didn't back out, however, on helping Cuadra's defense, admitting that because he loved Cuadra he contributed $70,000 in cash to help pay for a defense attorney.[15]

Nep Maliki, another frequent Cuadra escort client who harbored amorous feelings for him, would prove to be an interesting, if not terribly damaging, potential alibi witness. It didn't matter. Cuadra's feeble attempts to gain an alibi from Maliki and others were soon exposed. Uncovering that effort would take a lot of hard work—something investigators, particularly Hannon, never seemed to shy away from.

Virginia Beach and Pennsylvania investigators worked long hours trying to find Maliki. Often employed at fast food restaurants such as McDonald's and Wendy's, assistant DAs Melnick and Crake, along with State Police Corporal Hannon, spent the better part of a very hot day in Virginia Beach trying to find Maliki, visiting every McDonald's and Wendy's restaurant in the area, until they found him. "(Corporal) Leo Hannon really, really wanted to speak to Nep again," Melnick said. Maliki had been previously interviewed only briefly by Pennsylvania detectives. "We stayed another day in Virginia Beach and we began our odyssey on a blistering Saturday morning there, searching for Nep Maliki."[16]

He would prove difficult to find. A man of Filipino descent, in his 50s, who lives at his parent's home and often worked two fast-food jobs to support himself, Nep was someone investigators wanted to talk to because he "was delighted to be, I guess, a participant in Harlow's life," Melnick said.[17]

A day of searching ended around 5:00 P.M. Saturday evening at the back door of a Virginia Beach Wendy's restaurant, near the drive-through order board. Melnick and Crake, nearly sick from the almost 100 degree heat and humidity, stepped back as Hannon interviewed Maliki who stood in the back door of the Wendy's. It was a weird setting to collect what turned out to be key evidence. "I was standing off to the side in the blistering heat smoking a cigar and wondering whether Charles Dickens could create a better scene for one of his novels," Melnick said.

The interview became "a slam-dunk interview," Melnick said. "Nep Maliki pulls out of his pocket a hand-written, fake alibi (from Cuadra) that no investigator had found before."[18]

Crake was equally amazed at their good luck. "He's got this crinkled up note that he's been carrying around in his wallet for eight months," she said, noting it was a "big break."[19]

Melnick, Crake, and Hannon couldn't believe their good luck. Melnick credits Hannon for his bird-dog tenacity in digging up a key piece of evidence.

The note that Maliki produced showed the desperation sweeping over Cuadra as he sat locked up in a jail cell and sought help in building a defense against evidence that was quickly mounting against him.

In the June 13, 2007 note from Cuadra to Maliki, Cuadra wrote:

Hi Nep.
This letter is for your eyes only. Thank you so much for your help Nep. Like I said over the phone, if my lawyer needs you to testify for me in court, your

transportation and salary will be covered. He will give you a legal letter for you to present to both of your employers. I remember that you came over on January 24th about 7:30 A.M., maybe it was 8 A.M. You had on black jeans and a black heavy sweater. Black slip on leather shoes. There were several cars in the driveway. A black corvette (sic.), a black BMW, a yellow viper (sic.) and a silver nissan extera (sic.) parked in front of the house. My S2000 honda (sic.) was in the shop still, so I rented the nissan (sic.) in case it snowed. I had on a black leather jacket, blue jeans, and the hat that is on the blog website. You know the one where I am making a muscle. We met up for an hour, then you showered with me and left. I guess the thing we need to get clear is the time you came over. Did you work early that day after you saw me? At what time did you go to work that day? Please check with your work. Please ask these questions over the phone, not in writing.

It was clear Cuadra was *telling* Maliki what the agreed to alibi was as much as he was trying to recall it—complete with placing the Nissan Xterra in his driveway the day after a similar vehicle was spotted at the murder scene.

Other attempts were made by Cuadra and Kerekes to find alibis among some of their former escort clients, none of them successful.

The troubles with Joe's alibi

Joseph Kerekes tried, it seems, an evolving approach to explaining exactly what was or was not his involvement in the death of Bryan Kocis. He settled on the version that he agreed to as he pleaded guilty, that he was not at the Kocis home and did not personally or physically participate in slaying Kocis. Beyond that, the story has been a little muddy.

In July 2007, Kerekes granted a jailhouse interview to

reporter Ed Lewis of the *Times Leader* to explain himself. Kerekes wove a tangled story of how he and Cuadra made up the model application for Kocis as part of a legitimate business deal to link up their BoyBatter productions with Cobra Video. Kerekes explained that Cuadra using the fake name "Danny" was an attempt to keep Kocis interested, since they feared Cuadra would be viewed as too old (beyond age twenty-five) to be part of Cobra's target audience.

In this version, Kerekes said that Cuadra went to Kocis' home around 7:00 P.M. on the night of the murder and that Cuadra called him and said something was wrong and that he was leaving. Cuadra would later tell him, Kerekes said, that he smelled smoke in the house and heard a noise and fled.

Kerekes' story continued that the couple immediately left the Fox Ridge Inn and fled south on the Pennsylvania Turnpike to return to Virginia. "Harlow said he got there (and) the door (to Kocis' home) was partially open," Kerekes told the *Times Leader*. "He looked inside and saw an overturned table and smelled smoke. He said he saw someone on a couch or chair, and heard a noise upstairs, like someone was about to come down."[20]

The problem with this version is that it is completely at odds with the known timeline for the crime, eyewitness accounts from neighbors, and is at odds with physical evidence at the scene that showed no overturned table in Kocis' living room.

The timeline problems suggested by Kerekes' alibi were most troubling; such as the fact that Kocis was participating in a phone call with his attorney Sean Macias until at least 7:50 P.M., witness statements showing a white SUV leaving the driveway of Kocis' home around 8:20 P.M., and firefighters notified of a fire at the home at 8:34 P.M.

Kerekes was consistent with saying he stayed at the Fox Ridge Inn in Wilkes-Barre sending e-mails via a free Yahoo account while Cuadra was down the road in Dallas Township.

Investigators, however, learned through a flurry of warrants that the last time Kerekes accessed his Yahoo account was at 5:44 P.M. The account was silent, detectives found, until 8:36 P.M., just two minutes after the Dallas Township Fire Department was dispatched to the fire at the Kocis home.

There are other problems with Kerekes story. The state's Affidavit of Probable Cause and court testimony indicated that the Verizon cell phone Cuadra was using to communicate with Kocis prior to their ill-fated meeting was used for the final time at approximately 6:35 P.M. and the call was relayed by a cellular tower a few hundred yards from Kocis' house.[21]

Given that it takes at least twenty minutes to drive from the Fox Ridge Inn in Wilkes-Barre to the Back Mountain area and Kocis' house, when did Cuadra really leave the motor inn? A 6:30 P.M. departure time that Kerekes gives seems unlikely.

An investigator told the court during preliminary hearings that on the night of the murder "Kocis and 'Danny' (Cuadra) made arrangements to meet..." and that those communications were via e-mails, and "(t)he last communication occurred around 7:15 P.M."[22]

Another problem arises. If Cuadra left Kerekes behind at the motel room with the computer, was it Kerekes that sent a final 7:15 P.M. e-mail to Kocis forty-five minutes after Cuadra supposedly left the motel? Cell phone records refute the idea of Cuadra being on a cell phone telling Kerekes what to write back at the motel. There's only one other alternative that fits the facts, especially given the ubiquity of air card access in northeast Pennsylvania: the computer—and most probably Kerekes himself—were both in the SUV with Cuadra, as it headed up Back Mountain. How else to explain what has been documented to have transpired? It's a claim Kerekes vehemently denied, insisting he was not at the Kocis home.

Another troubling aspect emerged right after the murder as well, as signals from two cell phones registered to Kerekes were processed through a cellular tower on Country Club Road in

Dallas Township, a short distance from the murder scene, state police Corporal Hannon said. Hannon told the court the calls were made at 8:36 P.M., two minutes after firefighters were being dispatched to the Kocis home.

All of this raises the many big questions about Kerekes' alleged alibi: if Joe were at the motel during the time Harlow was visiting Kocis alone, why would two of his cell phones connect to the *same* tower in Back Mountain right after the murder? Was Harlow talking to himself? In fact, why were those two phones anywhere near the house at 8:36 P.M., when Kerekes maintains that Cuadra had arrived at about 7:00 P.M., smelled smoke, saw a body, heard a noise, and took off back to the motel? Put simply, that's about an hour's worth of slow-motion panic.[23]

The problem with all the denials, and really the entire unfolding defense, Cuadra and Kerekes had to construct is captured in what has become known as the Occam Razor principle. The Occam Razor refers to the principle that all things being equal, the simplest solution tends to be the best one. The more facts that defendants must contest and the more explanations they must provide, the more likely they will be convicted. The Commonwealth of Pennsylvania succeeded brilliantly in piling up a mountain of facts that left Cuadra and Kerekes searching not only for how to defend the facts piled against them, but also trying to decide which ones to tackle.

Joe keeps talking

It's not surprising Joe Kerekes once thought of himself as a good candidate to be a preacher. He likes to talk, sometimes too much, and may have terribly undermined his own cause while he waited out the tangled legal back-and-forth that dominated most of the nineteen-month period from his May 2007 arrest to his December 2008 guilty plea.

Given Kerekes' verbose nature, it's not unexpected that Pennsylvania investigators ran across jailhouse informants who claimed Kerekes detailed parts of the crime to them.

Robert Tolley was one of Kerekes' unit mates at the city jail in Virginia Beach while he awaited extradition to Pennsylvania. The thirty-nine-year-old Tolley told investigators that Kerekes openly admitted to killing "some guy in Pennsylvania."[24]

Another inmate, John R. Riggs, twenty-five, was housed with Kerekes for about a month at the Western Tidewater Regional Prison in Suffolk, Virginia. He told detectives Leo Hannon and Dallas Township Police Officer Todd Adams during two interviews in June and July 2007 about how Kerekes said the murder was necessary in order to make Kocis "disappear" in order to hire "some porn guy from another state" who was under contract to Kocis. Riggs, serving a sentence for a probation violation for a larceny charge, said that Kerekes placed blame for the murder on Cuadra, saying he stayed in the SUV in the driveway while Cuadra went inside and killed Kocis. Riggs' detailed account included remarks he said Kerekes made that indicated Kocis was already dead when Cuadra called him into the home, that it was "too bloody" of a scene to clean, that he assisted Cuadra in moving Kocis' body to a sofa in front of a large screen TV in the living room, and then setting a fire in the home.[25]

He also provided details that police did not know, that Cuadra had allegedly destroyed items taken from Kocis' home while the couple had fled to South Beach Miami, Florida after the murder.

Kerekes also gloated, Riggs said, about using sexual favors with police officers and attorneys to get what he wanted in Virginia Beach, but denied he was gay. He also reportedly admitted to taking Kocis' prized Rolex watch just because "I wanted it."[26]

Riggs said Kerekes seemed to be dominant at times with Cuadra, claiming he overheard three-way phone calls between him, Cuadra, and their friend Renee Martin where he heard Kerekes say that Cuadra should "keep his mouth shut" and "don't talk to anyone."[27]

Detectives and prosecutors were quite hopeful about Riggs' account. He had just over seven months to serve on his probation violation and then would be a free man. He seemed, unlike other jail house informants, to be one without a compelling motive or incentive to lie.

Detective Hannon and Dallas Township Detective Higgins found yet another jailhouse informant who recalled what the talkative Kerekes allegedly told him. Robert G. DeVaughn Rodden, forty-two, said Kerekes sought him out frequently for legal advice while both men shared a cell at the Virginia Beach Correctional Facility. [28]

Rodden, serving a five-year stint for a stabbing incident, said Kerekes talked freely about how he had traveled to Pennsylvania for the murder. He said Kerekes admitted purchasing a second knife to try and throw off investigators. Kerekes even detailed, Rodden said, a visit to the Wilkes-Barre Wal-Mart in the hours before the murder. The shopping list at the Wal-Mart was unusual. Receipts later seized by investigators revealed that among the Cuadra and Kerekes purchases were KY lubricant, condoms, and lighter fluid.

Rodden said Kerekes also detailed how he had lodged at the Fox Ridge Inn and had "made several phone calls" and used his computer to try and create an alibi for his whereabouts. He also claimed he and Cuadra were not gay, but were into escorting for the money only, and that Cuadra did most of the "mule work" of meeting with clients.[29]

Kerekes was confident, talking openly about whether he would turn "state's evidence" against Cuadra, Rodden said, and claimed that he was a wealthy man from his days in escorting and porn. Rodden said Kerekes also stated that "before he got to prison he was doing all kinds of drugs and having a good time."[30]

Rodden told detectives that Kerekes "pretty much told him how him (sic.) and that the other guy (Cuadra) did it," and that

Kerekes "probably put the kid (Cuadra) up to it, and now he's gonna hang him out to dry. I think (Kerekes) was at the victim's house, though, whether he did the stabbing or not."[31]

Rodden reportedly became disenchanted with Kerekes' casual attitude, one he described as "heartless" about Kocis' murder, quoting Kerekes as joking, "They haven't even buried him yet. They have him frozen somewhere." Rodden also quoted Kerekes as gloating, "They won't be able to get me for murder. Harlow went out to meet the guy, and he won't say anything…because I told him not to. I'll get out in five years and make tons of money off of this."[32]

The friend: Renee Martin

One additional informant who would develop along the way, the colorful and sometimes difficult Renee Martin. Martin knew Cuadra and Kerekes as a neighbor from Stratem Court back in Virginia Beach. During that time, she befriended the two men and began to learn more about their business. A "Navy widow" whose husband was often away on military assignments, she grew close to Cuadra, and at least for a time gained the trust of both men. It was a trust she would someday have to betray.

After Cuadra and Kerekes were arrested, Martin's role in the matter of investigating Bryan Kocis' death grew. In fact, Kerekes said the couple didn't know her well at all before the Kocis murder, but that "she was a big supporter of Harlow."[26]

At first Martin's contact with the two, while they were still jailed in Virginia, amounted to moral support and reading to them news reports and blog updates about their case.

Martin's increased role was aided, however, by her offer or agreement to facilitate "three way conference calls" between Cuadra and Kerekes (who were held in separate jail cells in Virginia Beach pending trial between May 15 and July 16, 2007). Tipped off to the "conference call" arrangements, authorities began audio taping the conversations. The recordings would reveal a painstaking effort on the part of Cuadra and Kerekes (sometimes with the help of Martin) to flesh out and consider various alibi approaches to defend themselves.

In one of the calls, Kerekes "tries out" one of his early alibis by saying he planned to fight extradition by proving he was never in Pennsylvania at the time of the murder. Martin replied, "Yeah, and the problem being with that is, you gave your photo ID for a hotel someplace in Pennsylvania." Martin told the men during the calls that "the truth is the best way" when considering a plausible alibi, something Kerekes agreed with.[33]

As a result, in one of the three-way calls Kerekes directly speaks to Cuadra and says, "Ah, Harlow? Listen, we have to go to Plan B. We went there."

Kerekes told Martin, "You've got to explain the truth to Harlow, that we were, ya know, *there*."[34]

Martin briefly balked saying she feared any discussion of alibis in her presence "because if they're listening in on this conversation, and I have three-way'd you, and you guys tell each other what you're supposed to tell each other, then y'all are gonna get me in trouble."[35]

Kerekes then interjected, saying, "Harlow, it's pretty, it's pretty much what we already know, remember what Plan B was, right?"[36]

"Plan B," it seems, was based on a "hypothetical" version of events created by Kerekes for the ever-shifting alibi, complete with a "once upon a time" introduction. Kerekes would later say the hypothetical version of events was "pretty much the truth," offering, "OK, once upon a time, there was a gay escort couple that, ya know, once upon a time that thought maybe working with this movie producer would be good, where as he had access to other young stars that would enhance one of the two (mens') career, so they set up an appointment to meet."[37]

Kerekes' version this time around notes that the "hypothetical version" of himself stayed back at the motel, while his partner went to the meeting. "When he (Harlow) approached the home, obviously there had been an intrusion and the door was open, hypothetically and supposedly then, he found what was there, and he supposedly and hypothetically ran and came back to the older one (Kerekes), who was in the hotel and they were scared."[38]

"Plan B" included discussions of how Cuadra was "in complete disarray" at what he allegedly saw at Kocis' home, and later cut up and burned the clothing he wore to Kocis' house.[33]

The recorded conversations revealed the growing tension between Cuadra and Kerekes, at one point Kerekes asking Martin to leave the line so he could talk to Cuadra alone, a request Cuadra objected to. Kerekes seemed determined to get Cuadra on board with the idea that he was not present at Kocis' home.

"I know, I know, I know," Cuadra said. "I, I, I know, I know Joe."

"And I wasn't there," Kerekes replied once more.

"Everything, everything's in my head, just be very calm, alright?" Cuadra pleaded.

Martin seemed to relish her role as chief information officer, legal adviser, and personal counselor. In the recorded calls, in addition to playing referee to flare-ups between Cuadra and Kerekes, she attempts to reassure both men that "it's gonna be good." She tells them that the criminal charges "may disrupt your lives for a momentary time" but that the two would be okay "eventually down the road, as long as everything, ya know, as long as everything comes out."[39]

She openly admonished Kerekes to stop "pressuring" Cuadra and that he was "stressing him out, it's ruining a conversation." Kerekes replied, "I'm completely stressed out, too."[40]

As the investigation wore on and prosecutors and detectives began debriefing Martin, they struggled at times to keep her focused. Her loyalties seemed to be in a state of flux, moving from intense loyalty to see Cuadra and Kerekes through their ordeal to wanting to help authorities solve a murder.

In May 2008, the DA's office contained an unsecured $50,000 "witness bail" for Martin, now living in Fort Worth, Texas, for her continued cooperation in the investigation. Prosecutors knew by now of her arrangement of three-way telephone conversations with Cuadra and Kerekes and that she had heard "incriminating statements" made during those calls.

Judge Olszewski ordered Martin to maintain weekly contact with investigators based on the DA's claims that her testimony would "provide substantial and important information about the defendants and their actions, and she was privy to the conversations between the defendants. Renee Marie Martin's testimony is material to help establish certain elements of the criminal charges currently pending against the defendants."[41]

The bond was used to ensure Martin's participation, something investigators couldn't be sure of until the very last minute.

Joe Kerekes' parents had seemingly had enough, and a day after their son and Cuadra (who they said they treated like a son) were extradited to Pennsylvania, they completed the sale of their Virginia Beach home. The timing of their move raised speculation they were tapping all resources they could to help fund their son's defense. However, Joseph Kerekes insisted the home was for sale prior to his arrest on murder charges.[42]

One anonymous Virginia Beach source, however, indicated the semi-retired couple had received a poor reaction from some of their neighbors and friends after Joe's arrest. The Kerekes' would eventually move west to Kansas to live near their other son's home and to be near their grandchildren.

The preliminary hearing

Once extradited to Pennsylvania, Cuadra and Kerekes faced a preliminary hearing. Pennsylvania District Magisterial

Judge James E. Tupper conducted the two day hearing in late August 2007 that included fourteen witnesses and forty photos of the murder scene. Preliminary hearings are required under Pennsylvania law in order to force attorneys for the commonwealth to present evidence that a crime has been committed and that the defendant is probably the perpetrator of that crime. Judge Tupper's role, which is normally to adjudicate traffic tickets and other non-felony cases, was to serve as a "gatekeeper" for the higher Court of Common Pleas.

Attorneys for Cuadra and Kerekes were ultimately seeking a dismissal of the charges but couldn't have been too optimistic about their chances. The hearing did provide them a chance to see inside the state's case for the first time and learn what type of evidence has been collected against the defendants so far. The state did not unveil every last bit of evidence it had, but it most certainly began to make a very strong *prima facie* case against Cuadra and Kerekes.

The state presented a videotape showing Cuadra and Kerekes in a Virginia Beach pawn shop purchasing a gun and a knife in the days before Kocis' murder.

Grant Roy was also called as a witness and recalled the now infamous Black's Beach meeting he and Sean Lockhart had with the accused duo on April 28, 2007. The Luzerne County Coroner also provided graphic testimony on the nature of the attack on Kocis.

The evidence mounting against the two so far was devastating, and there was little question they would continue to face charges. As expected, Judge Tupper found for the commonwealth, upholding the bulk of the state's charges of homicide, robbery, arson, abuse of a corpse, and conspiracy to commit murder, and allowing the case to go to trial.

Cuadra and Kerekes won a small victory, however, one they wrongly believed would be the beginning of a turn of luck for them. Tupper agreed to defense requests to drop burglary and conspiracy to commit burglary charges against the two. It was the first positive news Cuadra and Kerekes had received.

Pennsylvania prosecutors needed to be able to charge and prove one of eighteen aggravating circumstances in order to seek and/or receive a death penalty in the case. Since the Kocis murder was committed while other felonies allegedly occurred, such as burglary, robbery, and arson were committed, the death penalty remained an option.

"I just think it's great the burglary charges were dropped," Kerekes told reporters as he was led back to jail. "We didn't steal anything from that poor man (Kocis)."[43]

Cuadra let his new attorney, William Ruzzo of Kingston, Pennsylvania, do his talking. "If I can get the robbery charges dropped, I think that would take death out of the case." Kerekes' counsel, Frank W. Nocito also of Kingston, said he agreed and argued before the court that the goods taken from Kocis home could have been done so by any alleged perpetrator only as an afterthought once the murder was completed. "The thought of stealing the goods was done after the murder," Ruzzo contended. "The motive of the murder was the murder. It wasn't to take a Rolex watch and computer tower."[44]

Melnick was prepared for this argument. He countered that even if the burglary charge was removed, the arson charge remained a strong aggravating circumstance because of the "grave risk of death" it may have posed to responding firefighters.

As he was led away from the hearing to be held without bond, Kerekes blurted out to reporters, "I was never in that house, and I intend to get an expert to prove that." He added that "I'm confident my lawyer and the evidence will vindicate us."[45]

While Cuadra remained silent during most of his "perp walks" to and from the courtrooms of Luzerne County, he did respond during an October 2007 hearing. When a TV reporter asked him how he felt about the case so far, he replied in a low voice, "It sucks. I didn't do it. I didn't kill that man."[46]

Cuadra details "the plan" for acquittal

As the months dragged on and Cuadra struggled to form a new defense team, he wrote to Martin about "The Plan" that he believed would lead to his acquittal. Time behind bars had convinced him that "this shit's real as heck now."[47]

Cuadra told Martin that his image management would require "obtaining the means to hire attorneys that can tell a good story. That's all this comes down to," he wrote Martin. "A good looking defendant is harder to sentence."[48]

He asked Martin for her help in making sure no "fat pics" of him were posted online. "Remember, it's the jeans that made me look like I have a fat ass, not my fat ass that makes those jeans look fat."[49]

Cuadra apparently paid close attention to intense media coverage of his case. He told Martin, "Image matters a lot. Notice all the close up of my face? Yeah, they use that youth killer look to make those papers fly from the stand. Thank God I shaved."[50]

His letter to Martin suggested there was some "cleaning (of) Joe's image" needed, to fill in "hard edges" and improve his blog.[51]

Beyond that, Cuadra had some specific ideas in mind that he believed would help his cause:

- Ready and free flow of information to his attorneys, who faced wading through a tangled maze of evidence and information. "We need to make it easy for them or risk them blowing through it and missing stuff," Cuadra wrote.
- Work to transform "gossip (to) fact" and "make fake facts gossip."
- Secure witnesses and experts to "counter and destroy" the state's witnesses.
- Get pre-trial motions "right and tight," Cuadra

said, invoking a rather slick lawyerly term for a
man who was not admitted to the bar.

- "Get the image right," Cuadra wrote, alluding to
  his elaborate instructions on colors and types of
  suits, shirts, ties, and shoes he needed Martin to
  secure for him.[52]

Cuadra apparently also had launched a plan for supporters
of his to show up in court wearing "Free Harlow Cuadra"
T-shirts that they had purchased (although he allowed that if
supporters showed up at the courthouse who had not purchased
a shirt, they should be given one for free). "I need the jury to
understand that we have friends and family and (we) are not
society's trash," he wrote.[53]

By the time of the 2009 trial, the only Cuadra "supporters"
present in the courtroom appeared to be his until-recently
estranged family members.

In the months leading up to trial, however, Cuadra
was keeping a strong front in place, calling up his military
training, no doubt. "We have to be brave," he wrote to Martin.
"America did not win World War II because those brave men at
Normandy ran back when a bomb landed in their midst. The
troops took Normandy in spite of those bombs and victory was
secured because they were brave."[54]

Answering those nagging questions

In the days before his defense attorneys finally, apparently,
succeeded in getting him to shut up, Cuadra used his blog,
harlowcuadraonline.com, to post a variety of responses to
questions his "supporters" were apparently raising.

In April 2008, while sitting out a long stretch of more than
a year for his case to come to trial, Cuadra said, "My friends
and mostly (my) mom thought it would be a good idea to go
about this particular blog in a question-answer format." In
doing so, he basically hand-fed prosecutors free background

information they were unable to get from interviews with him, interviews he refused to grant investigators.[55]

Cuadra set off to answer "How I ended up in the middle of all of this?" and why the police intercept tapes showed Cuadra and Kerekes were willing to offer Sean Lockhart so much money to join their team. "Sometime around mid-2006, someone at LSG Media sent an e-mail to my Men4RentNow.com escort ad," Cuadra explained. "It was basically an application 'for your chance to work with Brent Corrigan himself' (and) it was extremely pretentious, so I ignored it."[56]

Cuadra said he had no idea who Brent Corrigan was, a claim Kerekes would contradict saying that Cuadra had an intense interest in Corrigan. It wasn't until he began looking for guys to cast in a new porno film for his BoyBatter site, Cuadra said, that he returned to the idea of contacting Lockhart. Cuadra said he reached out to Lockhart and got back a series of "bitchy responses" from Lockhart complaining about how the industry had used him.

Regardless, Cuadra moved the discussion toward payment rates that would entice Lockhart to be in a BoyBatter porno. "(Lockhart) eventually calmed down and basically wanted residual income along with other benefits," Cuadra wrote. "Keep in mind that I had no clue who Brent Corrigan was. Here is this bratty kid telling me that he wants half."[57]

Despite such concerns, Cuadra openly admits he first offered $10,000 and then $30,000 to Lockhart in order to get him to participate in the porno. These are substantial sums for any performer and if raised, would have wiped out nearly all of the liquid assets Cuadra and Kerekes possessed.[58]

The hunt for trace evidence

Popular TV shows such as *CSI*, *Law and Order* and *Forensic Files* have increased awareness and understanding of the value of trace or DNA evidence in solving crimes. It is, as forensic-science pioneer Edmond Locard (1877-1966) put it, because trace or DNA evidence "is evidence that does not forget. It is not confused by the excitement of the moment. It is not absent because human witnesses are. It is factual evidence. Physical evidence cannot be wrong, it cannot perjure itself, it cannot be wholly absent."[59]

In the murder of Bryan Kocis, the hope for trace or DNA evidence was soon dashed. "Obviously, DNA evidence was impossible," said Michael Melnick. "The DNA was just gone. The place was incinerated where the victim was. It was completely incinerated."[60]

Police also sought trace evidence from the Nissan Xterra, the rental SUV used by Cuadra and Kerekes to travel to and from Virginia to Pennsylvania. A small patch of carpeting from the vehicle was subsequently cut out and sent for testing, but no conclusive link could be made between the vehicle and Kocis or Cuadra and Kerekes. And although spotted by Virginia detectives in the Stratem Court driveway the day *after* Kocis was killed, the SUV "was rented two or three times until we got to it. We believe Harlow entered the building with an overnight bag, our working assumption was that he had a change of clothes, he probably had a garbage bag, and once he slew Bryan Kocis, everything went into the bag and that was gone," Melnick said.[61]

The bag, if ever recovered, would have been a treasure-trove of evidence. What's more, Kerekes told investigators in December 2008, as part of his plea agreement, that the bag had not been thrown away or discarded, Melnick said.

It would never be recovered, however.

That it was never found was more attributable to bad luck and bad timing, rather than for any lack of dogged determination by Pennsylvania detectives. Almost two years after the murder, detectives still went looking for that bag. "When we debriefed Kerekes in December 2008 (for his guilty plea), Kerekes said they did not throw away the bag. Detective Steve Polishan asked him, 'What happened to the bag?'…(and)

Kerekes said, 'When we went out (to California) in April 2007, we accidentally left the bag at the hotel.'"[62]

Melnick said detectives were jubilant. "We couldn't believe he was telling us this. The Pennsylvania State Police immediately launched into an investigation in December 2008 and they called that hotel …and believe it or not, the hotel actually had a record of a bag being left in the room. But they had thrown it out after no one claimed it."[63]

A circumstantial mountain becomes substantial

It's said that proof of guilt by circumstantial evidence resides in the proof of the facts from which guilt is inferred, or that guilt is the conclusion reached after reviewing all of the circumstantial evidence laid out, to the exclusion of all other causes.

In the case of Harlow Cuadra and Joseph Kerekes, the State of Pennsylvania was more than able to build a mountain of circumstantial evidence against the two. They had to as direct evidence was in short supply. But they succeeded in going the extra step that circumstantial evidence requires; proving those facts beyond the exclusion of all else.

When stacked up together, an overwhelming conclusion of guilt begins to build:

- Rental car records from Virginia Beach showing not only did Cuadra rent an SUV matching the description of witnesses in Pennsylvania, but returning it with mileage consistent with a quick round-trip to the murder scene.
- Two cell phones "hitting off" cell towers near the victim's home, both phones of which were registered to Kerekes.
- Pre-paid cell phone records (purchased in Virginia Beach) showing it was only ever used to call the victim's Pennsylvania home.

- Credit records showing Cuadra purchased an online background check on the victim just prior to the murder.
- A free Yahoo e-mail account set up in the days prior to the murder, and only ever used by someone at Cuadra and Kerekes' home and motel room to communicate with the victim.
- Superior Pawn Shop videotape showing Cuadra and Kerekes purchasing a gun and knife in the days and hours leading up to the murder.
- Statements from the victim's lawyer, Sean Macias, and his friend Robert Wagner that he was expecting a new potential model to visit his home on the night he was found murdered.
- A cash-paid registration from Kerekes at a low-grade Wilkes-Barre motel during the window of when the victim was slain.
- The absence of Cuadra and Kerekes from their normal routine, namely, missing from the Big House Gym in Virginia Beach for the period of January 23 to 25, 2007.
- Inexact statements on the part of both men, first denying they were ever in Pennsylvania, then admitting they went to Pennsylvania for a modeling audition and a middle-of-the-winter camping trip.
- Three eyewitness statements from the victim's neighbor that a silver SUV matching the description of the one rented by Cuadra was seen leaving the scene moments before flames were noticed pouring from the home.
- A similar silver/gray Nissan Xterra SUV confirmed parked in the driveway of Cuadra and Kerekes' home the morning after the murder. A routine license plate check of the vehicle by Virginia Beach authorities (at that point unaware of the murder in

Pennsylvania) showed the vehicle as registered to Enterprise Leasing Company and had been rented by Cuadra.

- Credit and background reports on both defendants showing a choking amount of debt about to overwhelm them.

- Statements from former employees of the duo saying they were concerned about the victim's business prowess and his control of the modeling fortunes of Sean Lockhart.

- Statement from Grant Roy in California that the two defendants were casually describing the interior layout of the victim's home, a home they later would deny ever having entered.

- Clandestine recordings from both the Crab Catcher Restaurant and Black's Beach in San Diego, California where Cuadra and Kerekes made incriminating statements. These included indicating where the victim's body was found in the living room, that the victim had consumed alcohol just prior to his death, and that his watch was missing, facts never released publicly.

- Property of the victim, namely two cameras with the serial numbers rubbed off, found in the possession of the defendants (and online inquiries made by Cuadra in the days after the murder about how to operate the cameras).

- Post-arrest letters sent by Cuadra to at least three former escort clients asking for their help in constructing an alibi for his whereabouts at the time of the murder.

- Audio tape recordings of the defendants in three-way calls with their friend Renee Martin, trying to develop secondary alibi scenarios as their first stories began to melt in the light of new evidence.

- Police statements that Cuadra blurted out "I remember this, it's a long tunnel" as he was extradited north via the Pennsylvania Turnpike, rendering impotent his initial claims that he was never in the state.
- Purchase of a second knife, identical to the one used in the murder and identical to the one originally purchased in Virginia to throw off investigators.[64]

CHAPTER 10

The Commonwealth vs.
Kerekes and Cuadra

"I'm sorry."
—Joseph Kerekes to Bryan Kocis' family

"I sit back now and think about the things that I did to make a living and I agree, I could (have) found a better profession, but at the time, I was not thinking about that…Sometimes we just need time to reflect on the things we have done."
—Harlow Cuadra

A guilty plea

On December 8, 2008, Joseph Kerekes confirmed swirling speculation and walked shackled into the Luzerne County Court of Common Pleas and pleaded guilty to his role in the murder of Bryan Kocis. He pleaded guilty to five total charges, including a charge of second degree murder, criminal conspiracy to commit robbery, theft, tampering with physical evidence, and criminal conspiracy to tamper with physical evidence. Six other counts were dismissed, including abuse of a corpse, criminal conspiracy to commit arson, robbery while inflicting serious bodily injury, arson resulting in death or serious injury, arson of a building, and criminal conspiracy to commit murder.

Judge Olszewski accepted the plea agreement that allowed Kerekes to escape any possible death penalty but required he accept a life sentence without the possibility of parole on the charge of second degree murder. On the other charges Kerekes was pleading guilty to, Olszewski sentenced him to another fifty-six months "beyond life" for conspiracy to commit robbery on Kocis, unlawful theft, tampering with physical evidence, and conspiracy to commit tampering with evidence. He ordered him to pay more than $2,500 to the Kocis family to cover funeral costs and for a $250 deductible on Bryan Kocis homeowners' insurance policy. Those fees would be deducted from jail salaries Kerekes may earn while incarcerated.

Although he faced life in prison without the possibility of parole, Kerekes' long and ultimately futile effort to flee justice was finally over. The journey would continue for Harlow Cuadra, however. A day earlier, a similar plea deal reportedly offered to Cuadra was rejected.

As part of his plea agreement, Kerekes was required to initial and acknowledge a series of fifteen statements contained in a Guilty Plea Colloquy affirming that he could read, speak, write, and understand English; that he was not under the influence of alcohol or any drugs as he signed the document; that he understood he was in court for the purpose of pleading guilty to criminal charges pending against him; that he had the right to a trial by jury, but that he was waiving that right; that a trial by jury would include twelve citizens chosen from Luzerne County and that his attorneys would have had the right to help select those jurors; that all twelve jurors would have to agree to his guilt before he would be convicted, and that during a trial he would have been presumed innocent until proven guilty beyond a reasonable doubt; that the state would have to prove at trial each element of the criminal charges against him beyond a reasonable doubt in order to convict him; that he was entering into a plea agreement with the state for the purposes of pleading guilty; that the judge could decide to reject the plea agreement; that if the judge rejected the agreement, he could withdraw his guilty plea and "be in the same position as if no agreement had ever taken place"; that he understood the terms of the plea agreement; that he agreed to plead guilty; that he had not been subject to any threat or force to offer his guilty plea; that no promises had been made to him to enter the plea, other than what was stated in the plea agreement; and that the plea agreement had the same effect as if a judge or jury had found him guilty on the same charges.

The colloquy was signed by Kerekes, his lawyers, and the DA's lawyers.

In court, the state detailed for the court the information Kerekes had provided as part of his proffer on the guilty plea about his participation in a plan to "eliminate" Kocis as a competitor in the gay porn business, and how he and Cuadra had come to Luzerne County for the express purpose of committing murder. Kerekes' plea allowed him to maintain his now-oft repeated claims that he was at the Fox Ridge Inn Motel at the time of the murder and that he did not physically participate in slaying Kocis. Prosecutors were not arguing that point any more, and instead began focusing on Cuadra as the man who actually killed the victim.

Kocis' family was permitted to provide "victim impact statements" as part of the hearing to consider Kerekes plea. Kocis' father Michael told the court, "We will never forgive nor will we ever forget what Mr. Kerekes did to this family." Assistant DA Melnick said, "This was the most catastrophic and momentous event that ever happened to the Kocis family.

They are seeking closure. It has been a rough road." For his part, Kerekes turned away as Mr. Kocis read his statement and later told the judge weakly, "I'm sorry" without elaborating.[1]

Judge Olszewski read in detail the charges Kerekes was pleading to and reminded him, "Mr. Kerekes, you're essentially giving up your life in society as you know it. In an instant, you will not be a free man for the rest of your life." Kerekes nodded in agreement and answered with a quiet "yes" to each charge the judge reviewed to assure he knew what he was pleading to.[2]

As he was led away from the courthouse, Kerekes had one more statement for reporters, answering a question saying he would "absolutely not" testify against Cuadra in any future trial.

Joe's testimony offers Harlow no hope

Joe Kerekes knows the details of Bryan Kocis' death—they were told to him, he says, by Harlow Cuadra. But his refusal to testify, to even lie for his former lover and partner, meant he could offer Cuadra no hope in his murder trial about to unfold.

"Harlow told me that he sat next to (Kocis), face to face with him on the couch, and they came in together to kiss and Harlow just reached behind his back and pulled out the knife and sliced him," Kerekes recounts, demonstrating with his hands how Cuadra moved in to kiss Kocis before cutting him.[3]

Kerekes adds a grisly detail that seems difficult, if not impossible, to believe. He claims, "Harlow told me that as he was cutting him, Bryan said, 'Why are you doing this to me?' and Harlow told he me said, 'This is to keep you from raping any more little boys.'"[4]

Pennsylvania experts and other forensic pathologists contacted, however, doubt that Cuadra was telling the truth. Pathologists confirm that any person who had suffered the gaping neck wound that took Kocis' life (including severing his vocal chords and esophagus) would have been unable to speak during or after the attack.

The brutality of the attack apparently bothers even Kerekes. Mentioning the twenty-eight post-mortem stab wounds to Kocis' body, prompting the original mutilation of a corpse charge, "tells me there was something really, really wrong with Harlow. I think he was really angry about his life, about (allegedly) being molested as a boy," Kerekes said, his voice trailing off. "And I think Harlow was angry with me, too."[5]

Preparing for an unusual case in Luzerne County

The media in Wilkes-Barre and Scranton had closely followed the story of the Bryan Kocis murder case. Rarely do stories come along in this quiet part of northeast Pennsylvania that include such sensational elements as violent murder, gay porn, gay escorts and prostitution, and clandestine tape recordings of suspects while on a nude beach thousands of miles away at the Pacific Ocean.

As a result, continued pressure was placed on Judge Olszewski to consider granting defense motions to move Cuadra's upcoming trial out of the county. Olszewski held firm and said the case would be heard in Luzerne County. He did allow a rather unusual set of "juror questionnaires" by Cuadra's defense team to go forward. Those seventy-one questions pressed potential jurors in the county about a variety of issues, including the publicity surrounding the case; their views on sexual orientation, pornography, and prostitution; the violent nature of the crime; and their views on capital punishment.

The questionnaires provided a brief pre-trial glimpse into what lay ahead. Questions posed to potential jurors included:

- Do you perceive that homosexuals are more or less likely to commit crimes or engage in criminal conduct?
- Have you, members of your family, or close friends ever:

—made a joke about homosexuals?

—referred to homosexuals by using a derogatory term such as "fag," "queer," etc.?

—felt uncomfortable in the presence of a homosexual, whether in a public facility, metropolitan area, or neighborhood?

—avoided situations where contact with homosexuals would be anticipated?

—avoided TV or media programs where homosexuals would be depicted simply because of that fact alone?

—commented about the propriety of homosexuals living in committed relationships?

—remarked or objected to the demonstration of homosexual civil marriage ceremonies?

—refused to associate yourself with homosexuals?

—commented on a perceived connection between homosexuals and disease including but not limited to HIV and the AIDS virus?

- Would you find the testimony of a homosexual less reliable than someone else's just because they were homosexual?
- Are you conscious of any prejudice or bias against homosexuals?
- Are you or any member of your family or close friends' members of any group or organization that advocates against homosexuality?

The probing questions went on, including a variety related to pornography:

- Are people engaged in the pornography industry more likely to commit crimes or to engage in criminal activity?

- Do you object to those who profit from the display of homosexual activities or pornography?
- Would the fact that the defendants (and the victim) were involved in homosexual pornography in any way affect your ability to be a fair and impartial juror?

Potential jurors also were probed on their views on capital punishment, including:

- Would you reject or reduce the weight of evidence presented by defendants to support a claim that life without parole should be imposed?
- Would you automatically hold that in a case such as this, the death penalty should be imposed, without regard to the weighing process for evidence?
- Do you believe the death penalty should be automatically imposed every time a person is convicted of first degree murder?
- Do you have any religious, moral or other objections to the death penalty to such a degree that it would prevent you from sitting as a juror or imposing a sentence of death? [6]

Experienced counsel

Attorneys for both the state and Harlow Cuadra brought a lot of previous experience to the trial, although their time to prepare was very different. As reporters noted, the state had twenty-six months to prepare its case for trial. Defense attorneys had three months.

Defense attorneys Joseph R. D'Andrea and Paul J. Walker took on their client on December 10, 2008. They were the last in series of attorneys who represented Cuadra along the way. D'Andrea and Walker were appointed to the case by Judge Olszewski after Cuadra's previous attorneys, Stephen

Menn and Michael Senape, were relieved of their duties after a conflict of interest was determined.

D'Andrea was well known to Luzerne County residents mostly because of his work defending a former Scranton, Pennsylvania police lieutenant in the shooting death of his wife. Walker met D'Andrea while both worked as assistant district attorneys in nearby Lackawanna County.

For the state, assistant DA Michael Melnick was an experienced criminal court litigator, as was assistant district attorney Shannon Crake. Melnick had eight years of experience as an assistant district attorney prosecuting high profile Luzerne County cases, while Crake had three years experience as a DA. Joining the state's team was Allyson Kacmarski, who joined the DA's staff about a year before the start of the Cuadra trial.

The Commonwealth of Pennsylvania vs. Cuadra

A total of 125 Luzerne County residents received summons to appear on Tuesday, February 17, 2009 to be considered as jurors in the case of the Commonwealth of Pennsylvania versus Harlow Raymond Cuadra. Jury selection started slowly—only one person OK'd for jury service after a full day of questioning of candidates. Prosecutors and defense attorneys, under Pennsylvania law, were each given twenty "strikes" or excuses to drop any particular person as a juror.

While potential jurors were excused for typical reasons, such as having heard publicity about the case, schedule conflicts, or health concerns, some were dismissed because of their openly stated prejudicial beliefs. One man said he did not support the death penalty, while another complained that the state of Pennsylvania never seemed to get around to executing anyway and therefore did not want to serve. Another told attorneys that "I'm prejudiced against (Cuadra's) lifestyle, gay pornography; I can't deal with that."[7]

As attorneys for both sides questioned an unnamed woman

known only as "Juror No. 99" she volunteered, "I just can't believe he did it. He looks like a kid." She was not seated for the jury.[8]

In the end, attorneys questioned 122 of the 125 potential jurors over the course of a week before settling on a panel of eight men and four women, as well as four alternates (three men and one woman). Among them were a retired Army depot employee, a retired postal worker, a restaurant hostess, a metro transportation employee, and a housekeeper.

Family members for the victim and for Cuadra were present during each step of the selection process. Cuadra, appearing each day in a suit and tie, offered a quiet "Good morning" to potential jurors on the first day and waved at them.[9]

The murder trial of Harlow Cuadra finally began on Tuesday, February 24, 2009 in Luzerne County Court of Common Pleas II. For four weeks, jurors would hear an incredible parade of eighty-six witnesses put on by the state in making their case for Cuadra's guilt. Cuadra's defense would start and finish in just one day.

There was little doubt in the minds of the two prosecutors who lead the trial against him: Harlow Cuadra was more than capable of inflicting the fatal blow to Bryan Kocis' neck. As Melnick put it, "Cuadra was a little, raw-boned (man) at the time. There is no question that he could do this, that he was able to do this against a middle-aged man who was not expecting this at all. My gut feeling is that Cuadra acted alone. Harlow was very wily in his sexual whims and clearly he was able to captivate people…with his charisma and Mr. Kocis fell for it hook, line, and sinker."[10]

Assistant DA Crake points out that "there seemed to be this effort to make (Cuadra) appear to be very weak and mild at the time of the trial" and that he had lost a great deal of weight between the time of his arrest in May 2007 and his trial in March 2009. At trial, Cuadra also sported never-before-seen framed eyeglasses that seemed to add to his youthful look and seemed to be placed on and off his face with great regularity, depending on what was occurring in the courtroom.[11] Cuadra himself supported that idea in a jail-house letter he wrote to one-time friend and confidant, Renee Martin. In it he admits to dropping his weight down to 130 pounds "with shoes on."[12]

Among the concerns Cuadra expressed to Martin in a pre-trial letter dated October 13, 2007 was the manner in which he was being portrayed on various websites. Objecting to the use of the phrase "Stud Wonder" to describe him on the www.boybatter.com site, Cuadra wrote to Martin that his "Plan" to be acquitted had a lot to do with image. He apologized to Martin "that you have seen how ugly ninety-nine percent of gay men are" and "it's terrible how they sit back and do nothing."[13]

Opening statements

In his opening statement lasting an hour, Melnick told jurors that Cuadra's actions were "the horror and heavy tidings given to the Kocis family in the new year. This is a case that stretched from the shores of the Atlantic to the sands of the Pacific."[14]

As Melnick graphically described the wound to Kocis' neck, the victim's mother, Joyce Kocis, wept. Melnick said jurors would hear Cuadra in his own words and his own voice describing how Kocis died quickly in the attack and that "Actually seeing (Kocis) go down made me feel better inside."[15]

Melnick said Cuadra wanted to lure "the Tom Cruise type of gay porn" to his company and Kocis was standing in the way of his plans.[16]

Meanwhile, Cuadra's co-defense attorney Joseph R. D'Andrea said in his fifteen-minute opening statement that "our defense is simple, Harlow didn't do it." D'Andrea asked jurors to play close attention to evidence they would hear that implicated others, such as Joseph Kerekes, Grant Roy, and Sean Lockhart in the murder of Kocis. "They hated him...they wanted him dead," D'Andrea said.[17]

D'Andrea centered quickly on what would become a foundation of the defense: the murder of Bryan Kocis was the work of Joseph Kerekes, not Harlow Cuadra. "Joe was the dominant partner," D'Andrea told jurors. "Joe was controlling and he controlled Harlow, both on the personal and professional level." Kerekes only cared about making money, D'Andrea said, and thought nothing of "prostituting his own lover, Harlow, to make money. Harlow sits here innocent and he has the protection of innocence throughout this trial."[18]

Key pieces of evidence tell the means

Although physical evidence linking Cuadra or Kerekes to the murder of Bryan Kocis remained nearly impossible for police and prosecutors to uncover, there were several key pieces of circumstantial evidence that helped them tell the story in trying to convict Cuadra at trial. Prosecutors wasted no time in getting to that evidence.

Among some of the telling circumstantial evidence found came from Scott Walsh, a security manager for the Wilkes-Barre Wal-Mart store. Walsh testified about $139 of items prosecutors alleged Cuadra and Kerekes purchased at 11:20 A.M. on the day of the murder using a credit card, including the rather conspicuous purchase of Ronsonol lighter fluid in snowy Pennsylvania in January. Barbeques end in this part of the country when the snow flies, and lighter fluid is not a hot seller during the winter months, Walsh said. In fact, Walsh told jurors out of the more then 5,700 Wal-Mart stores across America, the Wilkes-Barre store was the only one to sell any lighter fluid that January day.[19]

Cuadra and Kerekes' other purchases were less telling. Retrieved receipts would show the couple purchased Trojan ultra thin condoms, Magnum large condoms, KY brand "natural feeling" liquid lubricant, a slide lighter, a multi-tool kit, Jet-Alert caffeine tablets, ibuprofen and aspirin tablets, chewing gum, lip balm, and shower gel. Wal-Mart was unable to produce a videotape of the purchases, however, as the request for that came beyond the date which the store typically records over older tapes. No Wal-Mart employee could positively identify Cuadra or Kerekes as having made the purchases, either.[20]

Other circumstantial evidence came in the form of records of a pre-paid cellular telephone purchased by Cuadra and Kerekes. The pre-paid phone records recovered by police showed it was used sparingly during its short life span of January 22 to 24, 2007. Beyond its activation, the phone was used "a number of times" to call Kocis' home, police said. The first outgoing call being on the phone was placed on January 22 at 7:26 P.M., bouncing off a cell tower located on Bells Road in Virginia Beach, just a few hundred yards of Cuadra and Kerekes' home. The last call on the phone was placed on January 24 at 6:35 P.M. and relayed off a cell phone tower on Country Club Road in Dallas, Pennsylvania, just behind Kocis' home.

In addition, the February 10, 2007 search warrant of Cuadra and Kerekes' home yielded perhaps the most telling physical evidence. There police found numerous items, including two Sony digital video cameras (model numbers DCR-VS2000 and HDR-FX1) with their serial numbers "forcibly removed and obliterated." Kocis' friend Robert Wagner later positively identified the cameras as ones Kocis had purchased and were not present in his home after he was discovered dead. Police later confirmed that Kocis purchased the cameras at a New York City camera store in 2005.

Even more troubling for defense attorneys, investigators found a message board known as "The Digital Video Information Network" designed for individuals to read and post questions and answers about digital video equipment. They noted that on January 29, 2007, five days after Kocis' murder, Cuadra posted an inquiry on the site asking about the operation of the HDR-FX1 camera, the same type of camera missing from Kocis' home.

Circumstantial evidence it was—but it reflected quite poorly on Cuadra. Why, for instance, would anyone buy new cameras and then scrape off the serial numbers? Why would someone who said he never knew Bryan Kocis pay for a background check on him in the days just before his murder? Further, why would Cuadra purchase and use a pre-paid cell phone only for the purposes of calling Kocis? These were part of the difficult, or nearly impossible, questions the state placed before the jury with little or no possible rebuttal from Cuadra.

Melnick's prosecution team also focused heavily on crime scene photos and post-mortem photos of the victim. A deputy county coroner who retrieved Kocis' body on the night of the murder, and the pathologist who conducted an autopsy the next morning, both provided graphic testimony of how Kocis died.

Getting to a motive

Melnick then turned his efforts to establishing what police and prosecutors believed was the motive for Kocis' murder: Cuadra's greed and desperation fueling his desire to get Kocis out of the way in order to use Sean Lockhart in his gay porn videos. To establish motive, Melnick called a series of witnesses who testified that they were present when Cuadra (and his partner Kerekes) openly discussed the need of getting Lockhart involved with BoyBatter Productions, and what it could mean to them financially.

Cuadra's former friend Andrew Shunk said Cuadra and Kerekes "wanted to do a pornography film featuring Harlow and Sean Lockhart. They thought that by bringing in Sean Lockhart or Brent Corrigan, that it would bring in a six-figure profit (for) the company; that combining Brent Corrigan's experience in the pornography industry as well as Harlow's, that it would be a new phenomenon." Shunk said Cuadra had called him from Vegas during his meeting with Lockhart and Roy and was excited about the potential Lockhart's presence could bring.[21]

Shunk's one-time boyfriend, Adam Greiber testified he also overhead conversations about attracting a new star to the BoyBatter site, but said he never heard the name Sean Lockhart or Brent Corrigan directly. He did hear, however, what the hoped for result would be. Greiber said Cuadra claimed that the new star "would definitely bring their company to a new level. The initial company BoyBatter was already viewed as a leading Internet site; but obviously the sign of a well-known adult film actor would bring their company to the next level."[22]

Justin Hensley, who worked and lived with Cuadra and Kerekes, said that the defendant was focused on recruiting people "with stardom" because that could "help boost profit in a major way." Hensley told the court that he heard Cuadra say that "Cobra Video was a main rival and that was it."[23] He said that Cuadra and Kerekes were excited when they returned from their January 2007 trip to Las Vegas, but only mentioned Brent Corrigan's name in their discussions. They also proudly showed off a photo of Cuadra and Corrigan (alias Lockhart) taken outside a Las Vegas restaurant.

Cuadra's regular once-a-month escort client, Joseph Ryan said he heard Cuadra discussing Corrigan-Lockhart as early as May of 2006. Ryan said Cuadra had reported he had made contact with Lockhart via MySpace and that discussions were underway. "He was quite excited about it," Ryan said, and thought "it would be a very good match."[24] Ryan said he went online and looked up Lockhart's photos and videos and assured Cuadra he believed they would be a good match sexually in a porn video.

Ryan said he also saw a lot of online chatter about the ongoing contract struggles Lockhart was having with Kocis and Cobra Video. "I was very concerned about the pending (Cobra) lawsuit that had been going on," Ryan said, adding that he "relayed and advised (Cuadra) that he probably shouldn't do anything until the lawsuit was settled; or that if he wanted to do something, he should probably talk to Cobra (Video)."[25]

Ryan also testified that he had received a "grandiose" e-mail from Kerekes via the BoyBatter site that gloated about the pending arrival of Lockhart to their productions.

Lockhart and Roy also testified that Cuadra and Kerekes remained persistent and aggressive in their attempts to get Lockhart lined up for their site, on a per-scene fee basis.

Bryan Kocis' final contacts

Juror's also heard that late on Tuesday night, January 23, 2007, Bryan Kocis took a phone call that just days before would have seemed impossible. On the line that evening was Sean Lockhart, Kocis' one-time discovery and prized performer, talking to him about future projects. "For a long time, I viewed Bryan as a mentor," Lockhart remembered. "A lot of those conversations I had with Bryan that week were...for advice. That sticks out in my mind (that I was) approaching him based on his business experience...."[26]

It seemed Kocis' cell phone was always busy, and that continued into the night he died. Kocis spent time talking to several people, including his Los Angeles-based attorney, Sean E. Macias, a business litigation and intellectual property litigation lawyer.

Macias had tried to help Kocis maintain control of the screen name Brent Corrigan through a protracted battle, but he had not been a direct part of the settlement negotiations. According to Robert Wagner, by that time the Macias-Kocis relationship was getting "a bit contentious" and Kocis was growing weary of an expensive lawyer tab that didn't seem to be leading to a resolution.

Macias said he spoke to Kocis by phone at 7:50 P.M. on Wednesday, January 24, 2007, just moments before he was murdered. Macias described Kocis as being "in a good mood" during their brief conversation. "He was expecting a guest at his house.(As) I was chatting with him, he said that he had a model coming over; and he went to answer the door, and he answered the door, greeted someone and that's what I heard," Macias said. Unable to hear the name Kocis used in greeting his guest, Macias said he could only recall that it started with the letter "D." Macias said he never heard the other person's voice as they came into the house and Kocis returned to the line and ended the call.[27]

Getting Macias' cooperation with the investigation and for the trial of Cuadra would prove challenging. Melnick said Pennsylvania authorities were ultimately forced to get a subpoena served on Macias by the Los Angeles District Attorney's office to compel him to cooperate. Macias even balked at travel plans arranged by Pennsylvania authorities, insisting that two airline tickets be purchased so that he could be guaranteed an empty seat next to him.[28] "No offense to the residents of Pennsylvania," Macias said at trial, "but I had no desire to be flown out here. I had no recollection of the events that transpired. I mean, I knew what happened, but I didn't think I could offer any testimony, so I fought the subpoena."[29]

Robert Wagner testified that his friend Bryan was "excited" about greeting "Danny Moilin" because "He thought he was cute."[30] Wagner said he viewed e-mailed pictures of Moilin that Kocis shared with him. Wagner said he told Kocis that "I didn't think he would be particularly good for the company. He was muscular and older. Muscular is fine, but he wasn't, like, the twinky kind of muscular that Bryan tended to go for. He was big, flabby muscled."[31]

Kocis and Wagner would talk by phone for the last time during the early evening hours of January 24 as Kocis awaited his guest, and Wagner departed his workplace in New York City. Wagner said the call lasted only about ten minutes as he rollerbladed from his office at 90 Park Avenue to his apartment on Ninth Avenue in Manhattan.

During the call, Kocis was "about to do cartwheels" Wagner said because he had settled his lawsuit with Lockhart and LSG Media. Wagner said Kocis was also excited because "I think he was going to get some play (or sex) that night."[32]

An unanswered call

Among Bryan Kocis' small group of close friends was Deborah Roccograndi of Kingston, Pennsylvania, a former co-worker at Pugliese Eye Care. Although their lives were very different, Roccograndi considered Kocis to be her best friend. "We talked on probably a daily basis, and we usually would get together once a week," she said. "You know, he was like a girlfriend to me, my best friend. We talked, you know, personally."[33]

Roccograndi confirmed what others reported—Kocis wanted no surprise visitors at his home. She had tried once—bearing a birthday present—only to be told to wait outside and he would meet her there.

Kocis would discuss some of his business enterprises with her, Roccograndi said, but not in detail. She didn't approve of the porn business, and Kocis avoided telling her details that would make her uncomfortable.

She did know, though, that he had returned from California a happy man. "It was one of the happiest times in his life, because he had settled an ongoing (thing), the Grant and Sean thing," she said. "I mean, we've never seen him happier."[34]

Roccograndi said Kocis was so excited about events, in fact, that he had called her on his cell phone from the airport to let her know how the settlement had been worked out. They continued to talk during the days that followed and true to her word, Roccograndi placed a call to Kocis' cell phone (and then to his home phone) at 8:12 P.M. on Wednesday, January 24, 2007.

It was a call he didn't answer.

Eerily, in all likelihood, Roccograndi left her voice mail message at about the same time her friend Bryan Kocis was being murdered.

Lockhart and Roy and the California tapes

Testimony by Sean Lockhart was greatly anticipated, and

local media reported his presence in the courtroom on day four of the Cuadra trial drew the largest audience of curiosity seekers—rendering a standing room only gallery in the ancient Luzerne County Court Room No. 2.

Both Lockhart and Grant Roy had their testimony closely tied by prosecutors to the tapes and transcripts from their dinner and beach meetings with Cuadra and Kerekes in California in April 2007. Prosecutors painstakingly walked Lockhart and Roy through the tapes, the transcripts, a seven-minute video shot of Cuadra and Lockhart on the beach, and still photographs of the group as they met for lunch.

Attorneys for Cuadra, D'Andrea and Walker, raised no strenuous or substantive objection to the introduction of the tapes or the transcripts. The only objection raised was regarding the Black's Beach transcript. "The defense has certain issues with this (transcript) and has opposition to it being admitted on its face value," D'Andrea said. "We have no opposition to it being admitted as a guide; (but) there are some differences of opinion that we have of what actually some of the words are in the transcript."[35]

D'Andrea asked the court to provide jurors an instruction to use the transcript only as a guide, but not to use it as "an exact replica of the tape." Judge Olszewski declined D'Andrea's suggestion that he provide the jury a special instruction on the transcript, but permitted a statement on the record reflecting that it was being admitted over the defense's objection. The tapes and the transcripts were key pieces of evidence and likely would play a major role in any Cuadra appeal.[36]

Lockhart and Roy also provided key testimony that indicated the lengthy and ugly battle they had engaged with Kocis was coming to an end, and was coming to its resolution *before* Kocis was murdered. Their testimony included detailed explanations of their assistance to law enforcement officials who were focused on Cuadra and Kerekes as prime suspects. If anyone had any remaining doubt about any possible involvement by the two in the murder, their detailed testimony knocked that out (even if their lack of a motive hadn't convinced observers before).

Lockhart's admission creates an issue

Lockhart's testimony, incidentally, almost didn't happen. Under routine questioning explaining his background and business, Lockhart acknowledged under oath to Melnick that he had acted in gay porn videos before he was eighteen years old, a violation of federal and state laws.

Judge Olszewski immediately removed the jury and explored the issue of whether Lockhart should continue testifying without first consulting with an attorney. "He's just admitted to crimes," Olszewski said to Melnick and Cuadra's attorneys.[37] The judge said he was concerned that Lockhart needed to consult with an attorney, or the court needed to consider whether immunity was needed. "I'm not saying right now definitively that (Lockhart) must have counsel," Judge Olszewski said. "I'm raising the question, which I believe, is a legitimate one."[38] Olszewski said he was not raising the issue as one of misconduct by the district attorney's lawyers, but doing so out of "an abundance of caution" to ensure that Lockhart's rights were protected.

To resolve the issue, Olszewski summoned Lockhart and attorneys for both sides to his chambers and questioned Lockhart about the need for counsel. Olszewski told Lockhart in chambers that his response in court could equate to an admission to criminal conduct and "I think it's my obligation to, at least, advise you that you may want to consult with an attorney prior to being asked any additional questions."[39]

Lockhart was rock-solid in his desire to go forward. "With all due respect, this is something that has been going on for about four, five years now," Lockhart told the judge. "We went through civil disputes and we went through (a) very heated public battle; and we contacted all kinds of authorities about the matter, and nothing happened. So that's why today, I am comfortable being able to tell the truth despite being party to what happened."[40]

With that, Lockhart declined any counsel and questioning by prosecutors continued.

Cross-examining Lockhart and Roy

Under a withering cross examination, Lockhart and Roy remained steadfast in their telling of the story, including retelling of incriminating statements by Cuadra on Black's Beach in California.

Defense attorney D'Andrea continually moved questions with Lockhart and Roy toward the nature of the relationship they witnessed between Cuadra and Kerekes, just as he did with most every witness who had met the two. However, only Cuadra's friend Mitch Halford, was much help on that line of questioning. Halford said he witnessed Cuadra acting like "a puppy" and "a battered spouse" under Kerekes' influence and that Kerekes exerted unusual control over the younger Cuadra.

D'Andrea also tried to make headway with witnesses about the depth of anger that existed between Lockhart and Roy against Kocis, and raise questions about whether e-mails purporting to be from Cuadra were actually written by Kerekes.

When Roy was under cross-examination, D'Andrea engaged a provocative line of questioning meant to impeach Roy by highlighting his role as a pornography producer, and emphasizing the age difference between himself and Lockhart.

D'Andrea elicited from Roy that he was thirty eight years old when he began his sexual relationship with Lockhart, twenty years his junior at age eighteen. Emphasizing the age difference, D'Andrea remarked, "And you saw an opportunity to take this teenager and exploit him and sell him like a piece of meat, didn't you?"[41]

Roy denied that description and said the two men started their relationship in a purely platonic manner, with Roy offering Lockhart a room to rent. He said it was not until later that the two men fell in love with each other and started an intimate relationship.

D'Andrea took issue with that as well, asking, "You indicated...that you had an exclusive relationship with Sean (Lockhart), right? I guess that doesn't count all the men that were having sex with him in your films...How does one love somebody and allow them to have sex with multiple people?"[42]

Melnick had reached his limit and objected to the relevancy of D'Andrea's line of inquiry. D'Andrea immediately withdrew the pointed questions, but had succeeded in placing them before jurors nonetheless.

During the exchange, Roy became visibly irritated and defended gay porn as "art" and said that his reasons for producing porn were "to do something positive and creative and give these boys an avenue other than just being exploited by, like, a lot of the industry does."[43]

D'Andrea pounced and said, "So, as a gay pornographer, you're making it out to this jury that you're like a savior, you save young boys to give them a great opportunity while you line your pockets with money, right?"[44]

Roy disagreed with that characterization but D'Andrea pushed on: "Well, tell the jury how you're helping these young boys (by) engaging them in sex. Tell that to the jury."[45] Surprisingly, Roy took the bait and attempted to explain that his films provided young men "an opportunity" and that his productions offered the actors a chance "to come together, interact in a normal setting; like take them to dinner, showing them San Diego...we more or less try to make it a working vacation for them, an experience they couldn't get anywhere else."[46] Roy then took the unusual step of comparing work in gay porn videos as "an all-around experience" that some of his actors had claimed was "even better than Disney World."[47]

D'Andrea wasn't done. He later succeeded in getting Roy to admit that the people he hired for porn videos were actually "sex workers" and mocked his profession as "works of charity."[48]

D'Andrea then walked Roy through the lengthy battle with Kocis, including his admission that he started the "Cobra Killer" blog. D'Andrea also attempted to get Roy to admit he had engaged a conversation at one point in 2006 about hiring a "cleaner" to get rid of Kocis. Roy denied he ever suggested such a thing, instead saying a model made that suggestion to him and said "I laughed, I thought it was ridiculous."[49]

Also disclosed under cross examination was the fact that Roy had obtained a proffer letter from the U.S. Attorney for the Southern District of California that indicated they would not attempt to prosecute him on any related charges in exchange for his assistance with the Kocis investigation.

Through more than six hours of questions about intricate details of the wiretap recordings, D'Andrea repeatedly asked Roy to point out instances where it was Cuadra (rather than Kerekes) who was pushing for a video deal.

At one point, Roy had had enough, his overall testimony now covering more than twelve hours over two days. Roy declared, "Joe was the mouthpiece" and then stated, "I don't really want to go through this whole thing again right now."[50] Roy's statement drew a warning from the bench, "Well, you're *going* to go through it."[51]

Pinned to the wall by D'Andrea's insistence that he point out every single instance where Cuadra had interjected or pushed the deal, Roy folded and said, "I will take it back then" and agreed to D'Andrea's statement that "Harlow wasn't really interjecting, it was Joe on the financial side and the doing the deal side."[52]

D'Andrea didn't let up, however, still walking Roy through intricate details of almost every page of the transcript. D'Andrea was meticulous in noting repeatedly that the tape (and transcript) never indicated a direct statement by Cuadra that he had killed Kocis or was aware he was going to be killed.

"Read to the jury something in there where it says from Harlow Cuadra, 'I killed Bryan Kocis' or 'I agreed to kill Bryan Kocis with Joe Kerekes' or 'I planned to kill Bryan Kocis with Joe Kerekes,'" D'Andrea said, pointing to the transcript once again. "Read at least one of those to the jury and I'll sit down."

"It's not in there," Roy said.

"That's right," D'Andrea replied.[53]

The uncooperative witness

On March 10, 2009, almost two weeks into the trial, defense attorneys surprised most observers by opening their case by calling Cuadra's lover and former business partner, Joseph Kerekes to the stand. If they had hoped for Kerekes to help Cuadra's case, their hopes were dashed almost immediately.

Led into the courtroom in jail garb, including leg shackles, Kerekes who had previously pleaded guilty to a murder charge in the case, said he was not willing to testify. "I've been thinking a lot about my parents," Kerekes said. "I think it will destroy them to say something that I didn't do."[54]

Kerekes said to D'Andrea, "What I told you was not true" and with that, Kerekes was removed from the courtroom. As he left the courthouse, he was uncharacteristically silent, and didn't respond to reporters' shouted questions.[55]

Melnick said Kerekes' appearance in court as a potential defense witness was one of the more "bizarre" moments of the trial. "We had heard rumblings that attorney Joseph D'Andrea had interviewed Kerekes at the prison," Melnick said. "Then it became a little more imminent that they were really thinking about calling Kerekes as a witness at trial. I thought it was certainly an interesting legal strategy, but I did not think much of Kerekes as a witness."[56]

Melnick said Kerekes' previous participation in the hearings before Judge Olszewski regarding the potential participation of defense attorney Demetrius Fannick had eroded his credibility. "We thought that his being called as a witness was certainly a kind of a wild maneuver. The defense…called him and Joseph Kerekes took the stand in a spectacular drama and says he's not going to admit to…something he didn't do."[57]

Unwilling to answer questions, Olszewski quickly dismissed Kerekes from the stand. As he was led from the courtroom, Cuadra's mother shouted to Kerekes, "You stole my son!"[58]

Melnick said the turn of events seemed to startle D'Andrea who wore a look the prosecutor described as "What do I do now?" D'Andrea had reason, apparently, to believe that Kerekes could help Cuadra's case.

"I was ready to go into court and lie for Harlow," Kerekes said months after the trial concluded. "I had talked to his attorneys and I told them I would go in and back up their story about Harlow being at the house to model and that I burst in during a jealous rage and killed Bryan. But that (story) is not the truth," Kerekes said. "I'm telling you just as I told my parents this…I told them and I tell you, I did not kill Bryan. I was not (at the murder scene), I was back at the hotel and there is nothing that proves I was there."[59]

Kerekes said beyond the fact that he did not directly participate in the actual slaying of Kocis, he remained concerned by suggestions from representatives of the district attorney office that "more than implied" that if he provided testimony that was helpful to Cuadra, it could mean they would have to go forward with a more formal investigation of Joe's parents. "The DA indicated they may seek some sort of 'aiding and abetting' charge against my parents," Kerekes said. "I couldn't put my parents through anymore and they hadn't done anything wrong."[60]

CHAPTER 11
Harlow on His Own Behalf

"The right to testify (for one's self) is a mixed blessing."
—Dr. Sherry F. Colb,
Cornell University School of Law

Defense witness: Harlow Cuadra

Their plan to get Joseph Kerekes to pull blame for Kocis' slaying toward himself now out of play, D'Andrea and Walker took the unusual step of calling their next witness: the defendant, Harlow Cuadra.

Putting Cuadra on the stand was a risk. Without him and without Kerekes' testimony, it's unclear what direction the defense could have taken. They had failed in efforts to keep the undercover tapes and transcripts out of evidence. They had even failed to shield jurors from seeing some of the autopsy and death scene photos that they believed were inflammatory.

There were few options left.

Regardless, most criminal defense and prosecuting

attorneys agree, defendants testifying on their own behalf is a risky prospect. If the defendant is sympathetic and credible, they may help their case. More times than not, however, they don't do well under cross-examination and find their stories being picked apart bit by bit.

Defendants also face the problem that a mountain of circumstantial evidence against them creates: which part of that mountain do you go after first and do you risk confusing or losing the jury's interest if you try to take apart the mountain, rock by rock, pebble by pebble?

Interestingly, criminal defendants were considered "incompetent" to testify at their own trials under the Common Law of England and then the United States until the nineteenth century, according to Cornell University law professor and former U.S. Supreme Court clerk Sherry F. Colb. In the nineteenth century, defendant incompetency "gave way to the notion that the basis for disqualification the defendant's 'interest' in the outcome of the trial and could instead form the basis for witness impeachment following testimony."[1]

Since that time, however, defendants were allowed (and later guaranteed) a right to testify under oath on their own behalf. These rights are granted, the high court has ruled, in the Fourteenth Amendment to the U.S. Constitution.

"The right to testify is a mixed blessing, however," Colb says. "With the right comes an expectation on the part of the jury that it will hear from the defendant. Despite the defendant's right *not* to take the stand (and the judge's available instruction telling the jury not to draw negative inferences against the defendant for the exercise of this right), jurors nonetheless know that a defendant *could* testify if she wanted to, and this knowledge inevitably makes the jury wonder why the defendant has chosen not to take the stand."[2]

Mixed blessing or not, Cuadra was called to testify under direct examination before the jury by Walker. Cuadra told jurors, deep into his own testimony, why he thought it was important to testify: "I take the stand and what is said here is the only thing that matters. That is evidence. Not what (Mr. Melnick) says, only what is said here on the stand."[3]

Walker led Cuadra through the perfunctory data about his early life and family, including quickly introducing the financial and personal struggles Cuadra's mother Gladis faced in raising her four children on her own. "It was just my mother caring for us, and she did her best," Cuadra said. "She was a working mother."[4]

In the Navy

Cuadra said he joined the U.S. Navy after graduating early from his Homestead, Florida High School in order to escape conditions at home.[5] Although he was only seventeen at the time, his mother signed the Navy permission papers. "I flat out lied to my mother and I told her I would never go to war, I would wear a pretty white uniform and I would be out of harm's way."[6]

Cuadra said he knew he was gay at the time he entered the Navy, but did not disclose that fact under the military's existing "Don't Ask, Don't Tell" policy. "I don't mean this in a bad way, but it is a straight man's military," he said. "That's the way it is set up. That is the way it is."[7]

Despite concerns of being caught for engaging in homosexual activity, Cuadra said he met an ensign officer while working at a Marine-Navy medical clinic in 2000 and they started a brief flirtation that led to a "non-sexual" relationship.

It was also during his work at the medical clinic that a fellow sailor, who was serving more openly than Cuadra, began engaging him in online chats during down or slow times at the clinic. Through that, Cuadra ended up meeting Joseph Kerekes who had been in a chat room trolling for guys to meet for his escort business.

Over time, Cuadra said, Kerekes seemed to take it as a personal challenge to try and get Cuadra out of the Navy.

Kerekes himself had lasted only a month as a Marine. Kerekes even suggested that Cuadra go AWOL from his Naval assignment, something he refused to do. Cuadra said he refused to try and slip out of the Navy on anything other than an honorable discharge. "One day I came home and (Joe) said, 'Come on, come with me,'" Cuadra testified. "I went in (Joe's) car to a really high-powered attorney and (Joe) gave him a stack of thousands of dollars, like about five grand, and (Joe) said, 'I need you to get him out of the Navy and he'll only do if it's an honorable (discharge).'"[8]

Cuadra believes the lawyer enacted a policy under the National Intel Conditions that allowed him to depart, especially since Cuadra had good evaluations from his superiors and had had no disciplinary problems in the Navy. "(The lawyer) had me sign a letter saying that I was a practicing homosexual and that I was in love with another man and that the relationship would not end," Cuadra said. The letter asked the military to "please understand that I need to be separated from the Navy."[9]

It wasn't too long after he signed the letter that his Naval colleagues at the clinic knew he was gay and that he wanted out. Cuadra said persistent, several-times-a-day phone calls from Kerekes to the clinic asking for Cuadra helped tip off his fellow sailors. "It was getting really difficult to hide (being gay), and people just (said), 'Oh God, Harlow is gay.' I got the third degree and picked on and what not."[10]

Honorable discharge—dishonorable career moves

Once relieved of his Navy obligations and with an honorable discharge in hand, Cuadra said he set his sights on enrolling in Old Dominion University in Norfolk, Virginia. Cuadra said Kerekes even promised to help pay for his college education.[11]

It was not to be, however, as Kerekes continued to dominate his personal time and behave in an increasingly jealous manner about Cuadra's comings and goings. Despite such concerns, Cuadra said he moved into Kerekes' apartment. Shortly after that, Kerekes said he didn't want Cuadra going to college. "In typical Joe fashion, he changed his mind," Cuadra said. "Everything (at Old Dominion) was a go, and then all of a sudden he says, 'I don't want you to go to school.'"[12] Cuadra said Kerekes expressed concern that he would meet another man at college and fall in love with him. Cuadra was devastated, he said, facing the reality that he gave up his dream of a military career for Kerekes, and was now giving up his plans to go college and earn a degree.

The months passed and perhaps not surprisingly, Kerekes recruited Cuadra to join him in the male escorting business. But Kerekes created an interesting caveat for Cuadra: he was not to have sex with his clients or allow them to touch him. Instead, Kerekes pointed Cuadra toward clients who wanted escorts to carry out fetish or "sex scenes" with them—scenes that only played out under strict rules Kerekes had set for Cuadra to follow regarding contact with clients.

One client, he testified before amused jurors, only wanted to play with his feet, fully clothed. Another client wanted Cuadra to dress in a "leatherman" outfit and liked torture scenes, including cracking a whip. "People like to role play and stuff like that," Cuadra told the conservative Pennsylvania jurors. Cuadra said he found the whole thing "weird" but added, "I was making all right money. (Joe) was happy, and I was kind of curious about it."[13]

"Little by little" Kerekes grew more comfortable having his boyfriend out on escort calls and agreed that clients could now start performing oral sex on him if Cuadra did not reciprocate.

To ensure his "rules" were followed, Cuadra said, Kerekes would insert himself into escort calls where the client had only requested Cuadra, not both men. "It was very awkward," Cuadra said. "He was forcing himself into the call, but then after that, (the client) would never want to see me again with him. It was just very awkward."[14]

Even though he was earning up to $160 an hour for his services, Cuadra said he never personally kept any of the funds, instead turning them over to Kerekes. "I don't think that out of the years I've been with (Joe), I've maybe written a dozen checks. I never paid bills...(Joe) took care of everything, car bills, electric bills, everything," Cuadra testified.[15]

Kerekes would try to give some of the couple's escort earnings to his parents, Cuadra said, but because Kerekes' parents were aware of how their son made money, they often did not want to accept the funds. As a result, Cuadra said, Kerekes would give his mother a $100 bill for a small item from the store, and then refuse to take the change.

Cuadra "a battered spouse"?

Cuadra's comments about Kerekes' role in controlling the couple's funds was just the start of a lengthy soliloquy in which he attempted to show Kerekes as the dominant, controlling member of their relationship. Cuadra and his attorneys needed to drive this point home if their attempts to cast doubt on Cuadra's role in the Kocis killing were to succeed, and it was doubt they wanted shifted instead onto Kerekes. Kerekes even held on to Cuadra's personal ID and credit cards, Cuadra said. "If I did happen to go somewhere without him, he would pull (my ID) out of his pocket. I never carried a wallet at all. I didn't own one."[16]

Cuadra suggested in his testimony that his stepfather's influence over his adolescent life, including alleged routine sexual intimacy between the two, left him open to Kerekes' heavy influence over his adult life.

Cuadra also testified that from 2001-2007 he was isolated from his own family, partially by his own choice, and moved more and more toward Kerekes' extended family in the Virginia Beach area. As he testified that he had resisted encouragement from Kerekes' parents that he should reconcile with his mother, Cuadra began to sob. "I'm sorry, Momma," Cuadra said, looking to the gallery where his mother continued to weep loudly. "That was my thinking, (Joe's) parents were all I had. Joseph was all I had. That was it."[17]

It wasn't until he sat more than a year isolated in a jail cell, ignored or harassed by other inmates because of the nature of his crime and his sexuality, that he began to "discover exactly how much you could get played for years."[18]

Acknowledging that he had all the comforts of a regular life, he revealed though that he had none of the freedoms of a regular life. Shopping or going out on his own were unheard of, he said, with Kerekes always insisting that he be at his side.

Perhaps expanding the uneven nature of their relationship, Cuadra said, was the fact that customers rarely called to book Kerekes for an escort call. Most of the BoisRUs clients wanted Cuadra, he said. "(Joe) only escorted when he was able to get into one of my calls."[19]

Whether it caused Kerekes to be jealous is uncertain, but Cuadra began developing a regular set of reliable clients. "Everybody that I met, it didn't matter if they worked at a burger joint or were a senator, everybody that I met, they just called me again," he said perhaps too proudly in front of jurors.[20]

Kerekes' behavior, Cuadra said, also scared off young men they had recruited to work for them, and even some customers. Cuadra said the other boys working in the escort service "were probably my only friends, and I only saw them right before a call or right after a model shoot."[21]

Kerekes also fell into an almost daily habit of getting drunk and refusing to answer the BoisRUs phones once he was happy with the amount of money made that day. "When he achieved the $2,000 limit, it's party time," Cuadra said. "Anything else that came in after that, he would just give it to other guys, other escorts, or he would just simply turn off the phone."[22] The $2,000 daily limit had been reached and Kerekes was drinking heavily on the day of the shooting incident referred to by other witnesses, the one that drove Justin Hensley to leave for good.

Cuadra said on the day of the alleged shooting, Kerekes was "stinking drunk" by 2:00 P.M. and called his former pastor, Ronald Johnston, and left a troubling voice mail message. Cuadra said Kerekes "goes into this rampage and I basically, you know, Justin (Hensley) is in the house and he's embarrassing me and I'm, like, 'Joe, chill, you know?'"[23]

Trying to escape his raging, Cuadra said he went into his bedroom and put a NASCAR race on the large plasma TV. Kerekes wasn't having any of it, and walked in and unplugged the TV. As Cuadra attempted to plug it back in, Kerekes fired at the TV, Cuadra said.

He said Kerekes went back to get another ammunition clip to reload his handgun, but Cuadra was able to talk him down. Kerekes then set about destroying computers, chairs, and tables in the loft area of the couple's home, and threatened Hensley who had entered the room when he heard the shots. The incident ended, Cuadra said, as "Joseph collapses on the floor crying and that was the end of that temper tantrum."[24]

Cuadra assesses the competition

During his testimony, Cuadra provided somewhat inconsistent testimony about his knowledge or awareness of Bryan Kocis' company, Cobra Video. In some instances, Cuadra said he had rented or purchased Cobra DVDs only because he found the guys on the box covers attractive. In other instances, he seemed to notice specific details about the increasingly popular porn fare offered by Cobra. "I had several of (Cobra's) movies," he said. "The covers looked good quality...but back then, I didn't even care who Cobra was."[25]

He expressed similar disinterest in inquiries he said he and Kerekes received from Lockhart and Roy via the LSG Media enterprise. Something about their inquiry, though, caught Kerekes' eye, Cuadra said, as he later discovered Kerekes had added Lockhart to Cuadra's "friends" section on his MySpace page. Cuadra continually maintained in his testimony that he never personally e-mailed anyone and that the e-mails prosecutors had shown as part of their case were all written by Kerekes (even ones going out under Cuadra's name).

Cuadra did admit to writing one e-mail to Lockhart that assessed other gay porn producers in the market. Cuadra, who still claimed to have little or no knowledge of the business of his own BoyBatter site or of Cobra Video wrote:

> The problem with those companies is that they are ran by dirty old men that dont (sic.) give a shit about the newer generation.they want to keep us down. Glad I didnt.(sic.) I have gone broke twice already finaly (sic.) the site is making a decent amount of income for itself. I checked the cobra vids (sic.) that you did, and can't believe the way they are marketing them.
> Plus their edit work sucks. Anyways, co-producing sounds cool![26]

Lockhart and Roy had made it clear that no productions with Cuadra and Kerekes could start until matters with Kocis were settled. That didn't stop the back and forth communication, though, with Cuadra acknowledging that Lockhart had "politely told me to get toned. When he says, 'get toned,' that basically means lose weight. He wanted my abdominals to look better. You don't pop your abdominals out by gaining more weight."[27]

Cuadra said he only communicated with Lockhart via one live online chat. "I swear, I only had like one chat with him on that MySpace, that was it. I mean, Joe was a very jealous person and he would never just let me talk to people like that, you know."[28]

Performing in a porn video with Lockhart was something Cuadra was excited about, though. "We were going to be a perfect contrast to each other," he said. "That is what Grant

(Roy) said, the pairing was so perfect because I was slightly a little taller than he was, a little bit better defined, and so it would be a good contrast to one another."[29]

Meeting Lockhart meant Cuadra had "butterflies" in his stomach and so he and Kerekes took several drinks in the casino bar before Lockhart and Roy arrived for dinner. "They had a very nervous smile on their face," Cuadra remembers. "So the first time they meet me, they're kind of, you know, I can tell that they're nervous."[30]

Talking of killing Kocis

Cuadra's version of the dinner at Le Cirque included details that Roy would often lapse off into mini-rants about ongoing problems with Kocis. "It was an uncomfortable conversation regarding killing Bryan Kocis," Cuadra testified. "How that got that way is, Grant Roy started to talk about (their) settlement and...he would end every negative paragraph with 'F Bryan, F Bryan...'"[31]

It was during one of the rants, Cuadra said, that Kerekes added casually, "I would have killed him a long time ago." Cuadra said Roy responded that he had thought about that himself, but said if Kocis were killed, suspicion would immediately fall on himself and Lockhart.

As expected, Cuadra said he was not part of the back-and-forth between Kerekes and Roy about killing Kocis. Conversely, Roy and Lockhart offered a different version of the conversations during their testimony, saying it was Cuadra and Kerekes who suggested Kocis "go away" to Europe or Canada.

Cuadra did recall that Kerekes gloated that one of Cuadra's regular escort clients was affiliated with the mafia and "he does this sort of thing." He said he realized Kerekes was lying.[32]

"Then Joseph is the one who tells (Roy), 'You know, they would stick (Kocis) in a car, in the trunk of a car, drive him over (to) Canada, the border, and dump him off in the woods," Cuadra testified. "Grant gets a laugh out of it, like a chuckle."[33]

Sealing a deal?

As expected, Cuadra's version of business discussions over dinner with Lockhart and Roy varied again, even when it came to who wanted to proceed with working together on porn projects. Cuadra said it was Roy who pulled out a small tablet and began mapping out three video projects and how the money could be split up.

"Then Joseph...still assumed that he had to pay Sean something," Cuadra testified. "(Joseph) reaches into his coat and he pulls out maybe about $12,000 and he puts it on the table and slides it towards Grant Roy." Roy pushed the money back toward Kerekes assuring that the deal would require no "upfront" investment from BoyBatter, Cuadra said.[34]

Cuadra said Kerekes and Roy openly discussed him and Lockhart and "referred to us almost like a third person or something like...Joe wouldn't even look at me. Then Grant Roy treated Sean Lockhart the same way...They would talk about us, we're here on these opposite ends and they're looking at each other."[35]

Cuadra also told jurors that it was his impression that Lockhart was "swooning over me. He liked me a lot and kept saying that to Joe."[36]

If being talked about as if he weren't there bothered Lockhart, Cuadra said, it didn't show. He reported Lockhart continued to text friends on his cell phone and take calls. "(Sean) could care less," Cuadra said. "I'm used to being around company where you have to act right. So I'm just, you know, trying to be respectful."[37]

In their version of the dinner, Roy and Lockhart never mentioned any cash being literally brought to the table. Kerekes version was never heard.

Plans for after-dinner drinks were shelved as Roy and Lockhart begged off as of being tired. Cuadra said he and his partner Kerekes returned to their hotel room and met up again with Roy the next day on the floor of the Adult Video Network convention.

It was during this time together, Cuadra said, that he and Kerekes formed the idea that he may want to model for Cobra Video because of its popularity. Their thinking: if bringing Sean Lockhart to BoyBatter would help build an audience, so would working with Kocis' Cobra Video.

Roy's flirtations, Cuadra testified, were why he and Kerekes made an early departure back to Virginia and did not attend a major circuit party occurring at the AVN event. Cuadra said that Kerekes told him he could "absolutely not" attend the party because "he noticed the way Grant is looking at me, and, you know, it makes him a little uncomfortable. (Joseph) is a very jealous person."[38]

Before they even got home to Virginia, Cuadra said, Roy sent Kerekes a text message that said, "We're all good. We settled. We're feeling great. It's on. The Cobra suit is done."[39] Cuadra said he thought this meant they were OK to proceed with planning a shoot with him and Lockhart around the time of the GayVN Awards event in February at San Francisco's Castro Theatre. He also thought it meant going ahead with approaching Cobra Video for work, he told jurors, even though he said Kocis' criminal past made him leery of him.

No one has ever been able to verify or confirm any of the elements of Cuadra's version of events, a major stumbling block for any defendant.

While prosecutors had both Lockhart and Roy saying virtually the same version of events, Kerekes did not cooperate and there was no way to effectively counter with Cuadra's version. It became Cuadra's word versus the word of two others.

Cuadra's version served the purpose of helping explain why he would have ever gone to Dallas Township, Pennsylvania to see Bryan Kocis. Moreover, it also attempted to take away an alleged motive for Cuadra and Kerekes to act to get rid of Kocis. By telling jurors about an alleged text message regarding the settlement from Roy to Kerekes (no evidence beyond Cuadra's direct testimony was ever produced to verify), Cuadra inched toward eliminating motive. The mountain of circumstantial evidence was stacked against him, however, and an inability to find corroborating testimony for his own meant Cuadra and his counsel may have tried chiseling away at the base of the mountain, but they got nowhere.

Getting more specific

By now, jurors had heard gruesome details about Kocis' murder, and heard damning testimony from Lockhart and Roy that placed any planning for a murder at the feet of Cuadra and Kerekes. Telling the story of his life, giving his version of the events were all valuable, but Cuadra had no choice but to also detail his version of events on Midland Drive that night.

Immediately gone was Cuadra's earlier version told to potential alibi witnesses, the one where he had arrived at Kocis' house to find him slain, a small fire started, and fled when he heard noises. It didn't matter. Jurors wouldn't hear that version anyway, instead hearing the defendant trying to tell events in his own words.

In setting up the trip to Pennsylvania, which Cuadra insisted was to fulfill an appointment to potentially model for Kocis and appear in a Cobra Video, all of the preparations and planning were pinned on Kerekes. Cuadra said it was Kerekes who picked up a gun, the knife, the rental car, even the pre-paid TracFones inexplicably used to communicate only with Kocis (and for no other purpose).

Cuadra testified that Kerekes ordered him to drive to Pennsylvania on Tuesday, January 23, 2007, a nine-hour roundtrip they made in one day. During the trip, Cuadra said, Kerekes continued communicating with Kocis via a mobile Sprint PCS card attached to his laptop. Kerekes sent e-mails and photos to Kocis while Cuadra drove the rental car north from the Virginia Beach peninsula to Pennsylvania.

He said it was clear during this back-and-forth that Kocis seemed to know who Cuadra really was, knew what BoyBatter was, and wasn't buying the "Danny Moilin" act at all. He said Kocis even asked why he used the name Danny instead of his real name, Harlow, and whether he had an existing contract with BoyBatter. "(Kocis) knew who I was," Cuadra said. "I laughed. He knew who I was. I was a little nervous (but) he can care less. He didn't care at all that I was an escort."[40] Cuadra said Kocis knowing who he really was and that it did not bother him "made me feel a lot more confident, like, this is good."[41]

Plans to meet that first night, however, were immediately shelved. Cuadra said Kocis called him off. "He goes, 'Forget it. I'm too tired.' Something like that, something along those lines," Cuadra testified.[42] Cuadra's version again strays from what Kocis' friends and family reported. All of them reported he anticipated meeting his new model Danny on Wednesday, January 24, not Tuesday, January 23.

During the evening of Tuesday, January 23 and daytime hours of Wednesday, January 24, Cuadra said he and Kerekes filled their time poking around online, watching TV in their motel room in Wilkes-Barre, eating lunch at a nearby Friendly's Restaurant, and visiting a local gym. "I wanted to look perfect for Bryan," Cuadra testified.[43]

Cuadra denied the state's theory that he and Kerekes ran reconnaissance on Kocis' home on Tuesday evening, contradicting what was gloated about on the Black's Beach tapes recorded months later.

Cuadra did mention that Kerekes left him alone in the gym in Wilkes-Barre for more than hour and did not explain his absence. When he returned, a small bag containing condoms and other items (including lighter fluid) was stowed inside the vehicle, Cuadra said, which surprised him because he planned to do a solo masturbation scene with Kocis, a scene not requiring a condom. "Unless it's a movie, I don't perform oral sex on another person unless they're wearing a condom,"

Cuadra turned toward the jury and explained. "It has to be unlubricated or else it kind of burns your mouth with that chemical."[(44)]

"Time to see Bryan"

Watching the clock move slowly, Cuadra said, the couple returned to their motel room after the gym with food and a bottle of Chuck Hill Chardonnay and a bottle of champagne. His appointment with Kocis, he said, wasn't until the evening hours so "I had enough time to eat and shower up, get all nice and spruced up and ready. Joseph didn't eat anything. All he did was drink half of each bottle." Cuadra said he didn't drink and "from there, it was time to see Bryan."[(45)]

According to Cuadra, the plan was for Kerekes to drop Cuadra off at Kocis' house and then leave and come back later to pick him up. Cuadra said he took with him a backpack containing clean underwear, condoms, lube, and his ID. "(Joseph) pulled in and I got out…and I went right up," Cuadra explained.

Kocis answered his knocks at the door, Cuadra said, with wet hair, looking like he had just finished showering. "He opened the door wide, 'Danny, come on in!' He liked me a lot, and it was hard to look at him sometimes because he was so smitten over me. You know, like when somebody is, like, 'Oh, your dimples'…I felt really good though. This was going to be very positive, (a) very good thing. I did not feel like something bad was going to happen at all."[(46)]

Cuadra and Kocis sat on the sofa, he said, while the large screen TV played a werewolf movie that Kocis did not appear to be paying attention to. Glasses of wine were poured, Cuadra said, with Kocis drinking more than he did. "In between that, he had received maybe about three phone calls, about five minutes in length," Cuadra testified. "After he would hang up, he would apologize (to me for the interruption)."[(47)]

Cuadra said the meeting with Kocis felt a lot like the escort calls he had grown accustomed to. "I was basically there to entertain him, get it on film, and leave so that he can produce this thing, market it, and then I can benefit off of it," Cuadra said. "That was what I assumed I was there to do."[48]

During their meeting on the couch, they sat next to each other, Cuadra said, and Kocis was "a perfect gentleman. He never said anything lewd or anything like that. He didn't even touch me other than to hug at the beginning and kiss on the cheek. He was very nice to me."[49]

A heavy knock at the door

Cuadra told jurors the conversation was progressing nicely when "all of a sudden, when we were in conversation, you can hear like a rapid knock, like a knock, knock, knock"(Cuadra knocked his knuckles on the witness stand to demonstrate the intensity of the knocks).

Cuadra said Kocis appeared surprised by the knocking, but went to the door to answer it. Here, again, Cuadra's version of events not only cannot be verified, but also differ greatly from the pattern of behavior the state had demonstrated in its case. According to Kocis' family and friends, a knock at the door did not necessarily mean Kocis would have answered his door.

"So the minute, the second he turns the knob and cracks the door a little bit, Joe comes in and they fight a bit at the door," Cuadra said, his voice cracking with excitement. "Joe just busts in and he looks at me and then he looks at Bryan and he decks him right in the face; and Bryan fights back with him, but Joe is, they fight and they come over to the area where (I was)." The tussle between Kocis and Kerekes, Cuadra testified, knocked over the cocktail table in front of the couch and spilled the glasses of wine sitting there.(Photographs taken just after the fire was extinguished, however, showed the table in an upright position, and detectives said they found the wine glasses stowed in the kitchen sink.) "I'm yelling, 'Joe! Stop! Stop! Stop, Joe! What are you doing? Joe, what are you doing!'" Cuadra testified.[50]

Kerekes didn't stop, Cuadra said. "He grabbed Bryan, (and) Bryan is wearing like a track suit, it's all black, black top, black bottom (and) he's wearing white socks, no shoes on," Cuadra detailed. Pinned to the couch, Cuadra said, Kerekes began punching Kocis in the face and "I grab Joe by the belt loop by the back of (his) pants and I'm trying to get him off of him," Cuadra said, but reported Kerekes struck him with a fist in the mouth, knocking him away.[51]

"Then (Joe) goes in his pocket, he takes out a knife and it's not that, it's not that Sig Sauer, it's that little one, and he slashes him right across," Cuadra said. "Bryan immediately grabs his throat and he starts yelling at Joe, 'What are you doing? What are you doing?'" Cuadra said. "Except you can hear gurgling, like the blood is going into his throat; and I'm, like, 'Joe, what are you doing?'"[52]

It was a question Kerekes would not answer, Cuadra said, as Kocis lay dying. He said Kerekes ordered him to "just get the fuck in the car," an order Cuadra said he followed and waited there for about fifteen minutes before Kerekes returned and the couple fled. Before leaving, however, Cuadra said Kerekes loaded several of Kocis' personal items, including computer towers.

Cuadra said he never noticed any fire while they were still at the scene and only learned about that later from media reports he read online.

Cuadra described a frantic scene that followed. He said Kerekes almost immediately pulled into a nearby gas station to get rid of the paperwork and laptop computer belonging to Kocis, thrown into a trash can adjacent to the gas pumps. From there, he said, a still angry Kerekes took the back seat and ordered Cuadra to drive back to Virginia.

"I'm driving erratic as hell, I'm scared," Cuadra said. "He's telling me, 'Stay in a straight line, Harlow. Slow down, speed up.' I don't know what to do."[53]

Despite his stated fear at what he has just witnessed,

allegedly watching his lover and business partner brutally murder another man, Cuadra said he stayed in the vehicle and continued driving. Eventually, Cuadra said, he began arguing with Kerekes about what had happened. "Then he starts on me," Cuadra said, retelling how he said Kerekes accused him of breaking their agreed-to escort rules: "You were going to fuck him. You were going to fuck him all night long, weren't you?"

It was then, Cuadra said, Kerekes struck him as he drove into the night southward. "I drove all the way back home nonstop, (stopping) only once to get fuel, that was it," Cuadra said. He tried to ask him again why he had done this, Cuadra said, but Kerekes kept telling him to "shut the fuck up" or would strike him and add, "Baby, not now. Not now."[54]

Later he said Kerekes began coaching him that the two of them could never talk about what had happened ever again. Cuadra said he saw problems with that, noting that many others knew they were planning a trip to Pennsylvania, including Kerekes' mother.

Figuring out their stories and keeping them straight would come later. For now, Cuadra said he was tired when he finally arrived home in the pre-dawn hours and collapsed on his bed and slept for hours.

"I completely shut down after that day"

Cuadra described for jurors the days after he returned to Virginia as ones where he "completely shut down." He said he cringed as he heard what he thought was Kerekes on the phone gloating to Lockhart the very next day about having hired a hit man to take care of Kocis. Despite Lockhart's testimony to the contrary, Cuadra denied he ever spoke to Lockhart the day after the murder. Cuadra did confirm a subsequent call came in a few hours later from Grant Roy in which he told Kerekes to stay away from him and Lockhart.

The empty weeks that followed found Cuadra and Kerekes seeking out legal advice from their attorney, Barry Taylor, who warned them to stay away from law enforcement and Lockhart and Roy. The couple only visited their home a few additional times to pick up items as they stayed a week or so at a time at various Virginia, North Carolina, and Florida hotels.

The day the search warrant was served on their home the couple fled even further south to Florida, but not before raising some additional cash by pawning Cuadra's Rolex watch that he considered "a wedding band" from Kerekes.

Cuadra told jurors it was at this point he wanted to come forward to talk to police because he had been identified publicly as "a person of interest" in the murder of Bryan Kocis. Conflicts about whether Taylor represented Cuadra or Kerekes combined with Kerekes' insistence that he keep quiet, meant Cuadra never came forward to talk to investigators.

Hidden away in a small condo in South Beach Miami, Florida, Cuadra said he continued to struggle to eat, sleep, or keep his spirits up. He said Kerekes refused to let him go anywhere on his own, and he rarely left the condo. The couple paid for their expenses, he said, with about $100,000 in cash Kerekes reportedly had hidden in a backpack.

"At first, Joseph started drinking everyday, early in the day now," Cuadra said explaining their nightmarish refugee life. "He didn't even wait until the afternoon anymore. Early in the day, he was hammered."[55]

By now, spring had arrived and authorities continued to piece together, bit by bit, who had killed Kocis. It was also during this period that Roy and Lockhart reached out to investigators and began filling in some of the holes in the story. If Joseph Kerekes knew that, he certainly would have never e-mailed Roy and Lockhart about jump-starting their porn production plans. His entreaties to them, perhaps reflecting the alcohol abuse that was occurring, included an open threat to Roy and Lockhart about the Kocis murder followed quickly by a hasty "I'm sorry." It was a familiar, brutish style that Kerekes personified, Cuadra said: act rash and violently and quickly apologize and try to make amends.

Cuadra said he experienced more wrath when he allegedly challenged Kerekes for having reached out to Roy and Lockhart to restart their porn project. Cuadra thought it was a bad idea, but if Cuadra was having any effect at slowing down Kerekes' moves to get back into porn production, it didn't show. Soon the infamous trip to San Diego was in the works and meetings with Roy and Lockhart were set up that ultimately would bring the end to freedom for Cuadra and Kerekes.

Cuadra said his continual badgering of Kerekes and his expressions of opposition to going to San Diego brought on another violent outburst. "He grabbed me and he pinned me to the wall and he said, 'So what? I killed him. So what? I got away with murder. It's on the back burner,'" Cuadra said Kerekes yelled.[56]

It was part of an emerging pattern, Cuadra said, during their final days of freedom where he said Kerekes abused large amounts of alcohol and was often "out of control" and was "self-destructive." Whatever Kerekes' behavior was, it didn't cause Cuadra to flee or refuse the trip to San Diego. In fact, he went along and was recorded in both meetings with Roy and Lockhart as being an active participant in the current plans.

Cuadra's story: It was all Joe

Back when he was arrested in May 2007, Cuadra provided an unprompted outburst for investigators while he sat at the Virginia Beach Police Department awaiting questioning: "Joe didn't do it," the detectives said he offered without prompting.

His story was going to change.

By the time of his March 2009 trial, Cuadra had turned that statement on its head and basically argued that the murder of Bryan Kocis and all related activities to that were all Joseph Kerekes' idea.

So why did he change his story? In Cuadra's words, beyond being frightened of Kerekes, he said he worried Kerekes would get the death penalty. "I said, 'Joe didn't do it' (because) I felt bad even saying everything I had said…I did not want them to kill Joe. You know, I love him. He had already killed somebody, but I didn't see a reason why somebody else should die."[57]

Cuadra's attorney Paul Walker then led him through tedious and lengthy explanations about various statements he was recorded making during the luncheon and beach meetings in San Diego. A classic example, prior to meeting with Roy and Lockhart, Cuadra said Kerekes got threatening: "He scolds me real bad. He reprimands me. He gets right into my little zone and he's, like, 'Harlow, you're going to sell this. You're going to sell it, you're going to sell it.'"[58]

From there, Cuadra said Kerekes controlled everything he said or offered on the tapes, including specific information about Kocis' home and stolen property that had never been released publicly before. On the tape, it sounds like a coordinated effort with Cuadra and Kerekes trying to move forward with their grand plans to make porn movies with the great Brent Corrigan character. At trial, however, jurors were asked by Cuadra and his counsel to believe that the tapes just reflected a frightened defendant doing as he was told by a dominant, threatening Kerekes.

"Then when I thought that part of the conversation would be over, Joseph starts talking business again (with Roy), and obviously, that's going nowhere," Cuadra claimed. "So Joseph gives me this little look and pushes me towards him, like, 'keep talking, keep talking, make (Roy) happy.'"[59]

Cuadra used this explanation to cover why he was recorded saying that Kocis had died quickly. He said he was saying whatever it was he thought Roy wanted to hear. He also said his comments about "feeling good" about seeing Kocis go down was just more of Kerekes coaching him. He testified that Kerekes told him, "Baby, you got revenge" for what his stepfather allegedly did to him.[60]

"I was very immature out there (on the beach), but I was

scared," he said. "That was not me. That was not something that I would do. You know, Joseph promised me that if I did that, that would be the end of Sean and Grant, and I would never have to talk to them again, never have to deal with that again, that he would put it behind us and that we can go on with a life."[61]

Cuadra even offered jurors alternate theories on why and how police investigators were able to uncover his approaches to former clients, begging them to help provide an alibi for the day Kocis was murdered. As expected, it was all Kerekes' idea.

He described for jurors an elaborate "communication system" inside the Virginia Beach Correctional Center (where he was initially housed) that Kerekes used to keep in contact with him. He said notes slipped to trusted inmates would be carried to and from Cuadra and Kerekes in exchange for a candy bar or other favors. The notes from Kerekes, he said, ordered him to seek out alibis.

Later, under cross-examination, Cuadra said Kerekes even tried communicating with him in elevators inside the Virginia Beach Correctional Facility when both men were brought in for hearings. "Sometimes, after certain court hearings, they would stick both of us in the elevator together," he said. "They would make us face the wall of the elevator and he would be side by side with me; and he would bump into me like playfully, and I would look at him. You know, there never was any security. He could have bitten my nose off."[62]

Three-way phone calls that Kerekes and Cuadra conducted later on, set up by their friend Renee Martin, were also Kerekes' idea, Cuadra said (something Martin also confirmed in her testimony). It was all too much for him, Cuadra said, and eventually contact with Kerekes ended and not only did their physical paths diverge, but so did their stories. Kerekes eventually admitted guilt to a portion of the crime and accepted a plea agreement. Cuadra wanted to go to trial.

CHAPTER 12
Bringing Cuadra's Trial to a Close

"Mr. Melnick, you're the only one out of ninety (witnesses)... the only that that is calling me a murderer or an accomplice or a conspirator. Your statements, Mr Melnick, are not evidence."

—Harlow Cuadra fighting back under
cross examination

Cross-examining the witness

No one could blame assistant DA Michael Melnick if he relished the rare chance to cross-examine a defendant in a major murder case. It's an unusual circumstance and one many prosecutors would undoubtedly savor. Melnick did not disappoint. He was well prepared and alternately polite and bombastic in his approach to Cuadra, a man who had openly declared himself on the witness stand "a gay porn star" in the heart of conservative northeast Pennsylvania.

Melnick started by reminding Cuadra of his "plans" sent

to his friend Renee Martin on how to pick apart the growing mountain of state's evidence and to put the victim, Bryan Kocis, on trial. Melnick also gained ground by emphasizing that Cuadra had successfully pulled (Melnick called it "manipulated") more than $70,000 from one of his former escort clients to finance his defense.

Melnick then read back to Cuadra a transcript of a taped phone conversation between him and Martin where he cast himself as "poor Harlow" and admitted that he would rather go to "the slammer" by himself than implicate Kerekes. "My self-esteem was so low at the time that (Kerekes) gave me this, I just wanted to protect him," Cuadra said. "That is basically it. I knew that by everything that had happened, that they would give him the death penalty if he did come to trial and he knew that himself."[1]

Melnick continued to pick apart what he called Cuadra's portrayal of Kerekes as "The Terror of the Tidewater" and his strong influence over Cuadra's actions.

Particularly damaging to Cuadra's claims was another taped three-way conversation between him, Kerekes, and Martin. Apparently still believing he would take the blame for the crime, Cuadra is recorded as encouraging Kerekes to keep the BoyBatter and BoisRUs enterprises going. "Honestly, I need you to run the escort service," the tape recorded Cuadra saying to Kerekes. "I need you to run the porn site. I need you to film these kids." The tape captured Kerekes replying, "I will. So even though Renee is saying move to Dallas, you want me to stay here (in Virginia)?" Cuadra replied on tape, "Yeah. I would actually want you to stay there. I need you to film kids."[2]

This was more damning evidence that flew in the face of Cuadra's repeated claims that Kerekes was the dominant, abusive, and sometimes violent boss of their operations. Here on tape was Cuadra mapping out their company's future with apparently Kerekes at the helm while Cuadra served a jail sentence. Cuadra denied to Melnick that he was ordering

Kerekes to do anything. "I was not giving him orders, maybe it may have sounded like an order, but I don't tell Joseph Kerekes what to do."[3]

Melnick's relentless references to the tape transcripts, and even offers to have the phone conversations replayed for the jury, seemed to irritate Cuadra significantly, with the defendant offering an exasperated, "There is a lot more that goes to that, Mr. Melnick. There really is. That (tape) is not the whole picture. It is just not."[4]

He also questioned why Cuadra would describe Kerekes repeatedly as this "tyrannical figure," yet "despite that you had multiple three-way conversations with him and Renee Martin time and time again."[5] "Yes sir, I loved him," Cuadra replied. "I missed him. The first year being incarcerated was so difficult. It's, you know, somebody treats you like dirt and you don't have the guts to just leave them, you feel like you just need them, and now all of a sudden I was liberated from him, but I couldn't, I didn't know how to act."[6]

Cuadra attempted to offer a similar explanation when Melnick confronted him about one telephone call taped with Kerekes from the jail in which Cuadra is recorded as cautioning his partner while discussing alibis and explanations: "Don't make my hole too deep for me to crawl out of, you know. I know (investigators) don't believe that I opened the door and saw the body. I know they don't believe that."[7]

Perhaps sensing he had put Cuadra on his heels and off his more confident direct testimony, Melnick began questioning him about an undoubtedly even more painful period of his life involving his alleged childhood molestation. He asked that if his childhood was so damaging and awful, why did Cuadra make his alleged molester the beneficiary of his $50,000 life insurance policy upon enlisting in the U.S. Navy? "Stockholm Syndrome," Cuadra said. "Even my mother, to this day, tried to get me to stop forgiving him so much. It's hard, but I forgave him for years of that (sexual abuse) and I wish him well in life.

Maybe I'm too soft, I'm too easy to forgive people, but that's just the way I am."[8]

Melnick even tried to demonstrate how Cuadra's Naval training as a hospital corpsman may have assisted or instructed him on working with knives, the undisputed weapon used to kill Kocis. "I never had knife training, sir," Cuadra said. "I knew how to give sutures. That was about the extent of poking or withdrawing blood, but (I) never made incisions."[9]

The state was successful in getting Cuadra to disclose that most, if not all, of the couple's credit cards and bank accounts were set up using Cuadra's name and credit. Kerekes' previous bankruptcy had made it difficult or impossible for him to obtain credit on his own, and by showing Cuadra had more control over what credit the couple could access helped diminish the argument that Kerekes controlled Cuadra in all matters of life.

The cross-examination also served to emphasize that Cuadra had at least *one* open chance to flee from Kerekes, if he in fact needed one, when he went *alone* to Mitch Halford's home to borrow a truck. Cuadra said he feared Kerekes would kill Halford if he tried that, and so he took the truck and went back to flee south with Kerekes.

Cuadra's participation in interviews with producers from MTV and HereTV! were also highlighted by Melnick to help demonstrate he was making his own choices about what to do and what not to do. It was a good opening for Melnick to pursue, because in the HereTV! audio-taped phone interview, Cuadra had to acknowledge that he is heard on tape saying it was his idea to come to Pennsylvania to see Kocis: "Even when I wanted to come to Pennsylvania, not physically, but (Joseph) fought me on it. 'No, no, no. I don't want you meeting with that queer. Blah, blah, blah.' I'm like, dude, come on!"[10]

Cuadra began to weep quietly on the witness stand and could only muster in response that he didn't realize he was being taped for a documentary, and his old stand-by response: it was all Joseph Kerekes' idea. Kerekes was "wicked" and "twisted," Cuadra said.[11]

Retelling the murder scene

Melnick then asked Cuadra to explain why he claimed Kocis had cried out, "Why are you doing this?" as he was attacked, when the pathologist indicated that Kocis' neck, vocal cords, hyoid bone, and carotid artery were all destroyed with one swoop of a knife.

First Cuadra said it was because Kerekes "took that swipe out of the side of his neck when he got him on that couch, it wasn't all the way because I was tugging at him to stop." But Cuadra admitted "memory is a tricky companion" and that as best he could remember Kocis said something before dying. "Maybe he said that before he sliced him, because he got him on the couch first and they were struggling; and then he went into his pocket and pulled out that little knife and that's when he did that," Cuadra tried to explain.[12]

Inconsistency in Cuadra's story also came up as Melnick walked him through photographs taken at the murder scene shortly after the fire was put out. He succeeded in having Cuadra admit that the cocktail table was not tipped over in some violent fight, as he had described earlier, but Cuadra had an explanation for that too: "Please keep in mind that Joseph stayed in the house for about fifteen, twenty minutes" and could have righted the table and put the wine glasses back in the kitchen sink, he said.[13]

Cuadra again struggled to keep his story straight on what Kocis' behavior had been the night he died. During direct examination from his own lawyers, Cuadra said Kocis had acted "as a perfect gentleman" and had not done or said anything lewd. However, under intense questioning from Melnick he embellished the story to say Kocis "had his hand on my penis. He answered the phone and was able to get to the door at the same time." Melnick drew a few snickers when he responded, "And would you agree with me that it would be inconsistent to be answering the phone, that he's dragging you by the groin (and) going to answer the doorbell? That should be pretty hard to do?"[14]

On a few other topics, however, Melnick was less successful in getting Cuadra to contradict himself. Little headway was made in directly implicating Cuadra in any alleged reconnaissance work a day before the murder at Kocis' house. Despite cell phone tower reports that showed his phone in use near the Kocis home, Cuadra stuck to his assertion that at least twice, once while he slept in the motel room, and once while he worked out at a local gym, Kerekes left on his own without telling Cuadra where he was.

Cuadra vs. Melnick

The defendant and the prosecutor openly sparred on more than one occasion—perhaps not unexpectedly. Prior to the trial, Cuadra told documentary producer John Roecker (via a jailhouse telephone interview) that he viewed Melnick as "a smart guy" but one who "looks like he could be a hard ass," who had had the wool pulled over his eyes by other witnesses. "It's hard to believe that someone that smart like this prosecutor is…would continue to hound us like this," Cuadra said.[15]

Cuadra seemed to take most umbrage when Melnick would identify him as the killer of Bryan Kocis. Cuadra defiantly declared that the only person saying that he had killed Kocis was the district attorney, not any of the witnesses. "Mr. Melnick, you're the only one out of ninety, out of ninety, I counted them this morning, ninety people that have taken the stand for you, (and) you're the only one that is calling me a murderer or an accomplice or a conspirator," Cuadra said, motioning to a slip of paper he pulled from his breast pocket with the number ninety circled on it. "You're the only one. Your statements (Mr. Melnick) are not evidence, only what is said up here on the stand."(The state actually called eighty-six witnesses and the defense two.) [16]

He later asserted that Melnick had "coached" witnesses

who testified against him.

He also alleged from the stand that Lockhart and Roy were lying and had joined "in collusion to get their stories straight to be able to make you (Melnick) happy so they can go back to San Diego and carry on with their lives."[17]

For his part, Melnick attempted to paint Cuadra as a coward who worked to get out of the Navy just as U.S. military forces were ramping up their efforts to begin protracted military conflicts in both Afghanistan and Iraq. Cuadra's attorneys strongly objected to that line of questioning, and the court agreed.

Melnick tried a bit more, prompting Cuadra to shout out, "I am not a coward!"[18] Cuadra's attorneys admonished him not to answer and asked the judge to remind Melnick that he cannot continue to ask questions that the court ruled were irrelevant.

Cuadra repeated his claim of having lived like "a battered wife does" and made excuses for Kerekes' behavior; he said it hurt him to speak poorly of Kerekes after the fact, and that before he got away from Kerekes he spoke up for him to others. He said, "I mean, I saw a very sweet side of Joe that nobody else ever did see. I was defending Joe to people."[19]

In Cuadra's mind, "(Kerekes) had a lot of chances to get away with this and to blame it all on me, but he plead guilty to murder and he came here willing to cooperate, but he changed his mind and leaves."[20]

During this same period, Cuadra reminded Melnick through tears, "I have always held onto my innocence, always."[21]

Continuing down this line, Cuadra opened his own summary argument on Kerekes and his theory of why he did not try to defend himself: "He was guilty of murder, and Joseph Kerekes pleaded guilty to murder…in his conscience, he's ashamed of it. (When he was here in court), he could look no one in the face. He looked down to the floor and left as fast as possible. He is guilty of murder. He killed Bryan Kocis."[22]

Seeing an opening, Melnick added, "Now that you mention the subject, let's follow up on that. (Kerekes) admitted he was your accomplice…" The words were barely out of the prosecutor's mouth when Cuadra's counsel Walker strongly objected.

"Your honor, I would object to that," Walker said. "I don't know that there has been any admission in court."

The judge agreed. "That is absolutely false and untrue, Mr. Melnick," Judge Olszewski said. "And I don't want to hear that question again."

Melnick tried to explain, but Olszewski had heard enough.

"I don't want to hear that question again. That is the last time I am going to tell you (that). The question was most improper," Olszewski said.[23]

The judge has a question

Interestingly, at the end of Cuadra's testimony, Olszewski himself posed a question to the defendant (in front of the jury). The judge asked him whether he was stating Kerekes had anything in his hand when he allegedly burst into Kocis' home and asked for more clarification of Kerekes' alleged movements immediately after Kocis was slain. The judge also had Cuadra confirm that Kerekes drove the SUV away from Kocis' home and was wearing the same clothing as when he went into the home to allegedly attack Kocis.

Cuadra offered, "Your honor, his hands were clean, no blood on them, so I assumed that he had washed them in either a bathroom or a sink."[24]

The judge's question and Cuadra's response would later prove important to some of the jury members. One juror, Jim Scutt said, "I've shot deer, many deer in my life and the femoral artery or any artery will squirt blood like a fountain."[25] He made a mental note of Cuadra's claim that Kerekes did not take anything into the house with him and that he had on "a nice pair of jeans on and a shirt." From that, Scutt asks: "I guess he drove back to Virginia Beach in blood-laden clothes?" It's a claim he doesn't believe, noting that it was Cuadra who said he took a backpack into the home with him, not Kerekes. "If you sliced someone's throat to the point of decapitation, you would have blood all over you," Scutt said. "Joe (Kerekes) wasn't in there killing him."[26]

Judge Olszewski's question ended twenty-four hours of testimony on the stand for Cuadra and the defense rested. No other witnesses were called by D'Andrea and Walker.

Closing arguments

In presenting closing arguments to the jury, both defense and state attorneys took about an hour making their case, with Cuadra's defense attorney Joseph D'Andrea going first.

D'Andrea told jurors that first and foremost his client was innocent. He said Cuadra lacked the physical ability to have killed Kocis. "The horror that was inflicted on Bryan Kocis by his killer was terrible," D'Andrea said. "But a mystery remains, who is Bryan Kocis' killer?"[27]

D'Andrea asked jurors to remember the seven-minute videotape they had watched of Cuadra and Lockhart tossing a football back and forth on Black's Beach in San Diego. "I hate to be so condescending, but it was almost feminine," D'Andrea said of his client's throwing ability. "Harlow is not a jock. Harlow is not the muscleman who has the physical ability to kill."[28]

D'Andrea's argument about Cuadra's football throwing style did not impress at least one of the jurors. Juror Tom Stavitzski, a former football player and coach, told his fellow jurors that he knew many strong players who couldn't throw a football well.

Regardless, D'Andrea continued to poke at the state's circumstantial evidence, including the state's contention that Cuadra purchased condoms and lube before going to Kocis' home. "You're not worried about safe sex if you're going to kill someone," D'Andrea said. "At best, my client was a witness to a crime. My client didn't have to testify. He didn't have to sit here and be barraged for two days. He waited for two years to talk to you folks."[29]

"Motive, money, Kerekes," D'Andrea said were the three things jurors needed to know about who killed the victim. He said Kerekes and his "relentless" pursuit of Lockhart required that he remove Kocis as an obstacle. Motive, money and Kerekes when added to the questions without answers raised by prosecutors, D'Andrea said, and jurors had no choice but to find Cuadra innocent.

For his part, Melnick started off by saying that he could agree with D'Andrea on one point: "Joseph Kerekes is a murderer, but Joseph Kerekes isn't on trial. This wasn't a solo act."[30]

He said he also didn't care how Cuadra threw a football and that nothing disproved that Cuadra was "ripped" in his muscular development from being a "gym rat." "(Cuadra) certainly had the strength to behead and nearly decapitate Mr. Kocis," Melnick said.[31]

Melnick walked jurors through the now well explored mountain of circumstantial evidence looming over Cuadra and his freedom. He noted that Cuadra had purchased lighter fluid the day of Kocis' murder from a Wal-Mart store in Wilkes-Barre, but did not smoke. It was also the only lighter fluid sold anywhere in the U.S. that day by Wal-Mart, Melnick noted. "(Cuadra) doesn't smoke, nor does Kerekes but they're buying lighter fluid in the dead of a Pennsylvania winter," Melnick laid before jurors.[32]

Melnick reminded jurors that Cuadra operated what was considered, in the gay porn business, a mediocre website. "But you heard him. What did the defendant call himself? 'I'm a gay porn star.' He was a wanna be. He wanted to be a big deal."[33]

Melnick asked jurors to question seriously Cuadra's

testimony by considering: "Was the defendant telling the truth? He has the most at stake. He has a significant interest to lie and fabricate, and you have to take that into account. Does it ring true or is it complete, unadulterated fiction?"[34]

Cuadra's own words were damning, Melnick said, as he read from a letter Cuadra wrote trying to work up an alibi. "Innocent people don't need alibis," Melnick declared.[35]

Judge Olszewski took more than ninety minutes to read particularly detailed instructions to the jury about their deliberations, admitting from the bench that "these are the longest instructions I've ever given to a jury."[36] Olszewski told jurors that Cuadra could be found guilty of homicide in the case whether they believed he actually killed Kocis himself, was an accomplice to someone else killing him, or was part of a conspiracy to plan the murder of Kocis.

The verdict: Guilty

Jurors took three hours and thirty-four minutes (including time taken for smoke breaks and a lunch) to make up their mind. Deliberations were heated at times, jurors reported. On an initial vote, all eight men on the jury voted to convict Cuadra, two of the women voted to acquit, and two said they were unsure, confirmed two jurors, Stavitzski and James Scutt, III. Seated around a large round table in the jury room "everyone started giving their theory of the case, and two of the women were saying, 'I don't know if they proved enough,' and you know, some of us were very passionate about his guilt," Stavitzski said. "We would tell them all of the reasons we thought he was guilty, we would go over our theories, but it was getting a little heated."[37]

Some of the men decided to back up and avoid angering fellow jurors, something they thought would be unproductive to deliberations. A smoke break among the jurors who smoked and lunch helped ease tensions.

After lunch, some of the female jurors still remained

unconvinced and sought clarification about whether they could in fact find Cuadra guilty of murder even if they believed he was only an accomplice. The judge confirmed they could, and urged them to continue deliberating.

In the end, they found Cuadra guilty on all twelve counts he faced.

Cuadra sat silently and stared ahead as the verdicts were read. Perhaps heeding admonishments from Judge Olszewski, Cuadra's outspoken and emotional mother Gladis Zaldivar muttered quietly the word "No, no, no" over and over. Cuadra's sister Melissa told reporter Coulter Jones from the *Citizens Voice* that her mother was "hanging on by a thread" and that "We've believed in Harlow since the beginning that he's innocent. We know him."[38]

Kocis' mother and father quietly embraced one another and hugged and then shook the hands of Melnick and the rest of the prosecution team.

Outside the courtroom, Cuadra's mother had lost her ability to control her bubbling emotions. Cries and screams were heard as family members tried in vain to block her from the view of TV reporters and cameras. In broken English she cried out, "Joseph Kerekes! Joseph Kerekes! He is the killer, not my son!" As her family helped her make her way to the courthouse steps, Zaldivar was inconsolable. "My son is a victim! My son is a victim! I need my son!" she shouted and began to sob.[39]

The penalty phase: Life or death?

Under Pennsylvania law (and other states), the same jury that determined Cuadra's guilty or innocence must also consider a recommendation on sentencing: they would weigh whether Cuadra would be executed by the Commonwealth of Pennsylvania for his crimes or receive some lesser sentence. Pennsylvania law requires that the jury reach a unanimous decision on a penalty of death. Short of that, Olszewski would be required to impose a life sentence without parole.

Melnick and the District Attorney's Office had no reason to be hopeful the death penalty was achievable, as local media pointed out that it had been more than a decade since a Luzerne County jury had agreed to impose the death penalty on anyone. In fact, the *Times Leader* noted that since 1985, ten death penalty cases had been heard in Luzerne County and only one, the case of convicted child-killer Michael Bardo, had resulted in a death sentence.[40]

Melnick's argument focused on two aggravating circumstances he said existed that favor finding for a death sentence: the crime was committed as part of other felonies (such as robbery) and that Cuadra's acts put the lives of others at risk (to wit: firefighters who responded to the house fire set after the murder).

He repeated his suggestion that Cuadra had fled the Navy to avoid serving during a period of military conflict in Iraq and Afghanistan. "Did the defendant, as he's presenting, demonstrate selfless sacrifice or selfish indulgence?" Melnick asked.[41]

Cuadra's counsel Paul Walker focused jurors on what he said were mitigating factors in the defendant's favor, such as his basically crime-free background, his military career and service, alleged sexual abuse suffered as a child, poverty experienced as a child, and his mental and psychological state as a result of his relationship with Kerekes.

"The defense can also ask the jury to show mercy, which is a legally recognized mitigating factor," reporter Terrie Morgan-Besecker wrote in the *Times Leader*. "It, by itself, can outweigh all other factors in a jury's decision."[42]

Both sides presented testimony, all of it highly emotional.

Cuadra's mother and his brother José Cuadra outlined for jurors the difficult childhood and adolescence Harlow had experienced because of poverty and alleged childhood sexual molestation. His mother noted, "Before he was born, I fought for his life. And I fight for his life now. That is all I can say." She told jurors that she acted immediately when she learned her middle son may have been a victim of sexual abuse, and said, "It's embarrassing, I'm sorry, I didn't know, I didn't know," as she turned sobbing toward her son at the defense table.[43]

At least two jurors were unmoved by Cuadra's mother and felt she may have attempted to manipulate emotions of jurors in the courtroom, even "synchronizing" her weeping to that of Cuadra during key moments in the testimony. They also noted Mrs. Zaldivar positioned herself on a hallway bench near the jury deliberation room, and "every time we took that route, she was there crying," Stavitzski said.[44] "She'd be out on the bench, crying out loud," fellow juror Scutt confirmed, adding that a baby was sometimes present, who was also wailing and crying.[45]

Jurors Stavitzski and Scutt took note of testimony that revealed Cuadra had had no contact with his family for more than six years, and sent them no money during a period of time he boasted he was making hundreds of thousands of dollars as an escort and porn actor. "If you loved your mother that much, and she's that poor, why wouldn't you send her a couple thousand bucks?" Scutt asked.[46]

During the penalty phase, Kocis' father Michael also testified on behalf of his family about what the brutal murder and loss of his son had meant to their family. Calling Bryan "my first and only son," Michael Kocis detailed what he believed were the positive aspects of his son's life and asked jurors to forgive him for his inability to get out his entire statement without weeping. "We have been through hell," Michael Kocis said. "It will never be over for us."[47]

The jury speaks

"One-by-one, they walked past Harlow Cuadra without looking at him," *Times Leader* reporter Edward Lewis wrote about the scene unfolding in Wilkes-Barre. He noted the same twelve people who had found him guilty of murder "will walk past Cuadra perhaps for the final time today as they decide if he should spend the rest of his life in prison or be executed."[48]

Jury members took just over five hours before returning to the courtroom to report via their elected foreman that they were unable to reach a unanimous decision on the penalty of death. The jury foreman told the judge that the jury could not reach a unanimous verdict on one of the two aggravating factors argued by the state. Later jurors revealed that eight jurors agreed that it was Cuadra who had actually cut Kocis' throat, but four jurors remained unsure or disagreed. As a result, they never discussed the death penalty. "No one (knew) who did the actual deed of slashing the man's throat," juror Ellen Matulis told reporters. She said she believed Cuadra could have just been an accomplice of Kerekes in committing the murder.[49]

Matulis said feelings ran high among jurors during their deliberations. "I'd be a liar if I said voices weren't raised," she said. "Obviously, if you got people who want a death penalty, it gets tense. We carried a person's life in our hands."[50]

Another juror, retired postal worker Daniel Austin, said that he felt Cuadra's testimony was particularly unhelpful to his case. "He shot himself in the foot with the different lies," Austin said. "In my eyes, Harlow was definitely the one who did the actually killing."[51]

Matulis agreed that any thought of "reasonable doubt went out the window when (Cuadra) opened his mouth," noting that his testimony clearly placed himself at the murder scene.[52]

Juror Stavitzski agreed, noting that it was next to impossible to match Cuadra's version of the murder (and his claim that Kocis uttered words after having his throat slashed) with the physical evidence presented by the pathologist. "That kind of set everything in motion for us," Stavitzski said.[53]

Fellow juror Scutt said he felt "Cuadra talked in circles on the witness stand," but it was no wonder. "That entire prosecution team was writing down every word Harlow said on the stand, they were just writing and writing," he said. "So when Melnick got up there (to cross-examine him), they were handing him all kinds of notes, like it was a shark feeding frenzy."[54]

Cuadra's testimony became key for jurors, Scutt said, characterizing the defendant's testimony as "the only direct evidence" that jurors heard, "everything else was circumstantial evidence, there was no DNA presented, no eyewitness to point to Cuadra directly."[55] "The most important witness in any criminal case, no matter if it's homicide, burglary, or whatever, is the defendant himself, because he has the most to lose or gain," Scutt said. "So, you've got to look at the credibility of all witnesses. The defendant himself, you have to put a little more weight on how he testifies and Harlow Cuadra had two years to rehearse his testimony."[56]

Even with two years to polish his story, Scutt said Cuadra "still got up there and gave all of these different versions of what happened, and the guy was full of shit. I mean, I'm just being honest...he was full of shit."[57] Stavitzski agreed, noting "Harlow's testimony was erratic...he had more holes in his story than Swiss cheese."[58]

Some of the jurors found precise testimony and evidence concerning a specific "window" in which Kocis was likely killed most compelling. They noted Kocis' neighbor Amy Withers testified that as she bathed inside her home (located just a few feet north of Kocis' driveway) at 7:26 P.M., she heard a car door open and close next door. Representatives of America Online reported Kocis' open access to their services ended at 8:12 P.M. (reflecting the time when the computer towers were likely pulled by the perpetrator). Withers' friend Amy Zamerowski reported she witnessed the silver SUV backing from Kocis' driveway precisely as she drove by at 8:26 P.M. en route to her friend's house next door. Zamerowski said she was inside Withers' home only five minutes before another neighbor began knocking on the door, warning them to get out because of the fire at the adjacent Kocis home. Records showed the Dallas Fire Department was called at 8:32 P.M. and arrived on the scene less than two minutes later.

Service on a jury in any case is difficult, but that is especially so in a murder case and one where jurors are asked to consider the death penalty. Deliberations on the death penalty were unproductive, Stavitzski and Scutt said, because some of the jurors placed more weight in mitigating factors in Cuadra's favor.

After the trial, juror Matulis said her life "has been changed" from her experience and that "the shock of actually seeing some of this, it was mind-boggling seeing a burnt corpse, a heart cut with stab wounds."[59]

Scutt was also moved. "Don't think this wasn't difficult on me, because it was," he said. "Bryan Kocis was no angel, none of us are," he said. "It's like a boss of mine used to say, 'Everything travels in a big circle,' and (I think) the circle of life killed Bryan Kocis. He victimized people for profit in a not-so-honest business, and Harlow Cuadra just showed up in his life how many years later, working in the same not-so-honest business and he victimized Bryan Kocis."[60]

"Tell me who was more over the edge in life?" Scutt asked. "I would say Harlow Raymond Cuadra (because) Bryan Kocis, along with any other human being, didn't deserve to die that horrible death."[61]

Hindsight

In hindsight, defense attorneys D'Andrea and Walker both agreed that Cuadra's testimony at trial had "done more harm than he did good," but it was something they felt they had to do. D'Andrea defended having put Cuadra on the stand to tell his story to the jury. He said doing so allowed Cuadra to explain why the evidence collected by police investigators showed he was at the murder victim's home. Trying to "get around" that evidence, D'Andrea said, would be unwise. Their focus instead was on helping jurors to believe that Kerekes was the killer, not Cuadra.

Kerekes, who backed out of testifying for Cuadra's defense at the last minute, "again showed that (he) was trying to control Harlow Cuadra's life," D'Andrea said.[62] D'Andrea said he personally talked to Kerekes inside the Luzerne County Courthouse just five minutes before he was called as a witness, and that Kerekes was going to offer testimony to exonerate Cuadra of the murder. Between the time they talked, however, and when Kerekes was called, he changed his mind. "It appeared to be very evident the commonwealth's evidence was that our client was at the residence when this happened," D'Andrea told reporters. "It seemed imperative to me the position the defense had to take was that our client *was* there."[63]

D'Andrea seemed to take victory from the fact that the jury would not and could not recommend the death penalty. "Academically, it feels good that they said by their verdict that he wasn't the killer…the jury did not believe our client deserved the death penalty," D'Andrea said. In his view, if Cuadra had been a stronger witness, "we may have gotten a better result," but also supported the idea of having Cuadra testify. "He has to take the stand in a death penalty case, there was no question he had to," Walker said.[64]

"(Cuadra) wasn't the best witness," D'Andrea acknowledged. "We were hoping he would have been much more cooperative on the stand, not as combative (with the prosecutor)."[65]

D'Andrea said Cuadra's testimony at trial capped more than twenty years of frustration and silence about how his life had progressed, stretching back into his history of sexual molestation and intense poverty as a child. "He had a whole life of emotions that came out in twenty-four hours on the witness stand," D'Andrea remarked.[66]

For members of Melnick's team, including members of the district attorney's staff and state and local police investigators, the victory was sweet. Melnick's voice cracked with emotion as he talked with reporters at the trial's end, the gag order imposed by Judge Olszewski finally lifted. Words like "unbelievable" and "magnificent" came from Melnick's mouth as he declared his team "the hardest working trial team in Pennsylvania." The sentiment was shared by Melnick's boss, Luzerne County DA Jackie Musto Carroll who said, "In all of my years as a district attorney, I have never seen a trial team work so hard." Melnick heaped most of his praise, however, on police investigators who drove the case forward.[67]

Regarding Cuadra's testimony at trial, Melnick said his team had prepared for that possibility and assessed his performance as "very poor, contradictory, and utterly inconsistent."[68]

Melnick also said Kerekes surprise announcement that he would not testify, after apparently telling defense attorneys he would, was no surprise to Melnick. He said his interactions with Kerekes had convinced him that "the last thing I wanted was Kerekes as a witness on my side."[69]

As it worked out, Melnick said, Kerekes became "their problem, not ours."[70]

Paying for the blockbuster trial was the problem of Luzerne County taxpayers. Media reports indicated the county spent more than $112,000 to prosecute both Cuadra and Kerekes. "It was a very expensive prosecution," DA Musto Carroll acknowledged. Defending Cuadra and Kerekes would also cost local taxpayers, reportedly more than $25,000.[71]

Some final words

After the jury, judge, and lawyers had all exited Courtroom No. 2 in the Luzerne County Courthouse, only Cuadra and Sheriff's deputies remained as he sat in a chair next to his mother for a final good-bye as the winter darkness of an early March sunset took over the cold air outside. Cuadra's mother could no longer contain her emotions, and sobbed bitterly and deeply for her son as jail deputies removed Cuadra from the courtroom.

The following Monday, Cuadra was back in the courtroom before Judge Olszewski to formally learn his sentence. Reporters noted Cuadra, now in handcuffs and shackles "dropped his shoulders and leaned back" as Olszewski sentenced him to two consecutive life terms without a chance of parole for killing Kocis. Olszewski told Cuadra, "I certainly hope that a day does not go by for the rest of your life that you do not remember the tragedy, the grief, the pain, the endless pain, that you have caused."[72]

Following his sentence, tears began to fill Cuadra's eyes. Convicted and condemned to life in prison at age twenty-seven, he will be in prison for many more years than he was ever a free man. Both Cuadra and his mother quietly mouthed "I love you" to one another as he was led from the courtroom and returned to jail.

Bryan Kocis' father said sitting through the trial had been an ordeal, but one they had to endure. "You hear the lies, the lie after lie after lie…the dramatics that Cuadra himself put on that you know he was lying through his teeth when he was talking. To sit there and listen to that, it's all I could do not to explode," Michael Kocis said.[73]

Bryan's mother, Joyce, said she often sits in a chair next to a table holding the vase of her son's ashes. "People say, you know, have closure," she said. "Justice. We have justice, but we don't have closure. We don't have him."[74]

CHAPTER 13
Epilogue

"Much like Bryan's personal home and residence, my world went up in smoke and flames when he was killed. The truth is…when Bryan was killed, everything in my world crumbled to my feet. All of my plans, hopes and aspirations were put on hold until I could get a grip on the situation."
—Sean Lockhart

"If you pay enough attention, you can actually see people carrying their tears around like sacks of stones."
—Harlow Cuadra letter to "Natasha"

Joe Kerekes with time on his hands

Joe Kerekes will spend the rest of his life inside the Pennsylvania Department of Corrections unless a quixotic appeal effort succeeds in winning him post-conviction relief in the form of parole. That seems entirely unlikely, however, as Kerekes accepted a plea agreement that included a life sentence with no chance for parole. For now, the State Correctional Institution at Huntingdon, Pennsylvania is home. The prison, one of the state's oldest maximum facilities, opened originally in 1889 as a reformatory for juveniles, but was transformed into a maximum-security prison for men, and now operates as a "close-security institution," according to the Pennsylvania Department of Corrections. The Huntingdon prison walls and giant rolls of barbed and rip wire fencing dominates its dense, working-class neighborhood as it likely always has. Just a block in one direction is a wide tributary of the famous Susquehanna River, the Juniata River, and a few blocks in the other direction is the new Wal-Mart, proudly serving this aging town of just over 6,000 residents.

Kerekes reports he fills his days with weight-lifting and watching TV, or spending time in a day room area where inmates are allowed to congregate during certain times of the day. He resides in a 7' x 7' cell and gang-showers with the rest of the men in his unit. Joe's family, so far about his only visitors, can see him face-to-face and embrace him quickly in a community room carved out near the aging limestone arches at the front of the nineteenth-century fortress. Guests fill out forms and are sent through a metal detector, and often have their cars or bodies searched, prior to reaching the community room, before they can visit an inmate held at Kerekes' level.

The community room resembles the faculty office of any middle school in America, with rows of mismatched chairs taking up the center of the room and along one side of the walls bearing institutional-pink paint. No tables are provided to inmates or their guests. Those are reserved for the two or three DOC officers who remain in the room constantly.

Joe Kerekes bounded into this room one summer day in 2009 with seemingly more confidence than anyone else in the place. Family members and loved ones of the other seven inmates present whispered their visiting remarks quietly to the easily-identified inmates who all wore off-brown shirts and pants marked "DOC" on the back. Joe's jail garb fits his stature well, his looking more like light brown surgical scrubs than a jail uniform. The weightlifting he has resumed while in prison has helped bulk him up again to resemble more of his pre-arrest days. His ever-receding hairline is doing so in an attractive, orderly pattern, especially since Joe wears his hair very short. Take Joe Kerekes out of the prison, and he could pass any day, anywhere, as a suburban father standing on the sidelines cheering his kids at a soccer game.

But games, family, and a life outside of the Huntingdon walls are all but impossible. For reasons he seemingly is still struggling to explain, Kerekes accepted a plea "deal" or agreement in December 2008 that keeps him locked up for life with no chance of parole. In retrospect, it looks like anything but the best deal for a defendant, since Kerekes was not compelled and ultimately did not give testimony against his co-conspirator, Harlow Cuadra, who continues to insist he did not personally kill anyone. It is, however, a deal that allows Luzerne County prosecutors to feel comfortable. It's what the residents of Luzerne County, including Bryan Kocis' family, wanted.

Life without possibilities

Kerekes struggles with the reality of his life sentence. Since arriving at Huntingdon, he's befriended other inmates who are similarly situated on murder charges that brought life sentences, but who have the chance of parole. "I was misled," he says about the discussions with his attorney and the state that led to his guilty plea. Kerekes also feels he was threatened. Kerekes says he felt pressure from the district attorney's office to accept the plea or face the possibility that authorities would somehow seek to draw his parents into the investigation. He says the DA made it clear that his parents, because of their help in moving items from the Stratem Court home and helping their son prior to his arrest, could have been charged with "aiding and abetting" a criminal. "I couldn't put my parents through anymore," Kerekes says in a phrase strikingly similar to what he said during his aborted appearance on the stand in Cuadra's trial. "They hadn't done anything wrong. All they did was get some of my stuff for me and my dad went and picked up a car for me from the repair shop when I asked him to."[1]

The DA doesn't comment about people they have not charged (such as Kerekes' parents), but Kerekes says the pressure was real, including the spring day in 2007 when Harlow and Joe were still watching over their shoulder, waiting for the cops to swoop in. On one of those days investigators paid a visit to Joe's parent's house, and Joe called while they were there. Joe refused their requests to come and meet with investigators, with Joe recalling, "My mother was like, 'Joe, what is this all about? We need to talk to you, honey.' But I was not going to go there as long as the cops were there."[2]

His impulse that day, to leave his parents talking to the police while he and Cuadra went further underground, reflects just some of the impulsiveness that seems to have led to tough times throughout his life. Combined with a quick temper that is hard to conceal, he finds himself out of chances and out of a life of freedom.

Perhaps it was impulsiveness that led him to agree originally, and then recant, on a deal to come to Cuadra's trial and provide testimony that may have exonerated Cuadra of killing Bryan Kocis. "I was ready to go into court and lie for Harlow," Kerekes says. "I had talked to his attorney and I told them I would go in and back up their story about Harlow being at (Bryan's) house to model and that I burst in during a jealous rage and killed him." But "that is not the truth. I'm telling you just as I told my parents this, I told them and I tell you, I did not kill Bryan."[3]

Kerekes is back to telling the story he told investigators just before he signed his plea agreement: "I was back at the hotel (while Kocis was killed), and there is nothing that proves I was there."[4]

The DA believes Kerekes' version, but also know that Pennsylvania law does not provide any sort of "out" for a person who assists in planning, executing, and concealing a murder, even if they weren't present for the actual act. The lead prosecutor, Assistant DA Melnick believes Kerekes was likely to get the death penalty, and that is the reason he took the deal.[5]

"He was probably the less likeable in any possible jury's eyes," concurs Deputy DA Shannon Crake.[6]

Kerekes' dislike of prosecutors and investigators is, as expected, intense. A June 2009 visit by Melnick and Hannon to see Kerekes in order to "profile" him angered him considerably. Kerekes said Melnick and State Police Corporal Leo Hannon sought to conduct "a series of interviews (with me) in which they will probe my life, from babe 'till today, so they, law enforcement, can catch 'minds' like mine."[7]

Kerekes said he was told this was part of his plea agreement, but said, "I swore to them it was not part of my plea deal nor was I ever informed of the same. I met with them for a half hour...I clammed up (and) resisted this effort of theirs and told them I wasn't going to cooperate."[8]

Long days and nights

For now, Kerekes follows the prison doctor's orders and takes daily medications that include psychotropic drugs meant to level and control his personality, including anger and resulting impulsive acts. "I'm following all the rules and establishing a good record for myself so there will be no reason from my time here that they will say I cannot get a parole someday," he says hopefully.[9]

Spend a little time with Kerekes, and one notices a rather dramatic sadness that comes over him now and again. While his voice is up and he speaks fast about his unending love for Harlow Cuadra and their success as male escorts and porn producers, he does drift into melancholy. He finds himself agreeing with a painful description of him offered by his former pastor and mentor, Ron Johnston, that declared that a "dichotomy between good and evil" rages inside Kerekes. [10] When pressed how his internal struggles to make the right choices between good and bad are any more vexing than those of any other person, Kerekes adds, without explanation, "I've done some really bad things in my life. I have not lived a life that has pleased or served God."[11]

Looking back, he regrets leaving the church and seminary, and although he continually insists he is not gay and says he will never identify himself as such, he recalls with a low voice, "Harlow said to me once that I should have focused on being a pastor in (a gay) church."[12]

Prison seems to hold some relief for Kerekes. Gone are the days of having to hustle up thousands of dollars a day from online porn or sexual encounters from anyone willing to pay. Gone is the nice house that was mortgaged to the rafters with bill collectors at every turn. Gone is the worry that a life built on lies and innuendo must bring. The prison feeds him well, Kerekes says, and he enjoys most of his fellow inmates and the workouts they can undertake in the prison gym.

His biggest worry now, he says, is trying to overcome persistent insomnia.

A couple of years into his sentence, Kerekes learned of his father's September 2010 death via a telephone call from family members. Someone later posted a heartfelt, online condolence note from Joe expressing his love for his father that said in part, "I never met one single man on Earth with such meekness, piety, honor, patience, long-suffering and faith. You ARE the perfect Father, never pressuring, never hurting. Only loving, supporting, and uplifting."[13]

Covering a very unusual trial

Mark Guydish, an opinion writer for the *Times Leader* newspaper in Wilkes-Barre, offered a thoughtful analysis of the Kocis murder case. He noted Luzerne County residents had become accustomed to some level of controversy and problems downtown at the courthouse, but the courthouse remained "a majestic house, a metaphor for justice."[14]

Guydish provided a detailed description of Courtroom No. 2, where Judge Peter Paul Olszewski presided over the Luzerne County Court of Common Pleas. "Sweeping paintings" above Olszewski's bench depict a series of judicial virtues, including rectitude, courage, moderation, learning, and wisdom. "Into this larger-than-life setting walks Harlow Cuadra, a man with a name suitable for a sports car, or maybe a pulp-novel villain," Guydish surmised. "He looks more like an oversized Opie than the murderer he is accused of being, shoulders slightly rounded, as he strolls to his seat."[15]

The Commonwealth of Pennsylvania versus Harlow Raymond Cuadra had become "so big lawyers almost literally trip over it as they present their arguments. Cardboard boxes stacked under tables bulge with documents. Ring binders nearly a half-foot thick sprawl on the foot of desks," Guydish added.[16]

Cuadra's trial is and was a big deal for Luzerne County, but hardly the first or last big deal to come this way. What stood out here, Guydish pointed out, were the sometimes lurid details that emerged from a case that stretched from unlikely-Dallas Township "to late-night cocktails of Las Vegas casinos, the sandy beaches of San Diego, the hills of Virginia (back to) the cell phone towers of the Back Mountain and even a hotel in Plains Township."[17]

Times Leader reporter Edward Lewis, who covered the trial for local readers, also commented on the novelty of reporting on a gay porn murder trial. "Luzerne County sure has its share of high-profile and dramatic murder trials in recent memory," Lewis wrote. A reporter with more than a decade of experience covering courts and crimes, Lewis said "reporting about this case was certainly different than all the other murder cases that I've covered."[18]

It was Lewis who tracked down Cuadra before he had been charged and arrested with the murder of Bryan Kocis. Lewis also found himself logging onto gay porn websites and blogs of all types to learn more about his subject.[19]

Reporter Sue Henry from WILK Radio in Wilkes-Barre covered the trial for her listeners and offered her analysis: "You've got to hand it to Harlow Cuadra. He knows how to play the part. Although skies outside were overcast with a hint of drizzle, Harlow lit up a Luzerne County courtroom...with the performance of his life." Henry noted that Cuadra took the stand against the advice of his attorneys and "casually" told jurors about "his dual careers as a male escort and pornographic actor."[20] She quoted Cuadra as saying, "I fit the part and that's all that matters," noting that he sounded like a person answering a cast call for a play or musical, rather than a man fighting for his life and freedom. "Removing his square-framed glasses, the boyish Harlow faced the folks who might hold his life in their hands and detailed the fine points of the male escort/actor trade, mentioning the hungry nature of the newcomers and the quest for site traffic on an internet business," Henry reported.[21]

The Times Leader's Guydish tried to cut through all of the drama in some of his analysis of the case. "As you learn of the sprawling, seedy, even sadistic saga of Bryan Kocis and the two-week trial of his alleged murderer, Harlow Cuadra, it's easy to get lost in details that include nuances such as cell phone tower placement, or the storyline shifting from Virginia to Nevada to California to Florida to Pennsylvania," he wrote. It's tempting to get "stalled in the visceral response to the sordid topics" the trial presented, or that some had become "disgusted by the notion that you should waste time on homicide among homosexuals peddling porn and gay prostitution," Guydish noted.[22]

But Guydish made an important point often lost in the sensational nature of the trial. "Regardless of your response to the men involved or their actions and fates, there is something else more primal to remember. There are other characters who have been little more than flitting shadows on this stage. These people have families."[23]

At long last, Lockhart gets to make his denial

Almost a year after Bryan Kocis' murder and shortly before Harlow Cuadra's murder trial began, Sean Lockhart finally took up the issue of his former friend's death in a sustained form. In a December 15, 2007 blog posting, he discussed pre-trial preparations for Harlow Cuadra's upcoming trial and his expected return trip to Pennsylvania. "Let's face it, making comments or even acknowledging any of (the facts of the Kocis case) has been very difficult for Grant and me," he wrote.[24] Still cautioning that saying too much about the case put the chances of convicting Cuadra at risk, Lockhart said, "I can tell all of you definitely that Grant and I did not have anything to do with this heinous and wrongful act and that we are doing what we can to bring justice to Bryan's family, despite the very public and hurtful public feud carried on between us."[25]

Lockhart said he knew there were doubters and many who believed he and his partner were somehow responsible for the murder, "but until you find yourself in the position Grant and I have found ourselves in, you'll never be able to see from our perspective. When the world and your industry insists on implicating you as a murder suspect, nothing good can come of that. Grant and I put everything on the line to voluntarily take part in a two-day wire tap that ultimately provided the Pennsylvania authorities with evidence."[26]

Finally able to air his denials, Lockhart confessed that feelings of depression and low self-esteem overwhelmed him at times in the long months between the arrest of Cuadra and Kerekes in May 2007, and the Kerekes plea agreement entered in December 2008 and the Cuadra trial in March 2009. "Lots of damage has been done," Lockhart wrote in a February 2009 blog posting on www.brentcorriganinc.com. "All those who persecuted me and insisted I had everything to do with Bryan's death; they will never come forward and admit they were wrong. All those 'publications' and web portals that reported on it in the beginning...will never correct their assumptions."[27]

Lockhart reactions remain strong

Lockhart's career appears to be as strong as ever as he remains one of the most popular actors in gay porn. His latest efforts have been well-received, by fans, at least. In 2009, he earned thirteen separate nominations for the Gay Adult Video News Awards. Lockhart was nominated for "Best Supporting Actor," "Best Sex Scene," and "Best Group Scene" for his role in *The Porne Ultimatum*, a movie produced by Dirty Bird Pictures. Lockhart won separate nominations for "Performer of the Year," "Best Actor," "Best Bottom," and "Best All-Sex Film" for another role in another Dirty Bird production, *Just the Sex*. He also won a nomination for "Best Pro-Am Film" for *Brent Corrigan's Summit*, a film he directed.

In 2010, he was nominated and won awards at the GayVNs for "Best Web Performer" of the year and for "Best Amateur/ Pro-Am Release" of the year for *Brent Corrigan's Big Easy*. He also won a special "fan award" as "Best Bottom" performing in gay porn. The Fleshjack Company also released its latest plastic sex products, including a Brent Corrigan dildo, mouth, and anus formed from molds made by Lockhart and featuring his image in the promotional materials.

The 2009 GayVN Awards were punctuated, however, by an open attack on Lockhart by rival gay porn actor and producer Michael Lucas. Lucas sent Twitter messages to his fan base that he "had Brent Corrigan (Lockhart) kicked out of the GayVN Awards tonight...that criminal brat has put too many in this industry at risk already."[28]

At one point, Lucas even took to the stage of the awards as organizers attempted to present an award honoring the "Association of Sites Advocating Child Protection," interrupting proceedings to make his feelings about Lockhart known.

Later Lucas explained his actions by saying "I want(ed) to stress that the reason I am coming down hard on the industry reporters rooting for (Lockhart), and (the) judges embracing him, is that his claim to fame is that he was involved in child pornography. This made him a name and instead of being disgusted, they are mesmerized by it. That is revolting. I hold the conviction that we need to protect (the adult film industry) and our youths; it is a civil duty, a moral challenge, an imperative task from which we cannot escape."[29]

Lockhart's reply was to the point: "I've done everything I can to set it straight. I've issued numerous apologies in every venue that would talk to me. I've done everything I can to apologize."[30]

Despite this rather open harangue, Lockhart claims that Lucas once inquired about casting him in one of his films in 2006. "There were a few short e-mails back and forth between myself and one of Michael Lucas' assistants," Lockhart told blogger Jason Sechrest. Lucas acknowledged the approach to Lockhart, but said, he, like everyone else, was unaware that Lockhart was ever underage as a performer. No deal was ever arranged for Lockhart to appear in a Lucas production.[31]

Lockhart going mainstream?

One of Lockhart's forays into mainstream productions, a non-sexual role in the 2008 gay spring break romp, *Another Gay Sequel: Gays Gone Wild*, was marginally successful and presented Lockhart in the part of Stan the Merman (read: Mermaid). The film won a nomination for "Best Alternative Release" from the GayVN Awards, and featured other gay icons such as Ru Paul, Perez Hilton, Scott Thompson, Wil Wikle, and Jim Verraros. *Another Gay Sequel* had limited theatrical release, first in New York, Los Angeles, and Fort Lauderdale, Florida, but eventually was scheduled for runs in other large markets and has enjoyed significant success as a DVD rental as well.[32]

Lockhart also gained a credited, non-speaking part in director Gus Van Sant's Oscar-winning 2008 release, *Milk*.[34] "I don't think I'll make it as a mainstream (actor), but never say never," Lockhart said. "I have some talent and if you nurture it, it can grow."[33]

In 2008, Lockhart announced his new production company, Prodigy Pictures, was teaming up again with Dirty Bird Pictures, this time to produce *Brent Corrigan's Summit*. *Summit* was a follow-up to his earlier collaboration with Dirty Bird for the wildly successful *The Porne Ultimatum*.

Summit consists of Lockhart in the title role hosting nine other guys in a Lake Tahoe mountain cabin for a "reality style" orgy-fest. Established gay porno star Mason Wyler appears as did others from the Active Duty studios of Dink Flamingo. The film's script was co-written by Grant Roy.

Lockhart called completion of the four-scene, two-hour film "one of the sweetest victories of my life" after "a three-year journey, fraught with seemingly insurmountable obstacles, setbacks, and scandals. The Cobra civil suit prevented me from making money, but did not prevent me from being productive. Being fucked out of my first website and business venture set me back eight months. Then having the trial looming overhead for so long, all of these things have severely limited my potential. None of these things have persisted to stand in my way but if it's not THIS then it's THAT. They sky is now the limit…"[34]

How long does Lockhart plan to stay in gay porn? In a May 2009 post to his website, Lockhart notes "In a lot of ways, just doing porn is beginning to make me feel less of a person. The sad part is, there was once a market and a place for the difference between what porn is and what I want to do with the adult industry."[35]

Lockhart moves on

Sean Lockhart is many things to many people, but there is almost universal agreement that he is, often, dramatic. In the gay world, he might even be called "a drama queen" or "a diva."

He took up on his blog what had happened to him over the course of the years since he came to know Bryan Kocis, learned of his death, and participated in bringing his killers to justice.

Immediately upon returning to California after testifying in Cuadra's murder trial, he told his fans, "I feel completely and utterly deflated right now. While it may appear to be a hasty departure, the truth is, I'm not sure all of me is ready to put the polishing touches on this chapter of my life. I feel so…unfulfilled, like a spirit lingering and longing to carry out unfinished business."[36] He admitted to feeling overwhelmed with the idea of even trying to explain all that he had experienced. "Often times, I sit back and I wonder what the percentage is of my readers and fans that even have any clue that I've toiled with this predicament," Lockhart wrote.[37] "Much like Bryan's personal home and residence, my world went up in smoke and flames when he was killed. The truth is…when Bryan was killed, everything in my world crumbled to my feet. All of my plans, hopes and aspirations were put on hold until I could get a grip on the situation."[38]

If his bravado and self-centered assessment passed over the fact it was Kocis who ultimately suffered most, he didn't seem to care. He credited his ex-lover and business partner Grant Roy for being "the thread, and I was the needle."[39]

He admitted what anyone who read the transcript of the police intercepts of Cuadra and Kerekes could tell: he was frightened to death during most of those proceedings. "I had a job to do despite my fear of my life," he said during Cuadra's trial. "I had to play it off as if everything was fine."[40]

Citing his desire to "move on" and fight temptations to go back over the past and look for more ways he could have avoided struggles, he said, "It's best to just move on" and added,

"I'm growing tiresome of living this extraordinary life. It's time for me to just settle down and make a little porn."[41]

Moving on from porn, and from Roy, has been addressed by Lockhart more than once in his blog. In a July 2009 entry, he noted: "The truth is, right now in my life I'm in at a crossroads. My mainstream work is taking up more and more time than ever before."[42]

He also confessed differences were erupting between him and Roy about how to run Lockhart's career and their porn ventures. "The trouble we are finding is our past: which is varied and spotted with much misfortune," he said. "Though (Grant and I) love each other very much, it has become increasingly difficult to put our differences aside."[43]

Lockhart again hinted at leaving gay porn outright. "There's only so much you can create with porn and sex before you find yourself on a loop," he wrote. "In many ways, I feel I am outgrowing the adult industry. This doesn't mean I want to leave it behind. It does mean I need to find other ways to flex my artistic muscle. The deeper I get into the porn world the more I realize how *base* it is."[44]

A month later, Lockhart complained openly to his fans via his blog about the so-far lackluster sales of his latest porn venture, *Brent Corrigan's Big Easy* (sales figures that didn't prevent the epic from being named the 2010 Gay VN "Amateur/Pro-Am" gay porn feature of the year.) "I believe I have every right to voice these frustrations and feelings. I know I run the risk of coming off like a bitch. I understand people are losing their jobs *all over the world* at an alarming rate," but he lamented few sales from people who often claimed to be his supporters. Lockhart proclaimed: "If you think I'm angry, I'm not. I'm thoroughly disappointed. It's plain to see." [45]

He again raised the specter of leaving porn outright. "I'm not that lonely, sad little boy just looking for friends and admirers anymore," he wrote. "When I entered into this industry and even started writing (on a blog), I admit now that much of that was about self validation. I was desperately searching for approval and interest. I needed the attention because I was building my self esteem. I've grown up now and reality has set in. Validation and self confidence doesn't mean anything if you're living in a tent on the street corner of F Street in the East Village."[46]

The Kocis family and Cobra Video

Bryan Kocis' family has faded back into their private lives, the kind of privacy most families in the tight-knit communities of northeast Pennsylvania treasure. It was never their desire to be the lead story on the local TV news or the front page of the area's two daily newspapers. The murder and trial completed, more than two years of emotional ups and down were mostly over. As one might expect, Kocis' parents have given few interviews or comments since the trial. Their mourning delayed, their grief work lies ever around them.

Kocis' sister, Melody Bartusek, did offer comments briefly, both during the time of Cuadra's trial and afterward. Otherwise, she too seemed ready to move on with her life. She did not hold back, however, on a continued contempt held for Sean Lockhart. "(Bryan) was known for giving everyone the benefit of the doubt," she said. "Bryan made mistakes, but he was a victim of a horrible crime, and it was sad how many people forgot that. Sean Lockhart was Bryan's biggest mistake. He cared for Sean very much and Sean did nothing but hurt him."[47]

She said her brother was planning to keep a promise to get Lockhart out of the porn business and help him go to college, as he said he wanted to do. Lockhart claimed that those offers of help, however, came with strings attached that he remain in Pennsylvania and be romantically involved with Kocis.

Bartusek said, "I was with Bryan when Sean told him he wasn't coming back to finish his contract with Cobra, and that he was starting his own company. Bryan (had) just bought him a car. I will never forget how upset Bryan was. Unfortunately, Bryan is not here to tell his side of the story."[48]

The Kocis family is bitter about Lockhart's efforts to "make it look like he was the victim, but the victim was Bryan the whole time."

Kocis' sister takes issue with the claims that her brother did not check Lockhart's ID prior to making porn videos with him. "Sean lied from the beginning to get into the business, and then once he was in…he made a plan with Grant (Roy) to take Bryan for everything he was worth."[49]

Beyond the hard feelings that exist between Kocis' kin and Lockhart and Roy, the Kocis family does not believe Lockhart was involved in killing Bryan. "But I think if he wasn't involved at all, he should have warned Bryan of Harlow and Joe after the famous Las Vegas dinner," Bartusek said. "Grant and Sean did help the police, and for that we are grateful." She added, "The part that gets me so mad is that Sean has no remorse for anything he did and the hatred that he created against Bryan. I believe the events that took place and the public bad mouthing they did of Bryan led to the murder. I just wish Bryan would have never met Sean, maybe this would have never happened."[50]

Bartusek said she also is concentrated on "letting go of my anger toward (Sean and Grant) because they are not worth my attention and I have more important things in my life. Bryan and I believed in the saying 'What comes around goes around' and…ironically one of Bryan's other sayings he would tell me often is 'What doesn't kill you makes you stronger!' My life isn't ever going to be the same without him!"[51]

The Kocis family *is* convinced the right men were convicted of killing their loved one. They were pleased and thankful for the police and prosecutors who worked so hard in bringing the case to a close.

Disgusted at what she considers serial lying Cuadra conducted on the witness stand during his trial, she added, "I wish he (would have) got the death penalty, but I'm very happy he will be in prison the rest of his life." While still angry at Kerekes, Bartusek said the family was at least "happy that Joe owned up to what he did and at least apologized. It does give some closure. Harlow made himself look like a victim of Joe, but it was really the other way around."[52]

In October 2010, EuroMedia Distribution announced it had signed an exclusive, worldwide, multi-year DVD and licensing agreement with Cobra Video.[53] "We couldn't be more excited to be working hand-in-hand with Cobra Studios," said Hugo Harley, director of development for EuroMedia. "Beyond their still-popular back catalog, we will be overseeing a rebranding of the line and bringing some new releases and never-before-seen product to market. They have a strong brand and amazing content that delivers time and time again. We look forward to bringing their content to fans around the world."[54] Harley added that EuroMedia would also handle licensing of all broadcast, web licensing, and mobile rights for Cobra Videos. They also promised to release some "sure to be talked about (but) never-before-released scenes" from Cobra.[55]

The investigators

The men and women who dedicated countless hours of work on the Kocis case had little time to sit back and take a breath. In the two years after Kocis' murder, violent crime continued to rise in the community, including more than a dozen death penalty cases.

State police investigators continued to respond to requests from local communities to help investigate crimes, and local police continued their daily efforts to prevent and respond to crime. Sadly, the Bryan Kocis murder was not the first and certainly not the last to occur.

For Dallas Township Police Chief Robert Jolley and the seven officers on his department, their regular work serving the community goes on. Fortunately, the community averages only one homicide every seven to ten years.[56]

"What you do on a homicide case like this is that you bring in everyone that is available and you work it—you work it hard for the first two or three days," Dallas Township Detective Sergeant Doug Higgins said. "We had no idea how widespread this investigation was going to be."[57]

Higgins and Jolley said the investigation was "a huge effort." Both men expressed appreciation that Dallas Township supervisors were supportive of the effort to solve the crime. "I told (township officials), I cannot guarantee you when the end will come, but we need all of our guys out there working on this," Higgins said. "Their response to me was, 'Do what you have to do.'"[58]

And while the sexual orientation of the victims (and later the suspects) in the case would become known as gay, Higgins said that did not affect the investigation. "The way we looked at it is that we had a job to do, someone has been killed, and we were going to find the killer."[59]

Assistant DA Michael Melnick is satisfied with the outcome, especially the fact that both Cuadra and Kerekes are sentenced to life sentences with no chance of parole. "There is no parole for murder in Luzerne County," Melnick declares.[60]

Melnick's busy schedule continues, split between his work as a courtroom litigator for the district attorney's office and his private practice. The polite, cigar-smoking Melnick comes across as a conversational, friendly small-town lawyer, but in reality has established a reputation as a brilliant legal scrapper who stands up for the people of Luzerne County.

His law office, ironically on the busy Pennsylvania Route 309 in Shavertown, was along the route Cuadra and Kerekes had to follow from their motel room in Plains Township to the victim's home in the Back Mountain community of Dallas. While stopping short of calling the Cuadra-Kerekes case one of the biggest of his career, he does call the case very complex. Melnick is quick to credit local, state, and federal police investigators for their work in bringing the case to conclusion.

The judge in the Cuadra and Kerekes cases, Peter Paul Olszewski, Jr., stood for a ten-year retention vote in November 2009. In a rare outcome, voters turned Olszewski out of office. Although never implicated in scandals that swept two other Luzerne County judges from the bench under federal indictment, Olszewski's opponents nonetheless circulated a damaging photo of the judge unknowingly posing next to a convicted drug dealer. The result was catastrophic, with 33,800 county voters answering "no" to the question of whether to retain the judge; 22,471 voted "yes." Olszewski's loss was the first in decades for a sitting Luzerne County judge.

Harlow Cuadra appeals, and loses

While outspoken Wilkes-Barre attorney Demetrius Fannick did not succeed in representing Cuadra or Kerekes during their initial criminal proceedings, he did gain Cuadra as a client upon his conviction appeal. Fannick based most of the appeal, filed in August 2009, upon rulings he believed were in error; for example, allowing the Crab Catcher and Black's Beach transcripts into evidence, as well as items seized during searches of Cuadra's Virginia Beach home. Fannick also sought to have blocked from evidence on a retrial a video of Cuadra working out at the Big House Gym and autopsy photos of the victim.

The appeal allowed Fannick to continue arguing that he should never have been disallowed to represent Cuadra and concluded that the commonwealth's "evidence was insufficient to convict the defendant." Several of Fannick's appeal points were already addressed by Judge Olszewski prior to trial, including change of venue and use of victim photographs.[61]

In October 2010, the Superior Court of Pennsylvania upheld Cuadra's conviction and sentence in a five-page ruling. In it, the state's high court said Judge Olszewski's rulings in both pre-trial and trial proceedings were "well-detailed and well-reasoned." The judges added, "We can find no error in (the court's) factual findings and corollary legal conclusions."[62]

Seemingly undeterred, Fannick filed a new appeal to the Pennsylvania Supreme Court in late November 2010, perhaps the last long shot effort Cuadra could make to win release. It too failed. Defeated via the state's highest courts, it seemed unlikely Cuadra had any remaining hope of being released via this means.[63]

Harlow's life behind bars

Cuadra has talked little about his life behind bars to anyone but his immediate family and friends, but he revealed some of his experiences via a rather circuitous manner. In late 2009 and early 2010, on a web blog and YouTube videos posted by a young woman in England going by the name of "Natasha," published and later read and displayed on YouTube letters she had received from Cuadra.

Natasha told her followers that she had been writing to Cuadra and promised to show them one at a time. In her first letter from Cuadra, he details having received Natasha's first missive just as the paperwork arrived for Cuadra so he could proceed with his appeal. "That was an emotional moment," Cuadra writes. "In one hand could be the key to open the heavy door back into society, and in the other a letter from a stranger that had the guts to reach out to someone on the inside."[64]

In his reply, he told Natasha he read her letter first, putting off reading the appeal documents because "there was a lot of legal jargon and it took me a few days to read through it (it was thick as a phone book). Natasha, my head has been all over the place for days now and so please excuse how all over the place this letter is. Not until yesterday have I had any breathing room." He confessed that prison life "has been really tough. Not in a physical way, but pure mental. Most times I take my glasses off to avoid the stares and to blur out my surroundings."[65]

Cuadra was optimistic in his first letter, telling Natasha that he expected that in six to nine months, a judge could decide whether he could go home or would stay in prison for the rest of his life. He told her that "according to the legally inclined, the odds (on winning the appeal) are in our favor."[66]

A second undated letter was shared by Natasha online a few weeks after the first. In it, Cuadra updates her about the appeal process including his conclusion that a thirty-day extension granted in the proceeding was a good sign for his chances.

In this letter he also took up what he believed were contributing factors to his conviction, such as long-brewing Luzerne County judicial scandals and corruption investigations of county officials not involved with his case. "Not only did they (county officials) need to convict me in order to secure a bigger budget for the following year, but the Judge himself was up for re-election (he lost and is out of there)," Cuadra wrote. "Maybe they thought that my conviction would bury all of their bad deeds."[67]

He told Natasha to keep the faith, as time would prove him right. He also responded to her about their shared love of the band Green Day, and her comments about John Roecker's documentary about the "true life" of gay porn stars, a video he has never seen since it was released after he was incarcerated.

Again he offered a glimpse into prison life, referring to his new cellmate Paul (whom he called a "roommate") as "a nice guy" but that "we keep to ourselves around here. You must in order to make it day to day. Many of the guys in here are pretty much living people with dead souls. I think that is why most of the stuff I write is about the yaw and pitch of moral struggle."[68]

His third letter to Natasha (and the last one she published online) talked about the hot-humid Pennsylvania weather and Cuadra's happiness about weaning himself off the last twenty-five milligrams of imipramine. The drug, an anti-depressant normally sold under the name Tofranil, is prescribed mostly to treat depression and anxiety in adults, and to curb bed-wetting in small children, according to the drug's manufacturer. He mentioned to Natasha that he had received Prozac as a child, along with Ritalin and other drugs, all of which he said he stopped taking once he entered the Navy.

As he had in his earlier letters, he confessed, "I suffer every second of every interminable day. And it does not get easier; you just get sort of used to it."[69]

He contrasted his prison experience with that of "those who have sold drugs or killed people, maybe for them this has gotten easier because they are responsible for the world that they have created and now find themselves in. It's life on autopilot, almost like a groundhog day where the same day is repeated over and over." Always somewhat poetic, Cuadra noted that "the more time passes, the more you have missed, the more you have missed out on. If you pay enough attention, you can actually see people (in prison) carrying their tears around like sacks of stones."[70]

He repeated earlier themes about having to keep himself separate from "the undesirables" who were all around him. "You see people change around here, and it's never for the better. It makes it harder, but that's what I must do."[71]

Remain in prison is indeed what Cuadra has to do unless Pennsylvania's highest court reverses all previous proceedings and orders him a new trial. He remains housed on a life sentence at the State Correctional Institute in Coal Township, Pennsylvania. The medium-security facility is located about seventy miles southwest of Kocis' former home in Dallas, Pennsylvania. The facility housing Cuadra is about 100 miles away northeast of where Joseph Kerekes will spend the rest of his life.

The great porn machine grinds on

The murder of Bryan Kocis and the subsequent jailing of Harlow Cuadra and Joseph Kerekes did nothing to impact the ever-grinding machinery that produces literally thousands upon thousands of porno images everyday. The porn business, estimated to be worth at least $12 billion annually to its producers, is estimated to have as many followers as the National Basketball Association (NBA) and the National Football League (NFL) combined. Some have even touted porn as one of the few American economic sectors that is fully recession proof.[72]

Still a product that polite people don't talk about openly, porn is more likely hidden away on discreet files on a home personal computer. There are glimpses of mainstream acceptability. In 2007 then-San Francisco Mayor Gavin Newsom (now California's lieutenant governor) issued a proclamation for "Colt Day" in that city to celebrate the fortieth anniversary of Colt Studios, an established gay porn producer. Porn critics abound, some even fueled still by the ancient findings of the Meese Commission Report of 1986 in which the Reagan Administration once and for all declared porn was a big, bad business.

In 2012, the Los Angeles City Council gave preliminary approval to a plan to require porn producers to provide and require the use of condoms on a set in order to obtain permits to film, *Business Week* reported. The move by city officials to act amidst ever-growing reports of HIV transmission via "bareback" sex mirrored efforts by the AIDS Healthcare Foundation that sought a statewide California ballot initiative to require condom use in all adult films—gay or otherwise. New struggles face today's porn industry, beyond challenges related to HIV and AIDS transmission or even local obscenity measures. New online sources, such as www.xtube.com, present the same challenge to porn producers that www.napster.com and others presented to music producers. Customers can get an amazing amount of content online, for free. Add into that the merger of television and the Internet, seemingly embraced by producers of all kinds has meant that the "Google generation" of today may find it rather odd that anyone wants them to actually *pay* for their porn. Some estimates indicate that as much as 15 percent of the 100-most visited gay porn sites online offer free porn viewing. Getting it for free may be neat for the consumer, but the industry is reeling over how to react and survive.[73]

Some of the "reaction" or "will to survive" of the industry has taken on the form of producing more and more hard-core and kink content. Certainly the financial struggle has not slowed the desire for "bareback" or condomless content that Kocis produced. "As a small company, I am forced by distributors to shoot bareback content," gay porn producer Tyler Reed of USA Jock Studio told *The Advocate*. "Unless you have extremely high-quality models, sets, and so forth, distributors won't even touch the safe content anymore." Reed estimates that "bareback sells two-to-one, guaranteed. And if you put the word 'bareback' in the title, you're looking at three-to-one."[74]

Does it matter? Consider that four years ago, industry insiders said a porn website could expect 5 million "hits" or "visits" a day, and online porn site memberships have risen from 4 to 7 million subscribers throughout the first decade of the twenty-first century.

In May 2009, *The Advocate* reported in its review of the panic overtaking the porn community that DVD sales were down between twenty-five and forty-five percent overall—and that's for a DVD technology that most agree is bound for the graveyard.[75]

Whether he knew it or not, murder victim Bryan Kocis represented another new challenge to mainline porn producers. His home-based business was at the start of a huge wave of producers to come online. "Self-proclaimed producers from all walks flocked to adult entertainment, operating under the correct assumption that sex sells and the sort-of-correct assumption that there's an endless supply of customers," *The Advocate* reported.[76] As blogger Jason Sechrest said, "Everyone with a camcorder picked it up and said, 'Hey! I'm going to do that!'"[77]

Some mainline producers have tapped into what Kocis found early on by producing their own alleged "amateur" content, much of it focused on the "twinks" Kocis favored, or straight-guys-having-gay-sex genres. Successful examples include www.seancody.com, www.randyblue.com, and www.corbinfisher.com. "These companies are now some of the most lucrative in the business and offer top dollar for the right model," according to a report in *The Advocate*.[78]

Most predict the days of renting or buying one's own DVD from the local shop or online store is a thing of the past. Most customers will likely download the porn they want onto laptop computers or even more on mobile, hand-held computer devices. And while recessions come and go and porn producers will undoubtedly find ways to recapture their customers (and many new ones), gay activists lament the days when mainline gay porn studios were major contributors to HIV and AIDS prevention efforts and other political causes of importance to the gay-lesbian-bisexual and transgender communities. "(Gay porn) is a huge part of our culture," said online industry journalist J.C. Adams. "For many of us, porn was our first exposure to male intimacy and porn stars were the only openly gay or bi men that we saw or heard of."[79]

In the End

After all is said and done, the murder of Bryan Kocis was not dramatically different than the thousands of murders that occur across the nation each year. It had unusual aspects, given its ties to gay porn, and the small-town sense of security that it threatened in the hearts and minds of locals. But then, just as easily, locals and others can conscribe this case to the anomaly category. Observers of the events in Luzerne County can easily say they aren't involved in porn, they have engaged in no cross-country rivalries with others who seek to do them harm, they lead more everyday lives, and that something like this could never happen to them. But the people at the center of this case, Bryan Kocis, Sean Lockhart, Joseph Kerekes, and Harlow Cuadra are all products of those normal, everyday American lives and homes as well, though in differing forms. For their part, Kocis and Kerekes had very traditional, solid childhoods based on parents expecting them to do well at school, with extra curricular activities, including Scouts or church youth groups. And Lockhart and Cuadra represent the polar opposite, both coming from homes in transition without strong parental support at the top that caused traditional childhood boundaries to be blurred. The only "player" in this saga with any remaining hope or potential, it seems, is Lockhart who continues to construct an identity for himself both in and out of the porn world. His biggest advantage: he's alive and free to pursue what life holds next. For Cuadra and Kerekes, their lives essentially died at the moment of Kocis' death, all deaths borne in the margins of the gay porn subculture that placed the pursuit of pleasure above all else.

CHAPTER ONE END NOTES:

1. Melnick interview with AES, 6-9-09
2. Cuadra Trial Transcript p. 673
3. Cuadra Trial Transcript p. 680
4. Ibid.
5. Cuadra Trial Transcript p. 681
6. Melnick interview with AES, 6-9-09
7. Cuadra Trial Transcript p. 768
8. Melnick interview with AES, 6-9-09
9. Probable Cause affidavit
10. Cuadra-Kerekes preliminary hearing transcript
11. Ibid.
12. Cuadra Trial Transcript p. 1964
13. Cuadra Trial Transcript p. 1965
14. Cuadra Trial Transcript p. 701
15. Cuadra-Kerekes preliminary hearing transcript
16. Melnick interview with AES, 6-9-09
17. Ibid.
18. *Citizens' Voice*, 2-9-07
19. Ibid.
20. *Citizens' Voice*, 5-17-07
21. Melnick interview with AES, 6-9-09
22. Crake interview with AES, 6-9-09
23. Melnick interview with AES, 6-9-09
24. Puente e-mail to AES, 5-2-09
25. Cuadra-Kerekes Preliminary hearing transcript
26. WNEP-TV, Scranton/Wilkes-Barre, PA, 2-8-07

27. Ibid
28. *Citizens' Voice*, 2-9-07
29. Ibid.
30. Ibid.
31. Ibid.
32. Probable cause affidavit, p. 5
33. PAC Blog, 11-2-08
34. PAC Blog, 7-30-08, Material Facts Constituting the Probable Cause for Search
35. Higgins interview with AES, 6-9-09
36. Ibid.
37. Ibid.
38. PAC Blog, 11-2-08
39. Ibid.
40. Ibid.

CHAPTER TWO END NOTES:

1. *Allentown Morning Call*, 7-13-01
2. *Citizens' Voice*, 8-21-01
3. Rosencrans interview with AES, 4-21-09
4. Ibid.
5. Ibid.
6. Ibid.
7. Ibid.
8. Ibid.
9. *Citizens' Voice*, 4-5-02
10. Ibid.
11. Ibid.
12. Ibid.
13. Ibid.
14. *2009 Barron's Profiles of American Colleges, 28th Ed.* Hauppauge, NY: Barrons Educational Services, Inc.

15. U.S. Bankruptcy Court, Middle District of Pennsylvania, Kocis Voluntary Chapter 7 Petition filed December 17, 2001; and *Citizens' Voice*, 1-28-07
16. Cuadra Trial Transcript, p. 1986
17. Parsons interview with PAC, 6-18-09
18. Pennsylvania Secretary of State's Office, Business Entity Filing History, Entity #3096007 created on 9-20-02; and Division of Corporations, State of Delaware, File #3956494, incorporated 4-18-05 by Capitol Services, Inc., Dover, DE.
19. *Times Leader*, 2-4-07; and *Citizens' Voice*, 1-28-07
20. Parsons interview with PAC, 6-18-09
21. *Citizens' Voice*, 12-8-08
22. Parsons interview with PAC, 6-18-09
23. *Citizens' Voice*, 12-8-08
24. Ibid.
25. Ibid.
26. Cuadra Trial Transcript, p. 1977
27. Parsons interview with PAC, 6-18-09
28. Luzerne County Probable Cause Affidavit, 5-15-07
29. Gross, M.J., *Out* magazine, 10-07
30. Rosencrans interview with AES, 4-21-09
31. Gross, M.J., *Out* magazine, 10-07
32. www.jasoncurious.com, May-June 2006
33. Ibid.
34. Cuadra Trial Transcript, p. 470
35. J.C. Adams e-mail to AES, 5-15-09
36. www.dewayneinsd.com, 3-25-09
37. Ibid.
38. Ibid.
39. *Los Angeles Times*, 4-23-04
40. Ibid.
41. J.C. Adams interview with AES, 6-2-09

42. Ibid.
43. Ibid.
44. Ibid.
45. Ibid.
46. WBRE-TV, Wilkes-Barre, PA, 2-2-07
47. *Times Leader*, 2-1-07
48. *Times Leader*, 3-14-09
49. *Citizens' Voice*, 3-10-09
50. *Citizens' Voice*, 3-14-09
51. *Citizens' Voice*, 3-18-09
52. Bartusek e-mail to PAC, 7-7-09
53. PAC Blog, 3-18-09
54. Bartusek e-mail to PAC, 7-7-09
55. *Citizens' Voice*, 3-18-09

CHAPTER THREE END NOTES:

1. www.imdb.com
2. www.pornteam.com
3. www.radvideo.com
4. www.pornteam.com
5. www.radvideo.com
6. Ibid.
7. Ibid.
8. www.pornteam.com
9. www.radvideo.com
10. Ibid.
11. Ibid.
12. Cuadra Trial Transcript, p. 498
13. Ibid., p. 466
14. Ibid., p. 468
15. Ibid., p. 479-480
16. www.radvideo.com
17. www.jasoncurious.com, 5-5-06

18. Ibid.
19. Ibid.
20. Ibid.
21. Ibid.
22. Gross, M.J., *Out* magazine, 10-07
23. *Cobra Video LLC v. Lockhart*, U.S. District Court, Southern District of California, Case #3:06-cv-00293-B-LSP
24. www.jasoncurious.com, 5-6-06
25. Ibid.
26. Ibid.
27. www.dewayneinsd.com, 3-25-09
28. www.jasoncurious.com, 5-6-06
29. *Video LLC v. Lockhart, Roy & LSG Media LLC*, Original complaint filed 2-7-06, U.S. Federal Court, Southern District of California.
30. Ibid.
31. Gross, M.J., *Out* magazine, 10-07
32. www.jasoncurious.com, 5-2-06
33. Ibid.
34. Ibid.
35. Ibid.
36. Ibid.
37. Ibid.
38. Exhibit 2, Case #3:06-cv-00293-B-LSP: *Cobra Video LLC v. Lockhart, Roy & LSG Media LLC*, Original complaint filed 2-7-06, U.S. Federal Court, Southern District of California.
39. Ibid.
40. www.jasoncurious.com, 5-2-06
41. Exhibit 3, Case #3:06-cv-00293-B-LSP: *Cobra Video LLC v. Lockhart, Roy & LSG Media LLC*, Original complaint filed 2-7-06, U.S. Federal Court, Southern District of California.
42. Ibid.

43. Ibid.
44. Ibid.
45. Gross, M.J., *Out* magazine, 10-07
46. www.avn.com, 9-13-05
47. Ibid.
48. Ibid.
49. www.avn.com, 11-2-05
50. Ibid.
51. Ibid.
52. www.avn.com, 11-2-05 and 2-27-06
53. www.avn.com, 2-27-06
54. Ibid.
55. Ibid.
56. Luzerne County District Attorney's Office Evidence: Black's Beach Transcript, 4-28-07
57. www.avn.com 2-27-06
58. Ibid.
59. Ibid.
60. Cuadra Trial Transcript, p. 951-952
61. www.jasoncurious.com, 7-5-06
62. Ibid.
63. Luzerne County District Attorney's Office Evidence: Black's Beach Transcript, 4-28-07
64. Cuadra Trial Transcript, p. 952-953
65. www.jasoncurious.com, 8-30-06
66. www.gaywired.com, 3-22-07
67. www.cobravideo.com, 6-20-07
68. Ibid.
69. www.cobravideo.com; and www.brentcorriganxxx.com
70. www.xbiz.com, 6-22-07
71. Ibid.
72. Ibid.
73. www.avn.com, 7-16-07
74. www.brentcorrigan.com, 2-7-07

75. www.dewayneinsd.com, 9-4-07
76. www.cobravideo.com and www.brentcorriganxxx. com
77. Ibid.
78. Ibid.
79. www.xbiz.com, 1-8-08; and Luzerne County Court of Common Pleas, Civil Action #117 of 2008, filed 1-8-07
80. Luzerne County Court of Common Pleas, Civil Action #117 of 2008, filed 1-8-07
81. *Citizens' Voice*, 8-18-07
82. Ibid.

CHAPTER FOUR END NOTES:

1. Kerekes letter to AES, 5-4-09
2. Luzerne County District Attorney's Office Evidence: Crab Catcher Transcript, 4-27-07
3. Ibid.
4. www.nortfolkmaleescorts.com
5. Ibid.
6. WNEP-TV, Scranton/Wilkes-Barre, PA, 3-13-09
7. Times Leader, 3-14-09
8. Ibid.
9. Cuadra Trial Transcript, p. 2095
10. Ibid., p. 2095
11. Luzerne County District Attorney's Office Evidence: Black's Beach Transcript, 4-28-07
12. Cuadra Trial Transcript, p. 2095
13. Ibid., p. 2096
14. Ibid., p. 2096
15. Ibid., p. 2096
16. Times Leader, 3-14-09
17. Luzerne County District Attorney's Office Evidence: Crab Catcher Transcript, 4-27-07

18. Times Leader, 3-14-09
19. Ibid.
20. Ibid.
21. Ibid.
22. www.freeharlowcuadra.com, 10-13-07
23. Roecker, J., 2008 – Here! TV, "Everything You Ever Wanted to Know About Gay Porn Stars"
24. Ibid.
25. Ibid.
26. www.freeharlowcuadra.com, 10-13-07
27. Ibid.
28. Roecker, J., 2008 – Here! TV, "Everything You Ever Wanted to Know About Gay Porn Stars"
29. Luzerne County District Attorney's Office Evidence: Crab Catchers Transcript, 4-27-07
30. Roecker, J., 2008 – Here! TV, "Everything You Ever Wanted to Know About Gay Porn Stars"
31. Ibid.
32. Bankruptcy case number 98-29368, U. S. Bankruptcy Court Norfolk, Va.
33. Roecker, J., 2008 – Here! TV, "Everything You Ever Wanted to Know About Gay Porn Stars"
34. http://www.forums.viperclub.org, 7-29-04
35. Ibid., 2-15-06
36. Ibid.
37. Ibid.,
38. Ibid., 12-6-06
39. Cuadra Trial Transcript, p. 2105
40. Ibid., p. 2105
41. Ibid., p. 2105-2106
42. Ibid., p. 2108
43. J.C. Adams interview with AES, 6-2-09
44. Roecker, J, 2008 – Here! TV, "Everything You Ever Wanted to Know About Gay Porn Stars"
45. Ibid.

46. www.freeharlowcuadra.com, 10-13-07
47. www.boybatter.com
48. Cuadra Trial Transcript, p. 2107
49. www.xbiz.com, 1-13-09
50. Kerekes interview with AES, 7-2-09
51. www.jasoncurious.com, 2-10-07
52. Ibid.
53. www.norfolkmaleescorts.com
54. www.allamericanescorts.com
55. Ibid.
56. www.betheltemple.com
57. Kerekes letter to AES, 5-18-09
58. Ibid.
59. Ibid.
60. Luzerne County District Attorney's Office Evidence: Crab Catcher Transcript, 4-27-07
61. www.vfcc.edu
62. Kerekes letter to AES, 5-18-09; www.betheltemple.com; and www.josephkerekesonline.com, 9-13-07
63. Kerekes letter to AES, 5-18-09
64. www.josephkerekesonline.com
65. Gross, M.J., Out magazine, 10-07
66. Kerekes interview with AES, 7-2-09
67. Ibid.
68. Kerekes letter to AES, 5-18-09
69. Ibid.
70. Gross, M.J., Out magazine, 10-07
71. Kerekes interview with AES, 7-2-09
72. Ibid.
73. Ibid.
74. Ibid.
75. Ibid.
76. Kerekes letter to AES, 5-18-09
77. Ibid.

78. Luzerne County District Attorney's Office Evidence: Crab Catcher Transcript, 4-27-07
79. Cuadra Trial Transcript, p. 2132
80. Ibid., p. 404
81. Ibid., p. 405
82. Ibid.
83. Times Leader, 2-26-09
84. Cuadra Trial Transcript, p. 207
85. Ibid., p. 210
86. Rosalie Kerekes telephone call to AES, 6-1-09
87. Cuadra Trial Transcript, p. 414
88. Ibid., p. 427
89. Ibid., p. 427
90. Kerekes interview with AES, 7-2-09
91. Cuadra Trial Transcript, p. 414
92. Ibid., p. 428
93. Ibid., p. 428
94. Ibid., p. 218
95. Ibid., p. 429
96. Ibid., p. 430-431
97. Ibid., p. 434
98. Ibid., p. 2131
99. Kerekes letter to AES, 5-18-09
100. Gross, M.J., *Out* magazine, 10-07
101. Ibid.
102. *Citizens' Voice*, 5-17-07
103. Kerekes interview with AES, 7-2-09
104. Ibid.
105. Ibid.
106. Ibid.
107. Cuadra Trial Transcript, p. 1157
108. Kerekes interview with AES, 7-2-09
109. Ibid.
110. Ibid.
111. Ibid.

112. Ibid.
113. www.daddysreviews.com, 3-1-07
114. Ibid., 12-27-06
115. Ibid., 8-31-06
116. Ibid., 10-11-06
117. www.whoboy.com, 7-9-05
118. www.harlowcuadraonline.com, 9-10-07
119. Cuadra Trial Transcript, p. 1169
120. Luzerne County District Attorney's Office Evidence: Crab Catcher Transcript, 4-27-07
121. Kerekes interview with AES, 7-2-09
122. Childress e-mail to AES, 10-5-09
123. Ibid.
124. Ibid.
125. Ibid.
126. Luzerne County District Attorney's Office Evidence: Crab Catcher Transcript, 4-27-07
127. Ibid.
128. Ibid.
129. Childress e-mail to AES, 10-5-09
130. Ibid.
131. Luzerne County District Attorney's Office Evidence: Crab Catcher Transcript, 4-27-07
132. Ibid.
133. Times Leader, 6-25-07
134. www.harlowcuadraonline.com, 9-10-07
135. Ibid., 8-25-07
136. wwwfreejosephkerekes.com
137. Times Leader, 3-3-09

CHAPTER FIVE END NOTES:

1. *Citizens' Voice*, 1-26-07
2. Ibid.

3. *Times Leader*, 6-25-07
4. Pennsylvania Crime Stoppers news release, 1-27-07
5. WNEP-TV, 1-26-07
6. Higgins interview with AES, 6-8-09
7. Ibid.
8. Higgins interview with AES, 6-8-09; Dr. John Consalvo testimony, preliminary hearing; and WNEP-TV, 8-22-07
9. *Citizens' Voice*, 1-27-07
10. Kerekes interview with AES, 7-2-09
11. Kerekes letter to AES, 5-4-09
12. Cuadra Trial Transcript, p. 201-202
13. Ibid., p. 207
14. Kerekes interview with AES, 7-2-09
15. www.harlowcuadraonline.com, 4-07
16. Ibid.
17. Ibid.
18. www.julianpdx.blogspot.com, 2-07
19. *Times Leader*, 7-19-07
20. Kerekes letter to AES, 5-4-09
21. Ibid.
22. Ibid.
23. Ibid.
24. Ibid.
25. WBRE-TV, Wilkes-Barre, PA, 2-2-07
26. Cuadra Trial Transcript, p. 1996
27. Ibid., p. 1998
28. Ibid., p. 1999
29. Melnick interview with AES, 6-9-09
30. Ibid.
31. Ibid
32. Ibid.

CHAPTER SIX END NOTES:

1. www.jasoncurious.com, 1-27-07
2. Ibid
3. Ibid.
4. Cuadra Trial Transcript p. 852
5. Cuadra Trial Transcript p. 852
6. PAC Blog, 7-28-08, Material Facts Constituting the Probable Cause for Search
7. Luzerne County District Attorney's Office Evidence: Crab Catcher Transcript, 4-27-07
8. Ibid.
9. Ibid.
10. Ibid.
11. www.crabcatcher.com
12. Luzerne County District Attorney's Office Evidence: Crab Catcher Transcript, 4-27-07
13. Ibid.
14. Ibid.
15. Ibid.
16. Ibid.
17. Ibid.
18. Ibid.
19. Ibid.
20. Ibid.
21. Ibid.
22. Ibid.
23. Cuadra Trial Transcript p. 854
24. Luzerne County District Attorney's Office Evidence: Crab Catcher Transcript, 4-27-07
25. Ibid.
26. Ibid.
27. Ibid.
28. Ibid.
29. Ibid.

30. Ibid.
31. Ibid.
32. Ibid.
33. Ibid.
34. Ibid.
35. Ibid.
36. Ibid.
37. Ibid.
38. Ibid.
39. Ibid.
40. www.parks.ca.gov
41. Luzerne County District Attorney's Office
    Evidence: Black's Beach Transcript, 4-28-07
42. Ibid.
43. Ibid.
44. Ibid.
45. Ibid.
46. Ibid.
47. Ibid.
48. Ibid.
49. Ibid.
50. Ibid.
51. Ibid.
52. Ibid.
53. Ibid.
54. Ibid.
55. Ibid.
56. Ibid.
57. Ibid.
58. Ibid.
59. Ibid.
60. Ibid.
61. Ibid.
62. Ibid.
63. Ibid.

64. Ibid.
65. Cuadra Trial Transcript, p. 860
66. Ibid., p. 860
67. www.harlowcuadraonline.com
68. *Times Leader*, 7-19-07
69. Luzerne County District Attorney's Office Evidence: Black's Beach Transcript, 4-28-07

CHAPTER SEVEN END NOTES:

1. www.brentcorriganinc.com and www.gaypornblog.com, 11-6-06
2. www.brentcorriganinc.com
3. www.adultFYI.com, 1-26-07
4. Ibid.
5. www.brentcorriganinc.com and www.adultFYI.com, 1-26-07
6. www.brentcorriganinc.com
7. Ibid.
8. *Gaymonkey*, Vol. IV, Issue 4, Sept-Oct 2006
9. Ibid.
10. Ibid.
11. www.jasoncurious.com, May-June 2006
12. Ibid.
13. Ibid.
14. Ibid.
15. Ibid.
16. Ibid.
17. Ibid.
18. Ibid.
19. www.gaywired.com, 3-22-07
20. *Gaymonkey*, Vol. IV, Issue 4, Sept-Oct 2006
21. www.adultFYI.com, 1-26-07
22. www.jasoncurious.com, May-June 2006

23. Ibid.
24. Ibid.
25. Ibid.
26. Ibid.
27. Ibid.
28. www.chicagopride.com, 5-22-08
29. Luzerne County District Attorney's Office
    Evidence: Crab Catcher Transcript, 4-27-07
30. Ibid.
31. Ibid.
32. Ibid.
33. www.gaywired.com, 3-22-07
34. www.chicagopride.com, 5-22-08
35. Ibid.
36. *Gaymonkey*, Vol. IV, Issue 4, Sept-Oct 2006; and
    www.gaywired.com, 3-22-07
37. www.gaywired.com, 3-22-07
38. www.chicagopride.com, 5-22-08
39. www.gaywired.com, 3-22-07
40. *Gaymonkey*, Vol. IV, Issue 4, Sept-Oct 2006
41. www.imdb.com
42. www.brentcorriganonline.com, 6-23-07
43. www.gaypornblog.com, 11-6-06
44. www.brentcorriganonline.com, 6-22-07
45. Ibid.
46. www.brentcorriganinc.com, 11-28-07
47. www.brentcorriganinc.com, 7-16-07
48. www.imdb.com
49. www.brentcorriganinc.com, 11-28-07
50. Cuadra Trial Transcript, p. 801
51. Ibid., p. 1595
52. Ibid., p. 1596
53. Ibid., p. 1598
54. Ibid., p. 1598-1599
55. Ibid., p. 1598

56. Ibid., p. 1600
57. Ibid., p. 1602
58. Ibid., p. 1603
59. Ibid., p. 802
60. Ibid., p. 1604
61. Ibid., p. 1605
62. Ibid., p. 1605-1606
63. Ibid., p. 1606
64. Ibid., p. 1607-1608
65. Ibid., p. 1608
66. Ibid., p. 494
67. Ibid., p. 1611-1612
68. www.chicagopride.com, 5-22-08
69. Cuadra Trial Transcript, p. 847
70. Ibid., p. 847-848
71. Luzerne County District Attorney's Office
    Evidence: Crab Catcher Transcript, 4-27-07
72. Cuadra Trial Transcript, p. 504-505
73. www.chicagopride.com, 5-22-08
74. Ibid.
75. Ibid.
76. Cuadra Trial Transcript, p. 842-844, p. 978-979
77. www.chicagopride.com, 5-22-08
78. Cuadra Trial Transcript, p. 806-807
79. Ibid., p. 804-808
80. Ibid., p. 817
81. Ibid., p. 826-827
82. Ibid.
83. Ibid., p. 837
84. Ibid., p. 838
85. Ibid., p. 977-980
86. Ibid., p. 838, p. 982
87. Ibid., p. 982
88. Ibid., p. 984
89. Ibid., p. 839

CHAPTER EIGHT END NOTES:

1. Higgins interview with AES, 6-8-09
2. Ibid.
3. WTKR-TV, Norfolk/Virginia Beach, VA, n.d.
4. Higgins interview with AES, 6-8-09
5. Ibid.
6. Ibid.
7. Ibid.
8. *Citizens' Voice*, 7-24-08
9. Ibid.
10. PAC Blog, 7-31-08 reporting on Hannon's 5-15-07 synopsis report
11. Ibid.
12. Ibid.
13. Ibid.
14. Ibid.
15. *Times Leader*, 7-24-08
16. PAC Blog, 7-31-08 reporting on Hannon's 5-15-07 synopsis report
17. *Times Leader*, 7-24-08
18. *Virginian-Pilot*, 5-16-07
19. *Citizens' Voice*, 5-18-07
20. WNEP-TV, Scranton/Wilkes-Barre, PA, 7-17-07
21. Cuadra Trial Transcript, p. 849-850
22. Ibid., p. 849-850
23. Ibid., p. 849-850
24. Ibid., p. 849-850
25. Ibid., p. 849-850
26. Ibid., p. 994
27. Luzerne County District Attorney's Office Evidence: Crab Catcher Transcript, 4-27-07
28. Ibid.

29. Luzerne County District Attorney's Office Evidence: Black's Beach Transcript, 4-28-07
30. Federal Search Warrant executed on MySpace ID#87311731 regarding www.myspace.com/harlowcuadra, 3-14-07
31. PAC Blog, 9-23-08
32. Cuadra Trial Transcript, p. 1009
33. Kerekes interview with AES, 7-2-09
34. *Times Leader*, 6-25-07
35. Higgins interview with AES, 6-9-09
36. Melnick interview with AES, 6-9-09
37. www.harlowcuadraonline.com
38. Melnick interview with AES, 6-9-09
39. WTKR-TV, Norfolk/Virginia Beach, VA, 7-7-07
40. WBRE-TV, Scranton/Wilkes-Barre, PA, 7-17-07
41. Ibid.
42. *Citizens' Voice*, 7-18-07
43. www.harlowcuadraonline.com
44. Ibid.
45. Gross, M.J., *Out* magazine, 11-07
46. *Times Leader*, 10-1-07; www.freecharlowcuadra.com, blog posting by "HRC," 9-27-07
47. www.freelarhlowcuadra.com, blog posting by Gladis Zaldivar, 5-25-07
48. www.xbiz.com, 6-18-07; *Times Leader*, 5-19-07
49. Ibid.
50. www.jasoncurious.com, 7-2-07 and www.xbiz.com, 7-4-07; www.videoview.com
51. Ibid.
52. *Virginian-Pilot*, 5-19-07
53. Ibid.
54. Ibid.
55. Alleman e-mail to PAC, 7-11-07
56. Ibid.
57. Kerekes interview with AES, 7-2-09

58. *Virginian-Pilot*, 8-21-07
59. www.mls.com, Listing No. 0929975
60. *Alleman e-mail to PC, 8-8-07*
61. Luzerne County District Attorney's Office Evidence: Crab Catcher Transcript, 4-27-07
62. www.freeharlowcuadra.com, blog posting by "HRC," 9-27-07
63. www.harlowcuadraonline.com, 9-10-07

CHAPTER NINE END NOTES:

1. *Times Leader*, 2-12-08
2. Ibid.
3. Ibid.
4. Ibid., 2-21-08
5. PAC Blog, 3-6-08
6. Kerekes interview with AES, 7-2-09
7. *Citizens' Voice*, 3-7-08
8. PAC Blog, 3-22-08
9. Ibid.
10. PAC Blog, 3-27-08
11. Ibid.
12. PAC Blog, 7-9-08
13. PC Blog, 3-5-09
14. Halford interview with Pennsylvania State Police, as reported on PAC Blog, 5-17-07
15. PAC Blog, 11-16-07
16. Melnick interview with AES, 6-9-09
17. Ibid.
18. Ibid.
19. Crake interview with AES, 6-9-09
20. *Times Leader*, 7-19-07
21. Probable Cause Affidavit
22. Ibid.

23. PAC Blog, 5-13-08
24. Probable Cause Affidavit
25. Ibid.
26. Luzerne County District Attorney's Office
    Evidence: Crab Catcher Transcript: 4-27-07
27. Probable Cause Affidavit
28. Ibid.
29. Ibid.
30. Ibid.
31. Ibid.
32. Ibid.
33. Ibid.
34. Ibid.
35. Ibid.
36. Ibid.
37. Ibid.
38. Ibid.
39. Ibid.
40. Ibid.
41. *Citizens' Voice*, 8-27-07; www.courttvnews.com,
    8-24-07
42. Kerekes interview with AES, 7-20-09
43. www.courttvnews.com, 10-3-07
44. Ibid.
45. *Citizens' Voice*, 8-27-07
46. Ibid.
47. Cuadra letter to Renee Martin, 10-13-07
48. Ibid.
49. Ibid.
50. Ibid.
51. Ibid.
52. Ibid.
53. www.freeharlowcuadra.com, 4-18-07
54. Cuadra letter to Renee Martin, 10-13-07
55. www.freeharlowcuadra.com

56. Ibid.
57. Ibid.
58. Ibid.
59. http://en.wikipedia.org/wiki/Edmond_Locard
60. Melnick interview with AES, 6-9-09
61. Ibid.
62. Ibid.
63. Ibid.
64. PAC Blog

CHAPTER TEN END NOTES:

1. *Citizens' Voice*, 12-9-08
2. Ibid.
3. Kerekes interview with AES, 7-2-09
4. Ibid.
5. Ibid.
6. PAC Blog, 11-25-08
7. *Times Leader*, 2-18-09
8. *Citizens' Voice*, 2-23-09
9. Ibid., 2-17-09
10. Melnick interview with AES, 6-9-09
11. Crake interview with AES, 6-9-09
12. Cuadra letter to Renee Martin, 10-13-07
13. Ibid.
14. *Citizens' Voice*, 2-24-09
15. Ibid.
16. Ibid., 2-25-09
17. Ibid., 2-24-09; *Times Leader*, 2-24-09
18. *Citizens' Voice*, 2-24-09 and 2-25-09
19. Cuadra Trial Transcript, p. 1297-1298
20. Ibid., p. 1297-1298
21. Ibid., p. 201-202
22. Ibid., p. 1189

23. Ibid., p. 407-411
24. Ibid., p. 1161-1162
25. Ibid., p. 1161-1162
26. Ibid., p. 846
27. Ibid., p. 337
28. Melnick interview with AES, 6-9-09
29. Cuadra Trial Transcript, p. 340
30. Ibid., p. 487
31. Ibid., p. 489
32. Ibid., p. 491-500
33. Ibid., p. 1550
34. Ibid., p. 1552
35. Ibid., p. 1039
36. Ibid., p. 1040
37. Ibid., p. 788
38. Ibid., p. 788
39. Ibid., p. 793-794
40. Ibid., p. 795
41. Ibid., p. 1064
42. Ibid., p. 1064-1065
43. Ibid., p. 1062
44. Ibid., p. 1062
45. Ibid., p. 1062
46. Ibid., p. 1062
47. Ibid., p. 1062
48. Ibid., p. 1075
49. Ibid., p. 1071
50. Ibid., p. 1104
51. Ibid., p. 1104
52. Ibid., p. 1104-1105
53. Ibid., p. 1129
54. *Times Leader*, 3-10-09
55. Ibid.
56. Melnick interview with AES, 6-9-09
57. Ibid.

58. *Citizens' Voice*, 3-11-09
59. Kerekes interview with AES, 7-2-09
60. Ibid.

CHAPTER ELEVEN END NOTES:

1. www.news.findlaw.com, 1-7-09
2. Ibid.
3. Cuadra Trial Transcript, p. 2291
4. Ibid., p. 2071
5. Ibid., p. 2073
6. Ibid., p. 2073-2074
7. Ibid., p. 2077
8. Ibid., p. 2084
9. Ibid., p. 2085
10. Ibid., p. 2085-2086
11. Ibid., p. 2087
12. Ibid., p. 2088
13. Ibid., p. 2090
14. Ibid., p. 2092
15. Ibid., p. 2091
16. Ibid., p. 2098
17. Ibid., p. 2096-2097
18. Ibid., p. 2097
19. Ibid., p. 2099
20. Ibid., p. 2099
21. Ibid., p. 2102
22. Ibid., p. 2102
23. Ibid., p. 2103
24. Ibid., p. 2104-2105
25. Ibid., p. 2108-2109
26. Ibid., p. 2120
27. Ibid., p. 2125
28. Ibid., p. 2126

29. Ibid., p. 2125
30. Ibid., p. 2131
31. Ibid., p. 2133
32. Ibid., p. 2134
33. Ibid., p. 2134
34. Ibid., p. 2136
35. Ibid., p. 2138
36. Ibid., p. 2140
37. Ibid., p. 2134
38. Ibid., p. 2143-2144
39. Ibid., p. 2145
40. Ibid., p. 2165
41. Ibid., p. 2166
42. Ibid., p. 2167
43. Ibid., p. 2169
44. Ibid., p. 2172
45. Ibid., p. 2173
46. Ibid., p. 2176
47. Ibid., p. 2177
48. Ibid., p. 2177
49. Ibid., p. 2178
50. Ibid., p. 2180-2181
51. Ibid., p. 2181
52. Ibid., p. 2181
53. Ibid., p. 2183
54. Ibid., p. 2183-2184
55. Ibid., p. 2198
56. Ibid., p. 2203
57. Ibid., p. 2223
58. Ibid., p. 2206
59. Ibid., p. 2207
60. Ibid., p. 2211
61. Ibid., p. 2208
62. Ibid., p. 2241

CHAPTER TWELVE END NOTES:

1. Cuadra Trial Transcript, p. 2226
2. Ibid., p. 2227
3. Ibid., p. 2227-2228
4. Ibid., p. 2229
5. Ibid., p. 2238
6. Ibid., p. 2238-2239
7. Cuadra Trial Transcript, p. 2319; and *Times Leader*, 3-13-09
8. Cuadra Trial Transcript, p. 2230
9. Ibid., p. 2232
10. Ibid., p. 2251-2252
11. Ibid., p. 2252
12. Ibid., p. 2255
13. Ibid., p. 2256
14. Ibid., p. 2293-2294
15. *Times Leader*, 3-16-09
16. Cuadra Trial Transcript, p. 2321
17. Ibid., p. 2310
18. Ibid., p. 2232
19. Ibid., p. 2283
20. Ibid., p. 2296
21. Ibid., p. 2296
22. Ibid., p. 2284
23. Ibid., p. 2285
24. Ibid., p. 2353
25. Scutt interview with PAC, 5-30-09
26. Ibid.
27. *Citizens' Voice*, 3-12-09
28. *Times Leader*, 3-11-09
29. Ibid.
30. Ibid.
31. *Times Leader*, 3-11-09 and 3-12-09

32. Ibid., 3-11-09
33. Ibid., 3-12-09
34. Ibid., 3-11-09
35. Ibid.
36. *Citizens' Voice*, 3-12-09
37. Stavitzski interview with PAC, 5-30-09
38. *Citizens' Voice*, 3-13-09
39. Ibid.
40. *Times Leader*, 3-13-09
41. *Citizens' Voice*, 3-16-09
42. *Times Leader*, 3-13-09
43. *Citizens' Voice*, 3-13-09
44. Stavitzski interview with PAC, 5-30-09
45. Scutt interview with PAC, 5-30-09
46. Ibid.
47. *Citizens' Voice*, 3-17-09
48. *Times Leader*, 3-16-09
49. *Citizens' Voice*, 3-18-09
50. Ibid.
51. Ibid.
52. Ibid.
53. Stavitzski interview with PAC, 5-30-09
54. Scutt interview with PAC, 5-30-09
55. Ibid.
56. Ibid.
57. Ibid.
58. Stavitzski interview with PAC, 5-30-09
59. *Citizens' Voice*, 3-18-09
60. Scutt interview with PAC, 5-30-09
61. Ibid.
62. *Times Leader*, 3-17-09 and 3-18-09
63. Ibid.
64. Ibid.
65. Ibid.
66. Ibid.

67. *Times Leader*, 3-17-09; *Citizens' Voice*, 3-17-09
68. Ibid.
69. *Citizens' Voice*, 3-17-09
70. Ibid.
71. *Times Leader*, 3-21-09
72. *Citizens' Voice*, 3-17-09
73. Ibid.
74. Ibid.

CHAPTER THIRTEEN END NOTES:

1. Kerekes interview with AES, 7-2-09
2. Ibid.
3. Ibid.
4. Ibid.
5. Melnick interview with AES, 6-9-09
6. Crake interview with AES, 6-9-09
7. Kerekes interview with AES, 7-2-09
8. Kerekes letter to AES, 6-12-09
9. Ibid.
10. Kerekes interview with AES, 7-2-09
11. Ibid.
12. Ibid.
13. www.amosfamily.com/2010/09/fred-joseph-kerekes/comment-page-1/#comment-8656
14. *Times Leader*, 3-8-09
15. Ibid.
16. Ibid.
17. Ibid.
18. Ibid., 7-7-08
19. Ibid.
20. WILK Radio, Wilkes-Barre, PA, 3-10-09
21. Ibid.
22. *Times Leader*, 3-8-09

23. Ibid.
24. www.brentcorriganinc.com, 7-11-08
25. www.brentcorriganinc.com, 2-28-09
26. www.sfgate.com, 4-2-09; www.xbiz.com, 3-31-09
27. Ibid.
28. Ibid.
29. www.unzippedblog.com, 4-1-09
30. www.xbiz.com, 9-3-08
31. www.gaypornblog.com, 11-8-06
32. www.imdb.com
33. www.xbiz.com, 2-6-08
34. www.brentcorriganinc.com, 5-14-09
35. www.brentcorriganinc.com, 3-28-09
36. Ibid.
37. Ibid.
38. *Times Leader*, 3-2-09
39. www.brentcorriganinc.com, 2-21-09
40. www.brentcorriganinc.com, 7-31-09
41. Ibid.
42. Ibid.
43. Ibid.
44. Ibid.
45. www.brentcorriganinc.com, 8-18-09
46. Ibid.
47. Ibid.
48. PAC Blog, 3-18-09
49. Ibid.
50. Bartusek e-mail to PAC, 3-18-09
51. Ibid., 7-23-09
52. Ibid., 7-23-09
53. EuroMedia news release, 10-18-10
54. Ibid.
55. Ibid.
56. Higgins interview with AES, 6-9-09
57. Ibid.

58. Ibid.
59. Ibid.
60. Melnick interview with AES, 6-9-09
61. Defendant's Supplemental Concise Statement Pursuant to Pa. R.A.P. 1925-B, *Commonwealth of Pennsylvania v. Harlow Raymond Cuadra*
62. *Times Leader*, 10-18-10
63. Ibid., 11-22-10
64. http://www.youtube.com/watch?v=VFFMaQbFF3Q; http://www.youtube.com/watch?v=3BsalbNvoGU; and http://fuckyeahfreeharlowcuadra.tumblr.com
65. Ibid.
66. Ibid
67. Ibid.
68. Ibid.
69. Ibid.
70. Ibid.
71. Ibid.
72. *Los Angeles Times*, 3-3-07
73. *The Advocate*, 3-09
74. Ibid.
75. Ibid.
76. Ibid.
77. www.jasoncurious.com
78. The Advocate, 3-09
79. J.C. Adams interview with AES, 6-2-09